To Stan, enjoy (handwritten)

The Cry

Book Three in
The Magical Therossa Trilogy

Kathleen B Wilson (handwritten signature)

A Fantasy Story

by

Kathleen B. Wilson

Also by Kathleen B Wilson
The Secret of Tamsworth Forest
Therossa

Published in Great Britain 2019 by Brighton NightWriters

Copyright © Kathleen B Wilson

Cover artwork and design Kathleen B Wilson

ISBN: 9781798724521

Printed by Create Space

CHARACTERS IN THE THEROSSA NOVELS

In This World

Sue Dawson	Sister to Priscilla and Barry
Barry Dawson	Sue's younger brother
Priscilla Dawson	Sue's older sister
Aunt Moira	Aunt to Sue, Barry and Priscilla
Mrs Denton	Grandmother to Sue, Barry and Priscilla
Professor Harding	Searching for the other world
Cyril Grant	The Professor's assistant
Alfie	Professor Harding's nephew

In the Other World

Sonja	Sue's other identity
Raithe	Prince of the realm and Sonja's twin brother
Ruth	Queen of Therossa and mother of Sonja and Raithe
Thane	Hunter and tracker
White Hawk	Thane's wolf
Saturn	Thane's horse
Shaman	A gifted healer
Neela	The Shaman's assistant
Annalee	Thane's sister
Tansy	Tracker and friend of Annalee
Amos	Tracker and horse expert
Lex Ansell	Renegade leader

Zeno	Lex's stepbrother
Nenti	Renegade guard
Miccha	Renegade guard
Roddo	Renegade guard
Deena	Snake queen
Tam	King of Therossa
Vance	Tam's boyhood friend, also Thane's father
Oran	The evil priest, also the king's distant cousin
The Druzuzi	A tribe of people living underground with great magic
Sheeka	Red dragon
Silver	White dragon, daughter of Sheeka
Evonny	Black dragon
Firefly	Red dragon
Griffen	Green dragon
Sapphire	Blue dragon
Rainee	An elderly lady
Scrap	Her small dog
Jasper	Gypsy Ferryman
The Goddess	
Fleura	Mentor of the Goddess
The Keeper	Guard of the Enchanged Land
The Rotund Lady	
Bajahi	Very large black cat
Jacques	A gypsy
Cailli	A tracker
Zuboarra	Chief of the gypsies
Elina	Servant to the gypsies
Tug	Servant to the gypsies

CONTENTS

Prologue   The Story So Far

PART ONE

PART TWO

PROLOGUE
THE STORY SO FAR

Many months ago Sue was abducted from her family who ran a hotel on the outskirts of Tamsworth Forest. She was whisked away to a land of magic, a very different world from the one she had been brought up in. Not happy with this transgression, Sue looked continuously for a way back home, especially on learning the truth about her heritage, which her grandmother had kept from her. There was a mystery shrouding the forest about a young lady who went missing while walking in it. That was years before her time, but she discovered that young lady had been her mother. Her mother had fallen in love with the King of Therossa and given birth to twins.

Sue made many close friends while in the magical world of Therossa and the people of that land knew her as Princess Sonja. But her brother Barry, back in Tamsworth Forest, tracked her to this magical land and urged her to come home with him and live once again with her sister Priscilla and Aunt Moria in the hotel. Very much against her will Sue gave in to him and bitterly regretted her decision. She had to part from Thane, for whom she had great feelings, and White Hawk his beautiful wolf companion. On discovering no one had missed her and never expected her to return she decided to find her own way back to Therossa. She left the hotel late at night saying goodbye to Priscilla and Barry and ran into the forest. But at night everything was so different and enemies of the Queen were waiting for her. Just as she realised Barry was following her she was caught up in a malicious fog which ate away at her memory. Sue spent many weeks underground in the icy caves of the Drazuzi people. With no memory she would never escape. But Raithe her twin had given his sister a magical ring when they last parted "to keep us in touch" he said, and it was through this ring that he managed to convey to her she must get out into the air for her memory to return.

It was during her escape from the icy caves that Sue met a mysterious cloaked man who on several occasions came to her rescue. For her safety he took her to the home of Deena the Snake Queen and left her there for her protection. Deena took the liberty of making her a member of the snake cult. This act saved Sue's life on many occasions, not only hers, but people with her. On leaving Deena, Sue went in search of her brother Riathe who has been captured by the Queen's enemies. She learnt the identity of the cloaked man and came face to face with the Dragons. Sue and her friends love the Dragons. Skeeka the huge red dragon and leader of them all has a daughter names Silver. She is a beautiful white dragon who attached herself to Sue. Together they made a pact to clear Therossa of their enemies. Now that Tam, the King, has been rescued from captivity everyone in the country is in favour of this, except the Queen. She doesn't want Sue to have anything to do with dragons.

NOW READ ON . . .

Sentinel

Pale horse, standing silent and so still –
Timeless creature in a timeless field.

Who is your master, when owls shadow the moon?
How do the clouds of a slow dawn look to you?

Have you been left behind, a relic of evolution
As you stare unwavering at a clump of grass

Or is it we who have grown blind,
Unable to see what you have always seen?

Tim Shelton-Jones

PART ONE

CHAPTER 1
UNEXPECTED MEETING

Huddled on the hard back seat of a shabby limousine, Priscilla stared dejectedly through the dirty, steamed up windows. The car was speeding along, which made the buildings outside appear blurred as they rushed by. Unless she stirred herself to wipe away the condensation the windows would remain misty. Rain lashed nonstop against the vehicle and it made her feel depressed, not for the first time did she regret having started this journey. With nothing better to do than listen to the rain beating down hour after hour, the muscles of her jaw tightened. She overcame the urge to scream.

Darkness closed in and still the car rushed along. Intermittent light, shed from many street lamps dotting the road, became diffused. Priscilla tentatively moved her legs to ease the feeling of cramp in her limbs, she had been travelling in this car for several hours. Ever since the liner docked at Southampton and she had found the limousine waiting for her. It had taken several moments to overcome her surprise on seeing it. Aunt Moria was not one to pander to anyone's comfort, least of all that of her niece. Had it not been for the glass partition between her and the driver, Priscilla would have spoken to him. But the partition did not open and he showed no interest in her presence. His eyes were fixed on the road ahead. Only occasionally did he glance into the mirror to make sure his passenger was comfortable. Her airs and graces were off-putting and kept everyone at a distance, including him.

Lassitude swept through her body and she closed her eyes. This allowed her final goodbye thoughts to her parents to return. Priscilla had no interest in travelling with them to India, neither did she want to stay in America, several months in that country had been enough for her to find out it did not live up to her expectations. Already she was missing Barry and Sue. Her parents decided Priscilla should return and spend a few more months with Aunt Moria at the hotel on the edge of Tamsworth Forest.

She had already forgotten how bored she had been the last time she was there and how much she hated the forest. Priscilla stubbornly insisted she still wanted to go to her aunt, even though she knew that Barry and Sue were not there. She harboured a secret thought in her mind, which matured as the months passed by. She hoped to find her way to this other world where her brother and sister were now living.

Priscilla's thoughts were shattered by the sound of the glass panel in front of her sliding open. A gruff voice filled the small cabin. She was piqued because she realised it must have been locked on his side and there was no way she could gauge the driver's age in the dark, especially with his cap pulled down low and the dim lighted interior of the car was shadowing his face.

2

"This is where you get out, miss. A room has been booked for your stay here overnight. I expect you will be pleased to stretch your legs." His words were clipped and ceased abruptly as he reclosed the partition. Before Priscilla could think up an answer, he opened the back door of the car, letting the wind gust in, and rain spatter over her face. At the same time her hair was whipped in all directions. She drew back angrily.

Her indignant protest died before it was uttered, because the driver had not waited for her to answer him and was already standing at the front door of a gloomy old building. Whatever else it was, it looked nothing like a hotel. It had no name or neon lights flashing. The wind gusted ferociously round the driver's body, making it almost impossible for him to stand. It flattened his trousers against his long thin legs and whipped his coat to flap around like an escaped demon. The squally elements did their utmost to snatch it off his shoulders.

She watched carefully as he banged on the door to rouse whoever was inside. Priscilla had no intention of joining him and getting wet or standing out in the thick shadows. Anything could be lurking there. Her eyes could barely discern the building in the dim light that was shed by a swinging lantern. It squeaked and groaned with every movement it made.

A large amount of airborne leaves blew into the limousine like flying bats and Priscilla shuddered as one or two touched her cheeks. She was full of disquiet and started to imagine all sorts of horrible things that might happen to her, all alone out here in the dark. The area was devoid of people.

3

When the front door opened a little way and light flooded out onto the gravel path, she began to breathe again. An ample woman with rollers in her hair filled the space. Priscilla sucked in her breath. She looked nothing at all like a hotel proprietor and never issued a welcome to the girl waiting in the car. Priscilla strained her ears, trying to hear what was being said which was impossible against the roar of wind. She noticed something pass furtively between them before the woman retreated inside and blocked out the light. The door was closed.

The driver returned to the car with a jaunty whistle on his lips. Ignoring Priscilla, he slammed the car door in her face and then spoke to her from the driving seat. "It seems there's been a hitch, miss." He sounded pleased as he imparted the news. "No one here has received a booking for you and..."

"Ten out of ten for using your brains," Priscilla cut in arrogantly. "You've obviously come to the wrong place. A fool could see this is not a hotel."

"Beg your pardon, miss," he retorted sharply, his voice becoming surly, "but this *is* the place – and as I was saying before you rudely interrupted me, I can't drive you all the way to Tamsworth Forest without having a rest first. So my uncle has kindly offered to drive you himself. You just sit back like you've been doing these last few hours and enjoy it." The last words were added sarcastically. "I will pick him up at the crossroads. You will be with your aunt in the morning." With that, he slammed the glass partition into place and turned back to concentrate on his driving, ignoring her completely.

Priscilla fumed silently, unable to tell him that it was news to her that any arrangement had been made.

She sank back on her seat, fastidiously brushing wet leaves from her lap. He revved the engine with unnecessary force, reversed carelessly into nearby bushes and then went roaring down the road.

Priscilla compressed her lips, willing some other vehicle to come from the opposite direction and slow him down. What was it with men that they had to show off? Ten minutes elapsed before it dawned on her they had not reached any crossroads. Was he to be trusted? Priscilla rapped on the glass sharply, shouting at the same time, "Why have we left the main road?" and she hoped he couldn't hear the fear in her voice. But the driver seemed oblivious that she had spoken at all. It was either that or he was pleased to ignore her. She continued banging until with a screech of tyres the car came to a sudden halt, flinging her against the glass panelling.

Rubbing her head angrily, Priscilla became aware that the car-lights were signalling to someone else. Fear gripped her throat. She was being hijacked. The driver scrambled from his seat and disappeared into the darkness, leaving her alone. Before she had the car door open, a tall, well-muffled man took his place behind the steering wheel and another man sat in the car passenger seat beside him. This man was as obese as the woman had been in the house that they had called at earlier.

The engine revved up again and with another roar, the car raced smoothly on its way. The newcomers did not turn round to acknowledge their passenger. She might just as well not have been there. Priscilla huddled back in her corner, resentful and angry. Fear would not let her sleep. The fat person lit up a cigarette, and as he offered a light to the driver, the tall man turned his head. Priscilla gasped. In that split second she recognised the gaunt face and shrank as far away as she could. Only one person she knew had a nose like that – Professor Graham Harding. In that moment she knew real fear.

* * *

Dawn broke over the forest, and early morning mist swirled around the car. Life stirred in the undergrowth. One thin spiral of smoke rose straight up to the sky. Lots of animals watched from a safe distance but nothing ventured near to the car. People were not numerous in this part of the forest. As time elapsed, the sun rose higher and its warmth dissipated the mist. Birds greeted the new day with their lively chirping. It was this sound which aroused Priscilla from heavy sleep, after spending an uncomfortable night in the car.

She was none too pleased with conditions after being used to the luxury of her parents' apartment in America. With a groan, she surveyed the cramped interior of the vehicle, noting that the Professor and his companion had disappeared. She rubbed the back of her neck and eyes with her knuckles to remove the gritty feeling she was experiencing. She stretched her cramped limbs and the memory of last night's fiasco swamped her mind. The sardonic face of Professor Harding rose unbidden before her. She wondered belatedly if Aunt Moria was aware he intended to return to the hotel. It was hardly likely he had informed her. Professor Harding was not that accommodating.

She shivered, even though the sun streamed unhindered into the car where she sat. The other side was blocked by dense foliage, which obstructed her view through that window. The sight of so much greenery did not lift her morale. She considered the forest to be an alien and unfriendly place. It was not where she had expected to find herself stranded this morning. She noticed the car stood in the middle of a small clearing but there was no visible sign of how it had managed to get there. Trees encircled the vehicle, eliminating any sign of access, and the surrounding grass displayed no tyre tracks. It was as though someone had picked it up and placed it there.

Priscilla continued to mull over the mystery of her situation, until she realised she was losing valuable time by not escaping while she had the opportunity, but where to go, she had not yet worked out. Any moment, either of the men could return and she had no intention of being around to greet them. Excitement at the thoughts of outwitting them made her forget the initial fear of the forest. Grasping the door handle firmly she gave it a push and was nonplussed when it did not open. Angry at this setback she tried again, but the result was still the same. It was locked, which meant the door on the other side would be as well. She pouted, sourly contemplating the two men. Professor Harding had more sense than she gave him credit for and she cursed under her breath. It didn't take long for her fear to return. She was his prisoner. He had no intention of letting her arrive at the hotel. But what did he intend to do with her? This hired car had all been a ploy. Aunt Moria had never sent it for her. As far as she was concerned, public transport was good enough for her niece to travel in. Just what was the Professor's game? Frustrated, Priscilla drummed her fingertips on the shiny upholstery, her pretty face creased with a scowl. Then she noticed her chipped fingernails. This increased the hate she felt towards the man who only a few months ago hounded her sister Sue until someone from that other world saved her and took her to safety. That was not likely to happen to her, she thought. She was on her own. Maybe Moria would raise the alarm when she did not turn up at the hotel and a search party would come out.

A movement by the trees caught Priscilla's eye and her body tensed as a man emerged. He was ungainly and big, and came lumbering towards the car, displaying in one podgy hand the keys that would open it. Instead of being jubilant that help had arrived, her heart sank. She should have realised last night that the Professor's companion could be no other than Cyril Grant. Now she had two obnoxious men to contend with. He ambled closer to the car, mopping his red face. Then he smirked, catching sight of her watching him. With actions deliberately slow, he opened the door and stood back while she staggered out. He was peeved she showed no sign of being appreciative – especially since it had been his idea to lock her in the car in the first place. "No gratitude," he muttered sourly. "Don't kids of your age say 'thank you' anymore?"

"For what?" asked Priscilla haughtily, and her nose crinkled fastidiously as the smell of his sweaty body reached her. She straightened down her skirt. No way would she give him the satisfaction of looking in his direction. "You've not given me anything," and she continued to rub down her legs to get the circulation flowing. Cyril Grant leered as he watched her and licked his thick lips. "You're a proper little madam, aren't you? Can't think why he's bothering about you." Getting no response, he added aggressively, "I suppose you want some food now?"

Priscilla did raise her eyes this time and stared at him defiantly, wishing she was a boy and could thump him like Barry would have done. "What I want," she returned icily, "is to be taken to my aunt who must be worrying herself silly wondering where I am." Then her eyes blazed with anger. "Maybe you could tell me," she said, "What do you mean by bringing me to this godforsaken spot? Which way is the road from here?"

"Full of questions, aren't you." Cyril's eyes turned to slits in the rolls of flesh on his face. "I'm not your servant, Miss Hoity-Toity. Just get a move on and come with me if you know what's good for you," and as she stumbled, added, "Take those stupid shoes off."

A wave of nervousness assailed Priscilla but she strove to keep it under control. Her heart pumped rapidly, and loathing for the man before her shone from her eyes. She carefully moved one step away. "Your mistake," she retorted flippantly, "I'm not going anywhere with you. I'm going to my aunt and she can get the police onto you, so don't try to stop me. I can go faster than you."

But Cyril was faster than she gave such a big man credit for. His fat fingers clamped round her arm like steel. When she tried to pull away, his nails dug in viciously. His expression warned her to be careful. She had gone too far. He was enjoying this confrontation, so she stopped struggling.

9

"You'll pay for this," she hissed angrily. Instead of being put out, he seemed to relish her retaliation, and pulled her along.

"Where are you taking me?" she asked furiously.

"Questions, questions, questions," he sneered, adding annoyingly, "I'm afraid you'll have to ask the guvnor."

"So he pulls your strings, does he," was Priscilla's unwise retort and she cried out as he lifted his arm and a blow fell on her face. With her cheek smarting and showing the bright red mark left by his hand, she clenched her teeth together and went with him without a word. He gloated, thinking he knew just how to subdue the girl, but Priscilla was not the type to forget. He led the way through the trees where the ground became very squelchy underfoot, the results of last night's heavy rain. Fresh smells from the earth and the scent of flowers were lost on Priscilla. She never noticed the beauty of her surroundings. She saw only spider webs and crawling insects while she fastidiously tried to avoid the mud and unexpected puddles. By the time she reached the Professor, her shoes were ruined, her feet wet and her temper barely held in check.

Surveying the scene before her, Priscilla hardly dared to believe what she saw. Three black tents were erected and standing in a straight line. The Professor had a mathematical mind and had set up camp in the spacious clearing as though he were still in the army. A couple of fallen trees were being used as seats. He could not be faulted on his choice. From this spot the forest thinned out and gave a panoramic view of the area. Seeing so many trees only confirmed Priscilla's thoughts. This was indeed Tamsworth Forest, although she could not see any signs of Aunt Moria's hotel. In fact, she did not recognise this part of the forest at all. Her hopes of escape were dashed. Did rangers ever come this far? There was absolutely no way she would venture anywhere alone. She was not being the pioneer type. Anything in those trees could attack her. It was full of hidden dangers. Better stay here. The evil she knew was better than the evil that was hidden in the forest. Priscilla looked morosely at the man sitting comfortably on the log and cooking sausages in a frying pan over a small fire. He smiled in amusement, noting her sullen expression. "Not your scene at all, is it, Miss Dawson?" he remarked pleasantly, as if he were discussing the weather. "Still, never mind. I'm sure you'll soon get used to it. Sit down."

Priscilla had not missed the underlying order in his voice. She chose to ignore it, the same as she did Cyril Grant. "I'm not staying," she returned tartly and tossed her head defiantly. "You had no right to bring me here without my consent."

"We are on our high horse, aren't we," he retorted. "What a pity." To her mortification Professor Harding laughed, although the smile never reached his calculating cold eyes. "Well I was never one to go against a lady's wishes. If that's what you want – then go. Please yourself, Miss Dawson."

He turned his attention to the sausages as though she were not there. He flicked them over with a wooden palette knife and they sizzled in the fat, giving off a succulent smell. Because she remained where she was, he repeated again, "You're at liberty to leave whenever you like."

Cyril opened his mouth to protest but he caught the Professor's eye and quickly shut it. Priscilla was at a loss. All keyed up to argue with him, she now felt deflated. He had called her bluff. Something rustled in the undergrowth and, shuddering, Priscilla looked in that direction nervously. She was already terrified, and it was daytime. What would it be like when it was dark and she was prey to any animal? She wasn't going anywhere and the Professor knew it. The smell from the sausages made her mouth water. Although she always thought barbecues were the lowest form of eating, she was hungry and wanted an invitation to sit down and eat. Maybe after she had eaten she would be in more of a mind to escape. Licking her lips and swallowing, she asked in a very docile voice, "Why have you brought me here?"

The man with the frying pan raised his eyebrows a fraction at her sudden capitulation. He stared at her like a spider with its prey and read her mind correctly. "I need your help, Miss Dawson," he stated bluntly. "Believe it or not, you are the only person who can help me. Sit down with us and eat while I tell you what I want you to do."

Priscilla could not refuse. Her stomach rumbled and let her down. The smell of the sausages was the only thing that mattered. She did not have to do what the Professor wanted. She glanced at him and the expression on his face made her quail. He did not trust her any more than she trusted him, but he held all the trump cards.

CHAPTER 2
ALFIE

Haze hovered over a small part of the mountains, clinging to the snow-capped peaks like a cloud. In spite of strong winds gusting through the high passes it proved unwilling to disperse. In the bowels of the earth a fire raged fiercely in an underground temple; a fire that shed no heat. It was the cause of the red glow reflecting off the tall columns of stone which arched over the vaulted roof. This was the home of the deadly black snakes, there were hundreds of them slithering around the outer edge of the fire. They moved in a mindless fashion, squirming over each other, having nowhere else to go.

Deena stood on the earthen floor, staring into the depths of the burning embers. Her thin arms were raised. She fixed her eyes on the very centre of the fire, not blinking as she chanted an incantation. Other than her, the temple was empty. She had no need for help from her followers of the snake cult who were all women, the power she possessed was strong enough to summon the mighty Evonny from his rest. When her rasping voice ceased, a roar resounded round the cavern. The fire combusted and from its very heart, the huge black head of a dragon appeared. It reared up; its long neck twisting round sinuously towards her. The red from the flames reflected off its black scales. Large dark eyes, heavily lidded, glinted at her. They were full of evil intent. Its

13

head was bigger than Deena's whole body. She was ageless and stood no more than three feet high, but in her small compact frame Deena wielded a power much stronger than these creatures. So used to giving orders, she did not wait for the outraged dragon to speak. Ignoring him, she said in her gravelly voice, which was sharp with anger: "You did not attend the meeting. You dishonoured us all by your absence. Your name did not appear on the pact which was signed. Will you please explain your outrageous behaviour? You are as much a leader as Sheeka."

Evonny unfurled his great leathery wings from the centre of the flames and reared up tall, towering over her minute figure. His mouth gaped wide and he engulfed her body with fire, but she remained unscathed and watchful.

"I will never agree to that pact," he roared, his voice thundering round the temple. "Sheeka is turning into a woman. We are a proud race and king of the skies. We are not made to be beholden to the humans. You can say what you like, but I will tell you now, I will never be beholden to a lesser power. If any come near my colony I will burn them up without any feeling of remorse. They should not be in our land. Sheeka is letting us down."

"You're a fool," Deena snapped back. "It is you who are letting down your people. Great things can be achieved by working together. Is your mind so befuddled as not to see that?"

Evonny was incensed. He began to solidify even further. A taloned claw emerged from the flames and moved towards her. From Deena's upraised hands came a bolt of light which hit the dragon's scaly body to remind him where he was. "Stop where you are this instant," she exclaimed furiously. "I brought you here to talk – not demonstrate your powers." As the dragon retracted his foot she continued icily, "You have already put yourself in exile, but I will do better than that, I shall see to it that your banishment is extended forever unless you come to your senses."

The dragon's black head snaked down with the intention of intimidating her. She could feel his hot breath on her face, but without so much as a flinch, she stood firm. His derisive laugh rumbled in his throat. "Don't bother, Deena. I shall never return to my brothers all the time Sheeka allows humans to ride him," Evonny snarled, and seeing his expression, Deena became cunning.

"Then that is a great pity. You will never see or mate with Silver," she murmured slyly, and that cut into his pride like a sharp blade. "She is Sheeka's only daughter and she has befriended the human King's only daughter. They go everywhere together."

Evonny paused, considering her words – but he was not without his own cunning. He turned to the wily old woman, a foxy expression in his half hidden eyes. "No one can stop me from flying where I wish, be it in my own domain or over the palace. No one in their right mind would stand up against me in a fight. I shall have Silver – just you wait and see."

"Only if you sign the pact," replied Deena.

"No, it doesn't mean that at all," the dragon roared contemptuously. "It means I will pick up a human girl and take her to my colony – and if Silver does not come to save her, I will kill this woman." Anger rumbled in his throat and he fixed Deena with hard eyes ending with

"This meeting has been pointless. You could have saved yourself a lot of energy by leaving me alone."

Unmoved, the snake Queen stared at the proud magical monster through the flames. Evonny was everything a dragon should be, except that he lacked common sense. When Sheeka befriended a human boy many years ago, Evonny deliberately caused a rift within the dragon colony. He did it because he wanted to rule the colony himself. He said Sheeka was getting soft, but the other dragons did not agree with him. Feeling unwanted, Evonny deliberately put himself in exile to build up his own colony, only a few followed him, but enough to cause trouble for the new treaty between the people of Therossa and the dragons. Deena's ingenious mind came to her rescue. Looking as though she were succumbing to his mighty power, she inquired innocently, "Would anything change your attitude, Evonny? After all, you have everything you need – haven't you?"

"Except the Crystal Horse," he replied. Evonny's powerful voice was querulous and his eyes took on a greedy look. Suddenly he rounded on Deena and thundered arrogantly "Get me that, woman. Get me the Crystal Horse and I will consider your treaty."

His roar filled the cavern and he congratulated himself on outwitting the small woman before him. He knew he was safe in continuing his life in the same old style. No one could approach the Crystal Horse. It was a mythical creature that had never been seen. What did it look like? It was born of the faeries, the enchanted ones. He did not wait for Deena to answer or to be released by her. He used his own magic and vanished before her startled eyes. Deena's arms dropped to her sides and she wondered for the first time in aeons if she should transfer her powers to another. It was not so very long ago that the dragon would never have dared to leave her.

* * *

Priscilla took a long time before deciding to accept the casually issued invitation to join the two men for a meal. There was something about the Professor's disposition that was not ringing true. Inwardly she knew the correct thing to do was to reject his offer and show some independence by walking off, but it was not in her makeup to put herself in a position whereby she would find herself all alone in an unknown part of the forest, and besides which, she was hungry. The idea of refusing food was intolerable. Edging nearer to the fire she sat down on a log, as far away from the men as she could get, and in return received a sceptical look from the Professor. Colour rose under her skin and she contrived to cover it up with a weak smile as she daintily picked up a hot sausage. She watched her captors surreptitiously from under lowered lashes, congratulating herself on pretending to be complaisant.

When the Professor deemed it to be the right moment to speak, his caustic voice demoralised her completely. "Tomorrow morning, Miss Dawson, you will make yourself useful and take me to your grandmother's cottage. You needn't look like that either," he added, noticing the dismay on her face. "I am a busy man and have neither the time nor patience for people who do not earn their own keep. Still…" with an effort he made his voice become condescending, "I must be fair. They say – one good turn deserves another."

Priscilla choked on his flagrant twisting of the situation. She did not owe him anything, she was his prisoner, and as such had no intention of helping him out, no matter what he wanted. Although to visit her grandmother was not exactly what she had expected him to ask. She glared at the arrogant man, who ignored her by offering Cyril Grant another sausage. He was full of pleasantries today. She became wary. In fact, Priscilla never knew he could be like this. Suddenly she lost her appetite. She sensed the hidden undercurrents within the group. From now on, she must try not to antagonise him if there was to be any hope of escaping. He was unaware of how ignorant of the forest she was. Priscilla could lose herself within one hundred yards. The layout of the forest was a mystery to her, and one she had no intention of solving. But she did not put it past the Professor to leave her stranded here. The thought put the fear of God into her. Priscilla gave herself a shake and tried to appear rational. In what she hoped was a normal voice, she asked, "What do you want my grandmother for?"

Professor Harding twisted his head towards her. His face was shadowed from the sun, and his cold grey eyes raked over her. Instinctively she shrank away. "Nothing you need to worry your empty head over," he answered dismissively. Then, as though he had suddenly thought of it, added, "I trust you are ready to repay all the kindness we have shown you by bringing you here. If it had not been for us you might still be stranded at Southampton Docks."

"Repay you!" Priscilla stared at him incredulously.

Cyril Grant cut in rudely, saying, "You heard him, girl. Stop being a parrot. You will take us both to your grandmother's cottage or it will be worse for you."

Priscilla sprang up from the log. "If it hadn't been for you two," she exploded, "I would now be with my aunt at the hotel. You have deliberately brought me here against my will. I demand to be taken back to the hotel immediately."

The atmosphere became electric. A strange bird flew across the clearing, unnoticed by the three people. An unfamiliar noise came from the trees, which only Priscilla seemed to be aware of. The Professor removed all the sausages from the frying pan, pretending she had not spoken. He had no intention of wasting his breath on her. While she fumed and tried to suppress her fear, Cyril leered at her, watching her humiliation with enjoyment. He lumbered to his feet at the same time as she did, and towered above her shrinking form. "You're not in any position to demand anything." His voice was malicious. "Your family has caused us enough trouble as it is already. If I had my way, girl, you would be pleading for mercy instead of having the audacity to bargain for conditions. Do you know what," he looked menacingly from her and then towards the trees, "there are still wolves in the forest. I heard some last night. If you don't co-operate with us, we will throw you to them."

Priscilla turned a sickly colour, palpitations starting up in her throat. He took a step towards her as though to enforce his words and out of control she shrieked "You wouldn't dare."

Her scream caused a flock of birds to take wing and Cyril's laugh was sinister. "You're suffering from delusions, my lady. I mean what I say." With that, his fat arm shot out and he grabbed hold of her. Priscilla was beside herself with fear. She had never been so terrified in all her life. "Take your hands off me, you brute," she screamed, and in sheer desperation kicked out at him. Her shoe caught him on the shin. As Cyril swore, the Professor snapped imperiously. "Leave her alone, Grant."

"She kicked me!" he roared angrily, but noticing the expression on the Professor's face, let his hand drop away. Trembling, Priscilla looked at her unexpected saviour. "Are the wolves still there?" she asked.

"I shouldn't think so," the thin man answered grimly, remembering the one which bit him several months ago. "Forget them, Miss Dawson, you're becoming neurotic. I need you in one piece for tomorrow."

It was now or never. He had to know she didn't know where her grandmother's cottage was. Avoiding eye contact with him, she said meekly, "I'm not taking you anywhere."

"I told you!" Cyril bellowed out. "She's deliberately being obtuse. Get rid of her, man. We can manage without..."

"Shut up, Grant." The Professor turned to Priscilla, his eyes glittering like ice. "Why?" he snarled, "haven't I made myself clear?"

"Perfectly." But she backed away for safety.

"Good," his razor sharp answer sliced the air. "Then what is the reason?"

"There ...there's one thing you haven't thought of."

The Professor's smile turned predatory. "I thought there might be. What is it?"

"I don't know where I am, I've never been here before in all my life. I have no idea how to get to my grandmother's cottage."

At last she had their undivided attention. Cyril started to bluster that she was lying and he knew exactly how to get the truth out of her, when to Priscilla's relief the Professor silenced him by holding up his hand. "I will give you the benefit of the doubt, Miss Dawson." His voice was curiously flat. "In the morning, all three of us will navigate the forest. I would..." he broke off and swung round as a loud resounding crack came from the trees. Nothing moved and silence reigned supreme. *An animal*, he thought, disregarding the noise, and turned his attention back to the girl. "I would suggest you try and get some sleep to make up for last night. Please make use of the middle tent and if you want to wash – Cyril will show you the way to a pool."

One look at Cyril's predatory face and Priscilla decided against it. When no move was made towards her, she asked in a quavering voice, "Aren't you going to tie me up? I might run away in the night."

This time the Professor laughed out loud. "Do you know what, Miss Dawson? I'm going to take that risk. You are free to roam anywhere you like. I would suggest though, that you take some sausages with you. You are going to need all your strength in the morning."

It was on the tip of her tongue to refuse, but common sense got the better of her. She picked up the plate of sausages and asked meekly, "Can I have a drink as well?"

* * *

21

Alfie followed the tyre marks even though he was surprised at the direction they were leading him. The sun shining from behind the trees made the forest look dark and forbidding because it threw shadows over his path. He followed the indentations in the ground, feeling sure they would soon peter out. He had never been on such a route before that was so unsuitable for cars. The weeds along the edge were overgrown and encroaching everywhere. Tufts of grass grew in the centre of the track and would soon stop the car completely. It could not continue moving on such a surface. At the next bend, he felt sure he'd see the car parked.

Alfie whistled to keep his disturbing thoughts at bay. Was it only three hours ago he had been standing in the hotel, talking to a distraught woman who wanted to know where her niece was. According to her, she should have arrived yesterday, but nothing had been heard of her. She was convinced there must have been an accident because of the foul weather last night. Only fools would have been out driving through that rain. Why had she not been notified about the cause of the delay? Alfie had done his best to allay her fears, and said he would retrace his steps, keeping a look out for the car; and if he found it, he would telephone her.

He set out, a fresh breeze touching his face, brushing away all signs of fatigue. It was the sort of day to be out in the open, hardly a cloud in the pale blue sky. Yesterday's storm was a thing of the past, with just an uprooted tree here and there to remind anyone it had ever occurred. He drove slowly along the deserted road looking for skid marks, although the last thing he wanted to find was the car upside down in a ditch. He meditated on his uncle, thinking how foolish he had been, making the trip to Tamsworth Forest in such weather. Not that he was complaining. Alfie was pleased to lose the job, but something about his uncle's attitude troubled him. So much so, he decided to search for the missing car in his own little banger. At that time of night it had taken him a long time to find his own car, and by then, his uncle was miles away.

At last he found what he was looking for — some tracks. The dark skid marks veered to the side of the road and were still fresh. He scanned the area carefully, looking for the car, and was relieved there was no sign of it or an accident. It had not landed in a ditch. The skid marks pointed to a narrow path. In the dark it must have looked like a secondary road – but why his uncle took it was a mystery. There was no way it was going to lead anywhere, unless by chance it did lead through the forest. Alfie parked his own car by the side of the road, locked it, and set out on foot, enjoying the fresh air and the walk. He loved being out in the open spaces.

As he ambled along, he found himself wondering about the passenger in the car. She had not been very talkative. She was a lovely looking girl, but self-centred and aloof. She certainly did not seem the type to love forests. In fact, she did not seem the type to love anything. He wondered how she got on with his uncle who was not an easy man to make conversation with. Before long he was perspiring and removed his jacket by slinging it over his broad shoulders. Thank goodness for the shade.

He trudged slowly along the track, full of expectancy, and could only think how good it was to be out in the open and on his own. The track took a sharp bend, and he stopped abruptly. The path veered off in three directions, and there was no car. Two tracks were churned up mud, perfect for showing tyre tracks, and the third so narrow even a toy pedal car would have had difficulty in getting through, let alone a limousine. There was no sign of broken branches which was proof a car never went that way. The more he looked the more he realised it couldn't have got any further than where he was standing. The car tracks had come to a halt.

Perplexed, he scratched his head and deliberated his next move. He churned over all the possibilities that could be the cause of this unexpected setback. Had his uncle reversed the car and backtracked down the path? Alfie did not think so. His uncle never made mistakes. That was one of his idiosyncrasies. It was obvious he could not stand here all day like a dim-witted fool. He had to make a decision, so he turned to his right and stepped on the path. Immediately the mud squelched up to his ankles. Alfie quickly returned to terra firma, looking with distaste at his shoes. His footprint showed up clearly in the mud. At least he had proved no car had ever gone along there, so straight on was the only other possibility – but even as he looked, he knew that way was impossible. This was getting ludicrous. It must have been hidden. Exhaling slowly, he looked in the most ridiculous places and drew a blank. Where was the car? It was not feasible that it could vanish in a place like this.

The sun rose higher. The flies became a nuisance circling round his hot face. It had taken him half a day to get this far and he had not met a soul. Pity he had not thought about sandwiches before he set off. If memory served him correctly, there was a bar of chocolate in his pocket. After rummaging around, he produced the soft mass and quickly devoured it. Licking his fingers, he caught sight of a man trudging down the lane with a gun over his shoulder, happily sloshing through the mud. Hope filled him at last. As he came alongside Alfie, he slowed his steps and stared at him in surprise.

"Good morning, lad. Not many people come along here. You took me by surprise." His greeting was gruff but he smiled pleasantly. Rangers were used to coming upon strangers. More often or not, they were lost.

Alfie acknowledged the ranger, and before he moved on, inquired casually, "You haven't passed a car up that way – have you?"

The ranger looked at him as though he were mad. "You're joking, lad. No car could travel in that mire. Take my advice and go back to the road and try the lane a hundred yards further on. That's made up. You might find one there if you've lost it." He chuckled to himself as though he had made a joke, touched his cap and continued up the track Alfie had given up on. Mud or not, he strode on going about his business.

Alfie waited until he was out of sight, then curiosity consumed him. He would search the narrow path. There was no harm in seeing where it led. Full of determination, he crossed to the opening and pushed through the bushes. The grass was lush on the other side and the trees seemed to grow closer together. There was no sign of any mud, and as he poked around, there was no sign of any car either. He paused; it was rather pointless to continue in the direction he was going since the path had vanished completely. Alfie turned round, squeezing through the undergrowth. He soon became lost to his surroundings and thought nothing of it, but after nearly an hour had passed, it suddenly dawned on him that he really was lost because he could not find his way back to the muddy path. It took a lot to make Alfie feel nervous, but this time he did feel vaguely uneasy. He had never got lost before in his life.

In the far distance he thought he heard voices, the first signs of humanity he had heard all day other than the ranger. He was drawn in that direction like a moth to a flame. Although he homed in on it, he never got any nearer the sound and eventually realised he was going round in circles. This was getting bizarre. He began to think the forest was playing tricks on him. With this idea still in his mind, he studied his position carefully, taking stock of what he was passing. It was then, quite by accident, he saw the car, and his mouth went dry at the sight.

Standing abandoned by the trees, it could easily have been missed; it looked like a vehicle that had been neglected for years. The bodywork was corroded. Profuse ivy covered most of the roof and its waving tendrils were creeping over the bonnet. Alfie blinked. He must be mistaken. This was a different car, one that had been here for years. Alfie made his way slowly to the rusty wreck and it was not until he saw the number plate that he knew for sure it was the same vehicle he had driven from Southampton. The hair prickled on his arms and legs and the temperature of the air around seemed suddenly to plummet. Alfie felt eyes were watching him from the trees and he turned round, frantically looking for a way out, still following the elusive sounds.

CHAPTER 3
A SHOCK FOR PRISCILLA

Flimsy clouds scudded across the heavens. A strong breeze made the treetops wave in unison. Alfie worked diligently in the clearing surrounded on three sides by forest. He tended a fire which roared with help from the wind and busied himself with cooking, anything to keep his worrying thoughts from taking over. Behind him three black tents stood isolated and gave the appearance of being empty. That is what saved the one and only occupant.

Within the middle tent, Priscilla felt awful. She was not usually prone to headaches but this morning her head thumped with every move she made. No sound penetrated into the confines of the tent from the outside. The caustic voice of Professor Harding and the everlasting whining from Cyril Grant were absent. Hopefully, that meant they were elsewhere. She peered through dark heavy eyes at the small gap where the tent flap didn't meet the other side and saw morning was already well advanced. She was a coward. It was fear that kept her where she was, certainly not the comfort of her surroundings. The tent was frugal, typical of anything belonging to the Professor; it possessed the bare necessities for survival. A blow up mattress and large rug, with one added extra which the Professor knew nothing about. The spider was large and hairy and leered down at her from its position on a bar. Priscilla tried to avert her eyes from it, but her sinews tightened, knowing it was there.

When the whistling started up, it came as a shock. Someone outside was rendering one of the latest tunes. The hammers began thumping in her head all over again. Priscilla pulled the rug over her head to blot the sound out. She had had enough. She was determined to find her grandmother's cottage today – if only to be able to sleep in a proper bed. Helping the Professor had nothing to do with it. After all the howls and strange noises which had petrified her in the dark, there was no way she was going to spend another night out in the open. Even her thoughts of finding the other world diminished. Aunt Moria and the hotel were looking more luxurious by the minute.

The whistling from outside still penetrated through the rug, no matter how hard she tried to close her ears to it. In spite of her frustration she found it hard to believe that Professor Harding even knew such a modern piece of music. Then it occurred to her, he sounded happy. If he was in such a good mood now was the time to go out and confront him. Hoping that Cyril Grant was not around, she pushed back the rug and stepped through the opening of the tent, only to be met by a gust of wind which blew her backwards. Staggering under the onslaught, she caught hold of the tent to keep her balance, and shivered. She stared across the clearing towards the man who was busy cooking. Not sausages this time, but bacon. Its heavenly aroma drifted across to her, tickling her nose so that she licked her lips in anticipation. Then she paused. It was not the Professor who was whistling. She noticed this man had thickset shoulders and looked in need of a haircut. That was something Priscilla noticed inadvertently without even trying.

Something made the man aware of her scrutiny and he turned to face her. He recognised her immediately but was also concerned. She looked nothing like the self-assured girl he had picked up at the docks. He wondered what she was doing here, and how she got on with his uncle. He waved an arm at her in greeting. "Come over here and have some of this tea I've made. You look as though you are in need of it."

Because he expected a rebuff he turned back to what he was doing. He didn't like girls. His knowledge of the other sex was sadly limited. They scared him to death. Yet she looked in need of help and he had a chivalrous streak within him. As he agitated the tea in boiling water Priscilla approached, finding it hard to push her lethargic body towards where he stood, wondering why he looked vaguely familiar. Her suspicious nature came to the fore; there was nothing sluggish about her mind. Keeping up a front of composure she asked, with a touch of belligerence in her voice "Where is the Professor? Why is he not here?"

Her abrupt greeting surprised Alfie. He gave no sign of it, but veiled his expression and eyed her carefully. "Because Professor Harding and Cyril Grant went to their car some time ago," he explained, although this was not strictly true. They had been gone hours, but she wasn't to know that. He was still feeling furious at the way they hadn't believed him when he spoke of the condition of their car. They wanted to see it for themselves. Now they had vanished into the night. He realised Priscilla was still waiting for a better explanation.

"They wanted to get something from it. They will be back shortly…I hope."

The pause was too long. Priscilla detected a lie. Keeping up an unsmiling countenance, she wondered whether to trust him. "Who are you?" she demanded coldly, almost as if it were her right to know.

"Alfie," he answered obligingly, and mentally congratulated her on being careful. Now everything should be all right. With a broad smile on his homely face he said with approval "Now that we've introduced ourselves, would you like some bacon?"

Priscilla stepped back, wary. "You don't know who I am," she pointed out stiffly, and jumped violently when Alfie slapped down the mug he was holding in exasperation. Who did she think she was? He swung round on her angrily, forgetting to be chivalrous.

"Will you stop trying to be so correct, Miss Priscilla Dawson," he snapped. "We are in the middle of nowhere and I'm offering you the hand of friendship, which believe me, at this moment, you are sorely in need of. You're in more danger than you realise. Aren't you the least bit worried about the absence of your companions?"

The volume of his voice made something snap in her mind. Now she recognised him. He was the driver who picked her up at Southampton and never spoke the whole journey until they reached the gloomy old house. He said something about his uncle driving the car. *His uncle.* Priscilla's heart missed a beat. This must be Professor Harding's nephew. She slumped down on a log, having no conception of how forlorn she looked. Already annoyed at his outburst, Alfie relented, and passed her a mug of tea, saying "Drink it while it's hot. Sorry there is no milk. I'll get you some bacon as well."

Clasping the mug tightly in her hands, Priscilla felt deflated. How could she expect help from him, knowing who he was? She watched morosely as he removed a few rashers from the frying pan. He looked completely at ease out in the open. She studied his face. There was no similarity in his features to those of the cynical Professor, and if she was fair, he had none of the other's obnoxious nature either. The tea made her feel better even though it tasted disgusting. Her frozen mind thawed out while she tried to make sense of what he said. To what danger was he alluding? They were in a perfectly civilised part of Tamsworth Forest because his uncle wanted to find the way to her grandmother's cottage. It suddenly dawned on her that he thought her grandmother might direct him to this other world where Sue and Barry were. A grim smile touched her lips because her grandmother had no idea where it was either.

Alfie asked her what the smile was for and Priscilla was confused. For some inexplicable reason, she told him.

Alfie seemed to know a lot about the mysterious other world. His uncle had never informed him, but he had picked up a great deal of information by listening to his conversation with Cyril. He knew some woman was involved. He was always going on about Ruth who vanished there years ago. When Alfie told her this, Priscilla froze. She never realised Professor Harding had a personal stake in this venture. Alfie regarded her quizzically. "Penny for your thoughts," he said, "I don't suppose you know the way yourself, do you?"

"Of course I don't." Priscilla's voice was flat. "There is no way I would search the forest for it. I'm not the outdoor type," and he silently agreed with her.

Priscilla brought the conversation back to his previous remark of 'you're in more danger than you realise'. Was he alluding to his uncle, or something else? Because he did not answer right away, she asked again. "What did you mean?"

Alfie studied her white strained face and wondered if he was doing the right thing by telling her what he suspected.

"Where do you think you are, Priscilla?" he asked gently.

"Tamsworth Forest of course."

"Well, you're in a forest, I grant you," Alfie pursed his lips. "But I doubt very much it's Tamsworth."

"Of course it is," she protested, and drew in a ragged breath, wondering what on earth he was getting at. "Your uncle brought me here on the night of the storm."

"I know. I followed you."

"Why would you do that?" Now she was really startled and again Alfie hesitated. Whatever he said he was sure she would not believe him, but for her own sake he tried. "I was concerned about my uncle's attitude. When he took over the driving he seemed to be full of frenzied anticipation. He had something else on his mind – other than delivering you to the hotel. Believe it or not, I worried about your welfare. The same as your aunt is worrying about you now."

"My aunt," Priscilla echoed, "you've seen my Aunt Moria?"

"I saw her yesterday." Alfie replied, and Priscilla wanted to scream at him to go on. Eventually he said "I called in at the hotel to check up on you, and before you say anything, I'm not in the habit of running after women." He heard her quick intake of breath but still went on doggedly. "She was worried about your not turning up. So was I, and I said I would search for you."

"Then why on earth did you come into the forest?" Priscilla's voice was barely audible.

"Because that's where the car went," he replied. "I was following the car tracks and felt most uneasy when I saw where they were heading. Then I found the car." He paused, and frowned. Some inner sense told Priscilla something was wrong. "Has it got a puncture?" she asked naively. That could be the only reason why they were still here.

He realised there was no way he could go round this. "The car was rusty and unusable, covered in ivy as though it had been there for years. It is completely cut off by trees and there is no way back to the hotel. Priscilla, look at me," he ordered, as she turned in the opposite direction to hide the horror in her eyes. "Somehow or the other, we have crossed into this other world. I don't know how or why, but I do know I don't know how to get back."

Stunned, this time Priscilla did look at him and to Alfie's dismay she shrugged. "Is that all, Alfie? I shouldn't worry. Your uncle will know the way back."

He took hold of her shoulders and wanted to shake her for being so obtuse. "Haven't you been listening to me? Priscilla, there is no way back. I doubt very much we shall see Cyril or my uncle again." He felt her trembling but refused to stop. "There is evil out there amongst those trees. Can't you feel it? It's after us now and we must move from here. We're on our own. There is just you and me. You've got to be strong and..." He broke off and swore because Priscilla slumped to the ground in a dead faint.

* * *

Completely at a loss, Alfie stared at her prone form and silently cursed his bad luck at having been landed with such a highly-strung companion. Derisive laughter from the forest made his skin crawl. He felt eyes boring into him. Yet when he looked, the area was deserted. Trees swayed in the gathering breeze. He wondered about the fate of his uncle and Cyril, and why whoever it was out there had not come forward to take them as well. He felt decidedly apprehensive.

It was some time later that Priscilla recovered from her indisposition and consented to make an exploratory journey with him through the trees to see if they could find who dwelt in the forest. Maybe those people could give them the help they needed. Priscilla was relieved when the black tents were abandoned. Something about her attitude made it doubtful to Alfie that anything he had told her had sunk in. He soon found out that her logic was not like that of a normal person. So long as nothing happened to her and she was not left on her own, Priscilla did not care what happened. She had no idea what was the best course of action to take, and was content to throw her lot in with Alfie.

They pushed their way through a strangely silent forest. The wind was the only sound to be heard. Alfie did not trust what he could not see. Each one of them carried a rug and water bottle because Alfie refused to carry it all himself. Priscilla made a scene, the first of many, by saying Alfie was no gentleman — to which he answered, he wasn't a packhorse either. When she discovered there was no way she could cajole him into doing what she wanted, she sulkily followed in his footsteps. The thickly growing trees hindered their progress. Most of the time they pushed through tangled undergrowth. Alfie soon found out Priscilla was a bad travelling companion, and even though he did his best to make things easier for her, she would continually lag behind and complain about every hindrance that happened. More and more frequently she insisted they were heading in the wrong direction because she thought Alfie had chosen to go uphill just to annoy her. Exasperated, he swung round to face her. In doing so, a branch flew back narrowly missing her face and she glowered at him indignantly.

"It's not too late for you to go back, you know," he told her impatiently, trying to keep a civil tongue. Perspiration ran through his hair and down his red face. The humid atmosphere of the forest caused his shirt to cling to his chest where patches of dampness showed through. His temper was on a short fuse. She stared at him defiantly. Her hair was awry and clothing dishevelled. She wasn't looking her best, and because Alfie didn't seem to care what she looked like, it niggled her.

"Then let's go back," she snapped. Her fear was making her intolerable to be with. "I can't see any point in walking in this direction. If we return to your uncle, he will know what is best to do. He is after all, older and wiser than you."

Alfie digested this statement in silence. She had already forgotten the Professor had disappeared and the area around the tents was not safe. He absentmindedly swatted a fly which had decided to make a meal of his arm, while surreptitiously watching her use a handkerchief to wipe her forehead. He jumped when she spoke.

"Am I growing horns or something? Why can't you find a proper path? Your uncle would have done so. He's a man who's got his head screwed on the right way."

His uncle, again? Alfie's face twisted with wry humour. "I'm sorry you think I'm too young to have any sense. I apologise for being so wrong. You had better get started if you're going back. It's going to take you at least two hours — even though it is downhill. I just hope he's there to greet you."

Priscilla stared at him, nonplussed. "But you're coming with me," she said angrily.

"No I'm not," Alfie retorted firmly. "You're on your own. I'm going forward. Tell you what though — if I see your aunt I will tell her where I last saw you."

"You're an unfeeling beast," Priscilla screamed in childish temper. "You know I'll get lost." One or two crocodile tears spilt from her eyes but Alfie had had enough. He was finding her an incredible nuisance and chivalry had long since gone out of the window. For the hundredth time he asked himself why he had foolishly poked his nose into something which was not his affair. A pretty face did not lead to congenial friendship. "You won't get lost," he said perfunctorily, "just follow the path back. You can't have forgotten it already."

Priscilla compressed her lips. If looks could kill, Alfie should have dropped dead. "You know there's no path — never has been one," she answered peevishly. Suddenly she changed her tactics and tried to sound more compliant, asking "Where are you taking me?"

Alfie placed his hands on his hips and regarded her through narrowed eyes. "That depends on whether or not you're still coming with me. I'm not going to put up with your complaining hour after hour. I'd rather be on my own."

Priscilla glared. "There's no need to be so unpleasant."

"I'm not being unpleasant, but neither am I going to be a nursemaid to you. If you can't act like an adult, stay here until someone else finds you, as they must have already found Cyril and my uncle."

The words were no sooner out of his mouth than the undergrowth near their feet thrashed violently. A creature hunting for its dinner found its prey, which let out a piercing scream. At the same time an eerie blast from a horn sounded in the distance. Priscilla forgot all about decorum and threw herself on the startled Alfie, clutching him until he was nearly throttled. Feeling unnerved himself, he pushed her away awkwardly and hoped she hadn't noticed the tell-tale colour mount up in his face.

"It's OK. Nothing to worry about," he said soothingly. "Follow me closely. I think the trees ahead are thinning out. At least that horn tells us we are not alone. Sooner or later we shall see where we are."

Trembling, Priscilla followed, but so closely he could feel her breath on the back of his neck. Alfie was thankful that fear had silenced her. The horn sounded again, followed by a chorus of howls. Then came sudden silence. That was far more unnerving than the noise had been. They pushed forward and unexpectedly emerged from the trees. The force of the wind hit them. They realised belatedly what a protection the forest had been. Gasping for breath and slithering to a halt, they found themselves on the very edge of a high jagged bluff. It took a moment to adjust to the sudden change of scenery and their eyes opened wide in wonder. Standing where they were, on the brink of a rugged cliff, they braced themselves against the elements because the wind buffeted their bodies and whipped their clothes like flags. It gusted savagely around them — almost as though it intended to sweep them off their feet. After the humidity of the forest, the air was now chilly. Priscilla stepped back a pace as strange sensations ran up her legs. The edge spread away in both directions until it disappeared into a blue haze. The actual forest from which they had just stepped, sprawled to within two paces of the drop, leaving a narrow path on which to walk. In this wind, that would be a very dangerous thing for them to attempt.

Below, when Priscilla could muster up enough courage to look down, she saw a vast valley intersected by ribbons of water which connected here and there to larger lakes. The water, roughened up by the elements, sparkled like diamonds as the sun was reflected off its moving surface. Trees and rocks scattered the landscape and black dots crawled slowly in a line like an army of ants out foraging for food. They were too far away to see what they were.

Priscilla sucked in her breath, looking in the far distance to where majestic mountains reared their heads to the sky. White peaks were dazzling as the sun came into contact with the icy summits. Just for the moment she was unable to say anything. A lump rose up in her throat and she turned to Alfie, her gaze grief-stricken. "I didn't realise how big this world was. How on earth will I ever find Sue and Barry here?" This time her distress was real. Tears of despair rolled down her cheeks. She looked so vulnerable; Alfie put his arms round her to give some sort of support.

"We'll find them, Priscilla," he said stoutly, hoping they were the right words to reassure her. "Together we will search the valley below us and ask anyone we meet if they have heard of Sue and Barry."

Priscilla badly wanted to believe him, but standing on the edge of a precipice with no visible signs of how to get down to the bottom, was not very auspicious. She moved away and stared at the panoramic view before her, watching four black specks in the sky, weaving around in circles and slowly heading in their direction. Alfie joined her, worried she might do something stupid, like stepping too near the edge. It might crumble beneath her feet. Side by side they stood, braced against the wind. Occasionally it was necessary to shield their eyes against the glare of the sun. As the black specks became bigger, it was obvious that what they had first thought were birds were something much larger and more powerful. Alfie was the first to find his voice and he growled incredulously, "They look like flying lizards."

Priscilla squeezed her eyes to slits to see them better. Her voice came out sounding like a scream. "They've got people on their backs. What on earth are they?"

Surprise at the sight made her mouth fall open. Alfie, very much down to earth, frowned as he concentrated on them and at length muttered sceptically "Although I don't believe it — they look like dragons to me. I must be hallucinating because they exist only in fairy tales. It's this place. Be ready to run for the trees, Priscilla, if they come too near."

To their disappointment the dragons veered off and were soon small black specs again disappearing in the distance. Priscilla was still mesmerised but Alfie gave himself a shake and tried to be practical. "We can't stand here all day. This wind will freeze us to death. Shelter is what we need. The forest is not safe so it's obvious we've got to find a way down."

The urgency in his voice brought Priscilla back to her senses. She looked dubiously over the edge and felt that funny feeling in her legs again, and hoped he didn't mean they had to climb down. The cliff was not sheer as it had at first appeared; ledges could be seen here and there, giving handholds, and undergrowth covered the rocky wall giving a degree of safety. Alfie's keen eyes soon spotted what looked like a narrow path and a little way down, where there was a darker shadow on the rocky wall, he speculated there might be a cave. If they were lucky this could be their shelter. "We're going down there," he decided, almost arrogantly, and his voice brooked no argument. "It will give us shelter from this wind. Come on."

Priscilla hung back aghast. "Are you mad? I can't go down there," she wailed in horror. "I'll fall."

"You haven't tried yet," Alfie retorted angrily. "Come on — give me your hand."

"You must be joking." Priscilla moved away. "I'm scared of heights."

Alfie counted to ten. He wasn't going to go through all this again with her and said between clenched teeth "Then I'm sure you won't mind if I go on without you. It's not safe to stay here."

"You're not leaving me here on my own," Priscilla gasped, her face turning white. "You wouldn't dare."

"Wouldn't I?" snapped Alfie, "then just you watch." He turned away from her and paused, his eyes opening wide with shock as he looked towards the trees. From all of them along the bluff, as far as he could see, white tendrils of mist were gushing out. Even as he watched, they thickened and grew denser. The mist was surging forward as though it had a mind of its own to trap the unwary. The hairs stood up on the back of Alfie's neck. There was something malevolent about its progress; it was not a natural phenomenon. The wind which was battering them, should have torn this mist to shreds, but still it came steadily closer — untouched. Her argument with Alfie forgotten, Priscilla stared, transfixed as the mist condensed and blotted out the trees completely. The first fingers of fog touched them and Priscilla gasped. "It's so cold yet it's burning my throat. What is it, Alfie?"

Alfie grabbed hold of her arm, dragging her protesting towards the edge. "I don't know," he snapped, "but we've got to get out of it." To Priscilla's consternation he stepped over the edge — and still holding her in a vice like grip, pulled her closer. He gazed at her through the swirling mist. "You're coming with me and don't you dare argue."

Priscilla coughed. She couldn't speak because her throat was cloying up. Once Alfie had his feet planted firmly, he dragged her after him. The terrifying drop was hidden by the bushes, which also stopped them from falling. The mist curled over the edge — hovered — and then followed them. Alfie had never known such fear and in desperation made his way lower — then he saw the cave opening. Without any hesitation he pushed Priscilla in and she shrieked as she went sprawling over loose scree. Alfie could feel himself losing all sense of movement in his limbs and a sickness rose in his throat. Without any warning he fell inwards on top of the unconscious form of Priscilla. The mist came into the cave and swirled over both of them — but neither was aware of it.

CHAPTER 4
A STARTLING DISCOVERY

In spite of their size, the four dragons swooped effortlessly through the sky and the afternoon sun reflected off their colourful scaly bodies. They were beautiful to watch. No wonder the lizard population had grown vain when everyone admired them. The people who watched the dragons from the ground, thought they moved at random like the birds but Silver led them through the skies without the slightest doubt that her decisions were the right ones. Her white body sparkled. She was a perfect foil against Sapphire, who was blue, and Firefly red, with Griffin coloured green. Silver was a princess of dragons and being the only daughter of Sheeka took charge whenever he was not around. She led them now on their daily reconnaissance over gypsy territory. They skimmed low over the undulating land and climbed steeply to the clouds above. All the dragons' human riders were stimulated and would never change their way of life.

Strong winds whipped back Sue's short golden hair as she glanced over her shoulder towards Barry. He sat proudly on Sapphire's shoulders, thinking the world of his allotted dragon; but it was doubtful if the blue dragon returned his feelings. She was of the old blood and still a little uncertain about carrying humans on her back. She did it for Silver's sake. Tansy and Annalee made up the foursome, riding on Firefly and Griffin, the two male dragons.

Sue found it impossible to speak with her companions. Conversation was difficult as the wind fragmented their speech so telepathy was the order of the day, and all were happy to use it except Barry. He still hadn't got the hang of it. Tracking the whereabouts of gypsy caravans on a daily basis allowed the humans a great deal of freedom. There were no hard and fast rules set. Far below them the beautiful countryside opened out a vast panorama to feast their eyes on. From the air things looked different. They received a completely new concept of Therossa. The dragon league, as it was now called, was an up and growing thing, with more and more people wanting to fly. But Tam had set a task for them to accomplish before he accepted any of the hopefuls.

Barry, riding at the rear of the little group, was vigilant in carrying out his job to see that they didn't miss anything. But it was not Sapphire's idea to be in that position, she was disgruntled and did very little to help him as he kept his eyes skinned looking for trouble. Over the past year Barry had matured beyond recognition, turning into a handsome youth who had the female population of Therossa at his feet, especially since he had discarded his glasses. Tansy and Annalee teased him unmercifully, but Barry grinned, not rising to their bait. Everyone knew there was a bond between him and the one-time hunter — ever since their captivity together with the Drazuzi.

The dragons were heading towards a high bluff fringed with trees that seemed to spread for miles in all directions. It was a part of the forest that ran parallel with the world from which he and Sue originated, so it was a place well known to both of them. Barry would have loved to get a closer look, not because his memories were bad, but because it was a connection with the past. For some unexplained reason, Silver suddenly veered off and the dragons automatically followed. Barry stared at the bluff until it disappeared from sight. He found his voice. He was sure he had seen two people standing there. Leaning closer to Sapphire's head, he threw caution to the wind and burst out urgently "Can you go back?"

Disgruntled, Sapphire swivelled her large head towards her usually silent rider on these missions and smoke belched from her nose. She beat her leathery wings to keep up with Silver and roared, "Too dangerous." Then she forged ahead, ignoring him completely.

Barry was not intimidated. "But I'm sure I saw someone standing on that bluff," he shouted back desperately. "You're supposed to do what we want." They were the wrong words, especially to Sapphire, but he didn't care. The dragon seethed at being ordered about by a human. Immediately she was on her high horse. Treaty or no treaty, she was not going to be spoken to like that. "There are no people there — now or ever," the dragon responded in a dismissive voice. "That is Drazuzi land. Settle down, boy."

The term 'boy' rankled. Barry thought he had an understanding with Sapphire so he used more authority the next time he spoke. "But I saw them. Please turn back so that I can check."

Sapphire answered that by increasing her speed and going in the opposite direction. Very soon the Bluff faded into a blue haze. Barry's fury knew no bounds and he kept twisting his head to look backwards. There was nothing to be seen. His frustration penetrated the dragon's thought-waves and with a resigned puff of smoke, Sapphire drew level with Silver, their wings almost touching. Human ears did not hear what passed between the two dragons, but unlike Sapphire, Silver's head snaked back to Sue and she said,

"Barry thinks he saw someone on the Bluff. It is not in our orders to investigate there, but Sapphire is convinced he will do something stupid if we don't. She said he is paranoid. We are near enough to circle back and pass over the Bluff just once more — so hold on tight."

Sue looked quickly at Barry's set face before Silver dived, circling to retrace her journey. Because of the dragons' unique telepathy, soon all four knew what had occurred and communicated it to their riders. For a while, Sapphire kept level with Silver, then for reasons of her own she fell to the back. They skimmed over the ground so low their shadows passed over the landscape and put the fear of God into the gypsies they passed. Excitement built up. Not often was the pattern of their routine flight altered and any stranger seen, wherever that was, was news. Once again the Bluff loomed up, and this time Silver approached closer, intending to circle over the trees. Shock took away Barry's voice. There were no trees to be seen. In fact, there was hardly any bluff visible. A thick sinister looking mist covered all but the base of the cliffs. Sue felt goose pimples rise up on her arms and she shivered as memory swamped her. The Priest was at his games again. No matter what the others thought, she believed Barry when he said he had seen someone. Why else was this overpowering fog smothering the area? The Priest was using his man-made ability to overpower some unwary person and wipe away their memory. The strong draught made by the dragons' wings failed to have any impact on the mist. It remained solid. Silver swerved away having picked up enough of Sue's thoughts to realise danger was present here. She issued an order to return home.

"We must inform the King at once about this phenomenon," she thundered and Sue clung on tightly as Silver accelerated her speed. The other dragons followed and Barry gripped Sapphire's neck as though he could hold her back. "You must not go away from here. You've got to land," he yelled furiously. "Someone is in danger. Why doesn't anyone listen to me? "

"Do not dare to tell me what to do, mortal boy!" Sapphire roared, glaring back at him with baleful eyes. "We are returning home, so be silent."

"Well I'm not going, so what are you going to do about that?" Barry shouted, and before he knew what was happening, Sapphire turned a somersault. He had already loosened his harness by twisting round and this action caused him to lose his grip as well. With a scream he hurtled through the air, landing with an almighty splash in one of the many lakes. The other dragons and riders were unaware of what had happened and Sapphire followed silently at their rear, the only one without a rider.

* * *

Surfacing from the water with noisy splutters and wiping his eyes so that he could see, Barry stared in disbelief at the scene around him. The middle of a large lake was not the best place he would have chosen to be. Quickly assessing his position, he noticed that land was some distance away and decided it was further than he could swim to easily. Already his clothing was pulling him down, boots being the worst offenders. Attached to his feet they felt like ton weights. His absence had to be noticed by the others, so possibly the dragons would be returning at any moment now to pick him up. He glanced hopefully up at the sky but only clouds were passing overhead, and disappointment overwhelmed him. He knew instinctively Sapphire was not going to broadcast to the others that she had deliberately dumped her rider. He just wished he could be there when they discovered he was missing. Anger against Sapphire gave him the spur he needed to get moving. It suddenly struck him that if this water had not been here to break his fall, he would have had a nasty accident. As it was, his ego suffered a blow he would find hard to live down.

Dogpaddling, Barry focused in every direction until he caught sight of the Bluff, which he noticed was looking more like a cloud with the mist shrouding the cliffs. He thought of the two people he had seen up there and wondered if they managed to survive the cloying influence the mist had on people's minds. He was determined to climb up to the spot once he was out of this water. By his way of reckoning, it would not take him all that long to retrace the distance — but distances could be very deceptive, as he well knew. First, however, he must get out of this water and the banks were a long way off. It was just his bad luck to be in the middle of a lake — the most inaccessible place of all to be. Taking a deep breath, he threw his body forward and started swimming, hoping belatedly there were no obnoxious creatures in the water. Swimming in clothes became laborious and the bank seemed to recede when he focused on it. After struggling for many minutes under difficult conditions, he realised he had hardly made any headway and debated whether or not to remove his shoes to relieve his legs of an unwanted burden. Barry decided against it. If he inadvertently lost them, being barefoot would make his situation ten times worse.

Barry paused for a moment to refill his lungs with air and wondered why there were no people around to help him. The whole area was desolate. Then suddenly something plopped behind him, causing ripples to spread across the lake, as coldness flowed through his blood and galvanised him into action. His strokes became desperate as he forged ahead, but it was hard going and he was tiring fast because his clothes hampered him. When another set of ripples spread out it was almost the last straw but apprehension kept him going.

Then his worst nightmare occurred as something clutched his leg. Fear covered his skin with goose pimples. His heart missed a beat and he violently kicked out to free himself. Whoever his underwater adversary was took no notice and grabbed his other leg as well. Suddenly he was completely ensnared, making swimming out of the question. The blood drummed through his head. Forgetting he was alone, he yelled out, thrashing the water with his hands at the same time. He was expecting to be sucked down at any moment. Beneath the water the attacker was biding its time, allowing Barry to tire himself out. Barry gulped in a mouthful of water and choked. An iron band enclosed round his chest making breathing difficult.

By now his emotions were out of control and he was in the throes of panic. Common sense came to his aid. He realised he had been struggling uselessly for several minutes, and although his legs were still firmly held, nothing below the water-line was trying to make a meal out of him. By moving his hands he could still keep afloat.

Barry relaxed, thinking that maybe he could get out of this — but the hope was short-lived. Something hard thrust itself into his ear. With a startled yell Barry twisted his head round and came face to face with two large dark eyes staring intently at him from out of a furry face. Too shocked and stunned to think coherently, he gawked at the apparition — and whatever it was thrust something roughly into his face.

At the same time, from the bank a voice shouted out breaking the silence and, looking in that direction, the first thing Barry saw was a caravan with huge wheels and secondly the woman. He could not understand her speech but her wild gesticulations made him respond. He looked again at the furry face of what he now knew to be a dog, and saw a rope in its mouth. Without more ado, he removed it gently from the dog's jaw and with difficulty tied it round his waist. Now was not the time to procrastinate. The woman may be one of the hated gypsies, but she was offering him help. He held his hands up, hoping she would realise it meant he wanted to be rescued.

She took up the stance of pulling and even from a distance he could see she did not find pulling easy. His body did not move but the dog was already streaking back to the bank. Eventually the woman must have realised she could not manage on her own. She whistled, and a horse appeared from behind the caravan. She tied her end of the rope to the horse and slapped him firmly on his flank. As he walked away, it was his strength which pulled Barry nearer to the bank. Within twenty yards of safety the woman decided it was enough and released the horse, which went back to his grazing. Barry's jaw fell — didn't she care that he was still out here? The gypsy turned to him and shouted out directions, but her gibberish went over his head. He just stared and he could sense her annoyance. Eventually Barry shouted out apologetically "I'm sorry. I don't understand you."

The woman was elderly and dressed in a long dark skirt. She put both her hands on her hips and her laughter came out like a bark. "So you're a gringo," she ejaculated, "I should have guessed. No gypsy would be daft enough to swim in that lake." She paused while her eyes appraised him in amusement. "Stand on your feet, lad," she added curtly. "You can wade in from there easily."

The futility of the action she suggested made him glare at her. "I can't. Something has got hold of my legs."

This time the woman laughed uproariously and Barry seethed, failing to see anything funny in the situation. To his amazement she stepped into the lake — then his amazement turned to horror because as she approached him, he saw she held a long knife in her hand.

The water only ever reached her knees, showing him clearly he was lying in shallow water and he felt all sorts of a fool, but also he was now feeling vaguely uneasy. His eyes never left the knife. She drew nearer and when she was within arm's length of where he stood, she handed the knife to him. "Cut yourself free, lad, I'm not into eating gringos at the moment — they give me indigestion. This lake is notorious for the amount of weed it produces, but not everyone escapes from it. Just consider yourself lucky. I'll get a fire going and you can dry out."

Leaving Barry feeling ridiculous, she waded back to the bank and wrung the water from her skirt with firm hands. It flapped wetly round her legs as she entered her caravan. Barry was glad she did not watch him hacking the weed away from his legs — it was unnaturally tough and took quite a time. Eventually he splashed his way from the water and followed her with his composure restored. Half an hour later found him relaxed and wrapped in a large colourful blanket. He sat with the heat from the fire playing on his face. His clothes were steaming, hanging from trestles made by tree branches that were pressed deeply into the ground. The dog, black and tan, which the woman called Scrap, took a fancy to him and sat close by his side. He was not a very big dog but he had a powerful bark. Barry tickled gently behind its ears, for the want of something to do, while all the time he surreptitiously studied the gypsy woman sitting opposite him. While she busily weaved, he noticed she was past her first flush of youth. A hint of grey touched her temples and Barry could not make out why she looked so different from the gypsy women Sue had described. She was not swarthy in appearance and when she spoke in his language her voice sounded educated. At any moment he was expecting the rest of her clan to appear. He wondered what she doing out here on her own with just one dog and one horse for company. Her tanned skin was heavily lined. Maybe she wasn't a gypsy, he mused thoughtfully.

"Have you seen enough of me to make up your mind if I'm trustworthy, lad?" she asked abruptly, her dark eyes examining him from beneath heavy brows. It shocked Barry out of his reverie and embarrassed him to have been caught staring. He had no idea she was watching him. "Sorry," he mumbled, colour mounting in his face. "I just wondered why you were alone out here. There is no one around for miles that I can see."

"Good job for you that I was around, lad," she retorted tartly. "You could have been killed falling from a dragon like you did. I don't hold with people riding them things like horses. It's not natural — and they're vicious beasts, especially that blue one. I've seen it before."

"You saw me fall," Barry exclaimed, dumbfounded, "but we didn't see you."

The woman laid down the material she was working on and studied him grimly. "Yes I did, and if you want to know, you're not a welcome sight. You lot seem to think you can all hound us at will — scaring us with your low-flying tactics. What have we ever done to you to deserve such treatment?"

Barry was at a loss and shifted uncomfortably under her stare. This was not the way he wanted the conversation to go, then unbidden he thought of Sue and Tug and the harsh treatment they had both received at the hands of the gypsies. He was about to elaborate, but she cut him short with uncanny insight. "We're not all alike," she continued brusquely. "Some of us want to live a peaceful life. You're rather young to be playing at being a marauder, lad."

"I'm not a marauder," Barry protested hotly, and tried to protect the dragon league by adding "we're trying to keep law and order. Your people attack us for no reason at all except to steal and plunder. I'm sorry if you think I'm rude after your saving my life. Shall I go away?" He made an attempt to stand and she snorted derisively, "Stay where you are, lad. How far do you think you'll get in a blanket?"

Barry lapsed into silence, but not for long. Curiosity made him say, "There is only one blue dragon — and I ride her. I've never ridden this way before. Are you sure about the colour?"

"Do I look half-witted, lad?" The gypsy woman's voice was cold and dismissive. "If I said blue, then I meant blue. That dragon comes over here with a black one. Now tell me black is the wrong colour."

Barry just stared at her. "We don't have any black dragons," he managed to say, but confusion filled his eyes. With a decisive movement the older woman stood up. He watched her while she tethered the horse to a post in the ground and then she whistled to the dog that immediately went to her. "Come on, Scrap." She scooped him up and gave him a hug. "It's time for you to go inside." Once she had settled the dog she returned to Barry and scrutinized him. He looked very dejected with his knees pulled up under his chin. "Where will you head, lad, if the dragons don't come back for you?"

Feeling he had outstayed his welcome, Barry pointed to the Bluff where the thick fog was still churning around. He almost heard her quick intake of breath. "That's no place to go to at night — especially while that mist is still there — and anyway, your clothes are not dry yet. You can sleep under the caravan tonight. You will be safe enough there, lad."

Barry, who wanted to be on his way, realised the sun was already setting behind the trees and shadows were covering the ground; there might be a lot of pitfalls out there. He gratefully accepted the offer, saying, "Don't keep calling me lad, I'm Barry."

Her eyes suddenly twinkled. "I like a lad with manners. You can call me Rainee. Step into my caravan," she invited, "and I will give you something hot to drink."

CHAPTER 5
THE BLACK DRAGON

Scrap woke Barry early next morning by bounding down the caravan steps and making a beeline underneath the caravan. His long fluffy tail wagged furiously, sweeping up dust on his way and causing a miniature cloud. He pressed his wet nose on the boy's face, making him jump. In the confined space below the caravan, Barry hit his head on the floor above. Without thinking he let out a yelp, and the dog barked in unison. Scrap was ready for a game but Rainee put an end to what she thought was unnecessary frivolity, by saying sharply "Get into the caravan, Barry, and dress. Your clothes are dry."

Barry's movements were slow as he crawled from beneath the caravan because he tried to be careful and not bang his head anymore. His limbs felt stiff from lying on hard unforgiving ground through the night, and what with his enforced swim yesterday, he ached all over. Modesty made him hug the blanket tightly to his body as he scrambled to his feet. Rainee watched him ironically wondering, not for the first time, where he came from. It was easy to deduce he was not from Therossa. She waited until he closed the caravan door behind him, and then resolutely cleared away traces of the fire, which could have told anyone she had been there, and deftly harnessed up the horse, so that when Barry reappeared, she was ready to move on.

He looked at her uncertainly on seeing all the signs of her imminent departure and wondered why she couldn't have said she was leaving. There was so much he wanted to ask her — like whether she was a gypsy or not. In their short acquaintance he classed her as a friend but he didn't have the nerve yet to ask her personal questions. This was unusual for him. He descended the caravan steps and said with a touch of irony in his voice. "I see you're on your way. I hope I haven't delayed you. Thank you for saving me, Rainee — I don't make a habit of falling off dragons' backs. I hate to think of what would have happened if you had not come along in the nick of time."

The gypsy woman regarded him unemotionally and waved away his thanks by saying gruffly "I'm worried about where you are going, Barry. I was hoping I had misheard you. You are a stranger here so you wouldn't know, but the Bluff is no place for a young lad like you to visit. It has a bad name in this area."

"That's silly," Barry protested, "it's only a cliff and I like climbing."

"But people disappear up there," Rainee insisted, "and strange though it may seem — I feel concerned about you."

Taking what she said at face value, Barry could see no reason why he shouldn't tell her the truth. After all, she had seen him flying a dragon so she must have seen all the others with him. So picking his words out carefully, he said, "I'm going there because I saw two people standing on the edge of the Bluff before the mist came down and swallowed them up. None of my friends

58

believed me but I'm going to climb up there and find out what has happened to them."

"Were they friends of yours?" asked the gypsy woman.

"Not to my knowledge," Barry answered. "In fact — I've got no idea who they were."

Rainee shook her head sadly and placed a hand on his shoulder as though commiserating with him. "Unless you've got the ability of a mountain goat you will never climb up there," she said soberly. "There is nothing alive at the base of the cliff — and come to think of it — there is nothing alive at the top either."

"Except for two people," retorted Barry doggedly.

"There are no people alive up there." Rainee's voice became sharp. "Only the Drazuzi live there and you don't want to meet them. They are not human."

"Don't be so silly — of course they are," Barry blurted out. "I've met them." Then he paused because the expression in her eyes made him wish he had remained silent. Rainee became suddenly withdrawn and it was as though a shutter had fallen over her face. He tried to think what was so wrong about what he said. Why shouldn't he have met the Drazuzi? Did she know something about them that he didn't — or could it be something to do with the Priest? His eyes took the liberty of searching her expressionless face for any resemblance between her and the Priest, but there was none. In exasperation he asked bluntly, "Will you tell me what is wrong? Because I have met the Drazuzi, and you act as though I've committed a crime. I think I should be allowed an explanation."

Almost brusquely she replied, "By what you have just said I've suddenly realised who you are and take my word for it — I am the last person you should be associating with. You had best be on your way and... "

"I'll make my own decisions, Rainee," Barry interrupted her angrily. "Please don't tell me what to do."

Rainee glowered at him for butting in. "Like I said," she continued sharply, "be on your way before your friends come looking for you. From here on we go in different directions." Without another word she turned her back on him and leapt up onto the seat to drive the caravan. With a touch of the whip she urged the horse forward. The horse complained with a plaintive whinnying and became skittish.

Rainee growled out an order but the horse tried to rear within the shafts. The action excited Scrap, who took his doggy life into his own hands by dancing round the horse's legs. Exasperated, the gypsy woman looked over her shoulder and as Barry murmured hopefully "I suppose there is no chance of any breakfast before you go?" she swung round on him and yelled, "boy, there is danger approaching! Get back under the caravan at once and take Scrap with you. Whatever you do — don't you dare let him run out."

* * *

Feeling utterly fatigued, Priscilla slumped against a boulder and watched with interest a large hairy spider crawl along her leg. There was no revulsion in her expression and she saw no reason to rouse herself and knock it off. No doubt if she moved it would topple to the ground. She was disinterested in her surroundings, a dark hollow where grey stone was covered in patches of lichen. The place was gloomy because the only light filtering in came from the small irregular opening at the cave mouth. Feathery plants struggled to survive along its jagged edge and one shaft of sunlight fell on the motionless form of a youth staring with unseeing eyes towards the light.

Priscilla contemplated him for a while, but his rugged features meant nothing to her. The glazed expression in his eyes told her that she didn't exist for him either. If only she could think clearly. Something had given her a headache and she licked her lips because her mouth was dry. But what had given her a headache? Where was she? What was her name and who was this man? She stopped thinking because it made her head thump too much, but she studied him for want of something to do. He had a nasty gash on his forehead. Blood that had been running down his face had dried. Was she supposed to do something about it? Why couldn't she remember anything?

The spider was now climbing up the front of her. Its bright red eyes stared at her face. Priscilla put out a hand and cupped the spider in her palm. She felt no qualms about touching it. Surely it would be better outside. There was no food in here for it. Struggling to her feet she managed to move unsteadily towards the entrance of the cave, stumbling over the legs of the other person. Her automatic apology died before it was spoken because he stared at her blankly and made no attempt to move or speak. Priscilla swallowed to ease the dryness of her throat and said huskily, "Do I know you?"

He turned his head slightly, but his expression was blank. It was obviously too much for him and he slumped back into his former position. "Shouldn't think you do," he muttered gruffly. "I don't know who I am myself."

Priscilla accepted that explanation because she didn't know who she was either. It brought back the same thoughts all over again. What was she doing here? How had she come to this place? The spider, trapped in her hand, started to make its presence felt by frantically trying to wriggle from the captivity of her closed fingers. She looked incuriously at the furry limbs endeavouring to squeeze their way out and just for one moment she knew she had power over it. But why should she need power? Leaving the immobile man where he was, she stepped outside and opened her hand. The spider scuttled to freedom, but freedom was back in the cave, and she was unaware of the red puncture on the skin of her palm.

The slight breeze lifted the hair from her temples and she inhaled deeply, looking over the beautiful valley below. Such spectacular scenery should have had the power to touch her memory. The majestic mountains drew her eyes in their direction. Fleetingly, she wondered if she came from there. Slowly scanning the valley floor she saw a colourful caravan with people round it and wondered if it were possible to get down to it. There seemed to be a very narrow path at her feet, but going downwards it was overgrown. Upwards it appeared well worn and not too far to the top. The decision was not hard to make. Without showing a vestige of fear, Priscilla started to climb. Alfie dragged himself to the cave entrance and watched her precarious headway. Something about her actions worried him. Only a mad person would attempt that ascent. Where did she come from? Should he stop her? While he was searching for an answer, Priscilla reached the top with a feeling of triumph — although why she should feel so pleased with herself she did not know.

The force of the wind hit her and she swayed, teetering on the edge. It was a long way down but the perilous drop did not concern her. She was overcome by a joyous feeling. It felt good to be alive. Lifting her head she inhaled the air, and it was then she saw a black speck in the sky. Unexpectedly, something worried her, but for the life of her she couldn't think why. The headache was receding and she didn't want to think about anything that might bring it back. The black speck drew nearer, and curiosity kept her feet firmly in one place because now she could see large black wings and a long tail. By the time it was close enough for her to see its eyes, it roared. Smoke and flame issued from its huge snout as it passed overhead. A tingle of excitement touched Priscilla — but at the same time she experienced an uneasy feeling. Why? It was a magnificent creature. As the early morning sun touched its scales, it sparkled. She wanted it to come back. With a degree of impatience she waited for it to appear again. The dragon circled sideways into her view, and levelling out, swooped towards her. As it passed over for a second time its eyes pierced her mind and a shudder went through Priscilla. She was completely lost in its spell. Fascinated, she stood there, wishing it would land. It was graceful as it moved through the air. She held up her arms to its supreme power. The dragon swept round in a circle and hovered above her — the force of air from its wings almost threw her off balance. Then she saw the huge talons and something snapped in her mind — but it was too late for her to do anything. It grasped her firmly in its claws. As the talons bit deeply into her flesh, Priscilla screamed. She looked down and there was nothing below her. Everything faded into oblivion.

Alfie, watching from the safety of his cave, knew something was dreadfully wrong, but he didn't know what it was. Why had she screamed? He tried to think but his head felt like cotton wool and the gash in his temple throbbed. He would think about it later. The warmth of the sun made him slide down against the wall and put his head back on the rocky outcrop and closed his eyes. The wind blew on his face and before long sleep overcame him.

* * *

Barry was none too happy. He would have liked an explanation as to what sort of danger was approaching, but now was not the time to argue. Alerted by the urgency in Rainee's voice, he made a dive for cover under the caravan and miraculously the dog followed. Scrap thought this was a game. Not often did people come down to his level. He tried to lavish kisses on Barry's face and playfully put paws up on his shoulders. A vociferous roar split the air overhead and the caravan shuddered. The suddenness of it made Barry cringe back as far as the wooden structure allowed. Scrap was now pressed hard to his side for safety, his little body trembling. The noise had terrified him. Fire hit the ground indiscriminately and the smell of burning seared his nostrils. A blast of heat smote his skin and at the same time he heard a shrill cry from the horse. The caravan rocked as the horse tried to escape from between the shafts. Barry wondered what Rainee was doing and whether she was safe. She was still out there, a perfect target for the dragon. This unprovoked viciousness was a side of the dragon he had no idea it possessed. Barry vowed he was never going to chase gypsy caravans again. He would throw in his lot when he returned and be a soldier with Zeno. The dragon circled over them again, his huge bulk casting a shadow. Then his roars petered out as he headed towards the Bluff.

More than anything, Barry wanted to see a close up of this renegade dragon which was causing so much wanton damage. He edged nearer to one of the wheels and crouched behind the spokes, hoping that in that position he would be unseen by the monster. Scrap whimpered, but made no move to follow. He watched Barry with ears flat against his head. Barry gave the dog a reassuring pat but his attention was fixed on the magnificent black dragon flying over the top of the cliff. Its size equalled that of Sheeka and the sun made it sparkle as its body glided round in graceful circles. When Barry realised a person stood poised up there on the edge of the drop, his admiration turned to horror. Distance made it difficult for him to discern who it was but the person showed no fear of the dragon. He or she was either brave or foolish. His mouth dropped open when he noticed arms opened wide as though welcoming it. The dragon hovered above the person, and only at the last minute did the person try to escape. By then it was too late. Barry saw huge talons stretch down and grasp the victim. His blood ran cold as a scream rent the air and shaking he dodged back because with a roar of triumph the black dragon was heading back in his direction.

Flames struck the ground again at random and several trees were turned to ash in the unprovoked destruction. If the caravan were hit there would be no escape for Rainee or himself. This was the nearest Barry had ever been to a dragon's wrath.

He wriggled his way back to the other side of the caravan so that he could view the dragon's flight away. The unfortunate prisoner dangled helplessly from his claws. Barry prayed that he or she was unconscious. Just as he decided it would be safe to crawl out, another dragon joined the black one and Barry's faith in dragon nature was shattered. The new dragon, circling round, was Sapphire. A feeling of anger surged through him. He had thought Rainee was making it up, but his eyes could not dispute what he had just seen. To think they had all trusted Sapphire.

He had not realised the shock had immobilised him until suddenly he saw two feet placed within inches of his fingers and Rainee's dry voice ordered him to come out. "The danger is over for today," she said and she moved away, not waiting for his answer. Barry suddenly remembered he had been given his marching orders before all this had happened, and a little apprehensively he crawled from beneath the caravan. He stretched. It was good to be able to stand upright. The smell of burning was strong when he inhaled. Some of the colourful paintwork had been blistered. But worse than that, around the horse's legs the grass was singed, showing what a narrow escape they had all had. Above all the damage, Barry's first concern was for the horse, because without him Rainee was not going anywhere. Although the horse appeared uninjured, he stood staring around bemusedly from his fear-filled eyes. Barry spoke to him softly and the animal did not object when his nose was patted. Rainee watched him, grateful for the distraction, but in the end she said gruffly,

"My plans have changed. Forget what I've already told you. There is no way I am going to leave you on your own after this episode. Dragons are devious and cunning, and mark my words — they will be back. They do not like their actions witnessed. So while we can — what do you say about having a spot of breakfast to build up our spirits?"

She was already moving away before she ceased speaking. She took his acceptance as a matter of course so was surprised when Barry braced himself and caught hold of her arm to stop her. He spun her round, and because he was annoyed at the way she changed her mind, missed her sudden wince when he touched her. It might never have happened. She controlled it instantly.

"I'm sorry, Rainee," Barry said steadily. "I'm still going to the Bluff no matter what you decide to do."

Rainee pulled her arm back sharply and stared at him as if he had gone mad. Her lips tightened. "Not after what you've just seen?"

"Yes." Barry's determination made her pause. She asked shrewdly, "Was that a friend of yours he carried away?"

Barry shrugged. "I don't know, but whoever it was — they were not up there alone. If I wait until someone comes searching for me, it will be too late to do anything. You go your way as you first intended. And I'll go mine. I've got no hard feelings about your decision. It's my fault you were still here when that dragon came. I'll forgo breakfast if you don't mind." So saying he spun round and with determined steps headed towards the Bluff. It seemed a long way ahead and he had hardly taken many strides before Rainee's sharp rejoinder made him pause.

"If you weren't so pig-headed, lad, you could stop and help me. But not to worry, off you go. I'll catch you up in my own good time."

Barry spun round, wondering what innuendo her words concealed. She stood proudly braced against the side of her caravan, eyes inscrutable as they studied him. He hoped she didn't mean what he thought she did. He could not allow her to follow him into danger. Scrap decided at that moment to jump up at her with a bark because he had been ignored long enough, and then Barry noticed how awkwardly Rainee pushed him away. His sharp eyes also saw her burnt sleeve and realised she had been burnt by dragon-fire. It was hard to tell if she was in pain because her lined face was expressionless. With a swear word picked up from some of the trackers, he was by her side in two steps. "Let me see your arm."

Rainee raised her eyebrows and said reprovingly, "I would not have expected such language from you, lad. There is nothing wrong with me."

"Don't treat me like a kid." Barry's impatience started to show. "Your arm is burnt." He held out his hand but she ignored it. "I do not need your sympathy. I did not call you back on my behalf. I thought I could have been of some help to you."

"How?" Barry was uncompromising and glowered. "What could you do?"

Rainee shrugged off his question and said instead, "Suppose you got hurt climbing the Bluff."

"Then I'd call for a Shaman."

"Why?" Rainee asked with unusual crispness. "I could heal you."

"You!" Barry did not mean his answer to sound so derisive and felt his face burn. "Are you a Shaman?"

"No, but I heal people."

"What are you then — a witch doctor?" Barry knew he was mocking her but he could not stop himself. Rainee kept her temper in check and said slowly, "I was a nurse — not that it makes any difference. Well I'm not offering help anymore, Barry. You've obviously made up your mind, so go ahead on your own. I just thought my caravan would be useful should you find someone injured."

There was a pregnant silence in which the two eyed each other. The trouble was — what she said made sense. Barry's resentment evaporated. Whoever she was with her cryptic remarks suggesting she knew who he was, she had saved his life more than once, and he had to admit, companionship was better than solitude. His cheeky grin returned and he said audaciously, "I'll stay with you on two conditions."

Rainee's eyebrows shot up a fraction. "Only two?" she asked sarcastically.

"Yes. First you'll give me breakfast like you offered to do a while back, and secondly you will let me see to your arm. I might not be much good, but I'm sure I could see to it better than you can."

Rainee laughed uproariously. "You're quite a charmer, my lad. I can see we'll get along famously."

CHAPTER 6
STORM IN A TEACUP

A rosy haze spread over the evening sky as the dragons landed gracefully one by one on the green in front of the Royal Palace. Soldiers watched the traditional landing ceremony from the walls they patrolled. It was now a familiar and much loved sight. Most people made an excuse to see the great beasts coming and going. At this time of day many people were loitering in the vicinity and as the dragons returned they were immediately surrounded by hordes of admiring children. Firefly and Griffin flagrantly encouraged the village children to surround them by deliberately preening and flexing their wings to show off their colourful bodies. It only went to show that the inborn conceit of the dragons knew no bounds. They would have basked in the children's admiration forever had not one voice brought everything to a halt by saying,

"Where on earth is Sapphire? Why hasn't she landed?"

Tansy turned from Firefly to regard her friend and saw Sue anxiously scanning the evening sky for traces of Barry. Since the dragons always flew in formation no matter where they went, being last in line, Barry should have landed by now. His absence did not worry Tansy as much as it did Sue, because he was always doing

70

unexpected things. That was part of his charm. Tansy tugged her arm with the intention of pulling her towards the palace where she knew Thane and Raithe would be waiting for them. Thane had overall control of the dragon patrols and she did not want Barry to get into trouble.

"Don't worry about him, Sue." She kept her voice deliberately calm. "He's always trying to get Sapphire to take him on little escapades. Maybe this time his charm has worked and she has done what he wants." She had forgotten Sue's dragon Silver was nearby and at her words, smoke poured from her nostrils. The eyes of the white dragon flashed warningly.

"Then Sapphire should have known better," she interrupted angrily. "We went out on a planned reconnaissance and as such we should have returned together — no matter how persuasive Barry's tongue is."

Sue bit her lip on hearing Silver's reprimand. It didn't lesson the anxiety building up within her. She recalled Barry's face when he wanted to return to the Bluff and Sapphire was not very accommodating. A sick feeling in her stomach made her say tentatively "I can't help feeling Sapphire has a grudge about Barry being on her back. She was not at ease this afternoon and I'm worried. It's something to do with that mist gathering over the Bluff. It bodes ill for someone."

"You're dead right there, but I shouldn't worry." Annalee joined them. Just like Tansy she tried to brush away Sue's concern. "We'll go and see the king right away. You're making too much of a drama over Barry being late. He'll turn up in his own good time, as he always does. You know he likes to show that..." She broke off with a stifled gasp. Then everyone followed the direction of her gaze. There was no mistaking Sapphire gliding across the sky. The brilliant blue scales of her body glistened in what was left of the evening sun, showing only too clearly there was no rider on her back. As she passed overhead, Sapphire roared and flames lit the sky. It was an act of defiance. Her intended message certainly reached the other riders, since all dragons were forbidden to make fire over populated areas.

Blood drained from Sue's face and Tansy's hold on her tightened in disbelief. Silver was furious and lowered her huge head, almost touching Sue's cheek. She rumbled ominously. "I will speak to Sapphire at once and search for your brother. You must not worry. This is dragon business. Go ahead with the others and report to the king about the mist. That is very important. I will return to you directly I have some news."

Lifting arms which were none too steady Sue hugged her scaly neck and said "thank you." She stood back as Silver's great wings unfurled and the white dragon took to the sky. Firefly and Griffin followed her as though there had been a command which the humans did not hear. Once the dragons had gone, the children dispersed and very soon the green was deserted. With nothing to distract their attention the soldiers returned to their duties.

The girls hardly noticed the officer in charge as they passed through the gate, too deep in their own conversation. They decided unanimously not to mention anything about Barry being absent. They did not want to pile trouble on his shoulders because Thane took his job of being the overseer to the dragon patrol a little too seriously. Sue was beginning to wonder if the old carefree Thane had vanished forever. All they had to worry about now was hoping the king did not notice Barry's absence. That was going to be tricky because he always butted in on any conversation.

The murmur of voices directed them to the room where Thane and Raithe were waiting. But Raithe was not there. In his place were Sue's father and old Amos, who heard everything but did not often speak. White Hawk was finding this all so boring. He sprawled out on the cool tiles in the corner, with eyes closed but one ear cocked for danger.

As the girls burst into the room he lifted his head. They didn't realise they had interrupted a serious conversation, but Tam was always happy to see his daughter. He gave her a welcoming smile which included her friends. Amos retreated a step to Thane's side and a warning look passed between them, as though their former discussion must remain a secret.

Meanwhile the king, ever courteous, asked them what was so important that they needed to get it off their chests. The girls had the grace to look ashamed and for the first time Sue noticed small lines of strain round her father's eyes. She pushed this thought aside because she wanted to give them her own information. Not only the king, but Thane and Amos listened to what they had to say about the Bluff, politely at first, but their expression was grave by the time they had finished.

Oran, a cousin of the king, was an unscrupulous villain who acted as Priest and ruled over the Drazuzi people. He was not above taking prisoners for his own ends. Usually, he plotted against the realm. For many months his activities had lain dormant but to suddenly receive news that his destructive mist was being used again; this was serious. The mist overpowered the unwary. It took away their memory. It must not be allowed to continue.

Sue paused for breath and the girls felt extraordinary pleased to be the first ones to impart the news. Tam placed a fatherly arm over his daughter's shoulders and smiled at them all.

"You did well not to interfere at the Bluff and to bring the news of Oran back to me at once. I call that real soldiering on your part." Sue sighed in relief. Her father had not missed Barry. But then he continued grimly, "I hope you realise, Sue, that I can't have your getting entangled with the Priest again. You must surely see that for yourself. Anything to do with the Bluff is out of the question for you. Your mother would never forgive me if anything happened to you." Sue's indignant gasp of protest was drowned by Tam's remark of "All the same, this situation is serious. Something must be done if he is trying to seduce strangers coming to this land."

"You think there are strangers involved?" Thane queried thoughtfully.

"Of course there are." The king's reply was adamant. He stared at Thane in surprise. "Why else should he send the mist?"

Thane scratched his chin as though mulling over something in his mind. His eyes rested momentarily on Sue and he said carefully, "I think there is something more devious going on. Would anyone have followed you to this land, Sue?" he asked unexpectedly.

"Me!" Sue looked surprise. "Of course they wouldn't. I've been here for too long now. Everyone has forgotten me."

"Are you sure?" Thane's eyes probed her face. "Think back to when you lived at the hotel."

The fact that he should delve so far back in the past surprised Sue. "What are you getting at, Thane?" she asked. "Aunt Moria is not likely to try and follow me here and Gran is much too old. Even Priscilla is in America. You've got to think of something better than that. The way I see it, two unfortunate strangers must have accidentally stumbled through the barrier and the Priest thinks they're important. So he spreads the mist."

Thane frowned. "That's too much of a coincidence."

"Well I came through that way."

She saw her father draw his eyebrows together because he noticed Thane was not satisfied. "You have some other ideas?" he asked casually.

"Yes I have." Thane's voice was grim. "I've had them for ages and they will not go away." He turned to Sue. "Think back to the days when you walked through Tamsworth Forest to visit your grandmother. Who was it that pursued…"

"No!" Sue choked. "No! Not him. After White Hawk bit him he disappeared."

"But he could have come back," Thane continued softly. "Professor Harding is a very determined man. He's not only after you, Sue. I'm afraid he is after the Queen as well."

"What!" exploded Tam indignantly? "Over my dead body will he get hold of the Queen." He swung round and faced the bemused Amos, "Find my son and make up a hunting party right away. If that man is in this country I'll have him found. I'll not have him getting involved with the Priest. I can't have two evil minds like that working together. I know I've banned you from going, Sue, but that doesn't mean I'm stopping Barry. I'm surprised the boy has remained silent for so long. What have you girls done to him — gagged him?" The king looked at the girls, and then beyond them. When he didn't see Barry he looked questioningly at his daughter. "Where is my nephew? I thought you were all flying together today."

There was a pregnant pause, and Thane was suspicious. The girls were never stuck for words. While Sue was deciding on what to say, Tansy shifted awkwardly on her feet and said lamely, "He didn't return with us. You know what boys are like."

"No I don't," Tam answered. "Why didn't he return? It is compulsory that you all stay together when flying dragons. That was agreed at the very beginning of the pact. Just who was my nephew flying?"

"Does that really matter?" asked Annalee in astonishment. "We don't always ride the same dragon," she lied blatantly, and saw her brother's face darken.

"I'm afraid it does," Tam exclaimed, an unusual crispness lacing his voice. "You do not know the trouble we are having with Sheeka. So who was Barry flying today?"

"Sapphire."

"Sapphire," echoed the king. "Did I hear you correctly when you said Sapphire?"

76

Amos was suddenly afflicted with a fit of coughing which he tried to control when Tam glared at him. Thane was already biding his time to speak severely to the girls who seemed to be breaking every rule in the book, but the king beat him to it. He swung round on his daughter, trying to keep his anger at bay. "Has Barry landed yet?" His calmness was deceptive. Sue felt her face redden as she cleared her throat and said, "No."

"I knew it," he thundered unexpectedly, and Sue shrank away from him in alarm. She had never witnessed such fury in him before. Was this all because of Barry? Did Barry mean so much to him? Tansy stood firmly by her side to give support, and so did Annalee. They watched the king breathing hard, fighting to suppress the displeasure he felt. Then Amos's voice was like pouring oil onto troubled water.

"I always told you no good would come out of flying dragons."

Tansy pursed her lips. "Is there something about Sapphire we should know — because if there is, I think we should have been informed," She caught Thane's eye and dared him to interrupt with a banal remark. But Amos added derisively,

"I'll tell you right now I don't hold with consorting with dragons — never have and never will. The whole lot of them are devious and not to be trusted. This pact with them should never have been made. Sapphire is proving my point by disobeying orders. They take everything and give nothing in return. Leave well alone if you want my advice."

"Well I don't," flared Sue, making Amos jump back in alarm, "because what you've just said is not true.

I would trust Silver anywhere and with my life if it came to that. She is my true and loyal friend. Why is there this concern because Sapphire… "

"Enough, Sue," exploded her father, a little put out that she could speak to Amos like that. "You are speaking of things you know nothing about."

"Only because you hold back information," Sue accused him, trying to bottle up her frustration and placing Barry's non-arrival on his doorstep. "What things don't we know about?"

"You don't know about Sapphire for a start." Her father's voice was harsh because he could not believe his daughter was speaking to him like that. "She is the sister of the black dragon Evonny who is trying to break the pact between us. I can't think how she was allowed to carry humans on her back. The fact that Barry is missing proves my point. I can see only one solution to this situation now."

"Which is?" asked Sue, keeping her temper under control with an effort, but the colour had drained from her face leaving her looking pinched and white.

"I am banning dragon-flying from this moment onwards — until Barry is found. Even then I'm not so sure I'm going to let it continue," Tam growled, and Thane thought he was going rather beyond what the situation warranted.

Sue reacted like a coiled spring. She pushed herself away from Tansy and Annalee, avoided contact with Thane and glared at her father. "That's not fair," she burst out furiously, letting him know exactly what she thought. "You cannot penalise all the dragons because one doesn't fit in. The villagers are accepting them and the children are losing their fear. Isn't that what we are supposed to be striving for? I thought you at least were in favour of our living together, but now it seems you are allowing this Evonny to get his own way. He really must be laughing at you." Sue paused to gulp in more air and her father stared at her in stony silence. She brushed a hand over her eyes, which were filled with tears of frustration, and added defiantly, "Well count me out of your new schemes. I'm still flying Silver whether you forbid it or not. The others can do as they please," and before anyone realised what her intentions were, Sue swung round blindly and ran out of the palace, past startled servants who were closing the doors, and they watched her form disappear into the dusk.

Behind in the palace, Tam was frozen to the spot by the flight of his daughter. He stood where he was with a dazed expression on his face, realising his irrational temper had snapped the fragile bond between them. This was a catastrophe he hardly dared dwell on. Someone had been successful in shattering his ideals. His fingers curled round the crumpled piece of paper that had been thrust into his pocket when the girls burst in. It was a cryptic anonymous message, which had made him suspect there was a mastermind trying to ruin his life and cause havoc in the palace. Thane had been astute enough to realise it came from Oran. The girls confirmed it with their stories about the mist. Tam felt drained and overwhelmed with remorse.

"What have I done?" His strong voice sounded unusually flat. "I lost my temper over something trivial. Now I have lost my daughter. Suppose she tries to return to her old life, Ruth will never forgive me."

His words hung in the air. They were all equally stunned, although the girls were with Sue all the way. Thane pulled himself together and tried to break the tension. "She won't do that, sir," he said gruffly, hoping he understood Sue by now and the way her mind worked. "I'll go and find her. Although you might not think so, she is just as worried about Barry as you are. Amos!" he called, turning to the old man who was wishing he had never spoken and stirred up so much trouble about dragons. "You go and find Raithe and tell him what has happened and get this hunting party organised — meanwhile, I will speak to Sue."

"It's nearly dark out there," Annalee pointed out. "You'll never find her alone. Let us give you a hand."

"No! I've got better eyes than yours to help." He called to the wolf and it was by his side in an instant. He saw Annalee's crestfallen face and added more gently, "I would rather go alone, sis."

Annalee nodded and turned back to the king. She and Tansy could not remember ever having seen him so dejected before. He was always a fighting man and an inspiration to all. All his life he had overcome problems. Tansy was wily enough to realise his repartee with Sue was only half the reason why this unfortunate situation had arisen. She was keen to delve deeper — when Tam felt more like his usual self.

* * *

When Sue reached the outer wall, she quickly retraced her steps and re-entered the palace through an open window, immediately making her way towards the indoor garden of exotic plants. Through these she passed like a shadow into the lesser-used gardens at the rear of the palace, causing Thane to lose vital minutes in his search for her. The heavy glass doors swung shut behind her and the click of an unseen lock should have warned her there was no way she could get back inside.

At the moment that was not an option. Returning was the last thing on her mind. Feeling let down by her father's attitude, her aim was to put as much distance between him and her as she could. She needed to be alone and sort out the jumble of emotions swirling through her head.

A day which had started with the joy of flying through the air, had ended disastrously. Sue was mad with her father for being so dictatorial, angry at Sapphire for upsetting what was a thriving concern, and annoyed with Barry for causing ripples that were to have a long lasting effect. Never to ride the dragons again was an unbearable thought. Even now, cloaked in despair, Sue could not believe her father had suggested it.

As she pushed on, Sue was aware that the thickening shadows were making the ground hazardous for walking. Every so often she stumbled as her toes caught up against proud roots. For safety's sake she paused. The sun had disappeared below the horizon and the narrow path she was following became hard to see. Unless she wanted to fall over some unseen obstacle, her best option was to stop. With enough distance put between herself and the palace, Sue sank down on one of the many seats dotted along the way. Night flying insects buzzed around her ears making strange whirring noises. Dark shadows swooped out from the trees, beaks snapped around her head. Before long, all these noises ceased to exist. She was far enough away from everyone so that the silence could wrap itself around her like a cloak. Solitude was what she needed. Sue hugged herself to keep warm.

The minutes ticked by. The chill evening air touched her flesh and she shivered. Every part of her body was cold, except for one hand, and she wondered if something had bitten her there. She rubbed it automatically with her other hand, feeling heat as it throbbed beneath her touch. Then the green light flared out and made her jump. The area around where she sat was illuminated and the trees stood out like ghostly forms. After months of lying dormant, the ring was summoning her. Why? Who would be trying to contact her? She gave a shaky laugh. It had to be her brother Raithe. The ring connected them both, it was their own special bond and was used only in an emergency. Surely he couldn't be in any danger. Not like he had been when they first used the ring. No doubt her father had asked him to contact her and find out where she was. Sue had no intention of falling for that one. She still felt out of favour with Tam. Thrusting the ring hand back into her pocket, she ignored it. At this moment in time she felt she was in an alien environment with no friends.

The pain in her hand became so unbearable, remorse smote her. Why should she make her twin brother suffer because of their father's attitude? Raithe wouldn't give her away. He would understand if she explained. Removing her hand, she gently rubbed the ring and its light became brilliant. It was too late to worry if anyone in the vicinity was searching for her, because she had given away the position.

"What took you so long, Princess?" a voice asked with asperity. "I am a very busy person. If you wear that ring you should be ready to answer its call. I do not expect to be kept waiting."

Shock robbed Sue of speech. It was not her brother's face looking out from the facets of the ring, but Deena's, the proud Queen of the Snake people. Her thick lips were firmly pressed together in annoyance and her dark eyes flashed like smouldering coals. "I suppose you can hear me?" the Snake Queen snapped testily, "or have you lost your voice?"

"Of course I can hear you," retorted Sue indignantly, "but I was not waiting around for messages coming from you. I never expected you to use my brother's ring to seek me out. That is a private thing between us both. Coming to that, I can't think of anything you could need me for — especially since we said our goodbyes months ago."

"We are touchy!" A gravelly laugh came from Deena as though she found the conversation amusing, then she added in cold hard tones, "You are one of us, Sonja — or have you forgotten, and for your information, I am powerful enough to use any artefact I wish to summon you, no matter to whom it belongs." Then she ended sharply. "I have work for you to do."

Sue was in no mood for this. "I don't believe you." Tension began to build up within her. "I'm not in any position to attend to your wants. The king would have something to say about that. You were good to me once and gave me shelter when I needed it, but I repaid you when I helped seal the pact with the dragons." A sob caught in her throat, which she hastily swallowed. "That makes us equal. I don't owe you anything else. You must realise I am now leading a very different life."

"Don't be so short-sighted, girl," Deena snapped angrily. "Do you go about with your ears and eyes closed? All is not well and unless you can help me again, the pact will be broken. Evonny will have won. Your words, I think, Princess, which you said a little earlier to the king."

Sue's jaw dropped incredulously and she caught her breath sharply. The Snake Queen knew everything. She felt herself being drawn into a trap. Trying to defuse the panic rising within her, she said firmly, "There is nothing I can do, Deena. My father has everything in hand."

As her words trailed away, a sudden pain shot through Sue's hand making her gasp. Deena's dark eyes glared at her from the ring — shining now like burning coals. Sue could almost feel her anger vibrating against her finger.

"You're the only one who can help." The Snake Queen's voice was sharp and imperious. "Someone came seeking you, Sonja, in all good faith, but Evonny has made this person his prisoner and their life is now in the balance. The only way to get this person back is to play Evonny's own game — and he is a dangerous adversary, far more than Sheeka."

Listening to the gravelly words, Sue felt herself go cold, and it had nothing to do with the night air. She had the feeling Deena had woven a net about her and was slowly drawing it in. She tried not to show her fear. "I don't understand," she whispered. "Who was looking for me? I've not lost touch with anyone."

Deena remained annoyingly silent, so Sue repeated urgently, "Who came seeking me?"

"I have no idea," Deena responded dryly, "but I can tell you they are far from happy and not feeling well and their life is in your hands. To get them back..." She stopped speaking because Sue cut in with, "Is it Barry?"

"Will you stop interrupting me, Sonja. I have not finished," Deena exploded angrily, but Sue went on as though she had not spoken. "It's Barry, isn't it? He's the only person who is missing. Tell me — did Sapphire take him into danger?"

"I have no idea," Deena repeated again, aggravated, "and I can't see that it makes much difference at the moment. Evonny holds this person as a hostage and it is in your hands to save them."

"Mine." Sue's voice became unsteady. She pictured Barry in dire straits. "Tell me what I have to do?"

"Evonny needs the Crystal Horse." A persuasive note entered the Snake Queen's voice, "and when he is given it, he will release his prisoner and drop his objections against the pact. Then you can continue to live your happy life."

Firmly convinced now that it was Barry who was in danger because he had not returned home, Sue was ready to agree to anything Deena suggested, without asking too many questions. Why on earth had she not foreseen this happening after Sapphire's behaviour? Disregarding her apprehension, she asked, "What is this Crystal Horse? Flesh or glass? And where do I find it? Why can't Evonny find it himself if he is so powerful?"

Deena did not answer and Sue thought she had gone, but looking into the stone she saw the ageless

Snake Queen still looking out, staring at her with an inscrutable expression on her face. "The mission is fraught with danger," she said at length. "No one really knows what the Crystal Horse is — but it has great power, much greater than the Shaman, or any of the dragons."

"A power that is greater than yours?" Sue couldn't help asking, but Deena ignored the question although her eyes smouldered. "The Crystal Horse lives in the Enchanted Land," she continued, "and access to them is almost impossible. Men have died trying to enter this realm. You, Sonja — have the power to break through the barriers that defy even the dragons."

Sue's expression could not have been more bewildered. "But I still don't understand. You're talking in riddles, I have no special powers. Against the Shaman and the dragons I am non-existent. A nonentity, you might say. What good would I be going to this Enchanted Land?"

"It is the fact that you have been initiated," retorted the Snake Queen. "Also, you are a woman. No man may enter this land so don't try getting help from Thane or the king unless you want to kill them. This is between you and me only. If, or when, you acquire this Crystal Horse — you must bring it straight to me. It is imperative you go soon because of the condition of the hostage. You must go alone. You understand? Anyone can direct you to the Enchanted Land."

"But I can't go," Sue protested, "I wouldn't know what to do. Tell me, Deena – Deena... Deena, come back," Sue ended with a shout. She rubbed the ring vigorously. "Deena... you can't leave me like this. What about Barry, where is he? Deena... come back." The bright green glow faded. The ring was dead. Darkness surrounded her and Sue was devastated. She felt so helpless. Barry was in danger and she couldn't do anything about it. Tears ran down her face. Why was Deena always so cryptic? "Barry," she choked, "Barry — where are you?"

"Calm down, Sue," said a male voice. Someone sat down beside her and gathered her trembling body in his arms; at the same time a cold nose pressed into her hands and she heard a soft whine. Thane placed a cloth onto Sue's face to wipe away the tears. "Sue," he said, "I'm sure Barry will be fine. He's too wily to get himself caught up in anything." He softly stroked her hair. She pressed her face into his shoulder and a storm of weeping overtook her. Thane's expression was grim. Now was not the time to tell her he had heard the conversation with Deena and was not happy with it. He did not trust the Snake woman. She was using Sue for her own ends. He made a silent vow he was not going to let Sue out of his sight — but Barry was a complication he had not expected. The tie between those two was strong. Sue was liable to do something stupid.

CHAPTER 7
REUNION WITH BARRY

Only one lamp shone out when Thane led Sue back into the palace. But the darkness was shattered when Ruth confronted her mother. Seeing Sue's tear-stained face she gathered her daughter in her arms and motioned Thane to leave. White Hawk stood his ground until he was shooed away as well. Thane hesitated for one brief moment; he wanted to talk, but Ruth was adamant. Signalling to his wolf, Thane made his way to the meeting hall where he knew Tam, Raithe and Amos would be rustling up volunteers to go to the Bluff.

Ruth took one look at her daughter's crestfallen face and shook her head at Tam's insensitive handling of the dragon affair. It was understandable Ruth should think that that was what ailed her. She knew nothing of Deena's words because they were locked away in her daughter's heart, and Sue had no intention of sharing them.

Like all mothers, she noticed the aura of fatigue about her daughter's face. Ruth administered to her needs and tucked her up in bed. Sue was thankful her mother did not question her, and as soon as her head touched the pillow, she feigned sleep. Ruth waited a while, masking her disappointment that there was not going to be any discussion between them. In the end she moved softly from the room, closing the door silently behind her.

Sue was far from asleep. She lay with her eyes fixed on the ceiling, turning over Deena's conversation in her mind. Why couldn't that woman give concise directions as to where the Enchanted Land could be found? But she shied away from making contact with the Snake Queen again. She could rouse Raithe since the ring was connected to him also. Yet according to Deena, no man could enter the Enchanted Land, and live. This only left Tansy and Annalee. Dare she involve them? There was no one else she could turn to. In her dilemma, she turned restlessly in the bed. Her skin become clammy as frustration gripped her in its relentless hold. By the time the first streaks of light crossed the sky, heralding the dawn, Sue found inner peace. She stumbled out of bed, but this time there was purpose in her movements as she quickly dressed. Her mind was made up, knowing what it was she was going to, and she was eager to start.

Quietly opening the window, Sue took in several breaths of fresh air. At this early hour the servants were not yet awake. In seconds she was over the windowsill and landing on the soft earth below. Taking a few seconds to get her bearings and eyeing the open gate some hundred yards away, she saw her first hurdle. Three soldiers stood on guard. Getting past them was going to be tricky. If they saw her at this time in the morning, they would either refuse to let her go through, or follow her instead, which was the last thing she wanted to happen. Darting from bush to bush, she made her way to the wall. So far, the soldiers hadn't noticed her. Their eyes were looking forward over the parkland — they did not expect anyone to break out of the palace. In trepidation she crept nearer the gate, keeping well within the shadows of the wall and hardly daring to breathe. Eventually, she paused, studying them, and one yawned. It had been an uneventful watch and the hours passed slowly for them. From snippets of their conversation that reached her ears, they were about to be relieved of their duty. Someone called out from the barracks, "Hey, you three — there's a hot brew here for you if you want it."

Grunts of approval came from the soldiers, and because no officer was on duty at this hour in the morning, all three left their post and ambled off in the direction of the barracks. Before their relief had a chance to come out, Sue slipped through the gate like a shadow and raced along the foot of the wall to some covering shrubbery. She paused, panting for breath. The feeling of freedom gave new strength to her legs. The thrill of adventure was returning. It had been so easy to get away. Even if she was seen now by one of the soldiers, she was too far away to be recognised. Half an hour later, things might have been different. Sue reached the last thicket of bushes before she was compelled to use the path.

A commotion started up behind her and someone blew a horn. At least a dozen horsemen thundered her way. Sue froze, and squeezed into the thicket so that she was hidden from sight. The thought that she might have been seen leaving the palace receded, because these men were prepared for a long journey. Zeno and Amos were leading the group. Raithe was near the rear with Thane, and the wolf kept pace beside them. Her heart nearly stopped beating when the wolf decided to investigate the thicket in which she was standing, but unknowingly, Thane saved her from discovery by shouting curtly to White Hawk and he obediently followed the men.

It took several minutes before she composed herself enough to continue on her way, but this time she kept giving anxious glances over her shoulder. By the time she reached her destination on a small hill overlooking Therossa's harbour, the sun was just about to rise above the horizon. There was plenty of activity in the bay, but there was no one where she stood. Sue raised her face to the sky. "Silver," she called out. "Can you come to me?"

Her heart thudded and she stared apprehensively at the clouds. Would Silver come after Tam's harsh words — or would Sheeka stop his daughter from answering a human's call? Sue had almost given up when she saw a small speck flying from the forest. It could have been anyone, but as she watched, Silver spiralled towards her and landed a few feet away. Lifting her huge head, the dragon eyed Sue curiously. "You called me, Sonja?" she queried, her voice like a low rumble of thunder. "You do realise there is a ban on our fraternising."

Sue's heart sank and she exclaimed hotly, "I haven't agreed to any ban."

If dragons could laugh, then Silver was doing just that. Her whole body quivered and trails of smoke issued from her mouth. "I knew you had nothing to do with it," she roared approvingly. "I could not return last night because your King has stopped us from flying with you, and Sheeka is being equally bull-headed about it all. He feels he has been badly slighted by the human King. At the moment, he is laying down the law on the plateau, but I wanted to come and tell you that Sapphire dropped Barry off her back near the Bluff." The dragon paused, because of Sue's quick intake of breath. She wondered if Barry had broken a limb. — but Silver went on blithely.

"He landed in one of the lakes. I suppose he can swim," she mused thoughtfully.

Sue laughed. It was an anti-climax. She was almost on the verge of hysteria. First from thinking Barry had met with a terrible accident, and then realising he was not the hostage Deena had been on about. It was almost too much to take in. Silver eyed her in concern, flexing her wings, then her head snaked in Sue's direction and she said, "Why have you called for me Sonja?"

Sue put an unsteady arm on Silver's neck. "I wasn't sure you would come," she whispered.

"You and I are bonded," the dragon roared indignantly. "We will always help each other. Now tell me what it is you want."

"Will you fly me to the Bluff?" Sue asked tentatively.

"You want to go now?" Silver's eyes opened wide and as Sue nodded she flapped her wings again and said, "Climb up on my back — let's go before anyone realises what we are doing."

Sue needed no second bidding. She clambered up onto Silver's back just as White Hawk burst from the trees. He sprang at Sue but Silver had already taken off. The wolf howled. Too late did Thane and Raithe appear running behind him. Sue looked over her shoulder. Dismay overwhelmed her at the expression on Thane's face. He did not look happy as they pulled their horses to an abrupt halt. He said something to Raithe and they both stared angrily at the gradually disappearing dragon and rider. Thane made one last effort to gallop after her, but Sue had no intention of stopping Silver. She saw Thane stop and let out her breath in relief.

* * *

Rainee insisted her caravan be moved to stand beneath the shelter of some nearby leafy trees, away from the scorch marks on the grass; and only when the gypsy woman released her horse from the shafts so that he could graze did she turn to Barry and allow him to bandage her arm. Under her curt instructions he smeared some lurid green ointment over the burn which looked nasty and inflamed, but she waved away his concern and told him not to worry. Instead, she thought it would be a good idea if he made himself useful by lighting a fire for their cooking. This seemed a very reasonable request to Barry, until she mentioned unnecessarily, "out in the open, lad, away from the trees where it is safe."

That riled Barry. A flash of annoyance ran through him. What kind of a fool did she think he was? He quickly shrugged this feeling away. Maybe her arm was paining her and making her touchy. He set to work willingly. First he dug a pit as he had seen Tansy do on numerous occasions, and hoped he could find the correct kindling to start the fire. He would have had to be blind not to notice Rainee's eyes watching his every movement. If she was trying to do it surreptitiously, she was making a bad job of it. He could give her a few pointers in that direction. Every time he casually looked up at her, her eyes suddenly turned away. It was unnerving to know she did not trust him and that made him all the more determined that she would not be able to find fault with his work.

Scrap became a pain to have around, because no one was playing with him, so his doggy antics were more

93

of a hindrance than a help, making off with anything Barry put down until, red in the face, he swallowed a strong urge to tie the dog up. He knew Rainee would never forgive him. He tried ignoring the dog, refusing to chase after it and put up with his furry body entwining itself between his legs. At last a pit was dug and the fire laid but Barry realised he had nothing with which to light it. Tansy carried a tinderbox — but Tansy wasn't here. He looked at Rainee who was suddenly absorbed with the water-butt and pretending not to notice his predicament, but Barry knew her better than that. She hadn't missed a thing. He said deliberately, keeping his voice pleasant, "Have you got two sticks I could rub together, Rainee?"

Immediately, Barry knew he had overstepped the mark because her face muscles tightened. Without a word, she walked stiffly into the caravan and came out moments later holding a couple of twigs, which she handed to him. "Any good?" she asked him in a clipped voice. Barry's jaw dropped.

"What am I supposed to do with these?" he asked, holding them up as though they might bite him.

She shrugged. "I really don't know, but it's what you asked for."

"Well thanks for nothing," Barry said rudely, turning back to his unlit fire. Rather than throw the twigs away, he carefully pushed them into his kindling. He knew he should never have spoken to her like that. She wasn't Tansy. Rainee did not suffer fools easily. Making up his mind to apologise, he swung round to face her again, but Rainee had returned inside the caravan. On the ground in the very spot where she had been standing was a tinderbox — obviously left there for him to find.

Feeling foolish for not having asked for it outright, he picked it up and set a spark into the kindling. With careful blowing on his part, the spark turned to smoke which suddenly ignited into a flame.

Barry fervently thanked the gods for looking down on him kindly. It was the first time ever he had made a fire. Within no time at all he had a fire to be proud of. Rainee watched him through the small caravan window and a smile twitched her lips. She returned down the steps and stood beside him, telling him he had done a good job and just as his awkwardness left him, she added dryly, "I may be a gypsy to you, Barry, but I do not have a crystal ball. Neither can I read minds. Please ask for what you want in future. I've no time for people who beat about the bush."

Rainee thrust a black bowl into his hands and told him to boil up the contents. Her action cleared the air between them more effectively than a lot of meaningless words would have done. She never reprimanded him again, and Barry treated her with respect. He wondered again who she really was; not a gypsy, he would bet his life on that. Rainee was nothing like the people Sue spoke of. Barry prided himself on worming information out of people, but with Rainee he drew a blank.

Half an hour later, the pair of them sat on old wooden stools from Rainee's caravan and consumed something that looked like soup. The warmth from the fire flushed their faces and made Barry feel drowsy. To overcome the tiredness which attacked his eyes, he kept looking constantly at the sky, until the gypsy woman mistakenly thought he was worried and remarked bluntly,

"You're wasting your time sky gazing. The dragon will not be returning. He has got what he came for."

Barry frowned, because to him that didn't make sense. "How did he know someone was waiting?" he asked in surprise, and saw the gypsy woman flinch. A guarded expression entered her eyes and her lips tightened. For once her demeanour was one of discomfort. Eventually, she said gruffly, "He was told."

"Told? How?" Barry put his bowl on the grass and gazed at her. "How does one tell a dragon his dinner is waiting for him?"

Rainee wondered how she got into this conversation. Regaining her composure, she rebuked him sharply, "dragons do not eat humans. Kill them — yes. Burn them — yes, but do not eat them for food. They have too many animals from which to choose."

Barry swallowed his revulsion, thinking of the person he had seen carried away. With an effort he forced himself to pursue this conversation. "But who would have told that black dragon someone was on the Bluff? He didn't come by on the off chance."

"Well you should know. You said yourself you knew the Drazuzi..." Rainee began, but Barry cut her short, violently. "That's not the way the Drazuzi work. They are slaves used by an evil master. Are you sure you didn't mean the Priest, Rainee?"

Another dreadful silence hung in the air and a stony expression covered Rainee's lined face. It seemed to be her refuge for not carrying on with their discourse. She stood up without another word, collected the bowls and turned away from him. Barry studied her thoughtfully and wondered if there was a connection between the gypsy woman and the Priest Oran. Utterly perplexed, he also got up to follow her, scanning the sky as he did so.

"I think the black dragon will return," he said, giving her a side-glance. "I saw two people on the Bluff — not one. He made a bad mistake. He'll have to come back for his deserts."

"That's enough foolish talk from you," Rainee retorted crisply, "Your eyes were probably playing tricks."

"My eyesight is remarkably good," Barry murmured doggedly, "and in case you hadn't noticed — the dragon is already on his way back."

A muffled oath left Rainee's lips and there was a clatter as the bowls she carried hit the ground, spilling what small amount of food was left in them. Scrap pounced on the food with a joyful woof, but found he could not easily grasp the bowls in his mouth. Rainee ignored the dog, her gaze following the direction of Barry's eyes. Barry watched the dragon's progress towards them in a state of trepidation, wondering whether to expect another attack, or should he hide again. Gazing directly into the sun hurt his eyes and made silver motes dance across his vision. Rainee did not seem to be having any difficulty in keeping the dragon in focus. She showed no sign of alarm and her laugh suddenly burst out and she said, "that's not Evonny approaching. This dragon has a rider on its back. It's obviously someone looking for you."

A surge of excitement went through Barry at her words and he tried to focus on the approaching dragon, again screwing up his eyes. As it glided nearer, he tried to determine its colour — which information Rainee supplied with a wry twist of her mouth. "It's white, and bears a distinguished visitor. It is the Princess of dragons."

The change in Barry was so unexpected that Rainee faded into insignificance. He ran out into the open space waving his arms above his head in spite of her warning. "Silver," he yelled out, "It's Silver. Sue's come back looking for me." Barry's voice was jubilant and just for a moment, Rainee was held in the thralls of nostalgia. She watched for a few seconds, then unobtrusively scooped up Scrap and disappeared into the caravan, locking the door behind her. She was not in the mood for unexpected visitors.

Barry felt the rush of air around him as Silver spiralled over his head, her talons spread out for landing. Sue's laughing face looked down on him and directly the dragon's feet touched the ground, she was off Silver's back and caught up in her brother's embrace. Anyone would have thought they had been parted for weeks instead of hours.

"You don't look any the worse for your experience of falling off a dragon's back," Sue exclaimed, holding him at arm's length and hiding completely the misery she had suffered at his expense. "Did you forget to hold on?"

Barry was indignant. "Sapphire flew upside down. What was I supposed to do?" he retorted grimly. "As it happened, I fell into a lake back there and nearly drowned. It was lethal with thick weed but Rainee saved me."

Since no one else was with him, Sue looked speculatively towards the gypsy caravan parked amongst the trees, and a horse grazing peacefully alongside. The area seemed deserted, but she was sure she saw a movement through the small window of the caravan — and that made her wonder. It looked as though someone was hiding in there. "Your rescuer seems to be unsociable. Who is Rainee? Why hasn't she come forward with you to greet me?"

"I don't really know. She's got a dog and lives alone, but I'm sure she's not a gypsy."

"Then let's go and make her acquaintance. You can introduce me." Sue started to walk determinedly towards the caravan, but Silver roared unexpectedly and a sheet of flame stopped her in her tracks. The singed grass smoked almost by her feet, making her skin prickle with alarm.

"Do not go any further, Sonja," the dragon thundered, glaring balefully from angry eyes. "This is no place for you. The woman living in that caravan is a social outcast. No one ever speaks to her. Your own father ordered it so."

Incredulously Sue stared at Silver, unprepared for her aggressive attitude. It was bad enough taking orders from her father, she was not about to take them from a dragon. A dull flush of indignation stained her cheeks and she exclaimed hotly, "I don't believe you. My father is not like that."

The dragon's eyes became watchful, but she displayed no more fire when she roared. "Your father banished her when she put your life in danger…"

"That's utterly ridiculous. I've never met this woman before."

"Well she's met you," Silver retorted, not giving an inch. "I do not understand the years you humans keep — but it was a long time ago."

Barry came to her side. "I like Rainee very much," he stated defiantly, shutting his ears to the disdainful snort from Silver. "If it's of any help — she has already warned me to get away from here. Directly I mentioned I had lived with the Drazuzi, she said she knew who I was, and it changed her."

"Did it? Was she threatening?"

"No. She just told me I shouldn't associate with her. Someone wouldn't like it."

"Meaning Tam, I suppose."

"Could be." Barry shrugged the name away, saying "but you know me. I always do exactly what I shouldn't."

Sue turned back to Silver, feeling uneasy. "Please don't misunderstand me, Silver, but in spite of what you have just said, I want to meet this woman who saved Barry's life and make up my own mind about her. If it's going to upset you, go home."

That annoyed Silver. It was obvious from the smoke and fire issuing from her mouth. She stood at her tallest and looked exactly what she was — a proud exotic creature, but within her intimidating and watchful stare there was grudging respect. "I will not leave you here, but if she harms one hair of your head, I will reduce her to ashes." The dragon retreated over the grass and settled in the sun, keeping one eye at least on Sue and Barry.

They made their way towards the caravan, Sue exclaiming about the burnt grass. In disjointed words, Barry told her about the black dragon and the hostage he had taken off the Bluff. Sue felt a shiver pass through her. Who was the one who had come seeking her? Was it Professor Harding? Barry choked on hearing her words.

"I can assure you the person dangling from his claws looked nothing like him, even though they were too far away for me to see clearly. If you had not arrived as you did just now, I was going with Rainee to search for the second person."

"So she's still prepared to help you?" Sue stopped dead a few yards from the caravan and Barry nodded vigorously. "Yes, in case someone gets hurt. She could heal them. She said she was a nurse."

"A nurse." Sue was clearly surprised. "Barry — this doesn't make sense. There are no nurses in this land. You mean a Shaman, don't you?"

"No I don't," Barry retorted fiercely, "she said..."

"Barry," interrupted a gruff voice, and Rainee stood on the caravan steps. "I should like to meet your sister again and see how she has grown."

The two exchanged glances. Sue moved forward to meet this woman whom her father had outlawed. She could not see any reason for it, and the woman had saved Barry's life. But to Sue, she was still a woman who struck no chords in her memory.

CHAPTER 8

A MAN WITH NO MEMORY

The interior of the caravan was gloomy. It was compact, and possessed only one window and a door. The bed served as a seat during the day and a bed at night. A colourful rug cheered up the otherwise sombre abode. Intricate cupboards lined the walls, but their contents remained hidden behind beautifully scrolled woodwork. Sue could not see any evidence of a light source — yet there must be something for the night. She climbed the steps hesitantly, not at all sure about being enclosed in such a small space. It brought back too many vivid memories of her captivity with the gypsies. But once inside, with the door left open, she was pleasantly surprised. It bore no resemblance to her former prison at all.

Scrap immediately wanted to make a fuss of the newcomer by jumping up to be patted, and Rainee shooed him away, offering her bed for Sue and Barry to sit on, reclining herself in a wicker chair. Outside Silver edged surreptitiously nearer to the caravan and the nervous whickers from Rainee's horse made that lady look through the window.

"Is that dragon of yours hungry?" she asked bluntly, turning to Sue, and Sue gave a guilty start because she had been caught staring rudely around her surroundings. Barry forgot his former repartee with Rainee and said flippantly, "She'll ask first if she wants to eat the horse. I shouldn't worry!"

Rainee raised her eyebrows at him and it was enough to make him flush. He knew that he was being impertinent again. Then her compressed lips suddenly twitched at the corners.

"You're incorrigible lad, but at least I know where I am with you." She returned her gaze to Sue. "I know you're full of questions. I heard your exchange with Silver. Dragons are notorious for not keeping their voices low, but that dragon is correct in being protective and you should listen to her. What your father did was appropriate for my crime."

Sue shook her head, confused. "But did you put my life in danger?" she asked tentatively. The older woman grimaced. Her heavily lined mouth spoke of endurance and hardship, the result of her solitary existence in the wilds. Rainee quickly shattered her thoughts. "I do not need your sympathy. According to the people who stacked the evidence of my crime against me, your father had no choice. Actually he was lenient. Had I been a man he would have killed me."

"I didn't realise you were that barbaric," Barry muttered, but he was ignored. Sue leaned forward; but Rainee's face was deep in shadow and equally unreadable. "I don't understand," she burst out impulsively. "It doesn't sound as if you had a proper trial.

I'm sure my father was forced into his decision," but Rainee jumped out of her chair, frustrated.

"He did what he had to do," she growled. "I was let off the ultimate sentence because he remembered how I had helped him in his time of need, which was when I first set eyes on you, Princess. That did not go down well with his enemies. As far as I'm concerned, that is all I'm prepared to tell you — so no more questions please. It is all in the past and can stay there. I am happy wandering around on my own with just Scrap as a companion, and anyone else who can take me at face value." Rainee stared at them sternly, almost daring them to continue with their questions.

Rebuffed, Sue rose to her feet and moved away towards the door and down the steps. "Thank you at least for seeing me," she said politely, but her voice was tinged with disappointment. She found it hard to quell her desire to ask more questions. Turning to her brother she muttered, "Come on, Barry. Silver will give you a lift home. Tam's worried sick over your whereabouts."

Barry eyed her reproachfully, not moving. "I thought you knew. I'm stopping here with Rainee. She is going to help me search the Bluff." Then he added airily, "Do me a favour when you get back and tell all my friends I'm OK then they will stop worrying about me."

"You're joking, aren't you," Sue retorted in astonishment. "Don't you realise that by now a troop of soldiers are heading this way to do exactly what you propose to do yourself. You might just as well come back with me."

"I'm sorry — but no." Barry was adamant. "There is still someone up there on the Bluff that the Drazuzi have failed to capture, and I'm not risking anything else happening to whoever it is. The black dragon has taken one," he reminded her sharply, "and I'm not going to let that happen to the remaining person."

At first Sue was too stunned to answer him. Then a smile lit up her face that made Barry uneasy. He knew that look. An idea had occurred to her and she didn't keep him in suspense for long. "If we speak to Silver, I'm sure the dragon will fly us to the top of the Bluff and save you the bother of climbing. Then I could help you search, and if anyone is injured up there — what better person is there than Silver to get them back to this caravan where Rainee can heal him or her? That was your original plan — wasn't it?" She looked sideways at the older woman and Sue's expression disarmed Rainee. It had been years since anyone had deliberately ignored the fact that she was an outcast. Even so, she gestured towards the dragon outside who looked as though she were fast asleep, but everyone knew she wasn't.

"Don't you think it might be a good idea to acquaint Silver with your plan? She might not approve."

Sue caught hold of the older woman's arm and drew her towards the dragon, taking her at her word, but she had to drag her forward when Rainee baulked. "You have nothing to fear," she remarked blithely, "Silver and I are bonded. She will help us if I ask. It is her way to be protective and she is sensible enough to realise people can make mistakes in their judgments. Once I have told her that you are my friend, she will not harm you."

The confidence in her voice gave Rainee courage to stare hard at the dragon and she saw one of its eyes open. For a brief moment she was in half a mind to turn back, but Sue still had hold of her arm and continued to speak. "I will ask her to fly Barry and me to the top of the Bluff — and to bring us back again." She paused, suddenly struck with a thought, and eyed Rainee questioningly, saying, "You will still be here when we return?"

"I have already given Barry my word," Rainee replied crisply, "although I think you are going on a wild goose chase. There is no one up there now."

* * *

Alfie shivered, and not for the first time. His head felt bad as though full of hammers and stabbing pains which were always worse when he tried to think. Blood congealed on his forehead and matted his hair. His lips felt dry and swollen. He tried to think again and ignore the headache, which was persistent. Why was he here — in this gloomy cave, slumped against the wall? Why had he not tried walking away? Was he alone? Had he been here a long time? Didn't he have any friends? Vaguely he seemed to remember someone had been with him — but if that was so, why had he or she left him here? Was this his home — did he live here?

Alfie's bleary eyes looked in all directions. A fuzziness was pressing down on his head. Why did it hurt him so much when he tried to think? Maybe he should leave this place. Alfie struggled until he was standing and attempted to reach the ledge outside where sunlight flickered on the lichen-covered stone. The whole world went spinning round and he caught hold of some rock to steady himself. When his equilibrium settled, he gazed out over the panoramic vista before him. The view did not spark off

106

his memory — it meant nothing to him at all. If he lived out there, surely there would have been something familiar to see. Alfie wondered how to reach the bottom of the escarpment. The way down discouraged him — it was too far and perspiration beaded his forehead at the thought of it. Maybe climbing to the top would be easier because it was nearer.

Alfie started to climb upwards. Climb was not exactly the correct word because he was down on his hands and knees, crawling. His hands grasped everything there was available to hold on to because he felt so dizzy. Twice he stopped as vertigo swamped over him. He was forced to take in deep breaths to steady his nerves. Why couldn't he remember why he was here? The thought kept bugging his mind.

The top seemed tantalisingly near, but he felt he would never manage to drag himself up that far. The slope was steep, casting deceptive shadows on the rough wall. When he halted to get more breath where the shadow around him was very thick it became even denser as another shadow speedily passed overhead. Gritting his teeth, Alfie looked up, but whatever it was had gone. If it was a bird, then it must be huge. Wanting to see where it had landed gave him just that extra strength to get his limbs moving again. He pushed himself to finish the climb, but already his chest was rasping, and he just managed to grasp the edge of the Bluff when a happy freckled face looked over the rim and stared at him in astonishment. For a moment, neither person moved.

"Sue! Quickly! Come over here. I need a hand," called Barry.

The face disappeared and Alfie heard footsteps approaching. Then to Alfie's amazement, two faces peered down on him from above. One was a girl and her eyes opened wide in her bemused face. He was not to know that both Sue and Barry stared in alarm at his precarious position and noticed immediately the unhealthy pallor of his skin. He had to be rescued from there before he fell. Barry reached down to grasp him, taking a firm grip round his wrist, and attempted to haul him up. It was no mean feat. Barry pulled, but Alfie was a dead weight, not being in any condition to help. After a long struggle, with Sue's help as well, Alfie lay panting on the grass like a landed fish. Sue eyed the stranger as though he were an oddity, and the gash across his forehead caused her unease. She exchanged a questioning look with Barry — a look that almost said 'who on earth is he?' He was certainly not a native of Therossa, dressed as he was. He had obviously come from their homeland.

Barry felt around for his water bottle, then knelt beside Alfie and raised his head, pressing the flask to his lips. Most of the liquid had dribbled down his chin but Alfie managed a few gulps and focused his gaze on the girl and youth hovering over him. With a pleading voice and desperation in his eyes, he asked "do you know who I am?"

Without being told, Sue knew he was suffering from inhalation of the mist and his memory was gone. She bent nearer and answered, studying him calmly, "we were hoping you could tell us that. Can you remember anything?"

"What am I doing here?" Alfie said, trying unsuccessfully to get up, his eyes darting round in all directions. He did not appear to have heard what Sue had said. His look was traumatic as he caught hold of Barry's arm. "I thought someone was with me," he muttered despairingly. "Did I leave that someone behind?"

It was Barry's turn to ignore his question. He could hardly tell someone in his condition that a dragon took whoever it was away. He tried a different tactic instead by asking abruptly, "what is your name?"

Alfie shook his head, and confusion overwhelmed him. "I don't know," he muttered wearily, and closed his eyes to blot everything out.

"This is getting us nowhere," Sue cut in briskly. "It could be some time before his memory comes back to him and I hate to say it, but I'm not happy with this place. I've got a feeling everything is closing in. The hairs on the back of my neck are standing up. We must get this man back to Rainee as soon as possible. I'm sure it is not safe here."

Barry agreed with her and they both helped pull Alfie to his feet. He swayed alarmingly in their hold and tried to fight them off. Sue called to Silver, anxiously looking up in the sky and shivered. She could feel eyes watching her from the trees, and the trees were so near, they were within touching distance. This place was wrong, soaked in evil. A strange sensation was coming from the thickly growing forest. She tried to push the sensation aside, but without any warning, the temperature plummeted and then she saw it — the suffocating fog drifting through the foliage in their direction.

"Watch out, Barry," she warned, and turning her attention back to the sky, yelled out frantically, "Silver, where are you?"

Darkness came overhead as from the trees there was a whirl of wings, a rush of air and Silver landed very near to the edge of the drop. Her huge head snaked towards Sue and smoke poured from her mouth. "Hurry, Sue," she urged, "the mist will soon engulf you."

They didn't need any urging. Already it was creeping towards them with a speed they had never seen before. Fear gave Barry and Sue the strength to hoist the unknown man over Silver's back and clamber up beside him. Fingers of fog surged across the remaining distance to touch the dragon. Silver roared and a ball of fire hit the mist, checking its advance. In that time Silver flexed her wings and took off, carrying all three easily to safety. She spiralled and levelled off, and within five minutes the dragon landed by Rainee's caravan.

She came running towards them to help carry their now unconscious passenger to the caravan. Sue glanced back at the Bluff and gasped, her throat constricted. Barry followed her gaze and inhaled sharply. The Bluff was once again completely shrouded in the deadly fog.

* * *

Sue wanted to help after rescuing the man who everyone had said was a figment of Barry's imagination. Rainee oozed authority and made her feel redundant, especially with her brusque refusal. The gypsy woman allowed Barry to help get the man into the caravan and then, to his annoyance, shooed him out. It was not as though she were being secretive because the door was left wide open and anyone could see right in — but with everyone inside, there was no room to move.

110

Sue wandered off feeling let down. Rainee may have been a healer, but Sue would have liked to challenge her about being a nurse. By the description she had first given them, it meant she must have originated from her old world — in which case, how did she fall foul of Tam and how did he get to know her? Mentally exhausted, Sue went and sat down beside Silver, where she rested with her long neck stretched out on the grass soaking up the sun. Sue watched the little dog tentatively edge himself nearer, but his eyes were fixed on the recumbent dragon and he wasn't sure if it was safe to approach. Sue clicked her fingers and his head went to one side, so she said softly, "come to me, boy," and with eyes full of trust, he wriggled on his stomach until he was by her side, admittedly the furthermost side from the dragon. A few moments later Barry came along and threw himself to the ground beside her, cupping his chin in his hands. He was rather put out by Rainee's attitude.

They both eyed the Bluff speculatively, and after a while, Sue said anxiously, "I think that mist is getting thicker and spreading further afield. Do look, Barry — it's nearly at the bottom of the cliff now. Suppose it reaches us?"

"Not a chance," replied Barry, gazing at the whirling chaos of fog through narrowed eyes. Being a logical person, he added, "We know the Priest sends it out to catch people, but he isn't powerful enough to send it all over Therossa. You're safe enough here, Sue, although it was touch and go up there. I've never seen a mist move so swiftly."

Sue was still uncertain. "I wonder why the Priest is so keen to capture the man we've just rescued? I haven't a clue who he is. I thought I might have recognised him but his face isn't familiar. Thane was under the impression Professor Harding had found his way through and has convinced my father to think that way as well. Before long a hunting party will arrive here. I actually saw it starting off."

"Great," Barry muttered dryly. "I can join them. I'm giving up on flying dragons after the way Sapphire treated me."

A little smoke escaped Silver's mouth, but other than that, she appeared to be asleep. Barry snorted. She had to do better than that if she wanted to fool anyone. Sue hadn't noticed. She continued to muse about the man in the caravan. "He's nothing to do with my father so it can't have anything to do with the royal household. That's what makes it all so mysterious. Oran is up to something."

"You're forgetting about the other person," Barry pointed out. "You know — the one I told you about that the dragon snatched off the Bluff." He put a hand out and lazily rolled Scrap over on his back so that all his legs were in the air. "They may be important to the Priest." At this point Silver roused herself. She raised her head, unblinking eyes surveying Barry.

"What dragon, Barry?" she mumbled.

"I don't know," Barry retorted carelessly, but his hand instinctively clamped on Scrap's back to stop him from running away, "Rainee called him Evonny. He was black."

Silver roared furiously. She lifted herself up and her forked tail thrashed the ground, causing a ball of dust to arise. The noise was deafening. Rainee came out from the caravan to see what it was all about. Scrap escaped Barry's hold and fled back to her, whimpering all the way.

"This is serious," the white dragon thundered, eyeing the fleeing dog contemptuously. "Evonny's actions could cause untold damage. Why does he want a hostage? Who is this person?"

"We don't know," answered Sue, dusting herself down, but suddenly she felt uneasy because in a way she did know. It was someone seeking her out — but who? Sue could account for all of her friends, which was what made this a mystery. She needed to find out the identity of this other person before she started journeying to the Enchanted Land. Then looking towards the dragon, she was aware that Silver was eyeing her speculatively. It made her apprehensive, knowing the dragons' ability to read minds. At all costs Silver must not find out what Deena had asked her to do, she was liable to tell Thane. So shrugging nonchalantly, she said, "We're rather hoping the man in the caravan will enlighten us when his memory returns, and seeing that he's been away from the Bluff for some time, it shouldn't be all that long now. It's the fresh air that heals those affected by the mist."

But Silver was still watchful. She knew Sue was withholding information but decided to bide her time until the boy moved away. Barry ignored the dragon's fierce intimidating stare in his direction and decided to give her something to worry about. "Sapphire was with the black dragon."

To his disappointment, Silver never batted an eyelid. She only rumbled, "That's not surprising since he's her father."

Barry grimaced and jumped to his feet, thinking, what was it about dragons that they made him feel inferior. At that moment Rainee hailed them as she emerged from her caravan, supporting the well-built youth with a white bandage round his head. Now perhaps they would learn something.

CHAPTER 9
NIGHT FLIGHT

As Rainee stepped onto the rough grass at the foot of the caravan steps, the young man stared directly at Sue and Barry. Interest flickered in his eyes. Something was stirring in his memory which he couldn't grasp, but before he could speak, Rainee pushed him down on the caravan steps, saying brusquely, "you need to conserve your strength, young man. That bang on the head is nasty and you need watching. It could possibly lead to amnesia. When you've got some food inside you, maybe you will feel stronger." She glanced obliquely at Sue, adding, "he hasn't fully recovered all his memory yet, but he does remember quite a lot. His name is…"

Not waiting to be introduced by her, the young man sprang to his feet and cut in, "I'm Alfie." He stretched out his hand, but having moved so swiftly, stumbled.

Barry immediately dashed forward and supported him with a strong arm. He stared into Alfie's pleasant countenance, thinking uncharitably how homely he looked, yet eyeing the firm set of his mouth, he suspected this youth was strong-willed as Rainee had just discovered by the look on her face.

Sue grasped his proffered hand. Her eyes automatically probed his face, until she realised how much she was staring at him. He quickly withdrew his hand feeling embarrassed and said awkwardly, "Rainee

115

told me your name is Sue, but I feel sure I've seen you somewhere before, both of you. Stupid — isn't it?"

"But how peculiar." Sue was looking equally bewildered. "I thought I knew you as well — as though we had met before." In the silence that fell between them, she studied his face again. "I think it's the eyes." Her voice trailed off as she tried to pinpoint where she had seen eyes like his before.

"Well it's not the eyes with me," Alfie frowned. "It's something about the way you look — I also feel I have heard your name before," he groaned, "my God, I do hate having only half a memory."

"I shouldn't worry if I were you," Barry declared airily, "Because it's all possible. You must have heard me calling to Sue when we rescued you."

Alfie accepted that explanation with a grateful smile, thinking how much he liked this lad, but Rainee broke up the conversation by asking for help in preparing a meal. Here Alfie proved to be very accommodating. Against Rainee's better judgement, he attended to the fire as though it were second nature to him, putting Barry out of a job, and he skinned a rabbit for cooking with the ease of someone who had done this job all his life — but when asked the simple question of where he came from, Alfie was baffled and unable to answer.

A lot later when Alfie was propped up against the caravan wheel, he stared morosely at a piece of rabbit in his fingers. In spite of the welcome everyone showed him, he felt really low at not having a complete memory.

"Don't worry about it," was Rainee's advice. "It will come back when you least expect it."

He did not look as though that remark helped him. Alfie concentrated on the dragon instead, who was lying on the grass making strange rumbles from her mouth while she dozed. At the beginning, the sight of her had filled him with dismay and he could not help looking at her suspiciously, but now he accepted her as part of the group. Only one thing had him worried and he asked curiously, "Do dragons change colour? I could have sworn that she was black the last time I saw her."

Sue laughed, and glanced warningly at Silver who had no intention of joining in the conversation, but she saw her tense. Something warned her to tread slowly. "So you do remember the black dragon," she said carefully, thinking that maybe this was going to be the breakthrough she was waiting for. When Alfie was relaxed and not trying to think, that would be the time when he would remember something.

"Yes, I thought at the time she was silly to go with him, but I didn't stop her — yet I had this feeling it was all wrong," Alfie answered spontaneously, then he realised there was silence around him. The others were all staring at him in stunned surprise. Barry found his voice first because he was the one who had seen the unfortunate prisoner taken away, but he had no idea at the time that it was a woman. "You said *she*," he muttered. "Who was *she*, Alfie?"

Alfie looked confused, wondering what he had said. Suddenly his head was thumping as though it contained a working anvil. He closed his eyes as a means of escape. It was better than looking into Sue's strained face and horror-filled eyes. "It's all a muddle," he muttered despondently. "I can't remember anything."

117

"Please try," Sue begged. "You've come so far." She touched his arm, but Alfie shook his head and her hand fell away at once. "It's all going round and round, and my head hurts too much to think. Please — don't ask me any more questions."

Rainee was suddenly supportive and by his side. She motioned to Barry. "Help me carry him back inside. I will give him something for the pain and something to make him sleep. It is going to be a hot and humid night so we can all camp out here — unless of course you intend to leave." She stared hard at Sue, but Sue shook her head.

"We're staying — if that is all right with you."

Rainee grunted, and Barry took hold of Alfie who seemed to have no will of his own but went with his helpers uncomplainingly.

* * *

Sue kicked at a tuft of grass to vent her feelings. The problem Deena had given her gnawed continuously in her mind, and she felt torn two ways. She would do anything to heal the rift between the dragons and her people, but was Deena's secretive way the only option? Why, after all this time, was she beginning to harbour feelings of distrust about the Snake Queen? The problem of the hostage was the worst of all, Sue had only just found out it was a woman. If only she knew the person's identity. She had to ask herself, would it make any difference to her if she did? Unfortunately, the only person who could help was Alfie, but he lay in the caravan and could not remember a thing. Another tuft of grass went flying through the air, the result of another vicious kick.

Finding the Crystal Horse sounded very exciting, an adventure to share with all her friends, but to be told it was a dangerous mission and fraught with unknown hazards put a different perception on the venture entirely, besides the fact that she must not tell anyone where she was going — and go alone. Had Deena picked her out to find this object of power because she was susceptible and easily got at? What was stopping Deena from going herself? And if it was what Evonny wanted to put things right, why did Deena want it put into Sue's hands? All this thinking was giving her a terrible headache. She bit her lip, nearly drawing blood. The obvious and sensible solution to all this, was to seek the help of Thane or Raithe — but according to Deena, that was to send them to their deaths. Was she being told the truth? Was it only women who could go to the Enchanted Land? Suppose she asked Tansy or Annalee? Sue immediately shied away from the idea. They were her friends and she was not going to involve them in something dangerous. Deena said it was imperative to go at once. Deena said... always what Deena said.

Sue stopped her pacing, and a crackling noise made her look back longingly towards the caravan where a large fire illuminated the surrounding sky. Rainee and Barry were sitting side by side like old mates, talking, with firelight playing on their faces. Scrap was lying across Rainee's lap. Something like envy touched Sue that she was not a part of it. She gave herself a shake to rid her mind of morbid thoughts and self-pity. She felt eyes probing into her back. Silver was watching her — silent, but ever vigilant. It was thinking of Silver that made her mind up. She called out to Barry. "I'm just going to fly around with Silver. I'll be back soon."

Barry waved an arm to acknowledge he had heard her, and continued his conversation with Rainee. Hesitantly Sue went up to the dragon that was watching her, and little did she realise that the large wise eyes of the mythical beast had picked up her distress. Silver automatically lowered her body and mumbled quietly for a dragon, "where to, Princess?"

Sue clambered onto her back and put both arms round her neck. "Anywhere, Silver," she said recklessly, "somewhere quiet. I want your advice."

Silver needed no second bidding. Silently she spread her wings and glided forward into the dark, rising to where the stars overhead glittered like diamonds scattered over a black velvet cloak. Sue held on tightly, her head resting on Silver's neck, and the rhythm of the flight made her feel ecstatic as they skimmed across the land, a land lit only by moonlight, which looked vastly different from what it did during the day. A warming wind blew through her hair, blowing away her troubles and relaxing her mind. Silver made no attempt to communicate and Sue was content to drift along, going wherever the dragon chose.

They passed over forests, mountains, rivers and seas, but still Silver surged onwards. It seemed an eternity to Sue, but all too soon Silver banked and swooped lower. The ground met them at an alarming speed and the dragon manoeuvred her body to land on a ledge high up the side of a mountain; Sue looked at the spectacular view below, all clothed in moonlight. The silvery light made the fast flowing river sparkle as it crashed over rocks. The mountains around them reared up, giving the impression of sharp white teeth. Flickers of light dotted the plain and Sue heard Silver say derisively 'gypsies' and dismissed them from her mind.

Sue slid onto the rocky surface, rubbing her legs to return the blood flow to them. The ledge was sheltered from the wind and the air felt warm. Sheer rock walls surrounded them, making it impossible for anyone to get near without being seen. Silver had chosen a secluded spot for Sue to unburden herself, but Sue had forgotten what she wanted to discuss. Curiosity had taken over.

"Where is this place?" she asked, and the dragon answered pointedly, "you wanted to talk, Sue. I'll tell you where you are afterwards."

The dragon settled herself comfortably, curling her forked tail round for balance. Sue leant against her wing until she was relaxed. It was just as well Silver had inexhaustible patience, because she had to wait a long time for Sue to disclose what troubled her. Sue started to speak hesitantly at first, but on not receiving any interruptions, gained confidence and before long it all poured out in a jumble of words.

Silver listened in silence as she heard about Sapphire, Evonny, the hostage, ending up with Deena and the quest she wanted Sue to accomplish. "The quest to bring back the Crystal Horse from the Enchanted Land." Sue paused for breath and there was silence. Eventually the dragon asked, "What sort of advice are you looking for, Sue?"

That cryptic remark flummoxed the girl and it made her wonder if she was being a fool. What did she expect Silver to do? Tell her to forget the whole thing? Tell her not to trust Deena? Tell her it was all a hoax? Sue shook her head and said, "I'm confused. I don't like the idea of all this secrecy and attempting this venture on my own — especially since I've got no idea of what I'm looking for."

"You're correct there," Silver roared angrily, "someone should go with you for support." That remark gave Sue a glimmer of hope, but it was a short-lived.

"I can't approach Thane, Raithe or my father," Sue continued slowly, "because they are men."

"Precisely," Silver snapped. "What is more, you cannot ask Tansy or Annalee to accompany you either."

Sue looked surprised, even though she had already ruled them out herself. "Why shouldn't I?" she asked, curiously.

"Because as Deena pointed out to you — they are not initiated."

Sue digested that and looked bleakly down to the valley below, wondering if she had made a mistake in confiding with the dragon. By the surge of anger rippling through Silver's body, she knew her thoughts had been picked up. "What is it that worries you, Sue?" Silver demanded impatiently, smoke issuing from her mouth. "No! Don't tell me. I can read you like a book. You will go on this mission no matter what I say — because of the hostage — even though at the moment you don't even know who it is. Just tell me this — what are you expecting of me?"

Sue opened her mouth but was instantly cut short by the dragon. "You can forget it. I cannot go with you." She heard Sue's gasp of dismay, but ignored it. "My power is not strong enough to break through the barriers which surround the Enchanted Land. Neither can Deena go, which must upset her very much. She has to rely solely on you. She cannot leave the caves where she lives. Outside those walls she has no power. Why do you think she wants to lay her hands on the Crystal Horse? She has told you the truth, but only part of it. Whoever lays hands on the Crystal Horse will have immense power." Silver paused — and then her last words were spoken so softly, Sue only just heard them. "Do you still want to go on with this, Sue?"

Sue shivered, wondering what the alternative was. "I certainly don't want to harm my friends and it wouldn't be fair for anyone to face what I think I have to. But I feel so alone. All I want is a companion to be with me."

"Who?" asked Silver abruptly. Her unblinking eyes stared at the girl under her wing. Sue didn't answer, but her thoughts were so easy to read, and she looked so unhappy that Silver pressed her gently. "Why haven't you asked Thane instead of me?"

"I've told you. I can't." Sue choked. "He would want to come with me and I can't allow that after what Deena has told me. She actually ordered me not to say a word to him."

"And you believed her," Silver roared in disgust. "Think clearly, Sue. Tell me — would you contemplate this venture if there was no hostage?"

She saw Sue waver, but then a resolute expression entered Sue's eyes and she said grimly "I want there to be harmony amongst your people and mine — but this is not going to happen unless Evonny has the Crystal Horse in his possession."

Smoke once again poured from the dragon's mouth. "What stupid thinking is that," she hissed, trying to subdue her fury. "Evonny having the Crystal Horse would be the worst thing to happen." A few more puffs of smoke disappeared into the night air before she added bluntly, "You are being used. There are three ruthless people trying to rule Therossa. Firstly there is Deena, the Snake Queen, who only does anything for her own ends. She is a powerful woman, more so than Sheeka or any of the dragons. She uses a different magic. Secondly there is Evonny who desperately wants more power so that he can rule over everything. Then thirdly there is Oran, the deposed king who never forgave your father for returning. He works his insidious magic underground while pretending to be a benefactor to the Drazuzi. The Crystal Horse would do no good in any of these hands. Deena has played on your emotions, Sue, to entice you to help her."

Sue felt herself tremble. Although she was annoyed at the way Deena was using her, she was still uncertain. It wasn't all lies. It couldn't be. The words 'the hostage will die' worried her considerably, because there was a hostage. Barry was in the clear — but someone else was in his place. "Silver," she queried tentatively, "is the Enchanted Land really as dangerous as I've been led to believe?"

"Yes."

"And it's true about men dying?"

Silver shifted her position. "I would not like to swear to it because men have died trying to get there," she said. "It could be the result of the magic or it could be something they did — who knows? What is essential at this moment is for you to make peace with Thane. When you flew away from him on my back, you did untold damage to your friendship and to my position in the dragon world. I would like to bet he has got your father to speak to Sheeka."

Sue gasped in dismay. "Oh no, Silver, he wouldn't do that."

"Huh!" A lot more smoke poured from the dragon's mouth as she declared, "he's a man, isn't he?" Silver rose to her feet and swivelled her neck towards the valley below and continued, "across the other side of that river, where the trees grow very thickly — although in this light you cannot see them very well — is the Enchanted Land. The water is the barrier. You die if you so much as put a foot in it. Now, young lady, that's enough for tonight. Climb onto my shoulders — I'm taking you back to Barry."

Half dazed and half apprehensive, Sue did as Silver ordered. She could not stop her mind from thinking of Thane. Surely he was not upset with her when all she was doing was trying to save him. But she had overlooked the fact that she had not given him a chance to choose for himself and that, according to Silver, was the cause of all the trouble. Their journey back to the caravan hardly registered with her but they could not have been gone all that long because as they landed, Barry was just getting to his feet and yawning.

"I'm off hunting and have one or two things to see to — but I'll be back in the morning," Silver rumbled. "Meanwhile — think carefully on my words."

Sue ran across the ground to the caravan and there was lightness in her step. Rainee eyed her thoughtfully and thrust a colourful blanket into her arms. "To put round you in the night, it can get very chilly," she said gruffly, "and you're outside a long time."

CHAPTER 10
PRISCILLA

Gathering clouds of a storm rolled in from every compass direction. Thunder roared continuously. The heavy claps reverberated over the wide expanse of sky where lightning flashed nonstop. The ominous dark clouds, low and virulent, scudded along, propelled by a gale force wind. Not a moment too soon Rainee herded them all into her small caravan. Outside, the wind tore their fire apart, sending fragments in all directions. Barry watched it being extinguished, and felt sorry for the person who had to relight it.

It was a tight squeeze inside the caravan, but the occupants did not complain. They were pleased the caravan was there to keep them dry. They manoeuvred themselves around until they were all as comfortable as they could possibly get. The humidity inside became oppressive. Their clothes clung to their bodies in the small airless place and perspiration poured down their faces.

Alfie looked a lot better this morning and did not seem to be affected by the atmosphere. His perky expression was a tonic to the others and a mischievous light gleamed in his eyes as he patted part of the bed near to him, indicating to Sue to sit on it. He deliberately ignored the scandalised expression on Rainee's face and when asked sometime later by Barry as to why he did that, Alfie admitted he hated to toe the line. Barry plonked himself on the other end, nearest the door and sat in the prime position to catch any breeze that might blow in. He saw the first heavy raindrops splatter over the steps. Rainee was the only one who could be said to be really comfortable, because she sat in her wicker chair, although she had Scrap on her lap and he radiated a lot of extra heat.

As the deluge of rain thundered down on the caravan roof, it sounded like a waterfall. Outside on the hard ground, huge puddles developed with alarming speed and started spreading, almost as though they were going to form a lake. Barry wondered if the plain was liable to flood, but rather than ask, he decided to sit and watch. In some ways the storm was exhilarating.

"This is all very friendly and cosy," remarked Alfie unexpectedly from his corner in the darkened space. He glanced at all the other set faces around him, which appeared little more than a blur in the gloom. "I rather like being in the dry when it's pouring with rain outside."

"I'd much rather be outside getting wet," Barry muttered gruffly, watching the water running off the roof. "It would be much cooler out there."

"Maybe," retorted Alfie amiably, "but I thought that while we're all packed in here, we could get to know each other better. After all — I don't know a single thing about any of you. So what shall we discuss to pass the time away?"

"It's perfectly obvious we're going to talk about you," Sue responded immediately. "Has your memory returned, Alfie?"

Rainee glared at her for bringing up a subject she considered to be taboo, and Alfie shivered because he picked up on some strange vibes that came from her direction. "Not everything. Some names still elude me — but I remember a lot more than I did." He looked obliquely at Sue. "If it's any help — I know where I came from."

Sue tried hard to keep her elation low because of upsetting Rainee, but Barry did not suffer from any such restraint and asked, "So where did you come from?"

"From just outside Southampton. Ever heard of it?"

"That's a long way from here," Sue remarked in surprise, trying hard to keep the disappointment from her voice. "I suppose you do know you're now in another world and I doubt that you'll ever find your way back again?"

"Of course," replied Alfie showing no alarm, but he was piqued that he had not impressed them. "We realised that when we saw dragons flying for the first time. I was shocked, but she went into raptures over them — well — it may have been revulsion, I suppose. I've forgotten."

That word 'she' that he mentioned so liberally, hung in the air and Sue took in a deep breath. "Doesn't 'she' have a name?" she asked carefully.

Alfie scratched his head, looking almost comical. If he felt relaxed, no one else did. A flash of lightning lit up the little room, followed immediately by a deafening clap of thunder. In that split second of light, Alfie saw a strange expression on Rainee's face — but just as quickly it faded. "I told you I can't remember names yet," he said contritely, "only names of people I have known all my life. She was virtually a stranger, but we got thrown together by unusual circumstances." He glanced at Sue's downcast face. "Don't fret though. I'm sure it will suddenly come back to me. She had such a funny name — I'm surprised it eludes me, but that's by the way. Would you like to know how I met her?"

"We would much rather know how you came to be on the Bluff," retorted Barry unhelpfully.

"No," Sue interrupted, "tell us how you met her."

Rainee moved sharply and said, "Let the young man tell his story in his own way — then question him afterwards if you must." The tone of her voice was discouraging, but Barry interjected smoothly, "That's what she is doing, Rainee. Go ahead, Sue."

"Hey! Wait a minute," interrupted Alfie. He didn't like the undercurrent he was picking up. "I'm not going to start a war between you good people. If there is anything wrong — I'll leave right now."

Neither Sue nor Barry answered him, but both looked pointedly at Rainee. Rainee's lips tightened and she said dryly, "put what I say down to old age and the knowledge I've acquired over the years. You should still be resting and taking things easy after that bang on your head Alfie, and the *Princess*," she heavily accentuated the word Princess, as she glared at Sue, "should realise that there are some things she must wait for. She is not living in the palace now but in my caravan."

A brilliant glare dazzled everyone's eyes. Lightning forked down outside and a thunderbolt shook the caravan. Scrap vanished under the bed and Sue clamped her hands to her ears, not believing what Rainee had said. To make matters worse, Alfie took the opportunity of leaning closer to her and whispering so that everyone could hear. "I'm so sorry, your Highness, if I've been a bit familiar. I didn't realise you had a title."

Sue clenched her fists into a tight ball and her eyes flashed angrily. Temper shattered her usual serenity. From Rainee, her eyes shifted onto the poor unfortunate Alfie. "Don't you dare start being obsequious to me," she snapped furiously at him. "I'm just plain Sue — so please remember that in future or you'll be no friend of mine."

Barry jumped at the unexpected venom in her voice. Alfie looked stunned, as though he had been dealt a lethal blow. He floundered, eyes widening with shock. Sucking in his breath, he shouted, "my God! You sounded just like Priscilla then."

"Priscilla!" yelped Barry at the top of his voice, shattering everyone's eardrums, and Sue choked, "was Priscilla this 'she' you keep alluding to, Alfie?"

Mayhem ran rife for a few moments while everyone spoke at once. No one even noticed that the storm was over and the rain had stopped — except Rainee, who surreptitiously slipped past Barry to see what damage had been done outside. Storms were commonplace in these parts, but this last one had been terrific. She felt no remorse for the row she had caused.

Alfie collapsed under the onslaught as though all his energy had been sucked away. He may have inadvertently delivered a mortal blow to his rescuers, but what assailed him was ten times worse. With his memory completely restored, he felt shattered. Everything fell into place like a jigsaw. He knew now why Sue struck a chord in his memory and he could hear Priscilla's voice sobbing in his ear, 'how on earth am I going to find Sue and Barry here?' His eyes were becoming embarrassingly wet. It had to be faced — he had failed Priscilla, allowed a dragon to take her away and not lifted a hand to save her.

The misery showing on his face touched something inside Sue, who was staring at him with tears in her own eyes. Her former anger had vanished and she reached out to Alfie and touched him. "Please tell us everything. We had no idea Priscilla had been here."

Sue's mind was in turmoil as much as Alfie's. She could not believe Priscilla had left America. Alfie told bit by bit in a shaky voice the story of her return. She could picture her sister's reaction on finding out Professor Harding had abducted her, and her horror in realising Alfie was his nephew. It must have seemed like the end of the world to her, finding herself in the forest. The fact that the Professor and Cyril Grant had been captured did not worry her — but the next part of Alfie's story made her go cold and Barry stiffen in anger. Alfie spoke about how they were trying to escape from the mist, and from there on it became a bit hazy. He no longer recognised Priscilla. He knew a large black dragon flew off with her but he saw her only as a stranger and was not concerned.

Alfie stopped speaking, misery clogging up his throat. Sue swallowed as her own mind was made up. She did not care about the Drazuzi having the Professor — but Priscilla's welfare was another matter. No matter what anyone said to her, she was going to find the Crystal Horse. Not for Deena, Evonny or Oran — but to get Priscilla back and even out the power in this land. There was no way she was going to stand by while a dragon held her sister hostage. Sue rubbed her eyes on a sleeve of her tunic and turned to Barry. "Let's go. Alfie needs some time alone,"

* * *

No one saw the flight of the black and blue dragon, because it was early in the morning. Also it was on a route that was not much used. People had learnt to keep away from the eastern range of mountains because they had a bad name and harboured many ferocious animals. Just before Evonny touched down on a granite ledge, which was the gateway to many caves beyond, he roared out in defiance and let his followers know he had returned. It was a ledge that a human being would have found difficult to reach, which is why he claimed it as his own personal property. He released the prisoner he was carrying and she fell onto the hard rocky shelf. The jolt brought her to her senses, wrenching her mind back from the darkness of unconsciousness. Priscilla saw her worst nightmare as the dragon towered above her. No longer did the black dragon look magnificent. At the sight of him Priscilla cringed away, her eyes dilating with horror. When a second dragon alighted beside the first, she felt she wanted to throw up.

Evonny regarded her through narrowed eyes, and quickly assessed how much trouble they could expect from her. Priscilla did not rate very high in his esteem. "Get this woman something to eat," he roared at Sapphire, and noticed with satisfaction that the prisoner shrank away from the volume of his voice. "She's all skin and bones, but we had better keep her alive."

Priscilla went cold at the thought that they might contemplate eating her. But one thing she could rely on was her voice. "You better had," she snapped back spitefully, "otherwise Sue will have something to say about it."

Why had she said that? They wouldn't have a clue about Sue. As the blue dragon opened her wings gracefully and flew from the ledge, she emitted a disdainful laugh.

"I think I know where a few rats live."

Priscilla retched, and was just getting over the shock that dragons could speak when Evonny made one step towards her. Her hackles rose; her face contorted with fear. She screamed — a high-pitched cry that reverberated through the archways of her prison.

"Don't you dare come near me, you evil monster. You have no right to keep me here. I'll make you sorry you ever laid hands on me." Her remark was ludicrous because she was speaking to someone ten times her size, but the dragon halted and roared, his voice rebounding off the walls of the cave.

"You dare to threaten me, you puny little human," he bellowed. Smoke and flames poured from his mouth making him look like the devil incarnate. "I could squash you like a fly with just one foot." As he spoke, he lifted a massive taloned foot and with a screech of terror, Priscilla scrambled to her feet and fled into the cave behind her, having the forethought to bend her head in case she banged it on the roof. She felt like a rabbit running into its bolthole. She crouched against the rocky wall, her heart beating rapidly, praying fervently that he was too big to come into the cave after her. Priscilla had no idea that dragons were the greatest workers of magic, and without any bother, Evonny shrank in size and entered. For one second she was stupefied, not believing her eyes. She was sick. Twitching his nose repugnantly, Evonny moved right up to her and she felt his hot breath scorching her skin. She made one last effort to lash out, but a roaring in her ears made the walls seem to tilt and she was falling.

Landing on the rocky surface, Priscilla opened her eyes quickly, not trusting the dragon, and was already on the defensive because she expected him to be looming over her — but the place was dark. For the moment she stayed where she was, wondering how she could have been so deranged as to think him beautiful — she must have been mad. Having established that she was alone, Priscilla peered through the darkness, wondering how the light had vanished so swiftly. She had shut her eyes only for a moment. The blackness pressed down like an overpowering force and coldness enveloped her body. It felt like pins and needles. A continuous breeze passed over her. The stone floor felt icy and sent shivers all through her. The sharp edges of rock dug deeply into her skin. She was sure her flesh had been cut.

Where was Alfie? Why had he left her alone to face this horror? Priscilla tried to think but her mind became confused. Of course Alfie wasn't with her. Some bestial thing had carried her away. Then thoughts of the black dragon came back to hit her forcibly. Somehow she had to escape from here before it returned — but where was here? Why hadn't she taken more notice of her surroundings while she was able to do so? Now it was so dark it was hard to make out anything. Priscilla squinted, endeavouring to pierce the gloom, but this action got her nowhere.

The darkness was impenetrable and made her start to use her hands and feel around. Maybe things would be better if she stood — so struggling, she regained her feet.

The simple action was difficult. Half her body felt numb, making her movements clumsy, and her head started to spin. Priscilla fell down on the ground again with a groan of despair and tried crawling. Hard sharp rock dug into her hands and knees.

Moving this way was not satisfactory, but it was better than standing up, even though she was dragging herself along like a lame dog. Eventually, tears of frustration filled her eyes and self-pity took over. She gave up and started to cry in real earnest, wondering what on earth it was Sue saw in this world.

* * *

It was the ferocious roar which penetrated into Priscilla's muzzy mind that jerked her back to an awareness of where she was. The intrusion was something she could well do without, especially the way she was feeling. Another roar came, this time with added venom. She attempted to open her eyes, but it was too much of an effort to accomplish. Priscilla's whole body felt stiff and cold. She hoped that whichever dragon it was would go away and leave her alone.

Something unexpectedly caught hold of her middle with such a vicious grasp, it was like razor sharp knives digging into her flesh. She screamed — or thought she did, but the only sound coming from her mouth was a muffled cry. Priscilla knew she was being lifted up, but there was no way she could struggle or prevent it from happening. Daylight blinded her, or would have done so if only her eyes were open. Priscilla could see brightness through the covering of her eyelids. None too gently, whatever held her dropped her onto something soft.

"If you don't eat your food this time, I will not bring you any more." The voice that spoke was arrogant, but did not have the harshness of the black dragon. Priscilla tried to open her eyes again but the covering lids did not obey her order, neither did her mouth when she tried to speak. They felt as paralysed as the rest of her body. With a choking sob she wished she were dead.

* * *

"Do you honestly think this is going to work?" The rancour in Sapphire's voice succeeded in stoking up the fire raging within Evonny. The two dragons stood out in the hazy morning sunshine. Flying on such a sultry day was a feat requiring too much of an effort to accomplish. High up the mountainside, a frenzied weeping could be heard. Because Evonny did not understand the ways of humans, the noise irritated him and he thrashed his long tail with uncontrollable fury. Fire smote the already blackened walls of the rocky outcrop.

"Don't you understand, Sapphire? She will bring me what I most desire," he snarled, and stared at the blue dragon with eyes full of evil intent. "Deena has promised me so. We don't have to listen to that wailing up there — let's fly somewhere else. Anywhere you like. Then we can forget our prisoner."

Sapphire's tail struck him across his glistening body. "You are a fool. You have no idea of what is happening. Don't you understand that if she dies you will have lost what you're wanting?"

"Die?" Evonny thundered, drawing himself up so that he towered above his daughter. The look he gave her was malevolent. "What makes you think she is going to die?" he roared.

"She is ill." Sapphire's look was equally baleful. "I don't know what ails her — but that is why she cries."

"Then make her tell you," came the unfeeling answer. "Heat up her abode a little. Singe her hair. A little burning never hurt anyone." Evonny's bestial laughter was full of madness, but it stopped only when Sapphire snapped, "Whatever ails her has taken her speech away. She can't talk."

"I would call that a good thing," the black dragon snorted, "Her squeaky voice gets on my nerves."

"Then you are foolish. We need to know what is wrong."

Evonny was suddenly silent. Then his eyes showed cunning. He fixed Sapphire with an intimidating stare. "You are weakening, daughter," he roared, "you're wanting me to cast her away."

Sapphire declined to answer him and they both heard the mournful wailing drifting down on the wind. Nearby, the other dragons living in the small colony showed their disapproval by making a continuous droning sound to mask it. "I've had enough of this," said Evonny. "If she dies, I'll get another woman. They're easy to come by. You go up and heal her. If she doesn't live, it will be your fault." With that threatening remark, he launched himself into the air and flew off, smoke and fire trailing behind him. It was a warning for everyone to stay away from him.

Sapphire flexed her wings and wondered why she had thrown her lot in with her father and his renegade followers. For a dragon, her expression was whimsical. She couldn't help feeling it had been more fun being Silver's friend. Unfurling both her wings, she pushed off from the rock and entered a strong air spiral that lifted her up to the set of caves near the top of the mountain, known to everyone as the 'City of Wind'. The layout of the caves was open plan, although this phenomenon had been formed over countless years. A set of seven caves were joined to each other by natural archways, three of which teetered on the brink of a sheer drop. The wind whistled through from all directions, keeping them clear of debris, and they were dry and airy — but comfortable was not a word used when describing what it was like to live there. For the prisoner there was no escape.

Sapphire landed daintily on one of the ledges, the only possible place to alight with any degree of safety. The noise of her landing and an extra gust of wind failed to move the girl lying huddled on the rug that she had brought up earlier. Sapphire was in no hurry to be acknowledged. She passed the time by preening her beautiful wings, hoping the prisoner would soon become aware of her, but she got no response. Priscilla was hardly aware of anything.

At the beginning, Sapphire upheld her father's actions a hundred per cent. She had seen it as fun to taunt a human female, but with Priscilla of course, that action had fallen flat. How could you taunt someone who did not appear to be aware of you? It had started off so well. The day Evonny scooped her off from Oran's land, she had been in good voice, screaming with the fury of a

139

mountain cat — spitting and snarling with eyes full of venom. Such phrases as 'when Sue finds out it will be worse for you' were received as idle threats, and cast aside. There was no-way Priscilla could do anything — and no-way anyone could find her. This cave was Evonny's stronghold.

Now, as she basked in the sun, Sapphire allowed her thoughts to mull over the words. It was unsettling to know Sonja was known as Sue — and Sue was Silver's friend. Could there be any connection? Her thoughts were broken by whimpers coming from the inert form on the ground. After the briefest hesitation, Sapphire stepped closer and noticed with distaste, the food was still there, untouched, and despite the great height, a score or more flies were around it. Her large head snaked down towards the girl's face, which was red and puffy. Taking into account all the crying she had done, that was not unnatural, but the heat radiating from her gave all the symptoms of fever. Sapphire was nonplussed. How could the girl develop a fever in these sterile caves?

With her long snout Sapphire nudged the body until it was lying on its back. One arm was flung out to one side, while the other, twice its size, was turning black. Sapphire's eyes travelled down to her hand, which lay open, palm uppermost, and in consternation she saw a puncture mark, red and angry, standing out like a beacon, the bite of the red spider. It needed more magic than she possessed to heal it — and time was short for the victim. Sapphire had to make a decision and she hoped her father would understand.

CHAPTER 11
AFTER THE STORM

The storm receded after the last shattering roll of thunder shook the world, and glimpses of clear sky began to show through breaks in the dark bank of cloud. It seemed to be a good omen for the men who had been travelling all night. The group of soldiers making their way along a little used track looked weary and dishevelled. Their eyes were stinging for the want of sleep, and water was dripping off their clothes, yet they still urged their horses onward for whoever it was that drove them. Under furrowed brows, Amos, utterly perplexed, stared hard at Thane's back, and his eyes showed clearly that he condemned the way the soldiers were being relentlessly pushed on. This was so unlike Thane, that it was completely out of character. Never before had he taken out his anger on his men, and Amos wondered what sort of devil was making him do so now.

He looked towards Zeno and Raithe for answers since they were always communicating with him. They were guarding the rear and trying to keep awake themselves by talking in an undertone to each other. They were as tired as the men and waiting to hear just one word — halt. When Amos complained to them, looking for some sort of support, Zeno shook his head. He had no wish to get involved in any conflict with Thane — and Raithe clearly thought, and said, that what Thane was doing had nothing to do with them.

Amos saw red. "Of course it has," he snapped, glaring at the pair of them. "He's treating those men abominably. I wouldn't treat my horse the way he's treating them."

"Then how come you are keeping up?" asked Raithe slyly, and Zeno looked at him subtly through half-closed eyes, but either Amos did not hear him or he was ignoring the remark and went on to demand: "How much longer does he think the men will stand this pace? We should have camped when the storm started, to give the horses a rest. What is the purpose of all this speed?"

"I think he wants to catch up with my sister," Raithe retorted, his voice rather servile. "He's got something on his mind and I'm not about to interfere. Is there anything else you want to know?"

Only Raithe could speak to Amos in this manner and get away with it — but all Amos said was "ah", and his wispy white beard bristled, then he kicked his horse and galloped to catch up with Thane, hoping to make sense of this mad dash.

* * *

A few miles further ahead of the horsemen, the atmosphere was subdued as the occupants of the caravan came out to assess what damage the storm had done. As they sloshed around in mud and debris, their minds were not quite back with reality after Alfie's story. There was an unnatural silence surrounding them. Each and every one was thankful the storm had passed over and they were able to escape the confines of the caravan where it had been so hot and sultry. The humidity had given Sue a headache. Luckily for them the caravan had escaped the brunt of the storm — the only damage being a smashed water butt — but when Rainee noticed her horse had gone, it seemed like the end of the world. The horse was her life. Somehow he had broken free of the restraints holding him, and fled. For once in her life, Rainee had nothing to say and she stared around in a bemused fashion. After what she had heard disclosed in the caravan, she wondered where events were going to lead her.

Unexpectedly, Alfie took over. It was obvious he was a man used to the outdoor life and very much aware of what disasters can befall one out of the blue. Through narrowed eyes he weighed up the situation. By the way they were all acting, nothing would be improved by nightfall, so he took charge. Alfie felt wary about giving orders — he didn't want to tread on anyone's toes, especially Sue's since he had learnt of her background. He wondered if it were permissible to give a princess a rather mucky job to do. He looked at the chaos around them and stiffened his shoulders determinedly. He knew what had to be done if they were going to get back onto an even keel. He approached Sue and Barry with tongue in cheek and asked them to see about finding kindling to light another fire while he helped Rainee to track down her runaway horse.

"It shouldn't take us all that long. He's left hoof prints in the mud that a blind man could follow. If you two could get this place shipshape, things will look a lot better."

I knew that job would fall to me, Barry thought sourly, but he refrained from saying it out loud. He admired Alfie for taking the initiative. He and Sue nodded although they were both feeling lethargic. It needed someone like Alfie to get them going. They watched while Alfie squelched away towards the Bluff with Rainee trailing behind him dragging a rope for the luckless horse. Scrap barked furiously from the caravan steps, demanding attention, but he wouldn't put a foot on the ground because he didn't want to get his paws wet.

"I can see a likeness to Priscilla in that dog," Barry muttered unkindly, then shrugging his shoulders, he turned his mind to the job in hand and walked in the opposite direction. Sue could have gone anywhere, but she had decided to follow Barry, which she did in a lackadaisical fashion, kicking about more rubbish than she was picking up. For most of the time her eyes were searching the sky, anxiously looking for signs of Silver who had not returned since leaving her the previous evening. It was so unlike the dragon to stay away after promising to come back to her — and Sue had so much to inform her of. Being a dragon, as soon as Silver was aware of the identity of the hostage, she would know exactly what to do, but Sue could not shake off this feeling of dread. Something was wrong, or going to be wrong. She and Barry hardly spoke. He was as morose as she, and kept scanning the far horizon for the signs of the soldiers. Unlike Sue, he needed Thane's help in getting Priscilla back. In his eyes, Thane was like a big brother who could not do anything wrong and made him feel important. Although the two of them kept together, neither spoke of what Alfie had disclosed during the storm, yet their minds were consumed with the subject. They had never been so restrained with each other before and Sue thought it must be something in the atmosphere that was affecting them. She did manage to say quite casually, "I think Alfie is cut up about the way Priscilla was taken. I get the impression he rather likes her," and for once in his life, Barry did not have any acrimonious remark to make about his sister, although the opening was there.

This was going to be a long morning. Sue bent down and picked up a couple of curved staves, which Barry promptly relieved her of and said with an air of superiority, "that's part of a water-butt," and looked at her rather patronisingly, adding, "we can't burn that. It needs saving for reconstructing." Sue could not resist adding, "Alfie knew what he was doing, putting you in charge."

She splashed through a deep puddle thinking what an impossible task Alfie had asked them to do, as whatever wood they gathered would be too wet for burning. She would much rather have gone after the horse and seen some action. She paused, gazing into the empty sky again, then observing that Barry watching her she gave herself a shake and turned her attention to the job in hand. It was as her eyes were levelling back to the ground that she saw a moving smudge on the horizon.

"Horsemen," she exclaimed suddenly, and her heart started beating unnaturally fast. Why did she think their coming meant impending doom? She wiped a wet hand across her face, leaving behind a muddy streak. She never mentioned to Barry that it could be Thane. His name stuck in her throat. Ever since her conversation with Silver she was rather uneasy about meeting him. Unconsciously she braced herself for his imminent arrival, but at her word horsemen, Barry was jubilant. "Great," he whooped, and raced off in their direction, sending sprays of water into the air. Wood collecting was forgotten.

Sue remained rooted to the spot in the centre of the puddle, not realising how vulnerable she looked. Then she took the full onslaught of White Hawk as he streaked across the waterlogged land and jumped up at her to lavish wet kisses of welcome on her face. Behind him, charging along at a furious speed, was Thane. He slithered to a stop and his horse's hooves threw up a fountain of dirty water that spread out and tiny droplets hit her in the face. Sue flinched, but did not step back. Thane was well ahead of his soldiers, but Amos and Raithe had kept pace with him and were only a short space behind, so were well within hearing distance. Thane quickly controlled his laboured breathing. He wanted to berate Sue for putting herself in danger, but unfortunately, these feelings were masked and he showed her only detached indifference and steeled himself against her.

Sliding off Saturn, Thane stood staring through inscrutable eyes, the eyes of a stranger, and did not speak. There was no trace of a smile on his face or a ready greeting on his lips. He asked no courtesy questions or made any attempt to touch Sue, although all he had to do was put out a hand. A hard lump rose up in her throat, which she could not swallow, and misery assailed her. This was worse than she ever expected. Facing her was a Thane she did not know and she felt deprived of a special friend. She pushed the wolf gently away as he spoke, and the chill in his tone made her shiver.

"I'm really pleased to see you had the sense to stop at a reasonable place," he said but the voice which fell on her ears was impersonal. He could have been speaking to another soldier and his icy glance swept over her making her feel about two inches high. His eyes rested momentarily on Barry, but did not linger there — they returned to Sue. "Before you do anything else stupid," his clipped voice continued, "you might like to know — although I doubt it — that by absconding from the palace without a word, you have upset your mother and father and all your friends. It is considered in this land common decency to say where you are going."

Barry's jaw fell open in surprise that Thane could chastise his sister as though she were a schoolgirl, and before Sue could compose herself, Thane went on with an edge to his voice, "we've brought along a couple of spare horses with us to take you back home."

Sue smarted. Bright colour stained her cheeks, igniting the temper that stirred deeply within her. Before this onslaught, her first impulse had been to throw herself in his arms, as White Hawk had done to her — but that feeling quickly evaporated and she no longer wanted to hug him or ask what was wrong. He had successfully erected a barrier between them with his unfair censure, so instead, since his attitude stung her so much, she replied, "Thank you for your concern, I hope it hasn't put you out, but it was totally misplaced. I am not in need of any horse. You could have saved yourself a lot of time and bother. I have other travel arrangements. I've got Silver..."

"You've got nothing." Thane's cold voice cut her off immediately. "Silver will not be coming back for you."

With an effort Sue forced herself to remain calm, but his words made her clench her fists. Changing emotions coursed through her as she stared into the face of someone she did not know anymore. Anger came to her aid because it was the one emotion controlling her now, and hurtful words were so much easier to say. "You've got no right stopping Silver from coming to me just because you're jealous of her." She didn't see the flare of anger light up his eyes but continued, "I don't know how you managed it. I'm surprised she listened to you after what the pair of us discussed yesterday. We have got things to do — important things."

Thane's whole body stiffened. He grew more infuriated with every word she said, but he held himself under control. "Such as?" he asked with a deadly calm which should have been a warning to her. His face could have been carved from granite. Behind him, Amos winced but did not dare to interfere. These two were going to end in stalemate. Sue set her mouth stubbornly and looked more mutinous than Barry had ever seen her before. "You wouldn't understand," she snapped. "Dragons have more sensitivity than you'll ever know. We've discussed our... "

"You've discussed your plans with a dragon!" Thane's voice was now rough with anger, He could barely suppress it. Eyes like glaciers swept over her. "You find talking to her better than a friend — better than someone who is flesh and blood!"

Sue ignored the warning again. "She is a friend," she shouted back indignantly, "but it's not that...." Her voice floundered; wondering why things were getting out of hand. It was Thane's fault for being so dictatorial. She glared at him. "She understands my position," she flared.

"And of course, I don't," Thane's voice snapped back, laced with a fury he did not attempt to hide.

Although the soldiers stood at a respectful distance, they were near enough to hear everything that was said. Barry was completely overwhelmed and upset that the two people he loved most were fighting. Raithe moved from behind to stand by his sister's side, ready to give her aid — but she didn't see him, and Thane was still speaking.

"It's gratifying to know where I stand with you after all this time," he continued ruthlessly, "but I can promise you I will not bother you anymore. Consider our friendship — or what I thought was friendship — is now at an end." Thane swung towards Raithe and said stiffly, "can you get your sister mounted and escort her back to your father, I've got to think about the Bluff. Barry!" He swiftly rounded on the bewildered boy. "Whose caravan is this?"

The question was asked curtly, so unlike Thane that Barry jumped, completely out of his depth at what was transpiring before him. Sue felt bereft as Thane ignored her and turned to Barry. Barry glanced at her unhappily, and Raithe, really annoyed, caught hold of Thane's arm and said coldly, "You're being a little high-handed. How about allowing Sue to explain her position?"

"She wouldn't want to. I didn't hatch out of an egg," Thane answered sarcastically, and through clenched teeth, added, "maybe she will tell you if you turn into a dragon. I couldn't care less what she does. Come with me, Barry," he commanded.

Choking back a sob, Sue watched everyone move away, and it was only because her brother put an arm around her and White Hawk nuzzled her hand, that she felt maybe things were not quite so bad. The anti-climax came when Thane turned his head and gave the wolf a curt order, which made him leave her. As he obediently padded after his master, Sue watched in distress and bit her lip to stop it trembling. Barry had no choice. He had to go along because Thane held his arm in a firm grip, nearly dragging him — yet Barry's reluctance was obvious and Thane must have been aware of it. White Hawk also kept turning his shaggy head to see what Sue was doing, and she was sure that, with encouragement on her part, he would have defied Thane. No matter how sad she was feeling, Sue was not about to drag the wolf into their squabble. Raithe gave her a brotherly squeeze and couldn't help thinking what a fool Thane was as he glimpsed her vulnerable face.

He had handled everything the wrong way. Raithe could have told him that this direct method of his would only succeed in putting Sue's back up — yet being someone sharing Thane's confidence, he understood the reason why he was so bitter. Being fair, Raithe also attributed half the blame to Sue. Giving her space to calm down, he gently guided her away from the puddle in which she had been standing and led her onto firmer ground. Only when he felt she was sufficiently composed, did he say tentatively, "no matter what it is you're thinking, Sue, Thane doesn't hate you."

That was entirely the wrong thing to say because she didn't believe him and her expression almost accused him of taking sides. "Who are you trying to kid?" She rubbed her eyes roughly with the back of her hand, but this had no lasting effect because she continued to look at him through a blur of tears. "The way he spoke to me in front of all his men tells you exactly what he thinks of me. What I don't understand, and never will, is, is this all because of Silver? What has Silver ever done to him?"

"Nothing, Sue," Raithe answered patiently, "it's what you have done to him."

"Me!" Utter surprise snapped her out of the doldrums. "All I've tried to do is save his life."

Raithe shook his head at her. "That's not much use if he doesn't know. Your biggest mistake is not involving your friends in your activities. Why do you disregard them all? You can't keep doing things on your own. You need support. Tansy and Annalee have been itching to be taken into your confidence."

"I've got Silver to help me," Sue answered immediately.

"And that's the cause of all this trouble," Raithe retorted. "No! Please don't say another word. Let me do the talking for a change. Thane has always been your friend — right from the moment you first came to this land. He has bent over backwards to look after you and fight your cause. Does that sound like someone who hates you?" Sue opened her mouth to speak but Raithe did not give her the opportunity and pressed on relentlessly. "When I tried to harm you at the very beginning, he tore strips off me. He's been your champion through thick and thin. Right now — you can take my word for it —

151

beneath that hard exterior he is showing to the world, he is hurting like mad — gutted that you chose a dragon to unburden yourself to, and not him, the friend who has always been there for you. Have you any idea what it is like to be disregarded?"

Sue shook her head. The anger consuming her dissipated, leaving her stricken with remorse. For the first time she realised how her actions must appear to Thane. Her voice was barely audible, but Raithe heard her say, "there were reasons I could not tell him what I was doing."

They had been walking back to the caravan where a barking dog waited to greet them, but Raithe paused and looked into her eyes, searchingly. "Your biggest mistake was not taking Thane into your confidence. I can understand your keeping things from our parents — but Thane could have saved you a lot of misery if only you had brought up the subject of Deena with him."

"But what's Deena got to do with it?" Sue stopped in her tracks, looking bemused. "What does he know of Deena?"

Raithe almost smiled at her naivety, but knew better than to let her see it. Instead he said humourlessly, "Well, he rescued you from her stronghold before she initiated you, and he heard you speaking to her the other night when she was blatantly blackmailing you to do her bidding. You were so upset at the time, he comforted you and decided to bring the matter up later, but, it seems our mother would not let him in the palace, and you, Sue, did not give him the chance. When Thane came to see you early in the morning you had gone, leaving no word. You had forgotten all about him and sneaked off to meet

Silver. He tried to stop you, but you know that of course. You saw us both. Since then, Thane has been having nightmares, thinking you were going to the Enchanted Land and getting yourself killed. I'm afraid Silver told him where you were — and seeing you safe and sound lit a fuse within him. Later, he is going to regret the harsh words that passed between you."

Sue looked to the far distance where Thane and the soldiers had caught up with Rainee and Alfie. Squinting through her eyes, she saw him and Amos approach them. Sue had a mad impulse to run in that direction and say she was sorry. Why hadn't she realised her conversation with Deena could be heard? Why had she let the illusion of the ring blind her to what was the truth? To say it was because she was worried over Barry was pathetic. Silver had known, and given her fair warning, but it was now too late to make any difference. She turned to her brother, grateful for his enlightenment on the subject, and her intentions of running after Thane showed clearly on her face. He said quickly, "Don't bother, Sue. He will be back to you soon."

"How can you be so sure?"

"They've taken all the horses. How can I take you home?"

"I could call Silver..."

"Stop it." Raithe rounded on her violently. "Haven't you listened to what I've been telling you? She wouldn't come anyway. Thane got her recalled by Sheeka."

"Thane got..." Sue clamped her mouth shut and said no more, but she looked as though she wanted to say volumes.

They had reached the caravan and sat down on the steps. Scrap was ecstatic to have company at last and was all over them. His tongue worked overtime, licking any uncovered flesh he could see until Raithe pushed him away disgustedly, wiping his face on his sleeve. "What sort of dog is that," he exploded, eyeing the furry bundle with distaste, and as Scrap's onslaught turned to Sue, he pulled her to her feet causing the dog to summersault backwards with an indignant yelp, and exclaimed, "Come on, Sue — let's continue the job you were doing before we interrupted you. You can tell me who lives in this caravan and owns that four-legged pest."

An hour later, Raithe knew as much about things as Sue did, and to her delight, he filled her in on Rainee. "She was the midwife at our birth. Your grandmother hated her, so I'm told, because she was strange, but Rainee saved me from being given away to farmers. She returned to Therossa with our parents and Amos. She kept the secret of your existence for years. It was at the time when there was trouble with Oran, about succession to the throne. Rainee fell in love with a waster. She didn't know he was a friend of Oran. No one knows what really happened after that. She was taken to the Drazuzi caves to meet Oran — and after he had got all the information from her that he needed, renegade soldiers were sent to your homeland to seize you. She was accused of betraying the king's trust, and for this she was exiled. There — now you have it."

Sue pursed her lips. "Except that we don't know what happened to her in the Drazuzi caves."

"Leave it," Raithe exploded. "It's all in the past and she won't thank you for digging it up. Come on now.

154

We've got to make a fire before Alfie and the villainous Rainee return." His infectious laugh brought the first smile he had seen on his sister's face for a long time.

CHAPTER 12
THANE'S DILEMMA

Without a backward glance at Sue, Thane closed his ears to Barry's protests, and headed towards the Bluff, knowing his soldiers would follow him no matter what their private thoughts of the situation were. He was furious at that moment; he didn't care. White Hawk followed through sheer obedience, but it was obvious from his backward glances that he wanted to stay with Sue. Thane was irked to notice this, but at the same time pleased the wolf had protective instincts towards her. He knew Raithe would protect his sister through thick and thin, while he and Amos went towards the Bluff.

In a way, he was pleased the Prince was there to keep an eye on her. She would have been a distraction coming along with him; things were liable to be dangerous. Professor Harding, his old adversary, had to be scoured from the caves.

"I reckon that's our quarry up ahead," growled Amos, looking at the two people following tracks of some sort in the chaos of debris left by the storm. Already he had recognised Rainee. He had no love for her. The idea of having to confront her again brought bile to his mouth.

Thane halted the soldiers, dismounted, and with Amos beside him, approached the two people ahead. They seemed to be completely unaware of their presence.

Thane issued a sharp command for them to stop. Alfie heard the voice and was surprised at the hostility it contained. He took his time, stretching to his full height before turning, and immediately noticed the tense expression on Rainee's face. From out of the side of his mouth he asked, "Are they friends?" to which she replied dryly, "not of mine."

Alfie eyed them through narrowed eyes and saw the waiting soldiers behind them. They looked tired, their clothing dishevelled and their faces expressionless. Then he saw Barry, standing apart with misery written all over his features. Beside him stood the biggest wolf Alfie had ever seen. He remembered his uncle had spoken about such wolves. They were vicious — one had bitten him. Right now he concentrated on the two people in front of him. He thought the older man looked surly and arrogant while the younger one was brusque; Alfie had his own way of dealing with them.

"This looks like an inquisition." He kept his voice deceptively light-hearted. "Or am I trespassing? Do you want proof of who I am, because if so I'm going to disappointed you all. I didn't bring any identification with me. Didn't realise you needed it for poking around in the bushes."

"No one is accusing you of anything, lad," Amos retorted. This was all he needed, another person with Barry's idea of wit. "We just want to ask you some questions."

"Why? Are you lost?" Alfie looked surprised. "I hope not, because I'm the last person to give you directions. Tell you what though," and not waiting for them to answer, he added, "ask her down there by that caravan. She comes from around here." With that, he turned his back on them, and grabbing hold of Rainee's arm, continued to study the ground. Only Rainee saw the mischievous twitch to his lips. His casual reference to Sue had made Thane see red and there was a slight stir in the ranks. He made Alfie jump by walking up to him.

"I take it you're a stranger in these parts." Amos joined in by adding, "in which case I would advise you to show a little civility. We are looking for two people trapped up on the Bluff."

"The Bluff, is that thing behind me called the Bluff?" asked Alfie.

"Yes."

"Then go no further, gentlemen — I am here. How can I help you?" Alfie's smile seemed genuine, but Amos knew he was laughing at them. He scrutinized the confident well-built youth and said grimly, "This is not funny, boy!" He hoped the reference to 'boy' would demoralise him, but Alfie seemed as bumptious as ever. "We are trying to help you and I suggest you listen. It has come to our understanding that you were not alone and some of your party is missing — captured by the Drazuzi people."

"That's right — you're spot on. Isn't communication good in these parts?" Alfie tried to look as though he was impressed. "I did not share my uncle's fate — or his friends' either. They went out in the night and never returned. Priscilla was my companion and we were trapped by mist. It followed us everywhere. She unfortunately fell foul of a dragon that came down from the skies and carried her away. I was rescued by Rainee. This is she." He indicated the silent woman by his side

158

and could not help noticing the subtle change in the old man's demeanour. To him, the name Rainee was like a red flag to a bull.

All eyes were immediately focused in Rainee's direction, but it was Amos who quivered with indignation. She braced herself for a disparaging onslaught of abuse, and the old man's eyes pierced right through her. "What did you do?" he asked sourly, "drag him through the caves? You certainly didn't climb up there." His narrowed eyes jerked towards the Bluff and Alfie's banter left him in a flash when he heard Rainee's quick intake of breath. "There is no call for you to deride Rainee," he said coldly, "she has healed me, for which I will always be grateful. Of course she never climbed up that cliff — that would be beyond even your ability, Granddad." He glared at Amos. "If you really want an accurate account of how I was transported from up there to down here — Sue," he jerked his head towards the caravan where he had left her, "Sue and Barry flew up on a dragon, and in spite of the mist, carried me down here with them. A very different dragon carried off Priscilla, so if you're searching for anyone, search for her. Stop asking me foolish questions so that I can go on tracking our horse."

"This Priscilla you keep mentioning," Thane demanded crisply, "did she come from your world? I seem to know the name."

It was too much for Barry to stay silent any longer. Before Alfie could answer, he extricated himself from White Hawk and flung himself forward, shouting, "she's my sister," at the same time, tugging at Thane's arm. "I want you to find her. Evonny has taken her as a hostage. I — I — I saw it all happen and I — I heard her scream."

Thane looked down on the young face staring up at him, twisted in anguish, and saw the tears gathering unashamedly in his eyes. Thane was frozen with shock at the sudden revelation, and a vision of the petulant girl he met ages ago in Tamsworth Forest built up in his mind. Thane couldn't get his mind round the fact that she was now in Therossa. Was this the cause of Sue's divided loyalties? "Sue is aware of all this?" he asked harshly, because he had to know, and heard Barry's emphatic, "Yes."

Silence fell amongst everyone during which a bemused Thane and Amos exchanged worried looks. Danger was more widespread than they had anticipated. It was coming from two directions. The Drazuzi, they knew, but the renegade dragon population was a shock. Already Thane was regretting his earlier row with Sue and his first impulse was to go back to her, but the situation here had turned serious and he had to see it through. Why hadn't he given her a chance to defend her actions? It was Alfie who brought the situation to a climax, by saying to Barry:

"I thought you were supposed to be collecting wood. Have you left it all for the Princess to do when you knew she's feeling low?"

Thane nearly threw himself on Alfie to throttle him. His expression was thunderous and the men murmured angrily behind him, but Amos held him back. There was surprising strength in the wily old man. "Leave it, Thane. He is deliberately goading you." His scornful look turned to Rainee. "I would have thought you would have rescued his uncle by now. Have you forgotten the way into the Drazuzi caves, woman?"

Rainee opened her mouth to speak but Alfie pushed her back and stood in front of her proud figure like a knight in shining armour. Indignation suffused his face and for one brief second Thane saw the likeness to Professor Harding. "I have always been brought up to show a certain amount of respect for the older ladies," said Alfie, "it's a pity you haven't learnt that courtesy. Her name is Rainee — not woman, in case you've forgotten, and if you don't mind, we've got to be on our way. We're looking for a horse. If these Drazuzi caves are where my uncle is, then I hope he's happy. I'm not looking for him — I've got more important things to see to with a runaway horse. Now, do I need your permission to leave?"

Alfie's sarcastic voice was belligerent and Thane drew himself up, but beyond the tightening of his mouth, showed no other reaction. "We seem to have got off on the wrong foot," he said stiffly, but his words were clipped, "please go on your way. We shall see you later. If you haven't got a horse, you're not going anywhere."

"May I go with them?" asked Barry anxiously, "Sue…"

"Sue's not in any danger," Thane cut him short. "She's got Raithe with her, and these two," He gave Alfie and Rainee a curt nod and sprang up on Saturn's back. "Come on, Barry — you're with me."

At a sharp word of command, all the men moved forward. Barry cast one last longing glance at Alfie and that lad felt compelled to shout out, "I'll look after Sue for you."

* * *

It was not until the group of horsemen disappeared round a bend in the Bluff, that Rainee regained her composure. She'd got exactly what she expected from the king's advisor. In this country people had long memories, and Amos had been at the centre of the row. She could not suppress the sigh of relief that escaped her lips. With Alfie as her unexpected champion she had got through it fairly well. The sigh forced Alfie to ask, "Why do you let them treat you like that, Rainee? You strike me as being a woman with plenty of fight in you. What's the story behind it all? Is it there some dark secret you're keeping to yourself?" It was said flippantly, but he suddenly thought of his uncle. He had plenty of secrets hidden away and no one living could prise them out into the open.

Rainee shrugged her shoulders, thinking how dramatically her solitary life had altered since Barry arrived on the scene. Things were changing rapidly. She turned to look into his inquisitive eyes and answered nonchalantly, "I should have liked to have kept it to myself of course — but that seems rather pointless now. The past is catching up with me. If Raithe is back at the caravan with Sue, he will have told her all about me by now, so I might just as well tell you. It won't make any difference, but at least you will be in the picture."

The story was sketchily outlined, but Alfie picked up the gist of it and whistled in amazement. He wouldn't mind betting now that he knew more than his uncle did. Everything his uncle had ever said was guesswork. He never had anything concrete to go on. There was a lot of intrigue in this land. He hated to think what kind of a hornets' nest his uncle would stir up before they threw him out.

Alfie put it all out of his mind while they continued to search for the missing horse. It was proving to be more difficult than they expected. The caravan had long since vanished from sight, and where they stood, they were completely alone. The humidity had gone but the heat was just as intense and swarms of flies hovered over what few puddles were still around. Before long they lost the tracks they had been following. The ground became very unforgiving, turning rocky near the Bluff. The pair of them searched diligently until their backs ached and the flies became a nuisance round their heads. Rainee's eyes stung from too much staring and there was no sign of her horse. She wondered if Alfie was aware that as a tracker she was no good. Without Alfie around the horse would have been lost anyway. Rainee was on the verge of throwing in the towel, but Alfie would not give up.

Rainee stopped and rubbed her back. She almost stamped her feet in frustration. She had got to find him. He couldn't disappear like this. There was absolutely nowhere to hide. She had had him for years and understood all his behaviour problems. Her whole life depended on having him to move her caravan.

Alfie swatted the fly on his neck and glanced at Rainee. Perspiration ran down his face, and he looked hot and flustered. "This is not getting us anywhere, so let's shout," he suggested. "If he hears your voice it might bring him in this direction. What's his name?"

Rainee stared at him blankly. "Name?" she repeated. "I don't know. He hasn't got one."

"He must have one," Alfie exploded. "Every horse has a name. How many years have you had him? What do you call him when you want him?"

"Just Horse," she said, "he's never run off before, so what does he want a name for?"

Alfie scratched his head. "Well, it's friendly for a start and it makes one feel wanted," he retorted incredulously. "I'm not going to stand here shouting out 'horse, horse, where are you?' People will think I'm mad."

"Then it's just as well no one else is around to hear you being ridiculous," Rainee snapped, thinking he was making a mountain out of a molehill. She wiped her brow with the back of her hand, enabling a strand of hair to escape from its tight confinement and make her look hot and dishevelled. In her eyes lurked a touch of fear that her horse might be lost forever. "I can't lose him, Alfie, I don't know what I'll do if I can't find him," she exclaimed.

Alfie took a deep breath. "Well we've got one more avenue to try. It's never let me down before." He put two fingers in his mouth and whistled. The sharp sound echoed off the Bluff and flushed out a few birds which agitatedly circled around. From not too far away they heard a muffled neigh.

"That's settled that." Alfie was jubilant. "He's answered my call. So from now on his name is 'Whistle'."

Rainee glowered at him. "That's stupid."

"So is calling him 'horse'," Alfie answered blandly, "but don't let's argue — we've got to find out where that neigh came from, since it seems to be beyond your horse to come out from wherever he's hiding."

They both stared around their inhospitable surroundings. The place was deserted except for them. Nothing stirred, as the birds returned to their nests. Having the idea there might be caves in the Bluff, Alfie asked Rainee if she was aware of any but she shook her head. It was going to be a long slog to find a horse that didn't want to show itself. They moved in the direction of the rocky wall at the base of the towering cliffs, and following it soon discovered that heat was trapped in this vicinity. They sweated profusely, attracting more of the biting insects. It was impossible to follow tracks now on solid ground. There was plenty of foliage and trees, but none of it thick enough to hide a horse. They walked for a while, poking into impossible places, but found nothing that could be called a cave. The search was becoming pointless.

Alfie stopped, trying to mask his frustration. "We'll have to turn round and go back. I'm sure that neigh didn't come from as far away as this. We must have missed something. I bet that horse of yours is watching us and laughing. I can feel it in my bones."

Retracing their steps was a lot more tedious. Rainee longed for a breeze to cool herself. Nothing moved in the air, but higher up she could see the leaves of trees moving from where they stood. As it was, the heat shimmered off the rocks, and it felt like a furnace. Inadvertently she kicked a stone and groaned, hopping on one leg. "Whistle again, Alfie," she muttered, "I've nearly had enough."

Alfie grimaced. "I hope you realise we could be drawing the soldiers' attention towards us."

"I don't care," Rainee snapped, "just do it."

Alfie whistled again and to their surprise the whinny they heard seemed to come from out of the rock. They stared at the rough granite in bewilderment, wondering if they were hallucinating. Alfie walked towards its base, feeling like an ant as the cliff towered above him. With the palm of his hand he pressed hard on the rocky surface, wondering if there could be a secret door. He wouldn't discount finding anything in this land. The weathered grey stone remained immovable. In places it fell back making little indentations, but continued onwards in the direction in which they were walking. By now Rainee was sure her horse had met with an accident. Alfie was not a person to be beaten. He went towards what looked like an indentation and saw that it cunningly concealed a breach in the rock face. Without pausing, he pushed straight in without any thought of danger and a startled hiss came from between his tightly clamped teeth. He was certainly not expecting the sight that met his eyes. No way could this be referred to as a cave since it was open to the sky but within a small cramped hollow were two horses and the one furthermost away from him, wedged tightly against the rock face, was the missing stallion. The other horse beside him was a piebald mare. The pair of them looked distraught and his unexpected approach did not help. With ears lying flatly against their heads, and eyes rolling wildly with fear, they stared at him. Alfie's first concern was that they might be lame, but when he reached over and touched Rainee's horse, it tried to shy away and the mare eyed him askance. For the first time he wondered where the mare came from. Had the storm driven them both here for shelter?

Rainee came close enough to peer over his shoulder and her cry of delight at seeing her own horse made Alfie feel good. The stallion turned his head and realising she was standing there gave a small wicker. She tried to coax him out with gentle words but the mare would not budge an inch and kept him blocked in. Taking a risk, Alfie pushed at the mare's rear so that she moved very slightly and allowed the restriction to be removed. The stallion trotted out and Rainee flung her arms round his neck, giving him a hug. The piebald mare's lip curled and she bared her teeth. She did not move and would not be coaxed out. Alfie was concerned. He stepped closer to her and paused when her nostrils flared and she snapped at him. Rainee said from where she was watching: "Come on, Alfie. Leave it there. We've got to get moving. The sun is on its way down and we've come a long way from the caravan. Sue will wonder where we are."

Alfie glared at her, not moving. "Are you mad? We can't leave this other horse behind in the condition it's in. It needs our help."

"It certainly needs someone's help, but not ours." Her voice was curt. "Someone will come along and find it."

Her disinterest in the mare surprised Alfie. It seemed that now she had found her own horse she had no sympathy for the welfare of the stray. They had not seen a soul all day — certainly no one else searching, only the soldiers who had long since gone. Alfie made a great pretence of looking in all directions, then let her see he was outraged. "I can't spot anyone looking for her and we've been around all day. Rainee, think what a second horse could do for you. Take her home with us and then

167

you would always have a reserve. Come on, show a little kindness and let me have a few oats out of your pocket to give to her."

"Certainly not," Rainee answered stubbornly, "that is not my mare. It's a gypsy horse and they're more trouble than they're worth. I don't want a pack of ruffians chasing me all over the land because I've helped myself to their property. Come on, Alfie, leave it there. It's getting late."

"You must be joking." Alfie was now shocked at the callous streak in her and there was disgust in his voice when he said, "This poor horse is in distress." He looked towards the mare whose sides were heaving, and foam flecked her neck. "I'm sorry, but I can't leave her like this." His tone was now adamant. "If no one collects her she will be food for predators."

"You're a fool, Alfie," Rainee snapped. "For the last time, that mare is not coming with us. I'm going back to the caravan. You stay here if that's what you want." She turned her back on him angrily and patted her stallion as she tied the rope round his neck, but when she pulled to make him follow her, he unexpectedly reared on his hind legs, shrieking out in fury. Her docile horse was suddenly a stranger. She jumped away in alarm waiting for him to calm down, and when he did he looked at her defiantly, then turned his head towards the mare and whinnied. The mare answered with a small neigh. Alfie laughed outright at Rainee's outraged expression.

"You can't beat that," he laughed, eyes creasing with merriment, "you haven't got a say in the matter, Rainee. The horses have made their own decision. That mare is coming back with us whether you like it or not. Let me have some of your oats now."

Reluctantly Rainee passed over a handful to him and watched while he went back to the mare. She tried to shy away but the rocky wall prevented that. Alfie spoke to her softly and daringly put out a hand to pat her nose. The mare's dark eyes probed him and a peculiar sensation went through him — then she accepted what she saw and blew softly on his face. He held out the oats in his hand and she took them. "I don't think we shall need the rope," he called out to Rainee, "these two will follow us all the way home."

CHAPTER 13
THE PIEBALD MARE

They had no problem with the two horses. Unfettered, they followed them all the way back to the caravan. It irked Rainee the way they nuzzled each other. One would have thought they had spent all their lives together. Rainee remained aloof and unhappy with the mare around. She could not give Alfie any reason for this except that it was a gypsy horse, so he gave up trying to convince her of its assets. When the caravan's familiar outline came into view, the sun was beginning to sink below the trees, throwing out a mauve haze across the sky, and a welcome coolness touched the night air. Ahead was a cheerful fire and two figures stood up, but a very much smaller one detached itself from them and came bounding in their direction with joyful barks.

Rainee scooped him up and cuddled his warm body against her chest, happy to be with her pet after such an arduous day. Her stallion only gave Scrap only a casual glance, but the mare came close enough to breathe softly over his furry head, causing Rainee to stiffen in alarm. Scrap had no such compunction himself. He gave the mare a few licks and struggled to free himself. Almost in a daze, Rainee let him go and watched her dog dance under the mare's legs, while the mare bent her head and nuzzled him. Rainee refused to meet Alfie's cynical gaze or to listen to his ironic voice saying, "I thought you said gypsy horses were more trouble than they're worth. Scrap seems to have taken a real shine to her. Maybe you should do the same."

Rainee sniffed at his taunt and not having any appropriate answer ready, marched away with purposeful steps towards where the aroma of cooking filled the air. Alfie decided to change his tactics. Licking his lips in anticipation he said, "It really smells wonderful whatever they're cooking. I'm glad Sue is domesticated. I wonder if she has forgiven you for blabbing about her royal connections. Why did you do it, Rainee? I would never have classed you as spiteful."

The older woman paused, her dark eyes veiled, and looking at him expressionlessly, she said: "I've really no idea — but what is done, is done, and you're not living under any misapprehension."

"Humph," Alfie snorted, "well before we get too near — who is this Raithe fellow who's with her now?"

"Her twin brother," Rainee retorted, moving on, "and he's a lot more royal in his actions than she is. He will probably have you clapped in irons if you put a foot wrong."

They were level with the caravan and within the circle of light thrown by the fire. The unexpected sight of twins with identical features made Alfie catch his breath. Raithe appeared far more elegantly dressed than his sister, even though at the moment his clothes were crumpled and smeared with mud. But he looked a very approachable person. Alfie saw nothing in him that resembled the person Rainee depicted — and again, he wondered why she did it. With Raithe standing by Sue's side, Alfie stared from one face to the other, then he

171

shook his head as though to clear it. "Am I seeing things?"

Sue's smile was mischievous. "Well, we are twins," she said, stating the obvious, "but we're not really alike." "She's the bossy one," Raithe put in quickly with a grin, and he held out his hand. "I've heard all about you, Alfie. I'm Raithe."

His grip was firm and Alfie felt he could make a friend of him, but being what he was, Alfie had to test the water first. He quirked an eyebrow and asked with a wicked glint in his eyes, "You mean Prince Raithe?"

From behind him Rainee stiffened, looking scandalised, and she compressed her lips, but Raithe put a finger to his mouth and said: "Shush. We're incognito today."

The answer was so typical of his own humour that Alfie laughed spontaneously, eyes crinkling up at the corners. Raithe joined in and slapped him on his back. Sue sighed with relief that the two of them were going to get on. It had been a hard day for her, trying to come to terms with Thane's indifference, in spite of her brother's encouragement. Raithe had been a pillar of strength, making her work so hard she had no time to brood. He amazed her when he went hunting, brought down two plump birds and snared a rabbit, then built up an extra large fire with wet wood so that she could cook them. The hours of the day sped by almost unnoticed and neither of them missed the other two or wondered if they had met any trouble — considering the time they had been away. Sue had been very happy in her brother's company.

She turned away from the overpowering heat radiating from the fire and saw the older woman slumped against the caravan wheel looking as though she no longer cared what happened to her. The day had been tiring for her, not being as young as she used to be. It had been an effort keeping her condition unnoticed by Alfie's sharp eyes. Her resilience was low and fatigue showed on her face — also fear. It lurked behind her eyes — but what had she to fear? Sue knelt beside her, gently touching her arm to make her aware of her presence. "You look tired, Rainee. Can I do anything for you?" she enquired.

Rainee raised her head, surprised at being spoken to. Her dark eyes looked suspiciously as though they were watering and she almost growled, "thank you, Sue. Would you tether my horse so that he doesn't wander off again? I must sit down and rest for a while."

"Consider it done," Sue said as she regained her feet. She stared through the half-light to where two horses were cropping together. "Where did the mare come from?" she asked curiously, omitting to add for fear of offending Rainee, "It looks like a gypsy horse."

"Alfie insisted we bring it back," Rainee muttered, looking in the direction of the horses with disapproval written all over her face. "No one else seems to want her except my foolish stallion. I hope it doesn't lead to any consultations with its owner."

"There are no gypsies hereabout," Raithe put in tactlessly on hearing her concern, "so I shouldn't worry. I must say though, that I find it very mysterious that you were able to find a stray so near the Bluff — and astonishing that it survived the elements on its own."

"I'll tie the horses up," said Sue and made to move away but Rainee's voice halted her. "Only tether my horse," she said gruffly.

"But I must tie up the mare —" Sue began...

"I said leave her," Rainee's voice was sharp, "if she goes — she goes. I can't worry about her."

Sue stared at her in disbelief. The callousness of the order caused anger to rise within her. About to protest, she caught Raithe's eye. He nodded towards the mare and muttered out of Rainee's hearing: "Just tether her and say nothing." Sue moved away.

Darkness fell immediately the sun disappeared, bringing with it a myriad of gossamer flies that were attracted by the light of the fire. Many came too close to the flames and shrivelled up, but hundreds more took their place in the suicide run. The humidity after the storm had given them perfect breeding conditions. In the darkness surrounding the fire, the air was blessedly clear of the flies. Sue had no difficulty finding the horses by their soft snuffles; the firelight reflected from their eyes as they raised their heads at her approach. Rainee's stallion stood aloof, but the mare came right up to her with a whicker. Sue pushed her aside so that she could pick up the rope and tether the stallion to a ring on the back of the caravan. He had plenty of slack now which enabled him to move around. The mare still followed Sue and nipped her shoulder gently.

"OK, lady, it's your turn now," Sue admonished with a laugh, "but I've got to find some more rope." She moved away but the mare dogged her footsteps like a shadow, and Rainee's stallion stamped his feet giving an angry cry. The mare tossed her head and ignored him;

continuing to follow Sue. Alfie appeared from the shadows.

"Here's a rope," he said softly, "I would advise you to tie them on the same ring."

When the mare put her head down to blow on Sue's face, with one deft movement she threw the rope round its neck. The mare immediately shied away, half rearing. Sue still held the other end and was in control — but as she went to secure it to the ring, the mare lunged unexpectedly and with a shrill cry galloped off with the rope trailing behind her. Sue stared after her, nursing a stinging hand.

"I guess Rainee knew what she was talking about," Alfie murmured. "You'll have to let her go, Sue."

But Sue hesitated. "What about the predators out there?" She vividly remembered another gypsy horse which had done the same thing way back in time – and it had been killed. She had blamed Thane for its slaughter.

"My guess is that directly you join the others, that mare will return." Alfie turned back to the group round the fire. "Come on — we're all waiting to eat."

Sue cast one more doubtful look in the direction the mare had taken and then gave in. Rainee gave her a sharp look. "You tried to tether the mare," she accused. There was no point in denying the fact. They all heard the mare scream out and the thud of her hooves as she galloped away. She sat beside her brother who was handing out pieces of meat. He tried to cheer her up.

"Sometimes a horse instinctively knows what's best for it, so I'm sure that mare knows what she's doing. Now eat, will you. After all, you did do the cooking. Incidentally, Rainee," he said as he turned his attention back to the older lady. "What have you got against that mare?"

Rainee munched on her piece of rabbit and flicked away the flying insects from her face. She swallowed the food and wiped her mouth with the back of her hand.

"I don't really know. There is something about it which is not right — and if it is not right, I don't trust it. In all my years of wandering about this area, I've never met a healthy horse on its own before."

"Well it's gone now," Alfie stated the obvious. "You couldn't see it for dust when Sue tried to put a rope round its neck." His words did not impress Rainee; and she retorted darkly: "It will be back."

Her words dampened the atmosphere. A chill fell over the gathering and it made Sue shiver. Why was Rainee making a drama over the mare's reluctance to be tethered? To her it was a perfectly natural thing to have happened. The mare was a free spirit. Raithe nudged her.

"Stop fantasising about that piebald mare. It's probably on its way home by now. We've got some hard thinking to do. We've got to decide our next move — because if Thane does not return with the spare horses, we're stuck here with Rainee and she will have a lot of unwanted guests."

"Worse things have happened to me," that lady retorted. "I could start taking you all to Therossa in my caravan." No one answered. Rainee did not know if she was pleased or annoyed that the idea was not received with any enthusiasm. Raithe said apologetically,

"It would take far too long, especially when there is Barry's sister to be rescued. I'm afraid we've got to rely on Thane coming back."

At the mention of Thane's name, Sue's eyes lit up and it made Raithe groan and Alfie sigh. He would rather be somewhere else if those two pompous men he had met earlier were coming back here. But in an instant everything changed. Something enormous streaked over their heads. A downdraught of air lifted their hair and caused sparks to leap from the fire. Some of them settled on Alfie, who yelled out and quickly brushed them off.

"What in God's name was that?" he gasped in alarm, immediately hoping he hadn't sounded too agitated. Rainee's horse could be heard whickering in the darkness, so Alfie quickly made a move in that direction. Rainee stopped him by saying sharply, "Come back, it's only a dragon." They all looked at each other in surprise so Rainee added hastily: "They do this sort of thing periodically. I think it is a test of nerves. Had it been daylight you would have seen it coming."

"What a darn stupid thing to do," Raithe snapped, "When I get back—" He broke off in midstream because the dragon had circled round and was returning for another low dive, almost sweeping the ground with its belly. Sue, who was crouching low, looked up and glimpsed the blue scales. Her breath caught in her throat.

"It's Sapphire," she choked, now completely bewildered. "What does she think she's doing?" Her voice was drowned out as a new roar reverberated through the air, accompanied by a spurt of flame. "If only it were daylight then we could see what she is doing."

The dragon passed over their fire for a third run, this time almost extinguishing it with her long leathery wings. Raithe turned urgently to his sister. "Use your ring, Sue, and give us some light."

Completely at a loss, Alfie wondered how one got light from a ring — but he was not about to make an issue of it, having just got used to dragons. He was beginning to accept almost anything these days, but a ring was stretching things too far. He could just about make out that Sue was lifting her hand when the whole area became illuminated with a brilliant green glare. For fifty yards at least, everything could be seen clearly. The magical light from the ring had a startling effect on the dragons. It illuminated their colouring, making their skins glitter.

Alfie and Rainee rubbed their eyes in amazement and saw the Blue Dragon staring at them in surprise. Nearby, in the process of landing, was a white dragon. Before Raithe could prevent her, Sue galvanised herself into action and was halfway across the distance between them before Silver's roar stopped her in her tracks.

"Please wait, Sonja!" The formal address filled Sue with disquiet. She saw anger flickering in Silver's eyes. "Sapphire has something to say to you."

All eyes went to Sapphire, who was glaring balefully at everyone, Sapphire remained silent, but from her snout wisps of smoke were issuing. Obviously she was ill at ease being caught in the light. Silver advanced nearer to her until she was able to press her claws down on Sapphire's forked tail. "Tell the Princess who the hostage is," she thundered.

"But I already know," Sue exclaimed, not giving Sapphire a chance to answer. "It's Priscilla — my sister," then her voice broke and became husky, "You've got to take me to her, Silver." Alfie swallow a lump in his throat, but he was still dazed at the unexpected sight of two dragons having a conversation.

178

"Wait until you have heard what Sapphire has to tell you." Silver's roar filled the air and a burst of flame touched the other dragon. The feeling of dread which assailed Sue grew stronger. Something had made Silver dreadfully angry, and she felt herself going cold in trepidation. Antagonism vibrated from the very being of the Blue Dragon as she mumbled venomously, "She is dying." The words came out starkly, with no thought of what the impact might be on the watching humans.

"No!" screamed Sue; she swayed, and would have fallen had not Raithe sprung to her side. He steadied her but she was too shaken to notice. "She can't be dying." Tears ran unchecked down her cheeks. She was incapable of saying anything coherently, but Alfie shouted out wrathfully: "She was perfectly well when that black dragon snatched her away. What have you done to her, you overgrown lizard?"

Sapphire flexed her wings and tried to rear up, but Silver detained her. "Nothing," she hissed. "The prisoner was fine until this illness came upon her."

The word illness brought a glimmer of hope into Sue's distraught mind. "Illness doesn't mean she's dying," she choked, clutching at straws. "Let me go to her. Please — one of you take me to her,"

Sapphire's eyes were watchful, but no longer malevolent. "It's too late. You die when you have been bitten by the red spider," she said bluntly.

A dreadful hush fell over the gathering, but the full impact of the words was lost on Sue, having never come into contact with the species, and Rainee pushed herself forward, and if anything, looked scandalised. "Are you trying to imply she was bitten here?" she demanded with

179

an edge to her voice. "I've not seen any trace of the red spider in aeons."

Sapphire rumbled with annoyance, allowing more smoke and flame to burst out from her mouth. "There are certainly no red spiders in the City of Wind where we put her," the dragon retorted aggressively. "It is perfectly obvious that she picked one up in her hand because that is where the wound is."

No one heard Alfie's muffled cry of, "Oh my God," because Sue screamed out almost hysterically, "you're wrong. There is no way Priscilla would pick up a spider. She hates them. You are trying to cover up your barbaric actions. I'll never, never forgive you for this."

"Wait!" Alfie looked sick and stared at her, his own face white. "I'm sorry — but you can't blame the dragons. I don't quite know how to say this." He paused, biting his lip. He now had everyone's attention and Raithe prompted him to continue, "I'm sure you'll find a way."

Alfie gulped. "In the cave where we hid from the mist, I saw her. You — you must understand neither of us knew what we were doing. The spider was running up her leg and she didn't scream. She picked it up." He nearly stopped on hearing Rainee's quick intake of breath, and with an effort continued, "she put it outside in the sun."

"Priscilla would never do that," Sue cut in defensively, and Raithe said, "Go on, Alfie."

Alfie swallowed. "The mist was to blame," he said. "She had no idea what she was doing — and — and I saw no danger in her action." His voice trailed off and he looked towards Sue, but she was filled with misery and confusion. Her heart cried out for Thane, but he had deserted her.

"We'll get the Shaman to her." Raithe could hardly bear to watch her anguish. He knew as well as Rainee, nothing lived after the bite of the red spider. Silver intervened, declaring, "there is no time left for a Shaman. She will be dead within hours, long before he could reach her." The dragon moved impatiently. "What she needs is a strong magic — now!"

"You have magic," Sue whispered.

Silver jerked her head irritably. "I am a dragon. I have no hands," she uttered fiercely, "but there is one human person who has our magic — if only he could be contacted." The dragon paused to let her words sink in. She saw the hope flare into Sue's eyes and pressed her point. "He is the only person who could give Priscilla a chance."

Raithe knew — as well as Sue — to whom she was referring, but he had to make sure and asked bluntly, "Are you referring to the king — our father?"

"Sheeka taught him everything," Silver answered simply, "but I doubt you would have time to contact him. Priscilla's life has almost ceased."

"Sue!" Raithe spun round on his sister, everyone else forgotten. The apathy fell away from her as she remembered the cowled man, as he had been when she first met him, under the influence of Oran. She remembered how she and Raithe summoned him when they were in acute danger. Well, Priscilla was in danger. Dared they do it again? Raithe obviously thought they should. "Come on, Sue. Let's use the rings. You know what to do."

Sue nodded dumbly and Raithe turned to Alfie and Rainee. "Stand back," he warned, "and do not be alarmed. We are doing this in the hope of saving Priscilla's life."

Although Rainee was used to magic, she showed her uncertainty by standing close to Alfie. He stood upright, shoulders braced, thinking, *I've seen all this before*, but even so, he still stared closely at the brother and sister to see what they were doing. Sue was visibly trembling through excitement as she lifted her hand with the emerald ring on her finger and pressed it against the one Raithe wore, a beautiful ring with a wolf's head. These were the magical rings, which their father had given them to keep in touch. An explosion of light came immediately. A score of birds took to the wing. The brilliance was more than the watchers expected, so overpowering they had to close their eyes against it. The strong light eradicated the green illumination, but made no difference to the dragons, and when they looked again, a cowled man stood in the middle of the glare. He straightened himself up, standing to his full height and allowed the cowl to fall back from his head, letting everyone see a grave face below his mass of hair the same colour as the twins'. Stern eyes surveyed the assembled people and dragons, but his gaze lingered longest on Rainee, whose lips moved but from which no sound came. Then he turned his attention to his son and daughter. His look of puzzlement made Sue quail. His voice, when he spoke, was resolute and carried clearly.

"What is so important that you summon me in this way?" he enquired. "I have stressed upon you both that the rings are for emergencies only. This does not seem to be a matter of life and death. Unless my eyes deceive me — you are in the middle of having a feast. Will you please call Thane? I should like to have a word with him."

"You'll be lucky," Alfie muttered inappropriately, and it was certainly not for the king's ears, but he heard, and his eyes swivelled round on Alfie, piercing through his bravado and making him feel diminutive. They were not the only disapproving eyes either. The look Rainee gave Alfie was scathing.

"Please," begged Sue, distracting her father's attention from Alfie by catching hold of his arm, "this is a matter of life and death," and Raithe added, "Barry's sister has been bitten by the red spider."

Between them, in swift words, the story of Priscilla's fate was told. When they spoke about Evonny, Alfie unnecessarily thought they needed his help with descriptive details, which brought a small smile to Tam's lips, but they all missed it by being so agitated. Tam quickly assessed the whole picture and knew exactly what had to be done. Deep down in his heart he was relieved his daughter had turned to him for help. He looked towards Silver, a penitent expression on his face, but at the same time keeping his voice full of authority. "I hope you can forgive my former transgressions, Silver — but I really do need your help in this crisis." He saw Sue move towards the dragon and added quickly, "you're not to take my daughter anywhere." Sue stopped in her tracks, almost as though he had struck her, but her father was still talking to Silver. "I need you to collect the Shaman and take him to the City of Wind. You might find him a little reluctant to make the journey." The ghost of a smile touched his serious face as he went on, "but I know you will overcome that — then I need you to stay with me, Silver." Tam turned to the other dragon looking on balefully at the proceedings and said to her contritely, "I will not forget you have helped us. I hope you will continue to do so, I still need you to keep Evonny away while we remove the hostage. Go now, my friends — and good luck. Speed is what we need — speed of the wind."

No one argued with his decisions. There was a huge downdraught, and sparks flew into the air as both the dragons took off. Tam turned back to the silent group behind him and saw his daughter's stricken eyes. He knew without being told she had wanted to go to her sister. His mood softened. He remembered the last time he saw her when they parted in anger. Lifting a hand, he touched her face saying: "I know you want to come with me — but for my sake, Sue, please stay with your brother and I shall know exactly where to contact you. I shall do my very best to save Barry's sister."

For one brief moment he stared at them all and then, in the space of a heartbeat, there was a flash of light and he disappeared. Two people were completely dumbfounded. Alfie said, looking rather dazed, "did I dream that? Did I actually speak to a king?"

* * *

Alfie took some time to interpret all that had happened. His mind boggled at the way people came and went — all being controlled by rings. He wondered how he could get hold of a ring like that. As the green light faded, so did his bravado. Once again they were enveloped in darkness and other worries took precedence. The atmosphere as they gathered around the campfire, deteriorated, in spite of Raithe's attempts to stimulate congenial conversation.

Rainee forgot all about food and sat with her chin propped in her hands. This incident had caused the past to come very much to the fore, especially after the appearance of Tam. She asked herself why she had taken her exile as a matter of course all those years ago. Why hadn't she fought to clear her name? By the way she acted, everyone thought she was guilty. Well it was not too late to change things. She was in a position to strike at the heart of Oran's stronghold. Then she bit her lip. That was dangerous thinking and detrimental to her safety. Oran knew he held the whip hand. Rainee thought about the mare, and coldness went through her. More and more her intuition told her not to trust it. It was too canny. Was it something Oran had conjured up? As her mind locked on to the piebald horse, she felt everything happening around them was due to its presence.

Sue was inconsolable. Why had Priscilla followed her to this land? An outdoor life was not for her. It was everything she hated. No bright lights and sophisticated nightclubs. What had gone wrong in America? She had sailed back home with her parents' blessing to stay with Moria, but instead of her reaching the hotel, Professor Harding had waylaid her. Alfie was taking Sue's predicament to heart. He had seen a spark of something deep within Priscilla, and was as distraught about what had gone wrong with her as Sue was. He now sat morosely beside her, staring out into space, punishing himself for things over which he had no control. No matter how many times they told him it was not his fault that Priscilla picked up a spider, he still did not believe them.

In the midst of all their pensive thoughts came the whicker of a horse and all heads turned immediately in the direction of the sound. Standing just outside the fringe of light was the piebald mare, swishing her tail. Her appearance was received in different ways. A look of 'I told you so' crossed Alfie's face. Raithe glanced at it thoughtfully, wondering what it was playing at, and Sue, who was about to get up and approach it, was halted by Rainee's venomous voice.

"Leave her where she is," she snapped. "That mare's more bother than it's worth. I can't think what my stallion sees in it. I think he is being used by her so that she can get close."

Raithe yawned, and in an attempt to avoid another conflict, looked round at them all. "I think we should all try and get some sleep. In the morning we can work things out. It's been a long day and we should try and put it behind us."

"I'll get you some blankets." Rainee struggled to her feet feeling stiff after doing so much walking. When she reached the caravan steps, she said unexpectedly, "You can sleep inside with me, Sue. Let the men stay outside and protect us."

Sue was still undecided as to whether to go up to the mare that was staring at her through dark eyes. Eyes that were hypnotic. She felt a strong compulsion to put her arms round its neck and go for a gallop, but Raithe gave her a push and broke the contact. "You go inside and sleep. I'll call you if Thane should return with the men."

There's not much hope of that, Sue thought miserably, but feeling low and unhappy, she complied with his order. As she disappeared out of sight, the mare snorted and moved back into the shadows. Although Rainee left the caravan door wide open, it was stuffy inside. She sat in her wicker chair, but Scrap decided he would lie beside Sue, and she did not have the heart to push him away.

Outside everything was quiet. The moon moved across the sky. The fire died down to a smoulder and the lads were wrapped up in their blankets. Because her thoughts would not let her sleep and Scrap made her unbearably hot, Sue tossed and turned. Eventually she slipped off the bed and stood at the open door, enjoying a slight breeze.

Not seeing anything move, she went down the steps and stood on the grass. She saw Rainee's stallion standing with head bowed; the mare was nowhere to be seen and for some reason she was disappointed. Then Sue jumped as a head was thrust over her shoulder and warm breath fanned her cheeks. The mare's soft whicker sounded in her ears. For some inexplicably reason she felt happy.

"Go back to the stallion," she whispered in her ear, and caught hold of the rope, which still dangled from the mare's neck. She led her away, but some slight noise made Rainee open her eyes to find the caravan empty. She rushed to the door in time to see Sue patting the mare's neck and heard her speaking in a low voice. She knew this was wrong and fear caught at her throat "Sue!" she called urgently, "come back in. That mare won't run away."

The sound of her voice made Raithe stir and sit up, looking bleary-eyed. Sue did not answer. She never heard the call. She was filled with a desire to climb up onto the mare's back and ride off to find Thane. In fact, the feelings were so strong she shouted back to Rainee, "I'm going to find Thane."

"What's going on?" Raithe was suddenly wide-awake. His eyes followed to where Rainee was looking. He saw his sister with the mare. He pushed the blanket aside and jumped swiftly to his feet. sensing there was something wrong. He was in time to see Sue jump on the mare's back. Rainee screamed out: "No!" her voice laced with terror, "get off her while you can. She's not your friend. She's evil."

The mare reared furiously at her voice and showed her large teeth as her lip curled back. There was nothing docile about her now. She tossed her head and screeched out, the sound waking Alfie as it drifted on the wind. Instead of going the way Sue had wanted, the mare turned in the opposite direction and raced off. Sue clung to her mane because the mare showed no sign of stopping. Without thinking, Raithe chased after her, cursing the fact he hadn't got a horse. "Jump off her, Sue," he yelled, waving his arms. "Do as Rainee is asking."

"I can't" Sue's voice screamed. She sounded terrorised. "I can't move. My limbs won't work. Raithe! Help me!..." Her screams faded as the mare made a phenomenal spurt and vanished into the dark.

Alfie scrambled to his feet, bemused, wanting to know what was happening. Raithe had no time to tell him. Instead, he grabbed hold of Rainee's arm demanding, "what did you mean by saying that horse was evil? Explain, woman."

Rainee's lips moved, but at first no sound came out. She was shaking, and sank onto the steps, trying to gather her thoughts. Eventually, when composed enough to speak, she said jerkily, "I sensed something was wrong with the mare directly I saw it — but everyone else loved it. I thought the mare was an apparition from Oran. Now, I'm not so sure it's anything to do with the Priest because she's now heading in a totally different direction — away from the Bluff. But whatever you say, I still don't trust that horse."

CHAPTER 14
CAPTURED

Not often could one catch sight of dragons lying in undignified positions, but the colony of Evonny dragons was oblivious to the world because Sapphire had put them all to sleep by weaving a special magic spell around them. Evonny himself had succumbed to it, which was unusual, he being the most cunning of them all. Sapphire rested on the ledge above where they were congregated, making sure the magic never lost its potency. Her appearance of contentment was grossly misleading, because inwardly she was petrified at what she was doing, knowing it was deliberately against her father's wishes. But everything was ready now. Silver could come and go without any confrontation with Evonny. The plan to rescue Priscilla was well under way.

Tam was the first to arrive at the City of Wind where his concealing black cloak kept him hidden from unwanted scrutiny. Since light could be seen for miles around from this high pinnacle, he disregarded it and tried to search through the chain of caves in the dark, hoping to find Barry's sister. A strong current of air was continuously rushing through the many hollow cavities, shrieking like a banshee in his ears. For his own peace of mind, Tam formed a barrier to keep it out and this enabled him to hear. Before long, his keen ears picked up the laboured breathing of the girl and he hastened to her side. Priscilla lay exactly where Sapphire had left her —

with the repugnant smell of food scattered by her side. He allowed himself a flicker of light and knelt down. He sucked in his breath at the sight of her. How thankful he was that he had stopped Sue from coming along. The condition of Priscilla would have been the last straw for a squeamish person, but Tam was not squeamish. He gently touched the bloated face before him. Her flesh was burning and she had fallen into a coma from which she would not wake up unless he acted quickly. For Priscilla there would be no return. His arrival had not been a moment too soon. Impatiently he glanced over his shoulder for the backup he had asked for — and it came in the shape of Silver as she landed easily on the edge of the drop. She deposited her rider on the rocky ground and flexed her wings because he had hung on too tightly. Anyone would have thought she had intended to drop him.

The Shaman's movements belied his age as he swiftly put distance between himself and the reptile. With remarkable agility for one so old, he ambled to where Tam was waiting, and even in the dark, some sort of aura danced around his bald head. The Shaman did not waste time by asking superfluous questions, having been well informed by Silver of the situation. He was exceedingly surprised at her clarity. Up until this moment, he had kept well clear of the reptile establishment. He knelt down on the other side of Priscilla, and by habit masked his expression as he studied her. With great gentleness he lifted up her swollen hand and winced at the vibes which were issued from it. Firmly, he pressed the tips of his fingers into the punctured skin. An angry hissing filled the air accompanied by a purple haze. Her laboured breathing was immediately relieved. Without another word, his claw-like fingers went to her wrist and he held it tightly. Slowly a nimbus of light crept up her arm, spreading until it encased her whole body and she looked as though she had a halo. Withdrawing his hand, the Shaman looked at Tam's worried face.

"This is far worse than I ever expected," he said slowly, "but I've done all I can for her here. She is stabilised for the moment and the venom has been halted, but it is still in her. She must be brought to my quarters for healing without any further delay. Can it be arranged?"

Tam's gratitude was obvious. He grasped the Shaman's hand and fought for the right words. "I'm deeply indebted to you for coming here."

The Shaman's eyebrows lifted quizzically. "Did I have any choice?" he asked, and glanced towards the dragon that was glowering at the pair of them from the cave entrance. "*She* would not take no for an answer — and I did try to refuse."

Tam knew a moment of remorse. His actions could not have endeared him to Silver and he guessed she had helped him because of her love for Sue. "I know what you mean," he answered sympathetically, "but I'm afraid we still need her help to get you and young Priscilla back to your healing rooms."

"Well, if it's the only way," the Shaman sighed, and stood up stiffly. Tam scooped up Priscilla from the ground and walked over to the watching dragon. He did not make the mistake of taking her for granted, but asked pleadingly, "May I put her on your back?"

Silver acquiesced with a nod of her head and he placed her carefully over the dragon's back, then helped the Shaman into a safe and comfortable position behind her. Standing back he said, "I'll be seeing you both soon, but first I must even things up with Sapphire before I leave."

"Evonny will find out she betrayed him, no matter what you do," Silver said sternly, giving him a baleful look, and Tam shook his head. "Not if I put her into a deeper sleep than his," he said. "He will have to use all his cunning to find out what really happened. I can't allow her to suffer because she helped us."

Silver snorted contemptuously, "So the great King is having second thoughts!"

Tam's lips tightened, not used to being rebuked by a dragon. "I will admit to being unfair," he said. "You may go to my daughter whenever you wish, and tell the others I'm lifting the ban. It was a stupid arrangement anyway. It took my daughter to show me that."

Silver wanted to roar with triumph, but the dragons below stopped her. She nodded her head once more to Tam, and took off without any warning. If the Shaman had nine lives, he lost eight of them right then — and Tam saw his terrified face as he clung on for dear life.

* * *

Tempers were frayed after the soldiers had spent a laborious day scouting around the Bluff looking for signs that might give them a clue as to where the Drazuzi openings were to be found. Their caves were cleverly concealed. Eyes rested unfairly on Zeno and Barry who were thought to know the whereabouts of the Drazuzi hidden domain. The two lads stared glumly at each other, failing to see why the onus fell on them.

"It was my devious stepbrother Lex who made a point of knowing where all the entrances were," Zeno muttered darkly when they were alone and out of earshot, "but since he and his men have been banished from this kingdom, they've taken all their secrets with them. I have as much chance of finding an opening as the next man. Oran is known to keep changing them. He leaves nothing to chance."

"And because I happened to escape through one, that doesn't mean I remember where it is," Barry added resentfully. "I certainly didn't stand around making notes. I ran."

Aimlessly they threw a few sticks onto the fire for want of something to do. The fire did not need any of their help — it was well laid and burning furiously. They glowered towards Amos and Thane nearby who were working out some sort of strategy, scratching marks in the earth with sticks as though they were drawing a map of the area. Another two soldiers further afield were preparing food, and three more were still out scouting. The rest were on guard duty. Those who had not been delegated to any special job — such as they — were endeavouring to catch up on some sleep.

Amos had chosen the area to camp overnight well. It was thickly covered with low scrub and there were plenty of trees to give shelter. Some defied gravity and grew malformed with twisted trunks out from the wall of the Bluff. A track of sorts could be seen going upwards, which wound precariously back and forth and was wide enough to lead a horse; but eventually it petered out. No one as yet had climbed up there.

After Thane's unfortunate treatment of Sue, and Amos's conflict with Alfie and Rainee, Barry was far from being enamoured with either one of them. If it were at all possible, he would steal a horse and go back to the caravan. His thoughts must have been written all over his face because Zeno kept close to his side and baulked at anything he tried to do. "It's not worth it, us kicking against authority."

In the end, it was Zeno who broke the monotony by indicating the path winding upwards. Half in fun, he said to Barry, "let's explore a little way up there."

Barry's face brightened immediately and he jumped to his feet. "You're on," he said. "Anything is better than sitting here doing nothing."

The soldiers doing the cooking chores looked up saying, "You can help us if you like," but the two lads waved the idea away. "No thanks, ours is a better option." The soldiers grinned and turned back to their task, but at that moment Thane looked up and saw Barry and Zeno moving away. "Not too far," he shouted out. "It will be dark soon."

Barry swallowed his irritation when Zeno murmured, "At least he didn't try to stop us."

Feeling a lot happier, Barry asked, "How far up do you think we'll get before it's too dark to see?"

"Not very far unless you stop talking," Zeno admonished. "Come on, let's get started. There must be a wonderful view from the top." With those words he started striding up the track.

The idea of their doing something on their own appealed to Barry, but as he tackled the sharp incline up the cliff, he felt the eyes of Amos burning into his back. The fact that he disapproved took away half the fun. There was one thing Barry had never got used to in this land, and that was the swiftness of nightfall. They had not ascended far when night came down on them like a cloak, and the path they were on disappeared from view. The only thing visible was the campfire way down below, and the men silhouetted around it. One of the soldiers, remembering where they were, shouted out for their immediate return.

Resignedly the two lads turned to retrace their steps; easier said than done. They could not remember where the sharp turns were situated, and one false step would send them hurtling down the cliff face. Zeno put hands to mouth and shouted to those below, "Can someone come up with a torch before we break our necks?" and Amos's gruff voice bellowed,

"If you want to do daft things when it's getting dark, it will be a good lesson for you both to feel your way down. Your eyes will soon become accustomed to the dark."

Barry shivered. "One of these days I'll find out what it is Amos doesn't like about me. Well, I'm not going to give him the satisfaction of failing. Let's get moving. I didn't realise how cold it was up here."

Zeno grasped his belt. "We must stay together and that will reduce our chances of having an accident. Shall I lead — or you?"

Barry decided to follow Zeno, who slowly felt his way downwards. They missed the first bend and fell with muffled oaths into a sturdy bush, but neither lad realised what a drop that bush had saved them from. It was dark. Breathing deeply, they extricated themselves and felt their way back to the path. Having worked out where the centre of it was, they started to shuffle down together, but a lot more slowly. Laughter floated up to them from below. Some of the soldiers saw the funny side of their predicament and were shouting up useless advice. Zeno did not see the funny side of it, and Barry was only half-listening to the exchange of words. The hairs were standing up on his neck and he didn't think the coldness around them had anything to do with the elements. His fear registered with Zeno, who stopped, alarmed.

"What do you think it is?" he asked in muffled tones, and Barry's answer of 'Drazuzi' made him equally as scared — then common sense came to his aid. "Some hope of that," he scoffed, "we haven't found an opening yet."

Barry shrugged, but wasn't mollified. "That's the trouble," he observed. "You never find an opening unless the Drazuzi want you to do so."

They continued their descent. Down below, someone decided it was time to do something about the plight they were in and was lighting up torches to come and fetch them. That's when the lads reached another corner and nearly fell over the edge. Their hearts thudded as dislodged stones went spinning through the air and angry shouts of, "Be careful up there. That just missed my head," made them pause.

"I think we'll wait here," Zeno muttered shakily, and as Barry agreed, an icy blast of cold air surrounded them. Barry knew what it was from previous experience.

"Run, Zeno!" he screamed out, and for the benefit of the soldiers below. "It's a Drazuzi attack."

The warning came too late. Zeno was not fast enough nor was he inclined to run anywhere in the dark. He felt as though his feet were clamped to the ground. A chilling breath fanned their faces and icy hands grasped hold of them. At the first touch there was excruciating pain and then they knew no more. Down below, the men relaxing round the fire heard the drama clearly. They were instantly on their feet, ready and alert. Thane cursed himself for having allowed the lads to go up there, so near to darkness, but in fairness to him, he never expected trouble. One look at the other men, and he knew they were itching to rush up there and rescue their companions, but he had to stop them. "Get more torches," he ordered harshly, almost glaring at them as though it were their fault, "you want to see where you are going if you're to save them — and arm yourselves as well. We're up against an evasive adversary. Just one word of warning — do not let them touch you or you will be lost."

The men scurried to do his bidding, pleased to have action at last and meet this elusive enemy. Barry and Zeno were popular, and because of this, there were far too many volunteers to go to their aid. Thane had to restrict their numbers otherwise they would risk pushing each other over the edge of the track. There was not enough room for the whole unit to go.

Amos touched Thane's arm, looking slightly cynical, and asked if it was wise to let all those men go up there when it was so dark. Barry may have been mistaken. There was no telling what was waiting for them."

"The Drazuzi soldiers of course," Thane retorted through clenched teeth. "If we can get up there fast enough, with luck we shall find the opening. Otherwise we shall lose two good men."

Amos's expression showed more clearly than words that he thought Thane was being hasty, yet the men were already stampeding up the steep track. Without more ado, Thane followed them. With light from so many torches, the place looked almost as bright as day. Signs were easy to pick up. It was obvious there had been many people here not so long before. There were broken stems, snapped-off twigs and scuffs in the earth, but of Zeno and Barry there was no sign. The soldiers did not give up. They searched every nook and cranny, looking for an entrance to the underground caves, but they drew a blank in whichever direction they looked. Thane could do nothing other than call the search off. One man still asked if he thought it was a good idea to climb higher. Thane shook his head, feeling completely helpless, galled to know that the Drazuzi had obviously been watching them for hours, and were no doubt laughing at their puny efforts to find them. Things were going from bad to worse and Thane took responsibility for all the failures on his own shoulders.

At first this expedition had been to find the Drazuzi caves and rescue two men known to be held there, but now, with the loss of Barry and Zeno, it was imperative to break in somehow and get them all back. The way things were going Thane was making an impossible rift between him and Sue. She would never forgive him if he allowed Barry to be recaptured. With an angry gesture he ordered the men back to camp.

The raucous laughter was missing. The soldiers realised this was not a game anymore. Thane mulled over the fact that Amos had refused to give them any light. Had he sent up torches when they had called for them — would the Drazuzi then have left then alone? He did not understand this dislike Amos held for Barry and Zeno.

Eventually the long drawn out meal was over. The soldiers were able to jump to their feet and disperse, but everyone had the uneasy feeling that eyes were watching them from above. A contingent of men packed the food away from predators and Thane doubled the guard, his reason being that he wanted an early start in the morning. This was news to Amos who asked in surprise. "Where are we going?" Every man within hearing range had his ear cocked for the answer. None of them wanted to desert Barry and Zeno and leave them to the Drazuzi.

"Back to the caravan," Thane retorted curtly. "That is where we left the Prince and he needs to know what has befallen his cousin. Also he has his own method of informing the king what we are doing."

"We're not going back to the city?" exploded one of the soldiers unexpectedly, nearly causing a riot. Amos went red in the face at his insubordination. "You will do what is ordered, soldier," he snarled. At his voice resentment stirred up in the ranks, but Thane put a stop to it immediately by saying sharply,

"Far from it, our journey will be twofold. I think I am correct in assuming that Rainee, the owner of the caravan, knows the way into the Drazuzi caves. I'm hoping, with a little pressure, to enlist her help to be our guide."

"You've also got a short memory," Amos muttered sourly. "Have you decided what you're going to do with Sue?"

When a soldier guffawed, he was nearly ostracised. Thane spun round, barely holding his temper in check, and snapped at Amos, "Take over here, I need to do some thinking," and he walked off into the dark with just White Hawk as his companion. The soldiers looked uneasily at each other, but with Amos glowering at them, they silently made ready for bed.

CHAPTER 15
TOO LATE

The elements turned in sympathy with the way everyone was feeling. A chill wind blew over the land. Low clouds scudded across the slate grey sky, preventing the weak sun from breaking through. In the early morning light, the soldiers trudged along the base of the Bluff with eyes alert for trouble. Although nothing stirred in the foliage below, or on the cliff top above, everyone felt that eyes were watching their progress. Occasionally a squall lifted dust and leaves, blowing grit into their eyes.

To the weary men trudging along behind Thane and Amos, they were finding it hard to keep their resentment under control. The whole enterprise had taken on a different meaning with the loss of Barry and Zeno. What had been a routine operation was now a venture fraught with danger. Only White Hawk was happy with the direction in which they were going, and he would have raced on ahead, had not Thane kept him on a tight leash and ordered him to stay by his side. It was purely a selfish action on Thane's part. He didn't want Sue to be alerted to his return. The wolf would have destroyed the element of surprise. He had such a lot to make up for.

It was midday when they approached the bend in the Bluff where they had encountered Rainee and Alfie the day before. The caravan was standing exactly where they had left it — but Thane halted, holding up his hand. It was obvious something was wrong. The lack of activity

202

and silence brooding over the place made his sinews tighten. The area on which they were advancing was devoid of life. Even the fire was out, and that was a crime; it was a necessity in caravan life to have it for cooking food and to provide warmth. It was disconcerting to find the place deserted. Not only were the people missing, there was no sign of Rainee's horse. Thane exchanged a puzzled look with Amos and the old man said grimly, "They're obviously still out looking for the horse. I knew they were not trackers."

"Maybe," retorted Thane, breathing hard and swallowing his apprehension, "but Sue and Raithe were left here. Where are they?"

Amos scratched his grizzled beard, but his sharp eyes observed that the area had been tidied up since they last saw it. "I should say they are exhausted after a lot of hard work," he said at length, "and are sleeping it off inside the caravan. They didn't strike me as people who would get up early. I doubt they've even thought of building up the fire."

Thane relaxed. He must stop getting jittery at everything. He managed a tight smile. "Then we'll light it for them and give them a surprise." He glanced at the soldiers fidgeting at the rear. "It will take the men's minds off what has happened." So saying, he urged his horse to a gallop forward and everyone followed his lead. The horses thundered over the ground but White Hawk streaked ahead of them and reached the caravan first. Instead of disappearing inside as Thane had expected, he sat on his haunches, raised his head and howled. The sound made the hairs stand up on Thane's neck. He knew the wolf had found trouble. His former worries surged back and swamped him. Amos issued a sharp order for the soldiers to halt, and with the curt instruction, "arm yourselves," went forward with Thane.

The caravan door stood wide open to the elements and the empty interior could be seen clearly. Instead of chaos, everything had been left neat and tidy with no sign of a struggle. Annoyingly, there was nothing to say how long the occupants had been gone. A frown drew Thane's eyebrows into a straight line as he contemplated Rainee's abode and wondered if the Drazuzi had attacked them during the hours of darkness. He cast that thought away as soon as it came. Although the Drazuzi could see perfectly well in the dark, it was well known they would never leave their caves unless under the cover of mist, and there was certainly none of that, the place looked as though the people who owned it had gone on holiday, but — and this was the thought that perplexed him, why had White Hawk howled? What did he sense? He looked towards the wolf that sat so still he could have been carved out of rock. He made no attempt to ferret Sue out. It was as though he knew such an act was pointless.

Already there was an uneasy murmur rising from the ranks. The soldiers were superstitious and becoming restless. Amos silenced them with the curt countermand to his first order of arming themselves, and told them to put their weapons away, but keep alert. "We need a fire going and some food prepared for when the Prince and Princess return," he said, "so jump to it." He turned to Thane and added in an undertone, "if those other two are still out searching for their horse, I can only say they are bad trackers. Do you think we should send a few men out to help them?"

"We don't know where they are," said Thane staring in every direction, the frown on his face deepening. What was it he was missing? Sue and Raithe had not been with Alfie and Rainee, but they were all missing — and where was that silly dog he had seen with them when having those unfortunate words with Sue? Everything couldn't be missing. What would the Drazuzi want with a dog — or a horse come to that? Rainee would never leave her animals to fend for themselves. Something was very wrong here.

The soldiers tethered their horses beneath the trees and set about obeying Amos's orders, glad to be doing something at last. There was a whistle on their lips to boost their morale. They received a glare from the old tracker. "Keep it quiet," he growled, "sound carries out here."

Thane bent and studied the ground carefully, watched attentively by White Hawk. With so many tracks criss-crossing each other, deciphering them was almost impossible, but to his consternation, he did pick up the tracks of an unshod horse – and that suggested there were gypsies. But search as hard as he could, there were no marks of caravans. It didn't make sense. A little further away he saw the imprints of dragons. If he hazarded a guess, he would have said there were two of them. Now the possibility that they had flown away arose, but the dragons could not take a horse or dog on their backs. It was stalemate again.

Amos suggested using White Hawk who was still watching them. Maybe the wolf could track by smell — he had done so before. The only objects at hand all belonged to Rainee, so Thane picked up a rug from the bed, took it over to White Hawk to smell and ordered sternly, "Find." For a moment, the wolf stood undecided, looking at everyone, and Amos said impatiently, "That's no good, Thane. I should think that woman's circled around this area a hundred times. You want to find something Sue or Raithe have handled." what?"

"Well I don't know." The old man chewed on his lower lip. "I just didn't think a rug was appropriate."

Before they got involved in another argument, White Hawk pointed his nose to the sky and with ears pricked up, howled —

"Fine," Thane retorted, his voice growing more frustrated, "like

then he bounded away in the direction of the cliffs. The Drazuzi was the first name that came to Thane's mind and his heart sank. He sprang swiftly onto Saturn and followed the fleeing wolf, with Amos close behind. They were within thirty spans of the Bluff when quite uncharacteristically White Hawk veered off from his original direction and dived into the nearby tangle of undergrowth which covered a large part of the land. An area that looked uninviting, with briars and nettles thickly matted together. Saturn gave one disparaging glance at this unexpected hazard, and refused to go any further. Thane slid from his back and withdrew a long hunting knife. Amos, realising what he intended to do, followed suit. The two men started to hack out a pathway using knives which were not meant to be used for the resilient green stems which defied the blades and used their own defences, long wicked pointed thorns, which jabbed into the men's skin. White Hawk got through by wriggling low on his belly, but neither of the men was prepared to do that.

An extra strong briar swung out and whipped across Amos's face. His language left much to be desired and his temper became fouler as he wiped away the blood with the back of his hand. Flies zoomed in on this unexpected nectar and so intent were they on brushing them off, both men missed the scuffle, which came from deep within the dense growth, followed by a threatening growl and a very small whimper.

"If that wolf's out hunting, I'll skin him," the old man spat out, feeling his cheek that was smarting like mad. Thane hacked back another bush, feeling very little sympathy for the fuss Amos was making over a minor scratch, when he stopped with a strangled ejaculation as his knife barely missed the small dog crouching beneath it. Amos stared over his shoulder and saw the shaking ball of fur from which two very frightened eyes surveyed them. Its ears lay flat back on its head, and only one foot away was the drooling muzzle of White Hawk. The wolf showed his teeth and loomed over what to him was prey. Amos pushed past Thane and quickly scooped up the little dog before the wolf's saliva could wash over him. White Hawk shut his mouth with a snap and stared at the old man indignantly. His muscles tensed and he was just on the verge of snatching back what he considered was his when Thane curtly ordered the wolf away. He stared for a moment at the dog lying in Amos's arms, quivering while the old man stroked it.

"That was very good," he said disgustedly, "the blanket you gave to White Hawk to sniff and follow thinking it would lead us to Rainee, must have been this little dog's bed." Amos tickled the dog under his chin and received a feeble lick in return. "When we get out of this infernal undergrowth, we can get this little chap to track his owner. That's if you can keep White Hawk off," he added.

Thane quickly turned his head to hide a smile. The pair of brown eyes belonging to Scrap had smote Amos. The little dog had managed to make Amos forget his dislike of Rainee. They pushed their way out of the undergrowth a lot easier than they had got in — and when they joined up with the horses again, Amos placed the dog on the ground. Scrap wanted to play after his close shave with the wolf, so he rolled on the ground and kicked his legs in the air to have his tummy tickled. When Amos did nothing about it, he sat up on the old man's feet and looked up at him with enquiring eyes. White Hawk turned away in disgust. He wanted to shake that furry thing and toss it in the air, but people he thought were friends had denied him his meal. Amos petted the dog, keeping a sharp eye on the wolf. When Scrap felt more like his usual self, Amos gave him a push and said, "Go to Rainee... Rainee." He repeated the name, and Thane watched with derisive amusement, but his expression vanished as the small dog raced towards the Bluff. Every muscle in White Hawk's body tensed again and he was just about to spring after him for a second chance when Thane hastily ordered him to stay. White Hawk sat, his amber eyes glowering, while Thane and Amos mounted their stallions and raced after the fast disappearing dog.

Scrap stopped at the foot of a rocky wall, jumping up and down excitedly while he barked. Pulling to a halt,

Thane studied the cliff face, and saw, far above the reach of the small dog, an opening. The opening was by no means large enough to admit a horse, even if it were possible to get a horse up that high — but a human could easily wriggle in and out and Thane assumed that that was where everyone was. Before he could wonder why they should be in such a strange place, Amos thundered up, sending scree in all directions, and even before he slid off his horse, someone had squeezed out of the hole. This person jumped down and Scrap was ecstatic with cries of welcome, even though they told him to shut up. Alfie stood in front of the startled men, a grin on his homely face. He pushed the dog away.

"You're not lost again, are you?" Alfie asked pleasantly, but Amos cut in harshly, "You're the one who is lost if you were up there."

"You're right," Alfie agreed, "and it seems that you're heading for the same place?"

"Why the hell should we want to go in there?" asked Amos feeling extremely exasperated, "I'm the one asking the questions. What do you mean by leaving the caravan unguarded? Anyone could have stolen it."

"Without a horse?" another voice broke in, and looking up, both men saw Rainee clamber out of the hole. Alfie gave her a hand as she jumped down and as she straightened her skirt, she gazed unsmiling at Thane and Amos. "To what do we owe this pleasure?"

All his former ire towards her returned and Amos demanded aggressively, "where are Sue and Raithe?"

"I've really no idea," Rainee retorted annoyingly. "They are certainly not with us as you can see. Well we won't hold you up, gentlemen. We have got to get back. Come along, Alfie."

She walked past them, a cynical smile on her lips. Alfie made to follow, but Thane detained him by laying a hand on his arm. "Where is Sue?" he demanded, meaning to keep his voice noncommittal, but it cracked when he mentioned her name. Alfie forgot about Rainee when he saw the anxiety in Thane's eyes. Alfie was not a person to hurt another one unnecessarily. Almost against his will he said slowly,

"She left us in the night." He saw Thane's jaw tighten as he assumed the wrong conclusion. "So she went with the dragons after all," he said, his voice cold and harsh. "I'm a fool to worry about her. She will always go her own way."

"You've got it all wrong," Alfie shook his head. His eyes were sympathetic, and he tried to break down the barrier Thane created. "Hear me out," he added quickly as Thane turned away. "A dragon did come in the night — two to be precise, and so did Sue's father. I don't know how they did it," He wavered slightly because the two men were staring at him incredulously. "Sue and her brother put their hands together and there was her father dressed in a black cowl. The dragons had brought news about her sister Priscilla dying." Alfie paused because he had a lump in his throat, which he hastily tried to swallow. "That I believe is why they summoned him — but when the king departed with them, Sue and Raithe were left behind. Her father ordered this and she was very upset. It took a lot to console her."

"Then where did she go in the night?" asked Amos.

Alfie was lost for words and he looked imploringly towards Rainee, but she ignored him and continued on her way with Scrap yapping at her heels. Alfie took a huge breath to settle his nerves. "It all started when Rainee and I found her stallion. It was coming on for sunset. There was a mare with him. From the very beginning, Rainee was against our taking it back home, but she had no say in the matter. A strong bond had grown between the two horses and it was a matter of having both, or none at all. I could not make out why Rainee showed such a dislike towards the mare. The mare took to Sue, it followed her everywhere — unnaturally so and it wouldn't be tethered. When Silver and the king were with us, the mare went missing, but it came back during the night, seeking Sue out again. She went to it, and for some reason, climbed on its back. Rainee went berserk — screaming out to her to get off it because it was evil." He paused, perspiration forming on his forehead as he relived it all over again. Amos stood transfixed and Thane asked roughly, "and did she?"

"She — she couldn't get off the mare," replied Alfie. "Some magic trapped her on its back. She was screaming to us to help her. Rainee thought the mare was sent by Oran, but now we're not so sure. It didn't head for the Bluff. In fact, it went in the opposite direction."

Amos gave himself a shake to clear his head. If he hadn't known for a fact that what Alfie said was distinctly possible, he would have been one of the first to accuse him of making up stories. He was shocked at what he heard. "So where is the Prince, now?" he asked through clenched teeth.

211

"He's out following her on Rainee's horse. Rainee was prepared to confront Oran. That's what we have been doing here, but that entrance is blocked."

"She can save herself the bother," Thane broke in ominously, "that mare came from Deena. Curse the woman for meddling."

* * *

There were two campfires burning when they returned to the caravan — the men had been busy. One had been specially built for Thane and Amos to have some privacy, which cut two ways. The men were well out of earshot and could let their hair down without facing any charge of insubordination for what they were speaking about. Food roasted on sticks in both fires and Rainee took over the cooking on the fire allotted to her. As the unrestrained laughter from the soldiers' camp reached her ears, a smile touched her lips. It sounded like old times when she went camping with her brother. She was always segregated, but this time she was with friends — at least she hoped so, as she surreptitiously watched Amos through lowered lashes. She didn't think she was wrong in her assumption.

The fire roared merrily, and Rainee provided stools and rugs to make her guests comfortable. They had a lot to discuss. Thane's face was serious. Before arriving here, his plans had been cut and dried. Rainee had to be approached and asked if she would lead them into the Drazuzi caves. He hoped that when he told her the Priest had taken Barry as a prisoner, it would ensure her help, and it did. She was horrified, and prepared to face the dangers she knew would beset them to get Barry out. She had a fondness for the cheeky lad and was not the least bit worried that he had royal connections. Thane was still mulling over his plans. It was his duty to lead the men — and he had been ready and willing to do so, until now. The news he heard of Sue changed it all. She faced untold dangers at the hands of Deena, more so because she still treated that woman as a friend. Then there was Raithe, he was travelling alone on an unreliable horse. Someone had to follow him. Thane wanted to volunteer himself but it was his place to stay with his men. His frown grew even deeper on his face and his shoulders slumped. He was so caught up in his own dilemma, he never noticed White Hawk on the other side of the fire, mesmerizing the small dog and licking his lips in anticipation. All he wanted was for the dog to run but Scrap had picked up on the vibes and pressed closer to Amos's legs — he felt he had an ally in the old man.

"How about my going?" Alfie suggested tentatively. "I'm a good tracker. I'm sure I could find the Prince."

"You don't know the land, lad. You'd be eaten alive out there," Amos growled, "but thanks for offering."

Alfie stared at him thoughtfully, and then burnt his boats by saying, "We could go together."

He never expected the old man to take him up on it, but Amos was alert at once, his eyes gleaming at the chance of doing something for Sue — then he caught sight of Thane's face and changed his mind. Making a supreme sacrifice, he said, "You must go with him, Thane — you're by far the better man. I can handle the men and I'm prepared to follow Rainee if she has no objections."

Rainee raised her head in surprise and stared at him speculatively. With tongue in cheek she asked, "Are you sure you know what you're saying? I might be leading you into a trap — which wouldn't be a bad thing after the way you have treated me over the years."

Amos coughed. He looked uncomfortable. Alfie wanted to pat Rainee on the back for standing up for herself against the grouchy old man. At that moment the wind gusted across the land and smoke billowed out from the fire into their faces. Thane made a snap decision because whatever happened, there must not be any bad feelings amongst themselves inside the Drazuzi domain or they would have lost the fight with Oran before it had even started. He should have remembered the friction between Rainee and Amos. He turned to the old tracker and said unemotionally, "You go with Alfie, Amos. Rainee will fare better with me."

"I won't have that!" Amos exploded, and all the soldiers at the other fire turned to look at him as he jumped to his feet. He glared at Rainee, his expression mutinous. "We're going together, woman," he growled indignantly. "I'm man enough to take orders from you — are you woman enough to bury the hatchet?"

"I...I..."Rainee stuttered, confused, and Amos pressed his advantage, adding, "I've just got one stipulation to make first to which you must agree."

With Amos towering over her, Rainee was filled with apprehension and felt very small. "What's that?" she asked nervously.

"You will allow me to deal with Oran," he replied, "that's not woman's work — it's mine."

214

END OF PART ONE

PART TWO

CHAPTER 16
THE GODDESS

It was a day of intermittent showers. Thane and Alfie were anxious to put distance between themselves and the men before nightfall. They made use of a short lull early afternoon and started off in case more rainfalls obliterated the few tracks that were still visible. Rainee insisted that Amos should supply a packhorse, which they could easily double up as a spare mount if needed. They left the camp behind with the goodwill of everyone ringing in their ears, and the wolf, suddenly alert, following them like a shadow. Amos couldn't hide the fact that he was pleased to see the back of White Hawk. He worried about the animosity he showed towards Scrap. As a fighter and protector the wolf could not be faulted, but to get him to differentiate between what animal was food and what was not was impossible.

As White Hawk walked away, he glanced over his shoulder at Scrap with a predatory gleam in his amber eyes, which Amos saw, and so did the dog. Scrap whimpered in fear and Amos picked him up protectively. The action brought a smile to Rainee's lips.

It was a long time since Alfie had ridden a horse and he was sorely out of practice. The stallion chosen for him had not been picked out wisely, as it had a wicked gleam in its eye, but for the moment it was placid and obeyed every order given to it by the greenhorn on its back. This gave Alfie valuable time to master his almost forgotten art of riding. For two hours they wandered along the track and there was no conversation between the two men. Thane's attention was focused on scrutinizing the ground and following the few tracks that had been left by Raithe. Alfie ambled after him and tried to enjoy the scenery – not that much could be seen of it. White Hawk eyed him with a certain amount of distrust; not quite sure what the intentions of this stranger were. But since his master had no hang-ups about him, he was content to follow.

The landscape changed dramatically and this kept Alfie on his toes. Everything in this land was unfamiliar. It was unlike his country, yet already he was growing attached to it. Before long it became sandy underfoot and the ground gradually fell away until a huge lake blocked their way. They had the choice of three routes. One turned inland, one following the shore and the third went along a narrow path where rocks reared up on either side. This path looked rather sinister. Turning to Alfie, Thane asked grimly, "How are you with a bow and arrow?"

He was not surprised when Alfie shook his head. "I haven't got a clue about them. We don't use them in our land. I'm good with my fists and have a black belt in judo — and somewhere on my person I've got a knife. Is that OK?"

"What is this judo?" Thane asked with a frown — and he mulled over the answer Alfie gave of 'unarmed combat'. He eyed him up and down, noticing he had the build for wrestling. The soldiers did it all the time as a sport, but would it be enough if they were ambushed? The area they were now heading through was inhospitable and known for sudden attacks on strangers, especially from gypsies. He wondered how the Prince had fared on his own. Thane drew on his own bow in readiness and nodded to Alfie. "Be alert until we reach the open."

Awkwardly, Alfie drew out his knife, and seeing it, Thane hastily bit back a smile. The weapon Alfie held would be useless if they met trouble. At the first opportunity he must give Alfie something more suitable. The brooding silence around them hinted at trouble. Their horses made no sound on the sandy soil, but that applied to any assailant as well. Raithe's prints were often overlapping and it was difficult to discern if he had branched off in any direction. Making up his mind, Thane shouted, "Gallop to the water!"

He spurred Saturn on and Alfie tensed, thinking it was action at last. He kicked the white stallion, which bunched up his muscles and charged after the other two horses. It was Alfie's first experience of such speed. As he clenched his teeth and hung on, realising he had no control, he found the gallop was actually exhilarating. Reaching the water's edge looking flushed and pleased, he slithered to a stop beside Thane and took in his surroundings.

The water was an unforeseen obstacle. To cross the expanse would make them lose valuable time because they would need assistance — yet going round the edge was unthinkable. The ferry, if that was what it was, stood unattended — a ramshackle affair which had seen better days; and the hut nearby was no better. From the one and only window came raucous laughter. The ferryman inside was enjoying himself and had no idea they were there.

Alfie steadied his mount which, after his first gallop, wanted to be off again. He stared hard at the ancient raft, which he assumed was to take them over the lake. Two stout ropes disappeared across the weed choked water and in between them, bobbing lazily about, was a small wooden float with its edges rotting away. On the far bank many people seemed to be congregating in a haze of smoke, which partially camouflaged several caravans. He looked towards Thane, a question on his lips. "Have we got to pull ourselves across to those people over there?" he asked, not realising they were gypsies, "There isn't room on that rotting wooden platform to swing a cat. We've got three horses — and somewhere a wolf. We'd sink directly we stood on it."

"True," replied Thane, "But we're not about to take that risk — or to disturb the ferryman. The sooner we get away from this spot the better." Thane slid from his horse, fell to his knees and studied the ground carefully. An accumulation of tracks churned up the sandy soil. Lots were made by unshod horses, which didn't surprise him, seeing there were gypsies on the further side of the lake. He regained his feet, stroking his chin thoughtfully and murmured, "I'm darn sure Raithe never used the ferry or came this way." He indicated the path heading inland. "Let's get out of here, quick.

At that moment, the raucous laughter ceased and something was heard to crash within the hut. A loud angry voice shouted out some unintelligible words, which were followed by a high-pitched shriek. A small figure tumbled through the doorway and fell flat on its face. Apart from the ragged clothing and grimy skin, it was hard to discern the person's sex until she had scrambled upright. Her black hair fell in long greasy strands to her shoulders and she was painfully thin. A puff of wind could have blown her away, but her voice made up for it. She shouted a few defiant words back to the hut, and Thane winced. It was all indecipherable to Alfie, but by the way it was delivered, he wasn't so sure he wanted to know what she said. The girl looked up then and saw them. Thane's hand tightened on his bow, sure she was about to shout out to the gypsy ferryman for help. Alfie felt a wave of distaste at the thought that Thane could be entertaining the idea of attacking this child. The child, however, ran nimbly over the ground on bare feet and stood in front of Thane's horse. A repugnant smell wafted past their noses. With her hands on her hips, and a cheeky grin on her face — a face which sported a black eye and swollen lip — she said audaciously in a language they both understood, "Take me with you, Mister or I'll shout to old Jasper that there be gringos hereabouts. We eat gringos."

"You're out of luck, youngster. I'm not crossing the lake – so clear off."

His dismissive attitude had been entirely wrong. Certainly not the treatment this ragged urchin expected. Her impudence vanished. As Thane sprang up on Saturn and tried to edge his horse around her thin body, she caught hold of the bridle with amazing strength and showed no fear of Saturn's teeth as he turned his head towards her and nipped. Alfie, who could not tolerate disobedience in a child, thought he could help.

"You heard him, youngster — scram," he shouted as he came alongside, the white stallion nearly running her down. She barely reached the top of his legs. The girl however pushed the white stallion away with her filthy hands and grimy nails, saying impudently, "Horses won't hurt me — I'm fey."

Alfie remained unimpressed. "I don't care what you are," he retorted, "Just clear off and let us by before we run you down."

"I'll yell for Jasper if you touch me," the girl threatened. "You do that," Alfie retorted. Thane shot him a warning glance because at that moment Jasper had come to the hut door — he was a revelation not to be missed, a scruffy individual with at least a month's growth of hair on his chin. His fleshy oversized body spoke of indulgence and gluttony. He was not alone, because behind him appeared another man with tight curly jet-black hair and golden earrings falling to his shoulders.

Thane's heart sank. Gypsies were on this side of the lake, he reflected, what bad luck for them. But for the little brat they could have been well away. The curly haired-gypsy saw him and shouted out something, waving a huge brawny fist. Then the ferryman saw his daughter and added his voice to the other ones, and it was not pleasant.

"Get moving," Thane hissed. Alfie needed no second bidding. He was just about to allow his stallion to have his head when he caught sight of the girl's face. The earlier bravado had miraculously vanished and fear had taken its place in her eyes. Her lips trembled as she held up two unbelievably skinny arms. "Take me with you, Mister," she pleaded, "Just a little way — away from him."

The few tears that trickled down her filthy face left channels of clean skin behind them, but her pathetically appealing stance found its mark. Alfie was lost. No way could he stand against a woman in tears. Always the knight in shining armour he leant over, and not thinking of the consequences, scooped her up, then immediately thundered after Thane.

His ears were closed to the two men yelling out oaths and threatening dire repercussions. Alfie's nostrils were assailed by an evil smell radiating off the girl's body; he gagged and nearly dropped her. She, however, shed her former fear like a skin and grabbed hold of the white stallion's mane, pulling on it.

"Faster! Faster!" she shrieked gleefully, and to Alfie's horror the stallion responded to her voice. It all happened in a flash. Thane was suddenly faced with a horse out of control and a little demon urging it on. That young witch had told the truth when she said she was fey. Tracking Raithe was forgotten. The white stallion had to be stopped before it did itself a mischief.

Alfie was hanging on for dear life. With the speed he was travelling — the only scenery he saw was a blur as it flashed by. Thane whispered in Saturn's ear and his stallion tried valiantly to keep pace with Alfie, but the white horse was going with a momentum that was very near to flying. It didn't take long for them to find themselves miles away from the lake but at last the two horses were galloping side by side and Thane was able to use his rope to lasso the runaway stallion and brought it to a halt. The white horse stumbled and stood with its head down, sides heaving and covered with sweat. It was nearly at the end of its tether.

Alfie slid off its back, concern for the horse's welfare written all over his homely face. He glowered at the girl who had caused the incident. She jumped to the ground, unconcerned, and tossed her head defiantly. "Told you horses do what I want," she bragged airily.

Alfie's chivalry evaporated. He had the uncharitable desire to shake her until her teeth rattled, but Thane pushed his way between the two of them and threatened the girl through his laboured breathing. "I'll settle with you later, kid. We don't try to kill our horses — even if you gypsies do. Come on, Alfie — they need our attention."

The girl was shoved unceremoniously to one side and from then on she was completely ignored. Her petulance made her scowl. They had called her a gypsy. They would pay for that insult. While her bad temper festered within her, the two men rubbed down all three horses and curried their coats until they were well groomed. Occasionally a waft of some bad odour made their noses wrinkle up distastefully and they both had the same thought. Their eyes fell on the girl, scratching herself with no hint of decorum.

"First things first," Thane muttered, turning his back on her. "We'll stay here for the night. We're on a rise and the trees will give us a degree of shelter. You water the horses, Alfie, and I'll forage around for wood to build a fire and — if we're lucky — she will disappear." They both openly glowered in her direction but no matter how many surreptitious looks they shot at her, she didn't vanish as they had hoped.

While they were out scouring around the area, the girl lit a fire herself, and took it as a matter of course that they would not thank her. Secretly they were amazed, but it galled them both that she had managed it. They had no intentions of commenting on it. Thane eyed her up and down critically, noticing how filthy the skimpy rags she wore were, too meagre even to hide a tinderbox. He suspected she was laughing at them deep down in her brilliant eyes.

Alfie trudged up the small rise, damp with perspiration, and saw her sitting there, toasting her bare feet before the flames. Then he saw red. The smirk on her dirty face made him erupt. Reaching down, he yanked her to her feet, and dragged her to a nearby fast flowing stream and threw her in. Whether she could swim or not, never crossed his mind. She screamed like a banshee as the water went over her head, yelling words at him that were gibberish. Eventually she stood up, her eyes glowering with hate. Thane came and stood beside Alfie. Looking down on the furious girl, he said pleasantly, "There are a few house rules if you want to stay with us."

She deliberately turned her back on him. "I am not interested in any house rules or anything else you have to say," she declared.

Thane shrugged. "Then that's a pity — but I'll say them anyway and you had better listen. If you are determined to stay with us, you will obey orders, and the first one is, clean yourself — if you don't, then I suggest you start walking back to Jasper."

Her mouth fell open in surprise. "I can't walk all that way," she protested indignantly, "You give me a horse!"

Thane stared at her quizzically. "I said walk," he repeated firmly. "Come on, Alfie — let's see about our meal."

* * *

Night arrived with the suddenness that was so customary in Therossa, but on this particular eventide, a freshening wind came with it which gusted through the thick green foliage above the travellers' heads. Its power was disturbing to the two people sitting below. A multitude of debris rained down covering them, and some of the particles landing in the fire flared up. Alfie hugged his large arms about his body and Thane glanced swiftly towards the horses in case they were feeling disturbed. To his surprise they were already beginning to sleep. For some reason the hairs on the back of his neck stood up as though warning them danger was surreptitiously creeping nearer. Then he grinned foolishly, thinking how paranoid he was becoming. If any predators were skulking around, the animals would be the first to give the alarm – and as it was, White Hawk, who had returned to them half an hour ago, was already sleeping, dead to the world.

The men had no feeling of remorse about their treatment of the gypsy girl. They excluded her from all comforts, contentedly unwinding after a long traumatic day. The wolf lay sprawled at their feet, so dangerously near the flames his coat was almost singed. His muzzle, lowered onto his huge paws, was red with blood after a successful hunt — and he had no interest in what was going on around him.

Rainee had sent them on their journey with plenty of cooked meat, rye bread and water flasks filled to the brim. They had enough food to stop them from hunting for quite a while. They left the gypsy a few yards away from them, having commandeered her fire. They didn't want her in their vicinity so, with fingers crossed, they hoped she had taken them at their word and was on her way back to Jasper. Their biggest mistake was that neither of them were concerned enough to investigate to see if she had really gone.

Alfie was the first to feel a little compassion. Something about that scruffy urchin worried him. He remarked drowsily, "We were a bit hard on her, weren't we? Maybe we should have given her something to dry herself with when she emerged from the water — such as a blanket."

In disbelief Thane turned on him. He could hardly credit Alfie had said that. "What we should have done was hold her down," he exploded, not in the mood to be chivalrous. "That girl had so much grease on her, I should think the water ran off her skin and she never got wet."

"Well it doesn't matter now." Alfie yawned. "We've got other things to think of." So speaking, he carelessly threw a couple of logs into the fire and watched in fascination as the sparks exploded from the wood. He was feeling fatigued. His limbs were aching from the unaccustomed riding. All he desired was to roll up in his bed and sleep. In spite of the heat coming from the fire, he shivered. He tried to shake the tiredness off and be sociable. "I suppose in the morning we shall continue to track Raithe."

That was a sore point and Thane scowled. Everything had gone horribly wrong today and he blamed it on that precocious brat who had persisted in following them. It galled him when he thought of the precious time lost in which he could have been searching for Sue. With an effort he tried to remain cool and said, "We'll have to return to the lake to pick up his tracks; and risk being confronted by Jasper and a horde of gypsies. But I'm not about to take that risk. We must assume we've lost touch with the Prince."

"Then what are our plans... " Alfie began, but broke off in midstream because Thane slowly reached out and picked up his bow, carefully notching an arrow. "What are..." he started again — but Thane cut him short. "Alfie... do you sense something wrong?" he hissed urgently.

Alfie stared around uncertainly. He could see as far as the firelight allowed, which just about picked up the horses. Beyond them was darkness, black and impenetrable, since clouds above obscured any starlight. He understood what Thane was asking. An unnatural silence surrounded the area and the wind was non-existent. He chewed on his lower lip. "If there was anything wrong, surely the animals would warn us." As he spoke, he prodded White Hawk with his foot, "Especially this one."

His prod was not gentle and normally White Hawk would have been on his feet with a snarl — but to their amazement, he remained insensitive to their touch. Thane's eyes narrowed and his fingers tightened on the bow. "Push White Hawk harder," he ordered grimly, "I don't like the look of this."

Startled, Alfie did as he was told but the wolf lay like an inanimate object. Thane then realised he must have been drugged and they began to feel very uneasy. In an act of defiance meant for anyone who might be watching them from within the darkness, Thane shot an arrow — not aimed anywhere in particular, but just to let whoever was out there know they were aware of their presence.

The arrow sped away but its flight ended abruptly as it hit an unseen shield and fell harmlessly to the ground. There was no need to warn Alfie to be on guard as he had already grasped a knife, small though it was and he tried to pierce the gloom with his eyes, but his body came up in goose-pimples as a low seductive laugh floated out from the dark, and a voice said, "Put that thing away, Mister, before you cut yourself. There is nothing you can do now because you are already my prisoners."

With surprising agility Thane leapt to his feet, glaring in the direction from which the voice came. He could not see anyone and anger seethed through him. He blamed himself for falling into this trap. Because of his own inadequacy, he had failed to pick up the small signs which had been flaunted before his eyes. He should have known by the superb control of a horse that she had the lighting of a fire without the use a tinderbox. All these things had been subtly camouflaged by the little girl act. Anger made his voice sound chilly.

"Only cowards hide in the dark," he said cuttingly, "Show yourself, girl. Is this your revenge on us for throwing you in the water? Just be aware I would willingly do it again. You smelt like a dead polecat."

229

The laughter ceased abruptly and in the silence which prevailed, they both felt jittery. When the girl decided to speak again her voice sounded puzzled. "How did you know it was me?" she asked. "You can't see in the dark. No mortal can."

Thane declined to answer the question. His voice still retained its cutting edge as he snapped. "Who are you? Certainly not the impudent gypsy you would have me believe you are. Your powers are remarkable, girl, especially as you were able to get near enough to my wolf and drug him — and the horses." He jerked his head towards the sleepy stallions. "Don't let's forget them."

He was rewarded with another tinkling laugh, which made his hackles rise. "I told you I was fey."

"Then why do that to them? If you are fey they wouldn't harm you."

"I do as my Goddess bids," she answered simply.

"Goddess?" Alfie repeated voice was full of awe and ridicule at the same time. "You've got Goddesses in these parts? Is she the sort of woman with a divine status and a halo round her head as she floats through the heavens dishing out retribution on people like me?" He paused for breath and ignored Thane's frantic warning. "I don't believe in all that mumbo jumbo," he continued recklessly, "So is your Goddess about to strike me down because I'm an unbeliever?"

"You would be dead by now if she did. Tell me, young man, Why do you blaspheme on things you have no knowledge of?" a soft seductive voice asked as a slender woman stepped out from the darkness, with a very young girl following behind her. Her mystical beauty held them tongue-tied as her aura engulfed them.

Thane and Alfie lost all control of their emotions. They gawked at the apparition, which glided forward to stand before them. Her lustrous long dark hair, black as a raven's wing, floated sinuously around her bare shoulders, reflecting a thousand stars as it swayed to the rhythmical movements of her body. Two compelling dark eyes gazed from her beautiful face; they were so magnetic, and both lads felt they were being drawn into them and drowning. Her diaphanous gown of silver shimmered as the glow from the flames caught it — as did the diadem of crystal encircling her head. The girl beside her presented no competition as the Goddess's charisma completely overshadowed her. She stood to one side, watching proceedings through glowering eyes.

The Goddess snapped her fingers and White Hawk raised his head and looked around. Without her making any manual signs, the wolf scrambled to his feet and padded to her side. This simple act proved to Thane that her power overrode his authority. Ruffling White Hawk's fur, she stared through half-closed eyes at Alfie, then concentrating on White Hawk she said, "What shall I do with this brash young heathen, wolf?"

Thane exhaled — not trusting himself to speak, but inwardly fuming. He was wise enough to realise the Goddess had the upper hand and he sincerely hoped Alfie was not going to goad her any further. They needed to wait until she revealed the reason why she was here. Thane lowered his bow and Alfie took his cue from him and made to put his knife back in his clothing — but to his horror, he found his hand fixed, it would not move in that direction.

231

Then some hidden power forced it towards his throat. The lethal blade, catching reflections from the fire, glinted as if with red malevolence. It might not be much use as a weapon, but its sharp bevelled edge could do a lot of damage to someone's soft throat. His terror made him utter a strangled cry for help as he fought to win a losing battle. Sweat ran down his face and into his mesmerised eyes — but there was nothing he could do to halt the direction in which his knife was moving.

Thane's fury snapped at last. With an articulate oath, he grabbed at Alfie's hands in an attempt to stop the momentum. His muscles bunched as he found his puny strength was no match against the power that motivated Alfie's hand. Even trying to prise his fingers open was useless — they seemed glued to the handle. In desperation he turned and glared at the watching Goddess.

"What's the matter with you?" he spat out furiously, "Can't you see he's a stranger to this land? He knows nothing of our customs, or your power. You are certainly not endearing yourself to either of us, or our King, whose business we happen to be on."

His words left the Goddess unmoved. A bright spot of red stood out on Alfie's throat and his mouth opened to scream. The Goddess did not move, but she snapped, "Enough is enough, Fleura," and the girl beside her mumbled something. "Stay." Alfie's hand relaxed and the knife fell to the ground with a thud. His knees buckled, and Alfie fell, his body shaking like a leaf. He turned into a gibbering idiot. Suspicion flooded Thane's eyes — he glowered at the girl accusingly, and then directed his look

232

to the Goddess. "So you have menials to do your dirty work."

The Goddess turned her head and surveyed the girl reprovingly. "You take your fun a little too far, Fleura," she admonished softly, "There was no need to draw blood. He is not a bad man. You must learn to discriminate."

The girl pouted. "He called me a filthy gypsy and threw me in the stream. He did not discriminate. It was only right to get my own back," she remonstrated.

The Goddess smiled sadly. "That is not what we teach you. Always remember you reap what you sow, Fleura — this time you chose the wrong action and let yourself down." The Goddess turned back to the dumbfounded Thane, who had his arms round Alfie and was endeavouring to help him to his feet. The way he looked at the precocious girl showed exactly what he thought of her. Thank goodness they had seen the last of her, she would surely go with her mentor, but the Goddess's next words squashed that idea.

"Fleura is going to be staying with you both." She pretended not to notice the way they both stiffened, with violent objections on their lips. "You are going to need a guide who knows the way to the Enchanted Land. Your Princess — unless she is extremely lucky — is going to be in grave danger. A lot depends on her outlook. Too many people are trying to make her work for them. She is going to be in need of true friends." A strange smile crossed her face as she added, "I cannot vouch for the way Fleura behaves. That will depend on how you treat her."

233

Before Thane could answer, she vanished into thin air. The wind suddenly gusted through the trees as though some hand had released it and he knew, without trying to move, that the shield had been lifted. The horses raised their heads and whickered. Only the girl stood before him, her eyes flashing with defiance. Thane hastily choked down the sarcastic remark he was about to make. He remembered she was no child. She was whatever she wanted to be and was volatile and dangerous.

CHAPTER 17
THE BUBBLE PRISON

Priscilla was thin and her bones stood out at strange angles. The illness had sapped away all her strength. Her once thick dark hair in which she had taken so much pride was now lank and lustreless; pulled back from her face and tied in an unbecoming ponytail. Her heavily lashed eyes looked bruised. On the rare occasion when she was asked to raise her hand, the skin covering her veins appeared translucent and the actual limb resembled a claw. Priscilla would never know how lucky she had been to survive the bite of a red spider.

Each day found her languishing on a low bed which was placed on the balcony of her room. This gave her a view of the city, which surrounded her on all sides. Although she saw domes, turrets and graceful spires rising to the sky, the beauty of the buildings did not inspire her imagination enough to make her want to investigate, and none of the people hovering in the vicinity of her bed aroused any emotion within her.

Priscilla wanted to go home, where everything was familiar. She must have been mad, wanting to come to this world. But one thing worried her and she never mentioned it to anyone. She had intangible visions of a good-looking fellow with a homely face and nice smile who had acted as her guide before she became ill. She had no idea where he was. Maybe he had decided to find his uncle, the odious Professor Harding. A slight shiver went through her — she never wanted to see the Professor again. Lots of people came to this room and insisted on speaking to her. They seemed to know her name and that she was related to Sue and Barry. This confused Priscilla even more because she was convinced she had never seen them before in all her life. One elegant lady with long black hair, told her she was Sue's mother, Ruth, who was the mysterious missing sister. She remembered the Professor wanted to know what had happened to her. The first smile in ages touched her lips, and seeing it, Ruth, who had been watching her from the door, came forward to stand by her side.

"How are you feeling today, Priscilla?" she asked in a low gentle voice, and Priscilla quickly averted her eyes before she let herself down by crying. She never did that sort of thing. That was for babies. Even so, she was upset because Ruth looked so much like her own mother, and Moria. Ruth waited a few seconds before she reached out and placed her hand gently on the girl's head. "When you're feeling stronger, dear," she went on, "You must try to go out and put some colour in your cheeks."

There was no response from Priscilla. The very idea of leaving this room terrified her. Ruth sighed. A change of environment would do her the world of good. She wondered whether to press ahead and tell her of Tam's plan, but the thought of a scene with Priscilla made her quail. She took the cowardly way out. Maybe tomorrow Priscilla would be in a better frame of mind, but at that precise moment, Tam entered the room, fully convinced his wife had informed the girl of his intentions, and said brightly.

"All is ready. The girls are outside with the dragons."

By Priscilla's response to those words, he could have just passed the death sentence on her. A strangled gasp left her lips and her face turned white. With eyes widening with horror, she squeaked, "Dragons!" In her mind she visualised the big black dragon which had held her hostage. "No! No!" she shouted and shrank away from him. "I'm not going anywhere. Please let me stay here."

There was a poignant silence following her words. Tam glanced at Ruth, realising his mistake, but he had no intention of backing down now. The Shaman knew what he was talking about when he advocated she should go away from here. He had Annalee and Tansy's support. They would stay with her.

So, ignoring the appeal in her voice, he said, "It's for your own good, Priscilla." His voice was suddenly brusque, yet kindness filled his eyes. "You are not getting any stronger here. In the forest with the girls you will get plenty of fresh air and freedom and learn a different way of life."

"If I can't stay here, I want to go home," Priscilla answered firmly, to which Tam retorted artfully, "Well, that would be a pity. Alfie will be heartbroken at your decision."

"Alfie." Priscilla looked up at him. Bright spots of colour stained her pallid cheeks. Tam knew he had been correct in his assumption that there was a mutual feeling between them. She was flustered and for the first time in ages showed interest in her surroundings. "Where is Alfie?" she queried tentatively.

Tam moved towards the window and called out to someone below, and then turned to give his whole attention to the languid girl watching him through feverishly bright eyes. "He is making his way in this direction but it will take several days to get here. He was more than upset on hearing about your illness and I had to be firm with him and stop him from seeing to you. Now I'm sure you wouldn't want him to see you like this — so consider my proposition. Go with the girls until you look like your former self."

The offer was tempting, but still Priscilla hung back and was not convinced. "I don't get on with girls," she muttered lamely.

Ruth laughed at her naivety and gave her a motherly hug. "You'll get on with Tansy and Annalee," she assured her. "They don't act like girls and they're dying to skive away from their work. As for the dragons," she paused momentarily, trying to assess Priscilla's reaction, "They are friendly ones. The two girls ride them all the time. One will be with you and introduce you to the thrill of riding on their backs. If you're anything like Sue, you will love the experience."

Priscilla felt the first thrill of excitement. The feverish look dimmed and a glow of expectancy took its place. "Exactly where am I going?" she asked, looking at Ruth.

"To my forest retreat," Ruth answered simply, "high in a redwood tree. Take my word for it. You will love it there — and when Alfie comes here, we will fetch you back."

* * *

The freezing atmosphere bit deep into their bones, their teeth chattered and Barry and Zeno felt they were encased in ice as they stumbled mindlessly along a dark wet tunnel; guided by forms they could not see. Their feet were numb and occasionally droplets of something icy hit their heads and ran down their neck. This added more shivers to those they already had. The unseen people propelled them along, causing excruciating pain to their flesh when they inadvertently touched their arms or legs. The slightest deviation on the part of the two lads caused an icy sword to penetrate their bodies. They had no way of knowing if it was accidental or deliberate.

Barry clung to Zeno to receive some warmth. Their bodies were the only source of heat in this oppressive subterranean passageway. Barry did not recognise Zeno, he was a stranger captured at the same time as he was, but he couldn't help wondering what he, or this other fellow, were doing in this dark inhospitable place because his memory had been wiped clean. Yet one thing was clear; if his momentum stopped, the sharp pains came back with a vengeance.

A glow appeared ahead and looked welcoming. It spoke of warmth, which he was eager to embrace. Barry was happy they were going in the direction of the light. There was no need now for anyone to chivvy them along, as eagerness filled their limbs and moved their legs forward — but it seemed to take forever to reach the light. When they did, they received a nasty shock because they were able to see their captors clearly.

The walls of the tunnel fell away and they found themselves in a huge subterranean cavern from which glowing light seeped from pitted walls. From this illumination they were able to see it was the meeting place of the most bizarre people they had ever seen. Barry quickly looked towards Zeno, thankful at least that he looked normal. Then a frown creased his forehead as he belatedly wondered what on earth he was doing here with this stranger. Surreptitiously Barry studied the blank face, realising he looked just what he was — a man without a memory, like himself. It made Barry wonder if he had any friends. If only his mind were not so fuzzy.

He looked closely at his captors. These strange people possessed huge heads, which at first glance appeared like skulls, covered with tightly drawn skin. The enormous dark eyes of their captors appraised the gawking lads. They were the only features about them that looked human. With bodies covered in a dark cloth, draped over bony shoulders for modesty, they looked like walking skeletons. The worst part of this vision was the massive hands and feet, which appeared gross and made their skin crawl. They looked like the kind of apparitions one met in a nightmare. As the boys were pushed in amongst them, the mutants fell back and made a pathway for them to walk.

At this point, Barry realised these people were more intelligent than he had thought. The two who had been leading them paused, and scrutinised the lads. They gave the impression of being in charge, but they looked no different from anyone else. One lifted a hand and beckoned them forward. The two lads stared at each other and some sort of recognition stirred in their eyes, but they dithered for too long and, from behind, someone gave them a push. The ensuing pain caused them to gasp and brought wetness to their eyes. Automatically they stumbled after the two skeletal people ahead of them.

The area was no warmer, for the entire glow from the walls was just an illusion. By the time the leaders stopped again, Barry and Zeno were dragging their feet, hardly caring what was going on around them. Something insubstantial shimmered before their eyes. An archway led them into the glow — maybe this time it meant there was a fire and they advanced willingly. The skeletal people who had guided them this far stood aside and pointed for them to go through the arch. They did not argue — it looked so inviting — they held each other up and stumbled through. The archway vanished and Barry and Zeno were trapped in an insubstantial bubble suspended over a bottomless chasm — but the sudden change from a freezing atmosphere to unaccustomed warmth sent them both to sleep.

* * *

Barry felt someone shaking him vigorously and did not take kindly to being dragged back from a dream. He tried to resist but the person shaking him was persistent. In the end, he gave in, mumbling a protest, which came out with slurred words, "Leave me alone."

"For goodness sake, man, open your eyes," said a voice, "We've got to escape from here." The final shake was much stronger than the others and Barry's eyes opened with a jerk. For a moment everything was bleary, and then he made out Zeno bending over him looking extremely harassed.

"What is it? Where are we? What's the matter?" Barry struggled into a sitting position but wished he hadn't changed his posture. The ground moved beneath him and he experienced a feeling of swaying two and fro, almost losing his balance. When he looked down, he realised with a shock there was nothing below him except a vast dark pit, and his stomach felt queasy when he saw the floor was transparent. Darkness swirled beneath their prison. Barry did not try to speculate what held them up; instead, he closed his eyes, because any movement on his part rebounded tenfold. "In God's name, Zeno — where are we?" he asked hoarsely.

"Some sort of prison," replied Zeno, his voice was shaky. "This looks a very fragile affair to me and I should think it could plummet down at any moment. It's got the texture of a balloon, so be very careful how you move," he added unnecessarily. "I've got no idea how it stays in mid-air." As he spoke, he looked upwards, expecting to see a huge hook, but the translucent sphere had no appendages and defied gravity by swinging where it was. Such a delicate prison could not hold two hefty young men suspended in mid-air forever.

Barry inhaled deeply, attempting to settle his nerve as he gazed down between his feet to where darkness swirled below like a devilish monster, hiding a multitude of dangers from his eyes. He tried ineffectively to penetrate the balloon and the darkness. "What do you think is down there?" he queried at last, unsteadily. "How deep do you reckon the drop is? This might be a ploy to keep us still up here."

Zeno had no ready answer. It was taking all his willpower to hide his own unease, and he felt it was up to him to show some sort of authority. They both felt a malevolent power surging up to meet them from the chasm. The inside of the sphere was pleasantly warm, and although it was completely sealed, air brushed their faces, enabling them to breathe. This ingenious invention could only be something conjured up by the Priest — and because of that, Barry had no faith in its durability.

He studied the balloon minutely, seeking out flaws, and reached to touch its shiny sides. It bulged out at once and took on the shape of his hand almost as though it were pliable. This gave him the idea of pushing his whole body against it — but the flexible substance merely adapted to his form, showing no signs of any breach in its makeup. It was indestructible.

Barry frowned, concentrating fiercely on how their prison was formed. It was translucent and light as a feather. There had to be an opening somewhere, otherwise how did they get inside? It was more pliable than rubber and porous enough to enable them to breathe. He wondered if his knife would be strong enough to cut through it, and with that thought, he started to search frantically through his pockets. Zeno watched him, eyebrows raised, and said dryly, "They've removed my bow and arrows — what makes you think they've left you with a weapon?"

Failure to find the knife goaded Barry to say, "I thought you were the one who wanted to escape."

"I still am, but don't you think you're going the wrong way about things. Use some of that grey matter of yours. If you had your knife you would make a cut in this sphere, and it would plummet down below, where anything could be lurking to devour us."

The other lad stiffened but the sense of that remark niggled. Barry returned to the centre of the sphere, by no means mollified. Hunching up his knees and glowering with anger, he let his fingers still search. "Someone has stolen my dagger — and it was the one Raithe gave me," he growled indignantly. "They must have searched us while we slept and I think that downright underhanded."

"You were not specially selected," Zeno answered calmly. "You're overlooking the fact that I was robbed as well. Look at it this way, Barry. The Drazuzi have not tried to kill us... yet." The last word came out belatedly.

"Is that supposed to make me feel better?"

"No — but there must be a reason for keeping us alive," he reasoned.

"You bet there is. It's called slow torture." Barry stared gloomily down to where the glowing walls depicted a narrow path. Unbidden, he started to visualise his life spent in a bubble from now on, and it was too hard to contemplate. He would go mad. It was little compensation to him, to realise that down by those glowing walls it was icy cold, whereas in this sphere it was nice and warm. The last thing he could remember was climbing the cliff face with Zeno — and then darkness had fallen. They had shouted for a light and someone told them to get down the same way as they had got up. Amos! Then everything became a blank until he woke up in this bubble. Suddenly he came out in a cold sweat. He might have been in this bubble for months. Surreptitiously he rubbed his chin to feel if he had a growth of hair — then he caught sight of Zeno looking at him with a grin on his face.

"It's not funny," he growled, going red, but Zeno was not listening. His eyes had fallen on a small figure struggling along the path, trying to carry a basket which was far too heavy for him. The person was obviously heading in their direction.

"I wonder if sound carries through these translucent walls," he mused excitedly. "We could shout for help."

Barry dampened that idea immediately. "The Drazuzi don't speak," he retorted sourly. Zeno, however, shouted, "Hi! You down there. Can you release us?"

Barry's attention was riveted at once. The figure down below with the basket stopped and looked at them. It had to be a boy; his stick-like arms waved in the air and his huge eyes watched them without blinking — then to Barry's disappointment he turned back to his basket.

"Told you," he grunted, and returned to studying his hands and wallowing in despondency, but Zeno whooped excitedly. "We're going to be fed."

"Wishful thinking," was Barry's servile answer, then he realised the sphere was slowly descending and he watched the boy becoming larger. As soon as they were level with the path, the bubble stopped, but it was too far out from the wall for them to think of jumping should the opportunity arise.

"Come on," Zeno rallied him, "Get ready to catch it," and Barry's mouth fell open with chagrin as he realised Zeno could pick up the language of these strangers the same as Tansy could. What was wrong with him? Why couldn't he? Was he thick?

"No." By the amused smile on Zeno's face, Barry knew he could pick up his thoughts. "You're just not tuned in to them."

Barry had no time to answer because the boy started throwing objects in their direction from the basket. Both Zeno and Barry could be forgiven for expecting the items to bounce off the outer wall of their prison, but to their amazement, the food passed straight through and fell at their feet. There was no breach in the balloon whatsoever where it had entered. Barry gulped, and his mind boggled. What had stopped it from passing straight through and out the other side? Delicious smells rising from the food made him realise he was hungry. He looked at the figure that was about to move away and shouted, "Thank you."

Unexpectedly the young Drazuzi turned. He stared at the sphere for a while before resuming his journey, but Zeno said quietly to Barry and told him the boy said, "Enjoy your meal. My name is Honda."

CHAPTER 18
FLEURA

Emotions had reached a knife-edge. The girl made no attempt to conceal her dislike of the two lads. They in their turn pointedly ignored her very existence. The Goddess had thrown them together, but she could not make them be friends, even though the girl was now clean and tidy and could no longer be described as a dirty gypsy.

From the very beginning of their journey, Thane stipulated that since she was coming with them, she was to ride either behind him or Alfie — or else walk. Her answer to that was instantaneous. She sprang nimbly onto the back of the packhorse, perching precariously amongst all the bundles, and glared at them. The stallion was already laden for the journey. Beyond twitching his ears, the horse showed no other sign of the extra burden. She looked down her nose at the exasperated Thane, and in no uncertain language implied she would sit where she wished. They were not her masters — and since she wished to ride that stallion they would just have to put up with it.

"In which case," Thane replied placidly as he turned to Alfie, "We will camp here for a few nights. Can you unload him, Alfie?"

Alfie, having just spent fifteen minutes loading the pack horse, stared at Thane as though he had taken leave of his senses. Then he saw Thane's wink, and understood.

247

Playing his part to perfection, he assumed a dour expression and walked back to the placid packhorse where he proceeded to remove water flasks and packages from its back. Fleura looked down on him from her lofty height with mocking eyes. They were not the eyes of a child any longer and they dared him to touch her. It was her downfall because she had never met anyone like Alfie before and he stoically ignored her presence as he methodically worked. But he was wary of her and battled with his emotions, which were running haywire, while he tried hard not to let her undermine him. Unused to being slighted, Fleura became deliberately obstructive — unaware that Alfie could remove her with a single blow from his hand should he choose to do so. She continued blissfully on with her campaign of harassment.

Alfie, being a gentleman, made no attempt to put his thoughts into action. After the incident of his knife, he was more wary of her. Before he realised what was happening, she started to act provocatively, allowing her bare legs to dangle where she knew he had to put his hands. Alfie's mouth went dry, he could feel his face burning. He looked towards Thane for help. Thane, rekindling the fire they had just let go out, said sharply, "Bring the flasks over here, Alfie."

Relief made Alfie all fingers and thumbs as he grabbed hold of the items with unnecessary speed, anything to get away from her. He knew the girl above was laughing at him. He could feel her supercilious smile creeping under his skin. He reached Thane's side and dropped the packages at his feet, and was about to move back for more when Thane caught hold of his arm.

"Don't give her the satisfaction of knowing she is unnerving you," he breathed softly, "Calm down, lad. She is playing the oldest game in the world. If she finds you are not impressed with her beguiling manner, she might ride out of our lives for good."

Ignorant as he was about anything concerning women, Alfie straightened his shoulders and walked stalwartly towards Fleura, but before he reached the patiently waiting horse, he heard her precocious voice say, "How very ungallant of you to think of leaving me. You had best remember I can do anything." Although she finished speaking with a smug smile on her face, both lads detected the threat underlying her words. Alfie looked uneasy, but Thane turned slowly to survey her. Instead of being impressed by her words, he answered insultingly,

"You can't do everything, young lady. There are some things beyond your capability."

As he expected, his words stung her pride, and anger turned her face into an ugly mask. The little girl had vanished and the former enigma returned. Her eyes were unveiled and full of loathing. "You dare to ridicule me, mortal," she spat. "Do you want me to show you what else I can do?" Suddenly the fire before Thane combusted and a sudden squall sent burning logs in all directions, spreading the fire over the surrounding dry grass and small shrubs. Added to that chaos, a deluge of rain then fell and extinguished the flames, soaking the two lads in the process. The stench of burning and the smoke suffocating their chests was not enough for Fleura. Lightning then struck in their direction and split the nearest tree to them down its middle. It fell with a crash, making the horses rear in terror.

With triumph blazing from her eyes, Fleura watched them with her arms folded; she wanted to see what their reaction would be. To her annoyance, Alfie did not look in her direction, but moved immediately towards the horses and calmed them down with a few soothing words, while Thane removed his jacket, squeezed out the excess water and returned to making up another fire. Fury made Fleura quiver. "Well!" she postulated, feeling decidedly peeved, "If that wasn't enough for you — do you want me to show you some more?"

Thane turned to her wearily, and said as though he were calming a rebellious child, "We've all got magic, Fleura, in one way or another. No one here doubts your magical powers. If I thought it would help, I would show you what I could do, but this isn't a contest of power. If I might remind you, you stated you could do anything, and I said you couldn't. That still stands." He held her attention without blinking and her eyes narrowed.

Alfie braced himself for another explosion of magic, but although Fleura was outraged that a mortal would dare to argue with her, curiosity suddenly got the upper hand. Shifting her position slightly, she snapped petulantly, "Then you've got five minutes to prove your words — if you can. After that you will wish you had never met me. Just what can't I do, mortal?"

Alfie hardly dared to breathe, but Thane was unperturbed and stared at her calmly. "You have no idea how to show friendship, generosity or compassion. Had you any of these attributes, we would not be fighting like this."

Fleura's mouth fell open in astonishment and somewhere in the air came a tinkling laugh. She eyed Thane uncertainly, and her voice became hesitant as she said, "If I don't stick up for my rights, you wouldn't listen to me. You would treat me like a child and, and throw me in the water."

Thane stepped towards her and his smile was genuine as he held out his hand, which she eyed suspiciously. "Be fair, Fleura," he said, "You did ask for it, appearing to us like you did. Suppose we call a truce now and start by trying to get on with each other?"

She slid reluctantly off the packhorse, showing an alarming amount of bare leg, which made Alfie quickly avert his eyes. "Why can't I ride on this horse?" she asked, ignoring his hand.

"Because he's already got a lot to carry and it wouldn't be fair to him. So! Will you ride with me?" he asked.

"No!" A wicked light gleamed in Fleura's eyes. She had not missed Alfie's reaction and still harboured a mischievous streak. "I'll ride with him," she said, and to Alfie's dismay, she pointed in his direction.

* * *

The ill-assorted trio travelled together for two days, and after that time had elapsed there was a remarkable difference in their compatibility. Fleura realised there was no need to flaunt her magical powers to gain attention from the two lads and they were extremely indebted to her for the knowledge she had of the terrain in which they were travelling. Fleura remained silent when Thane schooled Alfie in the correct way of using a bow and

251

arrow for hunting, and she turned a blind eye when observing their frustrated efforts at fishing — a job she could have accomplished with her eyes shut. Only when they asked for her help did she surreptitiously use a little magic. As she lost her arrogant mannerisms, the two lads found Fleura a delightful companion. She took turns in whom she rode with, but whenever possible, Alfie was chosen because she was aware her presence made him uncomfortable, and it delighted her to be able to make him flustered. To Thane's dismay she took great pleasure in plaguing Alfie with her womanly wiles, and she was elated to realised she had the power to embarrass him. Fleura saw no wrong in her actions, but Thane was sorely tempted to put a stop to her subtle manoeuvres because Alfie was turning into a nervous wreck.

After watching the two of them through half-closed eyes, Thane decided — rather reluctantly – that the lessons Alfie was receiving could only do him good, and to Fleura it was all harmless fun. By the time Alfie met up with Priscilla again, she would find he was a different character.

They were riding through the forest on their third morning, feeling the sun hot on their back each time they emerged from the shade of the trees. The heat made their skin unpleasantly sticky, attracting all sorts of insects. Travelling was not fun for the lads, but Fleura seemed immune to the biting insects. She had no sympathy for them. At times Alfie felt like swatting her instead of the flies. They kept to the forest because it gave them some protection, and the flies were not so voracious when under the shade of the trees. Large red wheals had already come up on Alfie's neck. They were driving him mad.

Each time he raised a hand to scratch, Fleura rebuked him as though he were a small boy. She was saved from his anger because with a suddenness that startled them, the track broke out from the cover of the trees, and a huge expanse of grassland was before them.

It spread undulating for miles. The heads of the tall grasses bent and swayed as a cooling breeze caught them. Thane saw three tracks before him and knew that one of them would eventually lead him to the Snake Queen's domain. It would take at least another three days to travel there because the mountains in which she lived were only an indistinct blur at the moment. Yet even as he urged his horse one step in that direction, Fleura twisted round to face him.

"Why are we going this way? This is all wrong. Our path lies along the edge of the forest."

Although he agreed with her, Thane did not acknowledge she was right. He wondered why he was so obsessed with Deena. Was it because he no longer trusted her? According to the Goddess, Sue was already in the Enchanted Land. He was about to explain what was in his mind to Fleura, when Alfie decided he had had enough and took the law into his own hands. "At least out there the air will be cool and clear of all these infernal flies," he exploded. Not waiting for anyone to agree with him, he slapped his stallion and urged him out into the grass. He never heard the sharp "No!" from Fleura. The breeze fleetingly touched his flushed face, and then it happened so swiftly — he was covered with flies and was blinded. Alfie screamed out in fear as the flies massed from nowhere about his head, so thickly they buzzed in his ears and hair. They entered his nostrils, and settled round his eyes and mouth. He waved his arms like a demented lunatic, beating himself uselessly.

With a hand raised, Fleura uttered one word and they all vanished, but for Alfie it was too late. The experienced nauseated him and he trembled, still beating his head with his hands. Fleura uttered a command and his stallion returned to where they stood, but she discreetly ignored Alfie's condition and spoke sternly to Thane. "We cannot go that way — it is not necessary. Anyway, the Snake Queen has nothing to do with the way the Princess was taken."

"Then who was?" asked Thane harshly.

"I am not at liberty to tell you but it is my job to get you safely to the Enchanted Land so that you are there to help her should she call for you. I will ride with Alfie now," she added abruptly, and so saying, she slid off Saturn and sprang nimbly up to sit in front of the neurotic lad. There was barely any skin on his face which had not been bitten. It was red and puffy and his eyes had almost closed. Fleura lifted both her hands and placed them gently on each cheek. Alfie did not move — then she leant forward and kissed him lightly on each eyelid. The release from irritation was instantaneous.

A shudder passed through Alfie and he stared into her beautiful dark eyes with a gratitude that almost overwhelmed him. He was now her slave for life and Thane turned away with a sigh. There was no way he was going to beat her. Alfie was much too chivalrous to ever snub her again.

White Hawk decided to leave them, returning amongst the trees. They rode onwards along the narrow track winding just within the tree line, and the sun made dappled patterns on the earth beneath their feet. They soon forgot the horrific scene with the flies. Thane studiously tried to ignore Fleura and Alfie, but they were by his side, which made it virtually impossible. She had a way of getting under his skin. The best that could be said about her was she broke the monotony of the journey. As they turned one of the many sharp bends in the track, they came unexpectedly face to face with a band of rowdy gypsies which they had not heard approaching them. One look at their swarthy, evil faces made Thane's hackles rise, and without White Hawk they were at a disadvantage. His hand went instinctively to his knife. He saw surly amusement cross their leader's coarse features. There were six of them against him and Alfie — the odds were not on their side. The men automatically spread out like a fan around the luckless trio, preparing to ensnare them in an ambush. Their main object seemed to be the girl and they calculated the best way to get at her. Then they recognised who she was.

Alfie had grasped his knife, but Fleura knocked it from his hand and took the initiative. With head held high she spoke with sharp, precise words, which held no meaning to Thane, but certainly did to the gypsies. They cowered slightly, showed yellow uneven teeth in something which resembled a grin, and passed them by as though they did not exist. Thane replaced his knife and exhaled slowly, wondering how they had got out of that encounter unscathed. Then Alfie had to spoil it by saying smugly, "I knew Fleura would save us. She's our guardian angel. What did you do to them?" he asked. Thane saw the hero worship shining from his eyes. It made him look sick.

Fleura caught sight of Thane's sardonic smile, knowing exactly what he was thinking. She turned her back on Alfie and said with childlike candour, "I just told them to get back to Jasper as they had been out too long; and he was mad because he had expected them back days ago. Had they forgotten what Jasper was like when he was annoyed?"

Thane's lips twitched. She was so well able to take care of herself. He wondered if the gypsies knew what a canny witch she was. With Alfie feeling slightly deflated, they continued on their way. Although the water flasks passed continuously between them, no one spoke. The only sound came from the birds flitting above their heads from branch to branch. The serenity of the day soothed their emotions and the warm atmosphere made them drowsy. This could go on forever. Then for no apparent reason the sun went in, making it very dark amongst the trees. The birds ceased to sing and from being hot, they felt chilly. From the depths of the forest they heard White Hawk howl.

Instantly Thane was alerted. He did his best to peer through the leaves overhead to see if clouds were accumulating, then through the spaces between the trunks of the trees ahead to see if there was any danger. Without warning, the sun reappeared and dazzled them all.

"That was not caused by the sun," Fleura enlightened them. "It was the passing of an evil shadow. We were lucky it never saw us."

Alfie felt a chill run down his spine, wishing she would speak in plain English. "What on earth do you mean?" He tried to stop his voice from rising an octave. "If you're trying to scare me, you've just succeeded."

256

The girl looked up and a shower of disturbed leaves dribbled down on them like confetti. Fleura's evil spirit returned, making loud roaring noises above their heads. After the brightness of the sun it was hard to see, unless they looked past the trunks towards the undulating grassland. Something huge crashed onto the topmost branches above their heads, and then it was gone with another roar as it flew out into the open. Flying low, because he carried a great weight, Evonny headed swiftly towards the distant horizon. They could all see clearly that he carried a dead horse, which dangled from his massive talons.

The sight sickened Thane and rendered him speechless. His lips clamped on his teeth. He was incensed at the blatant way the dragon had disregarded Tam's terms, which stated in the treaty they had made together that all horses were to be left alone and not hunted by dragons. Eyes blazing, he spat, "There are going to be many repercussions now that Evonny has deliberately killed a horse. Before we go any further, I'm afraid we have got to find out to what person that horse belonged."

"Rainee will be devastated when she hears," Alfie muttered, and Thane turned on him impatiently. "It's nothing to do with Rainee," he snapped testily.

"It was her horse," Alfie choked.

Thane stopped in his tracks. The hairs stood up on the back of his neck. He stared hard at Alfie, as he noticed the unnatural pallor on his face.

"Are you sure, man?" he asked sharply, realising what this meant. Alfie nodded. "It was the horse Raithe was riding when he went after Sue."

The words were almost dragged out of him, but the fact that he knew they were true numbed Thane. Had the Prince been killed? And what of White Hawk giving that mournful howl? He had to find out. He was being pulled two ways. Thane decided this was more important than the Enchanted Land — that must wait. Trying to keep his hands steady, he fumbled for the horn at his side, and noticing Alfie's surprised expression explained bleakly, "This is the only way to find out if Raithe is alive or dead." He lifted it to his lips and blew twice. The sound floated away through the trees, and he strained his ears for an answer. There must be an answer. He willed it with every nerve in his body. Fleura raised her hands with the intention of giving them both some sort of comfort, but Alfie uncharacteristically pushed her aside and listened with Thane. He missed her annoyed look. Thane saw it, but at that time it didn't register. Silence greeted them. Beyond the whisper of leaves, nothing else was heard. They had just begun to think the worst when the clear notes of a horn sounded in the distance.

Thane swung round on Fleura, forgetting for the moment who he was speaking to. "Take us to the place from where the sound of that horn came."

* * *

In a small thicket of long dry grass, surround on all sides by many rocks which were half submerged in sandy soil, Raithe crouched low, unable to move. His body was burning up and the whole landscape was being bleached by an intensive sun. The heat formed a shimmering haze just above the earth, and this made it hard for him to

258

concentrate when his eyes were at that level. Raithe had not moved for several hours, blissfully unaware his skin was blistering.

He could not blot out the horrifying sight of his stallion being killed ruthlessly before his eyes, just to become food for a dragon.

It played on his mind, and no matter how hard he tried, he couldn't blot out the cry of terror from the horse, which ended so abruptly. Although it was useless now, Raithe berated himself for not being careful enough and scanning the sky for danger before he wandered off. He had only left his horse unattended for a few moments, while he foraged for food in the scrub. Raithe blinked hard to stop emotions from overwhelming him. That was all the time it had taken for disaster to strike. The last time he saw his stallion alive was when the horse was grazing peacefully, his long tail swishing gently to remove the flies.

Raithe shuddered. He felt guilty at the hard way he had pushed the horse ever since leaving the security of the caravan. It was too late now to show remorse. He was completely lost with no means of getting back home or going forward. Then he thought of the descending shadow that had been cast from the dragon to blot everything out. He hoped he never saw another one. That would be etched on his mind for ever. How swiftly it had swooped down from nowhere and landed on the horse. The slaughter was over in seconds. Evonny missed Raithe only because he was foraging in the bush. The violent impact had been a great shock to his system. Raithe collapsed where he stood, without the physical strength to move.

All too clearly, he realised he had dug his own pit by travelling for miles, away from where anyone could find him. Each day he had eradicated his tracks so there was no chance of being followed by friend or foe. It was just a matter of time now before something or someone found him — a feral animal! Or a band of gypsies — either spelt death.

Raithe eventually realised the sun was on a downward path. If he was going to put up any kind of fight for survival, now was the time to start moving. Staying where he was would only seal his doom. It was not in his nature to give in, so feeling stiff, sore and rather dizzy, he slowly regained his feet. For the first few moments he felt tottery, but once the landscape stilled, he scanned the area around him and his heart plummeted. He could not have been in a more desolate place.

Averting his eyes from the place he had last seen his horse grazing, his gaze rested on the forest. That seemed to be his best bet. It was not all that far away, but in his condition it was going to be a long haul. By the time he reached the fringe of trees, his feet hurt and his head thumped to his heartbeat. Raithe grimaced, trying to forget how his skin was burning, and the dryness in his throat which made it difficult for him to swallow. He felt for his water flask and groaned. He had left it hanging on the horse.

With a stiff upper lip he reached the nearest tree and tried to climb. In his condition this took a very long time. He was never sure how he reached a convenient fork formed in the branches. He became aware he was bleeding. A trail of blood was on the ground for some carnivorous animal to follow. He knew he wasn't high enough to save himself. When it became dark, all the predators would be prowling below. Raithe didn't want to die. What was the point of sitting up here? he wondered. Surely to light a fire to summon help was his best bet.

Then out of the blue he thought of his sister. Sue could help him and arrange a search party if he contacted her. Raithe lifted his hand to expose the beautiful ring with the wolf's head — the one link he had to the outside world. He rubbed it gently, intoning his sister's name, but after three attempts he gave up. Nothing happened. Why should it? He had no idea where Sue was. Worries about his sister now flooded his mind, and in the middle of it all he heard the two blasts from a horn filter through the forest. Someone was near enough to save him. In his haste to reply with his own horn, his fumbling fingers dropped it to the ground. Raithe was forced to scramble down the trunk before he could answer it with his own message.

Not knowing how long it would be before any searchers found him, Raithe thought it prudent to re-climb the tree. He nearly dozed off, lulled because the birds had already roosted, but something woke him. In that short time the shadows had elongated and it was becoming dark amongst the trees. Looking into the sky, now a brilliant red and mauve, he could see a circling spec. He thought Evonny was coming back for him and beads of sweat stood out on his forehead. He was a fool if he had thought the dragon had not seen him. The tree he had chosen was not exactly the best one to be in, standing proud of the forest — he had best get down and try to hide amongst the other trees, but the moving speck hypnotised him. It was circling lower. Then he noticed that amber eyes were fixed on him at ground level and was approaching. With his own eyes dilated he watched as it came closer — then he heard Thane's shout. "Raithe, Raithe! Where are you?"

"Here!" yelled Raithe hoarsely, "Just in front of the forest."

Throwing aside his fear of the amber eyes, he slid down the tree, grazing his hands on the rough bark, and White Hawk appeared beside him. Raithe swallowed hard. He could not believe he was not going to die. Then Thane and Alfie cantered up to him and the next moment they all clasped each other. Everyone was speaking at once, until a clear voice exclaimed coldly,

"So this is the Prince of the realm. Would you introduce him to me?" It was a command from Fleura.

Silence fell immediately and the temperature dropped. White Hawk disappeared into the forest and Alfie wondered why Fleura had reverted back to her arrogant self. Raithe was the only one who stiffened, and his hackles rose as he tried to step towards the horse that held her slight figure. No one ever spoke to him in that tone. This was the first time he became aware of the girl sitting proudly on its back. A girl who dared to look down on him so patronisingly. At first, he saw only the girl, but as he scrutinised her with more depth, he realised that those eyes did not belong to a girl and he felt a surge of fear. How had Thane managed to get himself involved with the Goddess?

CHAPTER 19
CLASH OF POWER

The illusion passed swiftly. Raithe saw it was the girl again and her mischievous eyes no longer tried to penetrate his mind. She was appraising him for what he looked like. Raithe had been brought up to evaluate people directly he met them, and realised with a shock she was a vessel of the Goddess. For some undefined reason, the all-powerful entity was keeping a watch on whatever it was that Thane was doing, using this child before him as a medium. He turned slightly sideways to scrutinise Thane, and wondered if he knew the reason why her personality kept switching.

Fleura leapt nimbly from her horse, putting her hands on his burning skin before he realised what she was doing. He watched her impassively. She could have been the Shaman touching him as his skin was restored to its natural healthy state. Unlike the other two, he accepted the action, showing no emotion. "Thank you for that," he told her politely, "But it wasn't necessary. By the morning the burns would have been healed."

At this snub, Fleura almost stamped her foot and said petulantly, "You're not a bit like Alfie. He likes my ministrations."

Alfie was glad he stood in the shadows where no one could see the hot colour flooding his face. She made it sound as if they were having a clandestine affair. As he tried to cover his embarrassment, Thane grinned. "I wouldn't answer that if I were you, Alfie. Women have got devious minds. Anyway, look, you've got another female to contend with now. See who else is coming."

All eyes turned to the space beyond the forest. The arrival of Silver was heralded with a tempestuous gust of wind that had the power of whipping back the hair from their sticky foreheads. As the white dragon slithered to a stop, so the daylight vanished. It would have been totally dark had there not been an aura of light surrounding Fleura, which outlined everyone standing near her. They were soon to find out that the more annoyed Fleura got, the brighter shone her aura. As the cloud of dust settled after her talons had kicked up the ground, Silver flexed her wings and assessed the small gathering. Being such a highly tuned reptile, she could hardly miss the pinpoint of power exuding from the Goddess's disciple. Neither of them was pleased to see each other, but it was to Raithe that Silver addressed herself, thus brightening up the light surrounding Fleura — who was annoyed she had been disregarded.

"Sheeka has appointed me to be the bearer of his condolences to your people," Silver announced. "He is ashamed that one of us has broken the pact, made so long ago with your father the king." She paused in her tirade because she felt Thane's eyes watching her and could pick up on his thoughts that Sheeka could never be humble if he tried. She preened her wings before adding carefully, "Sheeka is prepared to be generous. He wondered if you would like another horse to compensate for the one Evonny has taken. He is more than willing to go out and pick one up for you."

"No!" Raithe shouted out indignantly, "Whatever next." He was extremely annoyed that Sheeka could think of purloining someone else's horse without asking. He was a cunning dragon with no compunction about anything. "He can't make a wrong right by committing another wrong. Just make sure Evonny is suitably punished and my father will deal with any compensation for Rainee."

"That is the trouble, Prince," the dragon answered politely, and a puff of smoke escaped her nostrils. "Evonny has already been punished and made to look a fool by losing Priscilla... "

"Who is this Priscilla?" Fleura interrupted haughtily, but still the dragon went on as though she hadn't spoken, "He had great hopes of a reward — keeping her prisoner — yet someone was responsible for making her vanish. In some way that action contributed to his taking a horse." She suddenly thrust her scaly neck forward as she picked up on Alfie's agitation. "What a stupid name that is. Whoever heard of anyone being called Priscilla?"

Silver was happy to feel the fury building up in Alfie – but to Fleura, it could mean only that Alfie had feelings for someone else. The light of her aura shone brighter and she failed to realise the dragon was egging her on. Silver was delighted when Alfie strode right up to her, forgetting his fears in his determination to put things right. "I think Priscilla is a distinguished name and it suits her," he retorted defiantly. "I happen to like it." Then he added, "How is she?" showing all too clearly his feelings for Priscilla were real. Fleura's aura was now like a hundred watt bulb on the verge of exploding, and Silver suppressed her laugh, but only just. Her body rumbled with mirth. She was elated at the vibes coming from the girl lurking in the background. Dragons had no love for the Goddess or any of her minions. From the very start she had not been deceived about who she was — or her intentions where Alfie was concerned. Trying, with great difficulty to be solemn, Silver studied Alfie thoughtfully and said, "Priscilla is progressing slowly, but the silly child is worrying about a certain person and it is holding her back..." and to Silver's delight, Alfie muttered gloomily, "It must be Sue."

Fleura's light nearly burnt itself out. Alfie thought only of Priscilla, thinking he was a fool if he thought she still remembered him. Then he suddenly caught sight of Fleura's pinched expression and smouldering eyes. He had not realised that by mentioning these other girls' names, he was making her resentful and jealous. Silver did, and revelling in the fact, drawled,

"I can't say it sounded like Sue, Alfie." She deliberately added more fuel to the fire and her watchful eyes saw the growing discomfort in the Goddess's spy. "It sounded something like...like..."

Fleura pulled Alfie back with surprising strength for someone so small. She stood in front of him like an avenging angel and screamed to the dragon, "Go back to where you came from, you beast of the underworld." Her face was laced with suppressed anger and her small body rigid while she reprimanded Silver. With eyes flashing furiously, she said, "You have given us your message — now leave this place. You and your kind are not welcome here."

Silver reared. Her tail thrashed over the ground. Smoke and flame played round her snout, lighting up her face, and Thane stepped forward, yelling, "Stop it, you two." He spun round on Fleura whose face was contorted with hate. "Silver is a friend of ours, young woman, and you will not speak to her like that unless you wish to suffer the consequences."

"What consequences?" Fleura snapped, snarling like an animal, "She is nothing. I can get rid of her anytime I like."

"Then what's keeping you?" mocked Silver. "Look! I'm here." The dragon looked every inch the magnificent creature she was, fierce, watchful and intimidating. "Get rid of me, little girl!" she taunted.

Goaded, Fleura rushed at her with hands raised, and a series of sizzling bolts shot from her fingertips and struck the white dragon with force. Silver's mouth opened wide and the girl was engulfed in flames. Alfie turned away from the sight, feeling sick and waited for the screams to fill the air. It had all happened so suddenly, Thane and Raithe were locked in limbo as the battle went on. The atmosphere became full of the smell of burning, and alive with flashes of light and vivid flame as the two magical creatures fought for dominance. It could have continued for hours since neither one of them was going to give in. Suddenly, like a blinding light, the Goddess stood between the two fighters — neither of whom showed any sign of injury or repentance. Amazingly, her beautiful face was composed. Without raising her voice, she acknowledged Silver and spoke softly.

267

"Forgive my overzealous pupil, daughter of Sheeka. Please go ahead and do what you came to do. I will speak to Fleura in private," and so saying, she vanished as quickly as she had come, taking the girl with her.

With their going, darkness was complete. The humans could not see a hand before their faces, but normality had been restored. The stallions nickered uneasily in the dark, and White Hawk emerged slowly from the forest to Thane's side. The situation altered when Silver set fire to a bush. It made everything on the edge of the forest look eerie in the glow. Thane and Raithe went to Silver, expecting to see her scales damaged, but the dragon was in prime condition after her clash with power. The confrontation ended in the only possible way it could — stalemate. Alfie remained concealed in the forest because after what he had just witnessed; his churning emotions made him want to vomit, and he felt indirectly responsible.

"I gather you had a reason for coming here to find us," Thane remarked dryly to the dragon who, annoyingly, was ignoring them both and busy gnawing at her talons to clean them, "So Silver, when you've finished preening yourself — are we going to be informed of the reason?"

Silver swished her tail round, sending leaves scattering in all directions, then she replied blandly, "I knew you were short of a horse after what Evonny had done — so I came along to give you a lift back to civilization…"

"And disrupt our guide in the process," Thane cut in with a grunt, only to Silver that sounded like a rebuke and it put her immediately on her mettle. "Her!" she roared furiously — and the rush of air from her mouth disturbed the flames licking greedily at the bush. "You can do without that meddlesome chit. What are you thinking about, Thane? Don't you realise the Goddess is using you?"

"Possibly, but she's also showing us the way to the Enchanted Land, and protecting us," Thane answered calmly, and when Silver snorted, he added defiantly, "And that's where Sue is, isn't she?"

"Yes. I had heard she was taken there," admitted the dragon, and drew herself up, staring at the two lads fiercely. Her eyes glowed like live coals in the firelight before she said craftily, "I can take you there much quicker than that girl can."

"Thank you, Silver — but no." The offer caught Thane by surprise. He could tell the dragon was annoyed at his refusal, so trying to soften his blunt statement, he pointed out that they already had three horses and White Hawk so there was no way Silver could carry them all, and they would not separate. He paused, and added firmly, "But there is something you can do for us." At this point, Alfie joined them, and he heard Thane say. "You take Alfie to where Priscilla is."

Alfie started in surprise and was astonished at the leap his heart gave at the mention of her name. Silver's head snaked down to Alfie and her enormous face was just inches away from his. He could feel the heat radiating from her mouth as she boomed, "Will you ride with me, young man? Maybe the Prince will accompany us."

Raithe stepped back hastily and held up his hand. "Not me, Silver. I'm searching for my sister with Thane, but Alfie would be wise to go with you. From what I've seen, Fleura has got her claws into him and that makes Alfie vulnerable."

It was the thought of seeing Priscilla again that swayed Alfie to agree and override his fear of sitting on Silver's back. Raithe and Thane gave him no chance to change his mind. At any moment Fleura could be back. They tied him on securely and showed him how to hang on, and above all, they both insisted he should relax. There was one thing in Alfie's favour. It was dark so he would never see the drop beneath him.

When he was seated to their satisfaction, they stood back and gave Silver room to take off. They watched until she disappeared from sight in the night sky. For the first time in ages, Thane relaxed, but he doubted very much that Fleura would be pleased when she returned.

* * *

Thane felt as though a load had been removed from his shoulders. Much as he liked the sturdy lad from Sue's homeland, Alfie had no conception of the perils and strange customs Therossa held. Raithe, whose mind was clever and astute and who was always one step ahead of any adversary, was going to be a far better companion to have while searching for Sue.

They made camp soon after the dragon took off, using the remains of the burning bush to give them light enough to find fuel to make up their own camp fire. As soon as it was burning, they cooked and shared their food, then relaxed to work out their next move, just in case Fleura never returned. Raithe yawned and boasted he could find the Enchanted Land with his eyes shut.

That night, several animals approached their camp, but the presence of White Hawk kept them at bay. Although their fire was burning brightly and the light just reached to where the horses were picketed, the stallions were fidgety. They were very vulnerable standing on the edge of the camp, but the wolf's surveillance made sure they were unharmed and nothing came too close. Of Fleura, to Thane's relief, there was no sign. That night, the two lads slept fitfully as nature took her toll of the different incidents that had befallen them during the day. However as dawn broke with a wisp of mist seeping silently through the trees, Fleura returned, appearing unannounced.

Outwardly she looked no different, although Thane thought he could detect an aura of reserve about her. She walked straight to where they were sitting in careless abandonment, enjoying their breakfast, and sat next to them. There was no greeting, especially from her, because she took it as a matter of course that she would be welcome. Her eyes roved around the camp area as though she were looking for something. There was no need to ask what it was — Thane knew, as did Raithe — but neither lad afforded her any information or gave her permission to eat their meal. They knew if she were hungry enough, she would be quite capable of helping herself. Suddenly she said fiercely, her eyes over bright, "Where is Alfie?"

Thane had been ready for this question the moment she arrived. "He left us last night," he retorted, as though the subject were of no interest to him. "That lad's got a mind of his own, and once he makes his mind up there is no stopping him. Here, have a leg, Fleura." He handed

271

her the drumstick of their gull, which she refused with a look of distaste on her face.

"Where did he go?" she demanded angrily, pushing away Thane's hand. She had no intention of being side-tracked. Raithe looked at Thane and quirked his eyebrows, pleased he wasn't the one to have to explain things to this little spitfire. Thane shrugged his shoulders nonchalantly and his answer was very offhand as he started to gnaw at the bird's leg. "I've got no idea. He didn't say. You really ought to have some of this, Fleura," he said as he waved the leg under her nose. "It's very good — or has the Goddess fed you?"

Fleura sprang to her feet and fury began to build up in her face. She almost stamped her foot with frustration as she declared, "you are trying to hide things from me, mortal, and I do not like that." Hatred gave her voice a cutting edge. "Did that white she-devil take him away?" Because Thane refused to answer, she stormed away, incensed. "I will bring down the wrath of the Goddess and she will force her to bring him back. No one defies the Goddess."

Thane's lips twitched; in spite of trying to keep a straight face, he could not imagine Silver being forced to do anything. Detecting his amusement, Fleura tried a different tactic. She had many in her repertoire. "You must get him back," she said as her eyes beseeched him. "Alfie has no idea how to act on his own in this land."

"And because of that," Thane put in smoothly, "He has returned to civilization."

"You mean he has gone to that...that... that thing Priscilla." There was so much disgust in the girl's voice and she so looked devastated, that for one moment the watching lads thought she was going to dissolve into tears — then without warning, her whole demeanour changed.

"It is time to leave," she announced with grandeur, "You spend too much time debating useless things. Today we should reach the Enchanted Land and my job will be done. Douse that fire and I will get the horses."

Raithe never was one to take kindly to being given orders, especially from girls like her. His jaw dropped with surprise, before he had time to control it. "I don't think so," he retorted ominously. "In case you haven't noticed, I haven't finished eating yet. Do you mind waiting?"

Fleura swung round on him as though he hadn't spoken, and before he realised her intentions, she made the whole fire vanish. He and Thane found themselves staring at a patch of burnt earth. All their utensils had miraculously packed themselves onto a surprised horse and Fleura's dominance became overwhelming. She stood looking down on them as though they were of no consequence.

"Come on! Jump up! What's keeping you both?" she asked sarcastically, and before Raithe could tell her, Thane forestalled him.

"Nothing," he retorted hastily, and got to his feet. "You're riding with me, Fleura."

"No I'm not," Fleura answered pertly, and he could almost see her quivering with rage. "I'm riding with this one," and so saying, she sprang up onto the horse Alfie used to ride. Raithe clenched his teeth and in four long strides was beside the stallion. He did not even bother to make eye contact with Fleura. With a swift movement, he

273

yanked her off, depositing her body unceremoniously on the ground and stood astride her.

"No one gives me orders and no one rides with me unless they have my permission," Raithe growled, "And I have not given it to you. Remember, young lady — I am the Prince and I ride alone."

"And I'm the protégée of the Goddess," Fleura shrieked in an unladylike fashion, "And you had better remember it. I can ride where and with whom I please."

"I don't care who you are," Raithe exploded, "I ride alone, so shut up."

Thane quickly stood between them, hoping he could do something to have a peaceful life. "Raithe," he warned in an undertone, "be careful. She can… "

Raithe interrupted, glaring down at him, in no mood to be pacified, "You worry too much. Shall we get started?"

Fleura raised her hands and sent a bolt of power to the Prince's back to knock him off the horse, when something growled behind her and the hot breath of White Hawk fanned her cheeks. Meanwhile, the bolt unexpectedly shattered before it did any damage. Thane gave up with a groan. He should have guessed the Prince was prepared to repel magic. The ring on his hand was glowing, protecting him. Fleura's mouth fell open, making her look gormless. "How did you do that?" she demanded.

Raithe grinned maliciously. "When you're older I'll tell you," he replied. He turned, looking at Thane. "Who is leading?"

Having met her match Fleura turned to Thane, who made room for her in front of him on Saturn. Beyond one or two terse directions, she never spoke and Thane missed her coquettish conversation. It was late in the afternoon when they drew the horses to a halt on the crest of a hill. Down below them ran a fast moving river, through a valley dotted with caravans. The smoke from their campfires formed a haze and there was so much activity beneath it. On the far side of the river, which was far too wide to cross easily, trees grew to the water's edge, and there was no sign of life. There was no need for Fleura to tell them they were looking at the Enchanted Land. What he did need from Fleura, was to learn how to cross it safely, since no man had ever set foot on that land.

* * *

If they were honest, Tansy and Annalee would have regretted their rash promise to Tam directly they came face to face with Priscilla. She was staring at the slumbering dragons. They could have felt sorry for the pale wan girl walking unsteadily before Tam and Ruth, but the trackers were watching her carefully, and saw her thin lips tighten with disapproval. They also noticed the displeasure exuding from her eyes as she stared aghast at Firefly and Griffin.

"You must be joking." Her irritable voice was loud enough to make the dragons open their eyes. "I'm not riding those disgusting beasts. Haven't you got a horse?"

The trackers were easy-going people, but at her words hostility flared up within them, and Tansy wondered how on earth Priscilla could possibly be connected with Sue and Barry. Tansy and Annalee could allow for the illness, which made her features sharp, but her disposition left much to be desired. The dragons flexed their wings and thin wisps of smoke escaped from their long snouts, making them look awesome, and Priscilla hesitated. She detected anger in their red eyes. Tansy swallowed her ire, and trying to be pleasant, growled.

"Dragons are the kings of the sky," she retorted grimly. "You need to be careful what you say in their presence because they understand every word you utter, and they can answer you back if they think you're worth it."

Priscilla shivered, knowing already she had jeopardised their friendship, but she was remembering her fear of the black dragon. She stepped closer to Tam, who automatically steadied her. Priscilla saw him as a soft touch. Her eyes filled with tears, and in a choked voice, said. "I thought I was…"

"I thought you agreed to fly with the girls," Tam cut in roughly, refusing to listen to her, "And there is no time to start like the present. Tansy!" He directed his voice to the most amiable of the trackers. "If you climb up, I will help Priscilla to reach you," he called.

Priscilla recoiled as he edged away. "But I must…" she began.

"Come along, dear." Ruth was beside her and caught hold of her elbow. She pushed her towards the pulsating beast and caught her husband's eye, watching her. With more determination in her voice than she felt, she said, "You're going to love every minute of this adventure and…" seeing Priscilla's mouth open again, added swiftly, "We'll send Alfie to you directly he arrives here."

At the mention of Alfie, Priscilla shut her mouth firmly. Although stiff with apprehension, she allowed the king and Ruth to settle her firmly in front of Tansy. She would love to have complained about the roughness of the scales she touched and the indignity of climbing up the dragon's body, but she resolved not to say a word. Rigid with fear, she clung to some horny part of Firefly and felt Tansy's arm creep round her waist. Then the dragon took off to the sky so smoothly she hadn't realised they had left the ground. The experience of flying held her spellbound. Annalee watched their departure with a grin on her face.

"This guy Alfie must be quite a fellow if he can shut her up," she remarked, "I can see we shall have to use his name a great deal if we're going to get anywhere with her," and not waiting for Tam or Ruth to reply, she urged Griffin to follow the other dragon.

CHAPTER 20
RAINEE LEADS THE WAY

The soldiers were ready, full of enthusiasm and friendly banter. They were ready to depart, lined up in twos with their horses chafing at the bit. The delay was all due to Rainee and she didn't seem to care. Amos was acting true to form, by saying one thing to impress Thane and Alfie, before they galloped off, and then riding roughshod over everyone else. Rainee made up her mind that she was not going to be the loser in this foray. Barry and Zeno were her main concern. She could have helped them without the aid of the old man, but her disappointment in Amos was great.

She had hoped that, through Scrap, the gulf between them would have closed. She spent a long time searching her caravan for artefacts, which had been long forgotten. She never expected them to see the light of day again, but if she was going to come in contact with the Priest, she wanted them in her possession. Their size was not large, but compact, and oozing with power. She hung one round her neck, tucked beneath her blouse, and the other secreted in the hem of her voluminous skirt. There was no way, after the way he was acting, that she was going to tell the old man about their existence.

The first stumbling block concerned Scrap. Amos raised his bushy eyebrows when he saw the dog in her arms, and he turned a funny colour when she stated he was coming with them. In all his military life — whoever had heard of a pint-sized dog being one of the team? At his first reprimand at the stupidity of such an idea, Rainee lashed out and asked what sort of a monster was he to leave a defenceless animal on its own when they might be gone for weeks. He could die or be food for predators before they returned. Amos accused her of being pessimistic and spreading unease, which could upset the men.

Rainee found it hard to control herself, and returned grimly, "Then I'll stay here and you can go ahead without me. If you take me, Amos, you take my dog." When she saw the relief spread across his grizzly face at such an easy way out, she added sourly, "But it won't do you any good if I stay here. Without me you don't know where to go."

The chagrin in his expression made her want to laugh, but she admired the way he backed down without losing face. With all the men looking on, he was full of solicitude as he helped her up on the docile mare — and with more exaggeration than the episode warranted, he handed her up the squirming dog and gave it a pat. He wanted to give everyone the impression that he cared for the dog, which in fact was true, because he did have a strange affection for Scrap.

Pleased that the niceties were over with, Amos strode arrogantly to the head of the column and urged the soldiers forward. Rainee waited motionless until the last two soldiers in the line came level with her. They were not much older than Barry, and one of them turned his head and said cheekily, "You had better keep up, Ma'am or you'll be left behind."

279

Rainee snorted disparagingly as she noticed they were all heading back the way from which they had originally come and she said scornfully, "I'm not following him," indicating Amos, "the old goat has got no idea where he's going. That's not the way to the Drazuzi caves."

The two young lads pulled up their mounts, and keeping them under control, assessed her, wondering if she knew what she was saying. Their bemused expressions made her realise that there was a need for a strong leader as one of them scratched his head and said uncertainly, "But we're going to where we lost Barry and Zeno, surely that's the correct place to search?"

"Poppycock!" she retorted, "That was not the real entrance. Just a little lookout. The one that stupid old man needs is in the other direction."

"Then why…" started one of the lads, when Rainee cut him short and said, "Why don't you ride up the column and tell him of his mistake?"

There was a horrified silence and the soldiers looked aghast. Didn't this woman know one never told Amos he was wrong? The nearest one to her spluttered, "I'm too young to die, Ma'am."

Rainee glared at the gutless boy. "You'll never get anywhere unless you assert yourself," she snapped. "Have you got a horn, lad?"

"Yes, Ma'am – but…"

"Give it to me please," she demanded. "The further he goes in the wrong direction, the madder he will be when he finds out."

She almost snatched the horn from his hand and put it to her lips. It couldn't be all that hard to blow. Her cheeks puffed up with air and a strange wailing sound echoed across the land, making the soldiers cringe, but it had the desired effect. The column stopped and Amos came charging down the line, exertion making his face red. He saw Rainee with the horn in her hand and nearly burst a blood vessel. How dared she interfere? He snatched it from her hand and spluttered.

"What damn tomfoolery is this? Who gave her that horn?" he snarled. The poor soldier in question looked as though he wished the ground would open up and swallow him, because the whole column had stopped and turned in their saddles. Amos had not finished — in fact, he had only just started. "That horn is the property of the Therossan army, and no one — no one," he repeated, "Touches it except a soldier. You boy have got a lot of explaining to do and it had better be good. Otherwise I'll have..."

"Who is leading this column?" Rainee cut in sharply, breaking up his tirade.

"What's that got to do with you, woman?" the old man glared, and under the ferocity of the glare she should have shrivelled up. "This is not... "

"It's not what?" she interrupted.

"I was going to say it's nothing to do with you, so stay out of military affairs," he snapped.

"I'll be only too delighted to leave military things for you to sort out," Rainee retorted, much to his surprise. "Meanwhile, I'll go in the other direction, and if it's all right with you, I'd like to take these two smart lads with me. I shouldn't think you would need them, going in the direction you're heading."

Amos suddenly realised where his bullheadedness was taking him. He was not going to be going anywhere without the knowledge Rainee held. He met her eyes — thankful deep down that she had stopped him from making an ass of himself. He mopped his brow, saying rather ungraciously, "You start to head onwards with these two lads and I'll join you in a little while. There's nothing like giving all the men a little exercise before they meet trouble. We'll do a circle and follow you."

Rainee's eyebrows went up and her lips twitched. "If only I was as wise as you — but I'm only a woman," she murmured. She knew Amos had heard her without looking at him, and knew that his face would be burning. She caught the eye of the two lads and exclaimed briskly, "OK, lads, best leg forward, we're leading the column now."

* * *

The further east the three people rode, the structure of the bluff changed dramatically. It no longer represented a cliff face, but had become piles of dangerous rock. It was unsafe to venture near and unpredictable to walk on. Before long, the area around it would become a forest. Where Rainee stood at this moment, contemplating the view and giving her horse a rest, she was looking at the broken down piles of rock where trees covered the surface. The growth of vegetation in this part of the land was vigorous, but it was not due to natural causes — someone along the way had given a helping hand to nature.

It would take some time to find the path she was seeking and break her way through all the foliage. She squinted against the sun, looking for a landmark she knew. It had been years since she was last in this location, and everything had changed beyond recognition. Deep within her, she was pleased Amos was not with her to gloat over her inadequacy.

Rainee sighed. One tree looked very much like another and there were more here than she ever remembered. If she was honest, she had not taken much notice of the layout when she escaped. Why should she? She never expected to return. Up until recently, it was the last place she ever wanted to come back to. Now everything had altered. Barry was in there somewhere — and she liked Barry. Her escort of two soldiers was supposed to be resting.

She gave that order so that she could nose around on her own and search. She glanced briefly at them over her shoulder. They had left their horses to graze and were having fun and games on the sandy soil with Scrap. She could hear his high-pitched yelps as he got excited. Of Amos and the rest of the column, there was no sign. If the two lads were uneasy about their absence, they kept their feelings to themselves, but Rainee bit her lip. By now the rest of the column should have caught up with them.

The situation was becoming a little unnerving. Rainee brooded over Amos. Besides being an enigma, he was not as young as he used to be, and since Thane, Raithe and Zeno were gone, there was no one he could leave in charge if he felt unwell. Rainee snorted. He had the constitution of a horse. The very thought made her smile. That man would go on forever, growing more and more taciturn as the years rolled by. Why was he always so hostile? Once he took a dislike to anyone, he found it hard to reverse his opinion. Rainee gave herself a shake. She must find the path before he arrived. There was no way she was going to give him the chance to deride her leadership. She turned her eyes back to the jungle of trees, which were being strangled by greedy vines. To break through seemed almost impossible but somewhere in all that growth was a special stone, shaped almost like a horse. That was the most important thing that would guide them to the entrance.

Something struck Rainee as strange. She realised everything had gone quiet and she immediately expected danger. Spinning round, she saw the lads had thrown themselves face down on the soil and Scrap was busy digging. Her smile of relief was short-lived. Coming towards her, in the sky, were three black specks. Now her heart sank — they had to be dragons. She almost forgot to breathe as she watched them become larger, and they seemed to be heading in her direction. What possible reason could dragons want her? At a certain point, almost as though there were crossroads in the sky, they veered off in the direction where she had left her caravan. Well, that would give Amos something to think about.

Her reverie was broken by one of the lads shouting at her and asking, "Do we need a fire, Rainee?" and Rainee nodded her head, still musing over the dragons, which the two soldiers had obviously missed. It took her mind off her search. They would need a fire, because when she found the opening for which they were looking, the horses would not be able to enter. A picket line must be established out here, with men to guard it. The two lads demonstrated how well they had been trained under Amos because soon there was a fire, and mouth-watering smells of cooking. Rainee gave up searching and walked towards them. She sat down and they all ate together. Neither lad had the courage to ask outright if she had found the opening, the answer was written all over her face. When the sun started to sink, the lads took matters into their own hands and started to build a shelter — they were thinking of her. For the first time, a tinge of unease settled on Rainee. Where were the others? Nothing should have held them up for this long. Something must have happened. She had not concealed her fear enough because one of the lads said, "Shall I go back?"

"No!" Rainee's answer was vehement and it stopped further questions, but caused an uneasy silence amongst them. In another half-hour it would be dark, Rainee was thankful for the fire, it gave off a feeling of safety, and while she continued musing, one of the lads saw a movement. Their fire had attracted the attention of a passing visitor. As the lad pointed behind them, towards where the bluff used to be, something red and shimmering came crashing through the trees. A chill descended upon the watchers, but it suddenly broke free of cover and took to the sky. A massive dragon carrying two people flew over their heads. It circled once and landed a small distance away from them amidst a shower of debris caused by its huge talons seeking a hold on the ground. The glistening scales of Sheeka glowed in the light from their fire. Two men slithered off his back and Rainee's throat constrict at the sight of them. The two soldiers quickly scrambled up from the ground and stood to attention as their King walked towards them. Beside him, with a broad smile on his face came Vance, Thane's father. The dragon tried to camouflage itself in the thick foliage until it was hard to see in the fading light. Sheeka stretched his long neck on the ground, giving the impression he knew he was in for a long wait.

"Your Majesty?" Rainee made a quick bob, but Tam held out his hand and grasped hers — chivalrous as ever. "There is no need for that, Rainee," he smiled, "You and I know each other too well. In fact it was not so long ago I saw you. I thought you might like to know that the earnest young man who stood beside you on that day is now safely in the palace being looked after."

"But I thought he went with… "

"It's a long story, Rainee," Tam interrupted, "And I shall tell you more, later." He turned to acknowledge the two soldiers, putting them at their ease before he turned back to her. It was the first time that she noticed the gravity of his expression. His eyes bore into hers as he said slowly, "I'm afraid I come bearing bad news. Amos has been taken ill. It is something to do with his heart, which he has been having trouble with for many years. I am only thankful he used the device I gave him some time ago and called for help. The Shaman and I came at once, realising that events had left the column without a leader. You see, I saw where you were heading as we passed over." He turned away from Rainee, giving her time to sort out her emotions, and to the soldiers, said,

"Make room for a large camp. The rest of your mates are on their way. I've brought Vance along to keep you all in order — is that good news or bad?"

His eyes twinkled as broad grins crossed the lads' faces. Vance was well liked by the soldiers. He made none of the caustic remarks which were Amos's stock in trade. Tam now turned back to Rainee who had composed herself enough to ask if Amos was all right.

"Well! I've left him with the Shaman and Acolytes. I dare say the wily old fellow has been doing too much. He will be returning to Therossa — that's why there are three dragons. Sheeka will remain here until you and I return from visiting Oran."

The words took Rainee's breath away. "Just you and I?" she enquired.

"Yes."

"But don't we need a few soldiers with us for backup? We've got Barry and Zeno to rescue..." Rainee's voice trailed away.

Tam looked at her sternly. "Rainee, I can't believe you are not armed. I know you well enough to know you would never go back in those caves without any protection."

Rainee felt her face burn and Tam's lips twitched. "With your armaments, and my special powers, the Priest will not know what hit him."

The turn of events made Rainee feel weak at the knees and just for one uncharitable moment, she was pleased Amos was incapacitated. Tam, however, brought her back to earth with a few well-chosen words, "I will give you some friendly advice, Rainee. Unless you keep your dog under control, you risk losing him and he could suffer a horrible death."

She turned swiftly and caught sight of Scrap edging closer to Sheeka — and he was barking out his defiance at the dragon's presence and doing some sort of jig on four legs. The dragon eyed him balefully, his huge body twitching. His very stance spelt out danger, and one snap of those massive jaws would finish the dog off for good. Luckily, at her gasp, one of the soldiers quickly scooped up the squirming dog.

"I'll look after him for you until you return," he said hastily, clinging to the dog that was bent on escaping, and Tam said dryly, "That will be longer than you anticipate, son. We're not leaving until morning and now believe it or not, Vance and I are hungry."

CHAPTER 21
RAGA

Barry was full of ill humour, and wanted to vent his feelings on someone else. The only trouble was, there was no one around to have a go at. But he was desperate at being cooped up in this balloon.

Thinking back to the last time the Drazuzi held him in their power, he remembered that he had the freedom to walk around. Barry conveniently forgot about the chains round his ankles, which had rubbed his skin raw, and the slavery he had been subjected to in wet icy caves. That was a far cry from the warmth of his present prison. He glared about the balloon as though it were the balloons fault – or even Zeno's for trying to ignore him. How much longer were they going to be kept in this floating globe? Barry looked towards Zeno and felt infuriated because he made no attempt to be supportive as he lay curled up in a ball trying to sleep. Barry had the urge to kick him. How could he think of sleeping while they were suspended in this living hell? How long had they been here? There was absolutely nothing to suggest what time of day it was. Outside the sun could be shining or it could be night. Outside! A wave of longing flooded over him. How many days had it been? It felt like months to him.

No one ever passed by their prison except Honda, the boy who threw food at them, and Barry had lost count of how many times he had seen him. The situation they were being kept in was not natural. Their prison moved only when the boy lowered it. Surely there was a way out of here. It could be that he wasn't looking hard enough. He must study Honda more closely. A strange light caught his eye. It was floating towards their sphere, materializing out of the darkness, and as it came closer, he saw it was another balloon-like prison, exactly the same as theirs. Barry's eyes opened wide and he pinched himself to make sure he wasn't dreaming. Then he pinched Zeno for good measure, who sat up indignantly, rubbed his arm and asked, "What was that for?" ruefully looking at what he thought was going to be a bruise. "If you don't mind, I would rather be asleep than face this view day after day. It's a pity you don't try it."

"Look, Zeno," Barry hissed excitedly. "We've got company."

Zeno awoke instantly and crouched beside him, all senses alert. His eyes goggled as the other sphere glided right up to them, and just like any other bubbles, directly the two touched each other, they became one. The excitement of the boys was short-lived however, because the occupants of the other sphere were not prisoners like themselves, but adult Drazuzi. Devastated, Zeno slumped back down to the base of the balloon, showing exactly what he thought.

"Goodnight, Barry," he muttered, disappointment touching his voice, "They're all yours to experiment with," knowing full well he was not going to get anywhere with them, not being able to pick up on their thoughts.

Although Barry shared his friend's frustration, he was also curious as to why three Drazuzi should attempt to contact them in this way, and his active brain wondered if this unusual phenomenon could in some way be a means of escape. He eyed the three grown-ups, all looking identical and absolutely sexless. He never could tell a man from a woman — then he licked his lips, uncertain as to how to speak to them. One Drazuzi stepped closer, and feeling the glacial chill ooze from them, Barry edged away as far as the balloon allowed, but had the distinct feeling someone said, "You cannot escape, do not harbour such thoughts." It made Barry study them intently, but he soon decided he was being fanciful. There was no way he could pick up on their thoughts.

"I've seen you before, boy. You were with Golden Hair," someone said.

Golden Hair! The Drazuzi were speaking of Sue. A surge of excitement took Barry's breath away when he realised he could actually hear them talk. He must concentrate now and try to answer them back. With great effort he tried to project what he was thinking about by looking at one of them. And crossing his fingers, said, "You were the one who helped us escape?" He wasn't really sure of his facts, but it was a shot in the dark since they mentioned Golden Hair. Maybe he had said the wrong thing because for a moment the Drazuzi were silent — then that voice filled his mind again.

"Why have you returned here?"

That wasn't what Barry wanted to hear and he was indignant. "It wasn't my idea," he blurted out, speaking normally, "You're the ones who captured us."

Everything became a jumble in his mind. After that outburst, words were mixed and became indecipherable as three minds spoke together. Barry picked up on phrases like "Too many prisoners," Too dangerous," "It would never work," when one thought stood out loud and clear. "Why are your friends outside looking for a way to get in?"

"Because you've got us in here I suppose," Barry retorted swiftly. "If you let us out of here, then they would go away."

More conflicting thoughts followed and flew through his head. Zeno never stirred from his position although there was no way he could be asleep. Barry's hopes were dashed when at last the Drazuzi spoke. "They will never find a way in, and if they did, the Priest would collect them up. We cannot save everyone from him." That remark made Barry stare in surprise.

"But he's already got us, hasn't he?" he asked, "And you didn't save us, did you?"

To Barry's consternation he heard a laugh. He had no idea they could make that functional sound and he wasn't sure he liked it. "No, boy. You are nothing to do with the Priest. Surely you can see the difference. You do not have to work — you are fed and you are prisoners here at Raga's pleasure."

"Then I demand to see this 'Raga'," Barry insisted without thinking, and was met with a blinding flash as the sphere vanished. He found himself once again alone with Zeno in their prison. Outside, the impenetrable fog of darkness churned and swirled. It was as though there had never been another sphere — that he had dreamt it all. Zeno lifted himself up on one elbow and stared at Barry quizzically.

"Ten out of ten for being able to talk to them at last," he congratulated him, "But it hasn't got us anywhere."

Barry bit his lip, chagrined. He didn't consider he had handled things very well. His mind was trying to sort out the conflicting thoughts in his head. Who was this Raga? He had never heard the name mentioned before and he was sure no one outside had either. Thane was trying to reach the Priest and Professor Harding — and he was under the impression they were together. There must be two different tribes of Drazuzi in these caves? No! That was impossible and he dismissed the thought. One of those Drazuzi had known Sue — and that one had helped her escape. Feverishly, Barry tried to think back. What did that Drazuzi just say to him; "We cannot save everyone from him"?

"Zeno!" He clutched his companion fiercely, making him jump. "I think we're in the middle of two warring factions — but no one outside knows anything about it. We've got to get out of here."

"How?"

"I don't know. You're the soldier. Think."

After a few moments of silence, Zeno said tentatively, "I can think only of Honda. We must work on him. Now that you've mastered the art of telepathy, there will be two minds against one. Do you reckon we can wear him down?"

After that the waiting was intolerable for the two lads. Time stood still and weighed heavily on them as they waited for the small Drazuzi boy to put in an appearance. Their anticipation reached fever pitch when at last they saw him struggling along the path with his panniers of food, but instead of feeling elated, they were disheartened. The worst possible scenario had happened. Instead of being alone as was the norm, he was accompanied by an older Drazuzi. The two prisoners looked at each other, swallowing their disappointment. Zeno murmured softly, having no idea how far his voice carried, "We've got to ignore him this time."

"But..." was the only word Barry got out because Zeno pressed his hand in warning. "They are one step ahead of us," he hissed, "I'm afraid you've made them alert. Now try to make out you're stupid."

Although Barry quickly grasped the situation, he still glared at Zeno. It took all his willpower to ignore the small boy as their prison was lowered and the small boy started throwing packets through the balloon — an action which had long since lost its novelty. Acting as normally as they could under the unrelenting scrutiny, Zeno caught the food and Barry stacked it into little heaps. When the boy had finished, and the sphere started to move away, Zeno shouted out, "Thank you," and turned his back on them. Barry though, still watching, thought he heard the words, "Do you never speak to them?"

Honda's reply obviously satisfied his companion and they both disappeared into the darkness. Moodily, the two lads surveyed the food. The novelty of its arrival had also worn thin and they were not hungry. They got too much of it. Surely the Drazuzi had enough sense to work out that they couldn't eat the amount they were given. Then unbidden, a thought came to them. Perhaps they were being fattened up to be used as a sacrifice. That subdued them for a long time because the thought persisted. Eventually, Zeno said tentatively,

"We really ought to sing to keep up our morale."

"Why?"

"Well — it would stop us from getting depressed."

"Much too late. I already am," was Barry's grim answer, and after that Zeno gave up. Barry aimlessly drummed with his fingers on an empty vessel and the noise he produced put Zeno's teeth on edge. He closed his eyes tightly to prevent himself from staring at the uninteresting phosphorescent wall, and he hoped, that in doing so, he could shut out seeing Barry and hearing the annoying noise. Their imprisonment together was wearing them down and they considered it little better than torture. Nerves were raw and picked up the slightest sound. This was something which had not been noticeable at the beginning of their captivity. If they stayed together in close proximity for much longer, they would end up by hating each other.

Barry's thoughts were just as morose. He would have given anything to see the sun again — feel the rain on his face — and even welcomed Amos's voice. How much longer would they have to endure this? What cruel fate had made that elderly Drazuzi come along with the boy? Had he asked too many questions when he spoke to them? Was Zeno correct? Barry cast a surreptitious glance at Zeno and saw the tension in his face. If the boy didn't come along again soon, they would both go stark raving mad.

It seemed an eternity before the young Drazuzi boy returned. The food they had last received had hardly been touched, but they somehow managed to hide it by stripping off a tunic top and covering it. They watched warily as he approached, anxious to see if anyone was with him. As far as they could tell, he was alone this time and he diligently lowered the sphere by holding out his hands, palms uppermost, and nothing else.

"Is that magic?" Barry asked of him, nearly making him jump, but the young boy was put at ease on hearing the admiration in his voice. Honda paused, staring at him uncertainly. "I have no magic," he said. "I do what everyone else does."

"Well it looks complicated to me," Zeno backed Barry up. "I wish I could move the sphere by holding my hands out like you do. In fact — I wish I could try."

"I wish you could as well," Honda returned politely, "But since you're inside, there is no way you can try. Are you ready for the food?"

"Couldn't we come out and help you?" Barry's request startled him and his eyes moved from one to the other — then he dashed Barry's hopes by saying unemotionally, "It is not allowed."

"OK then," Barry said, "Give us the food." He overrode the setback with a smile on his face which was far from sincere. Halfway through emptying the pannier, Honda was just about to throw a flask when Barry said airily, "What are our chances of speaking to Raga?"

The boy immediately showed nervousness, a rasping sound coming from his throat. "Who told you of Raga?"

Barry shrugged. "I thought we were his prisoners. Why shouldn't we ask?" he said.

Suddenly the food was being thrown with speed. Honda obviously wanted to get away. It was entering the balloon quicker than they could deal with it, and one package hit Zeno's face.

"Ouch!" he yelled, "Be careful, Honda. We only want to know about Raga and who he is. We thought you looked like an intelligent boy and could tell us."

Honda hesitated, looked around, and then said, "Raga is Great White Spirit — all powerful."

"That's why we want to see him," Barry pressed relentlessly.

"No one can see him," the boy choked. "It is impossible."

Barry snorted derisively. "I bet you've seen him," he couldn't help but say, and this time the Drazuzi boy answered emphatically, "No one see him. He is the Great White Spirit. He is everywhere. He has no substance."

The lads felt their hackles rise and Zeno gasped incredulously, "You mean you can see right through him. He's — he's like a ghost?"

There was no answer from Honda, who wanted to scuttle away, but Barry was determined to find out more and his relentless barrage of questions continued. "How come someone who's got no body, can order us to be imprisoned? Come on, Honda — tell us the truth. Why are we here?"

Honda ran, leaving his pannier behind in his rush. It balanced precariously on the edge of the ravine, slowly swaying to and fro. Before Barry and Zeno's astonished eyes, the momentum increased until nothing could save it and it toppled over.

"Goodbye food," Zeno muttered regretfully, thankful they still had quite a store, but the pannier remained on its side, where it fell, and did not disappear into the abyss. For a few moments it lay there in full view and Barry sucked in his breath.

"Do you realise what this means, Zeno?" he said harshly, and anger burned within him. "There is no bottomless drop beneath us. It is all an illusion to deter us from escaping. That shows there is a way."

"It's gone now." Zeno gestured towards where the pannier had been but it was no longer there, and Barry laughed humourlessly. "I bet it hasn't. It's another illusion. Honda is going to get it in the neck, but they are playing us for fools. Are you game to try and break out from here?

Zeno bit his lip, staring into the swirling blackness. It didn't look like an illusion, but on the other hand, anything would be better than being coped up in here, so he nodded.

* * *

Honda never came back anymore with their food and Zeno suspected he had been blamed for losing the pannier in a way which had betrayed a vital secret. The knowledge, however, did not help them. They were still trapped in a sphere and had no way of getting out. Frustration built up in them until it reached fever pitch. Whether by design or accident, the Drazuzi left them without any food for an exceptionally long time, and when a pannier did arrive, two adult jailors delivered it. It had been on the tip of Barry's tongue to enquire after Honda, but at the last minute he acceded to Zeno's better judgement and left it unsaid.

Hunger was the last thing on their minds as they dutifully caught the items thrown at them through the covering of the balloon. It still amazed Barry that such a phenomenon could happen, because when he touched the sides, the sphere merely stretched to the shape of his hand, which did not go through it as the food did. The job finished, the Drazuzi turned to leave, but one spoke, and a shiver ran through Barry and Zeno as his words filled their mind.

"You will be pleased to hear your captivity is coming to an end. Tomorrow we celebrate Raga, and you two are destined to take a leading part."

Barry shook off a wave of fear and yelled out, "Who is Raga?" but his question fell on deaf ears and the two Drazuzi vanished. The idea of their being sacrificed loomed even greater in their minds. Barry was beside himself with anger and pummelled the sides of the sphere in frustration, until Zeno begged him to stop. "It's like being on a choppy sea," he complained.

"There has to be a way out," Barry growled, disregarding Zeno's feelings. "I've no intention of being a sacrifice to some Great White Spirit." He glowered at the sides of the sphere as though he expected to see the solution pinned there — his eyes were filled with a mixture of savage determination, and fear. Then Zeno muttered speculatively, "It must have something to do with the way the food passes through the balloon."

"That's it!" exclaimed Barry. Tremendous excitement filled him and he picked up an empty vessel saying, "Why don't we try throwing something out?" Before he had finished speaking, he aimed the vessel through the sphere to hit the glowing wall beyond. To their stupefaction it did just that, and shattered — but when Barry tried to follow it, he came up against the flexible barrier. Grinding his teeth, he made a disgusting noise in his throat.

"Someone who runs this underground world is very ingenious," he said and threw himself down on the floor and stared moodily at the broken vessel, sparkling like a cluster of tiny diamonds. "I really thought I had figured the mystery out," he grumbled petulantly.

Zeno knelt by the smooth wall of their prison, prodding it experimentally with his fingers — then he grinned. "I think you have," he whooped excitedly, and to prove his point, he picked up another unopened package. "Your only mistake was to let go of it. When you throw it you have to keep a hold on it and go with it. Somehow that confuses the subtle magic, which allows the package to go out, and not you. Now, Barry, you grab hold of me and remember — if only I get through and you don't, then grab another package, keep hold of it, throw, and follow me."

He did not wait for Barry to contradict him, he pushed the vessel against the balloon wall and his arm went through — his body quickly followed. Zeno had the foresight to be ready for the jump. Barry was beside him in a flash, but too late to get through himself. The wall repelled him so he swiftly picked up another unopened package, pushed it through the sphere and jumped after Zeno. He was not as careful as his friend, he tottered on the brink but Zeno quickly pulled him to safety. Breathing hard, they looked around, both filled with elation.

They were immediately aware of the chilly atmosphere and the coldness exuding from the rough walls. Shadows fell around them and a feeling of danger pressed down. Barry jerked his head in the opposite direction to that the Drazuzi usually took.

"This way," he hissed, his voice seemed to echo. "Don't let's stand here until someone catches us," and with a shiver, mixed with dread and excitement, the pair followed the path away from the sphere — which remained hanging motionless in the air.

* * *

With help from the soldiers, the formidable tangle of undergrowth which hampered their way was soon cleared, but minor accidents occurred. Two unfortunate soldiers were badly cut by vicious vines and another received a bite from a bad-tempered fox whose den had been disturbed. These were flown back to Therossa by Sheeka, leaving the rest of the soldiers to stare at the awesome piece of rock they had uncovered. It resembled a horse, was twice the size of an average man and was eroded by the weather and badly pitted by the vigorous ivy. Rainee turned to the king, dirt smeared over her lined face.

"This is the place we were seeking," she explained. "From now on, except for a short climb to that cleft up there, it is easy going. There used to be a gentle slope, but that has long gone. Oran will not expect anyone to use this long-forgotten entrance. I dare say it was he who encouraged the growth to conceal it."

"Why was it used?" Tam was thinking how out-of-the-way the entrance was. Certainly not the way he would have approached the place. His brow furrowed. "I can't say I remember anything about this place, and I've been to Oran's domain before."

Her laugh contained bitterness. "This was the way the parasites of this world entered when they chose to live in luxury at the expense of others. Oran gathered them as a flame attracts moths. Those people who are still inside will never leave, they came under that condition. They live in the luxury that the Drazuzi supply and have everything they want — except fresh air and sunshine." Rainee shivered. "I felt trapped inside. My companion died, and to deter me from escaping, Oran holds that over me. His last words to me were, 'You will be hounded all your life out there — because of you, a man has lost his life'." Tam touched her in sympathy, but Rainee turned from him to a track leading in the opposite direction. "This leads to a huge lake which can be mistaken for a sea. It is the home of many of Oran's misfits and he has supreme power over it. He has a lot to answer for."

"Doesn't he just," muttered Tam shuddering with distaste and remembering the time when Thane and his daughter were using the submerged pathway to escape predators, but came up against Oran's monsters. He turned to face Vance standing stolidly behind him and said, "This is the parting of the ways. There is nothing to be gained by everyone barging in. If we're not out in three days, storm the place — but make sure you tell Sheeka where you are going. He will know what to do. I'm not expecting too much trouble, we should be quickly in and out — but one never knows. Our advantage is that we have the element of surprise on our side."

"Good luck, Tam." Vance gripped his friend's hand, wishing he were going in by his side. He was well aware of what conditions were like inside the caves. His nod indicated Rainee. "You've got a good guide in her," he conceded.

Rainee felt her colour rising and she hastily turned her face away. She spoke instead to the soldier holding her squirming dog. "If you look after him I shall be forever in your debt."

"Have no worries, Rainee," he replied. "He's a fine dog and I like him." The soldier hugged Scrap closer and received a wet tongue on his face. "I'll walk away with him so he doesn't see where you're going," he added thoughtfully.

CHAPTER 22
THE ENCHANTED LAND

Sue was bemused and angry that a horse could so quickly whisk her away from her friends. The last she remembered of them, they were screaming and yelling for her to jump to safety — if only it had been that simple. She was fixed to the mare's back more securely than if she had been locked in chains. Whatever mastermind was behind this contrived hijack, knew exactly what he was doing. This same mastermind successfully tampered with the way she thought — and made her think she was being taken to Thane. The docile mare had changed beyond recognition, moving along at a terrifying speed into the unknown. Sue caught only the vaguest blur of trees and rocks as she travelled, and not much more when the moon peeked occasionally out from behind a build-up of clouds. Her skin was burnt fiercely by the wind yet at the same time she shuddered with cold. She was not dressed for a night ride. It whipped through her hair and numbed her cheeks. Fear made her scream out for the horse to stop, but it made no difference to the mare, whose pace did not falter as she headed to a destination of which only she was aware.

With no leeway to move, Sue panicked and found it difficult to breathe. It was a long time before she realised there was a degree of movement in her head and she could look down. It was only when the sensation of weightlessness assailed her that she became startled and focused with watery eyes on the mare's head, whose mane spread out like streamers in the wind.

The horse had changed. It had no wings but was flying. She expected to see wings sprouting from its body, but instead the legs were curled up neatly making the rest of her body look like a missile being projected through the air. Any hopes Sue may have harboured of escaping were dashed. No one would ever be able to track this mythical beast. Rainee had been so right to warn her against it.

A feeling of hopelessness stole over her. Time held no meaning. She was being controlled by a superior mind. Only by remaining lethargic did she stay sane. It was a change in movement that made her aware the mare was spiralling downwards. Sue strained her eyes to pierce the darkness, and the last thing she remembered seeing before she braced herself for the crash was rippling water touched by moonlight. She hit something soft which eased her fall, but even so it jarred her body. Too dazed to help herself, she lay where she had fallen and allowed sleep to overcome her.

* * *

A soft breeze brushed a tendril of Sue's hair from off her forehead, and warmth from the sun was enough to make her slowly open her eyes. A feeling of lassitude swamped her, dulling her mind to whatever the immediate surroundings held. For several moments she lay in utter bliss, content to watch cotton-wool clouds drift across the heavens. An intricate pattern of leaves and branches framed the pleasant picture and she wondered why she had never been here before. Been here before? Something unpleasant knotted her stomach. Where was she? The idyllic illusion shattered as with sudden clarity everything swamped back in her mind; the flying horse from which it had been impossible for her to escape, the terrifying flight through the night — ending with the fall. There had been no way she could have fallen off by herself. Some clever devious mind had contrived the accident and made sure she was there.

It was thinking of her fall that made Sue automatically flex her limbs, probing for any physical injuries. The examination was over almost before it started because she knew her body was unscathed — but the horse was a different matter. Concern for the mare became uppermost in her mind. Gingerly lifting herself up onto an elbow, she stared around, hoping against hope it was not injured. She soon discovered that on three sides she was hemmed in by foliage, which attracted a multitude of colourful butterflies. At any other time the sight would have delighted her, but she was consumed with thoughts for the mare's welfare. As she twisted her head to look behind, a strangled gasp of amazement left her lips.

A quaint old man was sitting on a rock, dressed, as far as she could make out, in an assortment of mismatched rags. From his emaciated body, bones protruded out at all angles, giving his stature a grotesque appearance. His nose was ugly. It resembled something like the hooked ones found on witches, warts and all. This vied with long pointed ears which grew far higher than the top of his head, looking like an unkempt bird's nest. Beneath the grey wispy hair, his heavily lined face had the look of leather, but under bushy eyebrows, two vivid blue eyes stared at her with quizzical interest. Sue had the feeling he saw and knew everything. For one fleeting moment she wanted to hide. His gnarled hands grasped a stout stick, and yellow teeth held an evil smelling pipe. He puffed out smoke, which hovered above his head like a cloud. The impression he gave to Sue's bemused mind was that he was a misshaped elf — but that couldn't be. They did not exist. He was just some poor misshapen creature that lived here. Quickly realising how rude she was to stare, Sue opened her mouth to speak, but he beat her to it with a nasal growl.

"Have you got permission to be here, young lady?" He spoke without moving his position or his pipe. His aura exuded a chill, which was hard to disregard. "This is private land, so do you mind removing yourself."

The rebuff made Sue scramble to her feet and for a moment she was assailed by guilt. "I'm sorry, I don't know where I am."

"You're trespassing," was the uncompromising answer.

Sue bit her lip. "I realise that — but I still don't know which way to go to get off your land."

"The way you came in before you decided to go to sleep."

He was being cantankerous, and trying to remain calm, Sue took a deep breath. "If I knew that, I wouldn't be here now talking to you. I want to go home. Which way do I go — right or left?"

"Just please yourself," he answered.

"Don't be so stupid." Now Sue was beginning to lose patience. "It must be one of those ways. Please tell me which."

He puffed furiously on his pipe and his voice was cutting. "Do I look like an encyclopaedia?"

"Don't tempt me." It took all Sue's willpower to bite back the words that filled her mouth. Changing tack, she asked patiently, "Maybe you saw where my horse went? She's obviously wandered off and seeing this is your land, you must have some idea where she is."

"Horse!" the old man repeated the word as though she had said something terrible. "Filthy creatures — I can't abide them. There are no horses hereabouts — never have been and never will be while I'm in charge."

Sue flinched. "But I was riding one when I fell off and…"

"And you think I'm going to be happy with that explanation and let you search my kingdom for it?" the old man interrupted sourly. "You think again, girl. I've met your type before — and you're not even dressed for riding. Coming to think of it," He eyed her up and down insultingly. "I don't know what you're dressed for. Strangers are not welcome here — especially nosy ones."

Sue met his hostile stare calmly. "Where am I?" she asked finally.

"Right here," he snapped.

"Where is here?"

"It is where you are standing of course. Have you lost your brains as well as the horse?"

"This is utterly stupid." Sue's temper rose unwisely. He was being deliberately obtuse and she was beyond caring what his reason for it was. "I'm wasting my time talking to you. If you don't mind, I'll search for my horse, and directly I find it, I'll leave your land. I can think of better things to do with my time than speak to unhelpful people like you."

His bushy eyebrows rose but he made no attempt to move from the rock. His eyes watched her, making her uneasy. She had the feeling he was playing with her, but she had no intention of stopping to find out. She had to walk past the rock he was sitting on, and as she brushed past him, she expected his stick either to trip her up or hit her. She imagined him capable of doing any of these things, but nothing happened, except that he took in a deep draw on his filthy pipe and said complacently, "You'll soon be back."

"No I won't," she retorted, angry with herself for acting like a child. "I'm sure I'll find someone more helpful than you," and she walked up a grassy mound to where a few trees grew on the ridge. She felt a peculiar drag to her feet. At the top she had to pause for breath. Looking back the way she had come made her disappointed. Climbing higher had done nothing for the view. All she could see was the clearing where the old man sat. He now had his knees raised, and his chin was resting on them, his bony arms wound round them to hold them in place. A cloud of thick smoke surrounded his head and he had obviously given up on her because his back was still turned to her.

Sue grimaced, wondering why he had thought she would be back. That was the last thing she intended to happen. This place was big enough for her to find a homestead, and maybe the people would be friendly enough to help her and tell her where she was. The choice of which way to go was limited. There were only three paths to choose from and they all looked alike. The paths

309

were soft with grass and moss, and thick foliage bordered the sides. There was little chance of her wandering off and getting lost, but she held on to the hope she might find signs of the mare having passed this way.

Choosing a path at random, she poked around diligently looking for tracks but found nothing that even suggested a horse came this way. Well it could be the wrong path, but in her heart she knew there would be no tracks. The mare had been flying.

It was no use counting on the mare as a means of escape, she must use her initiative. She started walking along the path feeling fresh and relaxed — even the drag to her feet had worn off. It was good to be out feeling the warmth of the sun on her shoulders and hear the sound of birds twittering above her in the trees. It eased her worries. Also they were so colourful and restful to the eyes. At one point she paused to watch them, and insidiously the thoughts of Thane, Raithe and Alfie entered her mind. They must be so worried about her. She wondered what they were doing. If she found herself stuck here she would use her ring to contact her brother. The thought gave her comfort. She had nothing to worry about.

Sue followed the zigzag path, enjoying the butterflies as much as the birds. It seemed never-ending and she never came across any gaps in the foliage to denote another path going in a different direction. That did not worry her so much as not finding any habitation. Just when tiredness made her want to stop and sit down, she saw a clearing ahead and quickened her pace almost to a run. Breaking out into the opening, she pulled up with a gasp of dismay. Before her was the old man —

sitting exactly where she had left him, but with more smoke swirling around his head. Sue felt faint. How had she managed to come back to the exact place she had started from? She hadn't turned off anywhere. In fact, she thought she had been walking forward all the time. It would be humiliating if he turned and saw her, so she quickly slipped down another path — and when she thought she had gone far enough not to be detected, she paused, and sank to the ground.

A feeling of helplessness engulfed her and took away her earlier urge to explore. She could not shake off the feeling of pessimism that assailed her. Suppose this path led her back to the little old man as the first one had? It looked exactly the same. Sue closed her eyes, overwhelmed with indecision, and she very nearly dropped off to sleep — only to be roused by a voice in her head saying, "What's the matter with you — giving in?" Her eyes flew open, she was startled, thinking someone was with her, but her only companions were thousands of butterflies and colourful birds. The voice had been all it needed to get her going. Determined not to tarry, she was on her way again, searching for traces of the mare with renewed enthusiasm, but as before the path zigzagged along, unbroken on either side, making the outlook rather monotonous. It did not take long for her newfound resolve to start crumbling. She was on the same path. Sue turned the next bend in trepidation, only to find the path blocked solidly by a huge rock twice her height. Instead of seeing it as a disaster, Sue welcomed the sight with open arms. She was actually travelling in a different direction and the relief from that knowledge made her feel weak. To turn back now was not an option she was going to take.

Sue studied the rock calmly, realising it had to be climbed if she were to go forward, because on either side the foliage was thorny and impregnable. She soon noticed there was a lack of footholds in its shiny surface, and wished Thane was with her to give assistance because he could scale anything. She looked to her left and contemplated a nearby tree. Sue decided her best bet was to climb up it and wriggle along a branch, which conveniently arched over the obstruction. She could then drop down onto the top of the rock. There were plenty of thick vines to hang on to and the first part of the climb was accomplished with ease. Now came the difficult manoeuvre — to crawl along the branch. The bark was rough and cut into her hands and legs. Large leaves hindered her movements and slapped in her face with stinging regularity. Sheer doggedness made her persevere and by the time she fell down on the rock surface, parts of her arms, hands and legs were bleeding profusely. She lay panting where she fell and felt sick. It was quite a while before she sat up and gazed down the path, which continued on the other side.

The drop down was easy to achieve. It was nowhere as high as the side she had had to climb up. She jumped and stumbled along the track, stopping every so often to dab the blood away from her knees, which throbbed along with her hands. Sheer cussedness made her persevere, and she felt dirty and dishevelled. After a few more twists and turns in the path, she saw a haze of smoke. Her heart leapt. It had to be someone's home — but would the owner help her, looking as she did? She

312

would face that when the time came. She hastened her steps, eager to reach the place. It was not that far away — she could see the clearing just ahead. Sue fell out of the trees, exhausted, and felt her senses reeling. In front of her was the same little old man sitting on the same rock, surrounded by a cloud of smoke. This time, he turned round and looked at her. Removing the filthy pipe from between his yellow teeth, he said with satisfaction, "I told you that you would be back."

Sue had no power to answer him. She sank to the ground feeling sick and fighting to keep her tears at bay. It sounded as though his voice came from a distance. "I shouldn't sit there, girl — you've got another path to go down yet." His words stung her.

"I'll go in my own time," she choked. "Maybe you could tell me where I could find some water?"

"When you reach the last path, you will find a stream somewhere down it."

Sue's eyes hardened. "Is that before or after I arrive back here?" she asked sarcastically. To her disquiet he left the rock and walked right up to her, almost standing on her feet. A strange smell fanned her cheeks as he drew sharply on his pipe. His bright blue eyes pierced through her and in that instant she felt he knew everything about her.

"You've got a lot to say for a trespasser, young lady," he said. "I would strongly advise you to keep your comments to yourself unless you wish to find yourself in a worse place than this."

The prescience of danger pressed down on her and she quickly regained her feet. With bravado, she demanded bluntly, "Where am I?" although inwardly she felt vaguely uneasy because there was something about this place which did not ring true.

The throaty chuckle from the elf-like man sent shivers down her spine, and he returned to his rock and made himself comfortable. "You really don't know?" he asked, and to Sue's horror, he took great pleasure in informing her that she was in the Enchanted Land — and was not ever going to get away unless she succeed in all the tasks he gave her to do. Then he advised to go down the third path and stop asking silly questions.

CHAPTER 23
ESCAPE ATTEMPT

Masking her fatigue, Sue entered the third pathway, which she knew would look exactly the same as the other two, even down to its colourful birds and butterflies. Whoever was responsible for this place was a stickler for perfection. Resentment bubbled up in her until it was on the verge of erupting. Why should she do what he told her? Why didn't she ignore him? How came there to be a man in this land where none existed? Maybe he wasn't a proper man? He was an elf, wasn't he? But those blue eyes did not belong to an elf. This was the first time she had met such an aggravating, deviant and sadistic individual who was enjoying himself at her expense. He knew, just as she knew, this path would eventually return back to this spot. So why was she walking down it? Was she stupid or too scared not to please him?

A cold sweat covered her body, brought on by palpitations. She knew without being told that her host wielded magical powers and because of this she was treading carefully. It was a mystery as to why she had been chosen; why not Annalee or Tansy? Sue stumbled along, dabbing at the blood that still oozed from her cuts. It was something he had seen but chose to ignore. She tried to focus her mind on escaping from here. He couldn't control every part of this land — she was in a maze. The trouble was, mazes were known to be

315

insidious. She could get herself into a worse mess than she was already in. She studied the surroundings closely. The sides of the maze were constructed in such a way that each twig of the bushes was entwined perfectly with its neighbour. There was no way of breaking through such an intricate barrier. The only way was forward — and that led to nowhere. What chance had she got of escaping? She looked down and saw her ring. Her heart leapt. Why hadn't she thought of it before?

Once Raithe knew the difficulties she was facing, he would get help to her in no time. Making sure she was not being observed and her actions were private, she rubbed the green gem and wondered why she felt guilty for doing so. However, no matter how hard she rubbed the ring, or willed her brother to be there, the ring remained dead and unresponsive. A feeling of dread swamped her. Had something happened to her brother?

If she had not succumbed to trying to use the ring, Sue would have walked on quite happily, but now she knew she was completely cut off from any help, and that was devastating to her morale. She looked up at the sun, the same sun that was shining on all her friends. She thought of Tam and Ruth, knowing they would help her if only they knew where she was. Silver had already explained dragons did not have the power to fly over this land. Something repelled them. She was on her own.

Sue's thoughts drifted to Deena and the Crystal Horse she was supposed to find. It was all lies to cover some other devious purpose. Deena said no man could live in the Enchanted Land. Obviously she knew nothing of the man making her run round in circles. Sue pulled up her wandering mind with a jerk. Maybe he wasn't a man, but some lowly minion being subservient to a higher deity, in which case she was held here firmer than a fly in a web. She gnawed on her lower lip and decided she was not going to be taken into captivity without a fight.

After all that contemplating, Sue felt a lot better and more in command of herself. She continued to walk along the track with bravado and wondered how long it would be before she found the water. Although she realised it was a waste of time, she still kept her eyes alert looking for the smallest sign of something that might aid her escape. In spite of her newfound confidence, Sue became concerned when she noticed the shadows were thickening on the ground. This was a pointer that the day was coming to an end. Her stomach rumbled, reminding her it was a long time since she had last eaten. Food didn't seem to exist in this place, but on turning the next bend, she saw a raspberry cane well laden with fruit. Sue fell on it, not caring if it was real or an illusion. It felt real enough and the sweet juice dripped down her chin as she gorged herself with raspberries until she felt satisfied. She wiped her mouth with the back of her hand, leaving smears of blood intermingled with raspberry juice on her cheeks. Above it all came the sound of running water — the stream at last!

Sue quickened her steps, which brought her to the edge of the fast moving water — it was too wide to jump across, but a convenient flat-surfaced rock was in the middle, standing proud of the water by two inches. It made a welcome stepping-stone. Kneeling down and cupping her hands, she took a drink of the clear sweet water and saw small golden fishes darting towards the banks for a hiding place. Weed floated with the current and looked too real to be an illusion. Sue stared thoughtfully along the stream, noticing the foliage came down to the water's edge into which the leaves dipped now and again. She thought that if she waded along to find the source of the stream, it was something the old man would not expect her to do, and maybe — she crossed her fingers — maybe she could escape this way.

Sue stepped off the stone into the water and quelled the urge to wash away all the grime and dirt on her body, much as she would have liked to have done so, but time was against her. The water barely reached her knees and the ground beneath her feet felt soft and sandy as she walked along. She took only six steps for the unexpected to happen. The ground suddenly shelved and she was out of her depth. As the water closed over her head, she spluttered and choked. Then Sue surfaced and started to swim — not back to the stepping-stone, but onwards with the current. She must make full use of this opportunity. She expected to feel the bottom before long, and tried every few yards with her feet, but was doomed to disappointment. Nevertheless her resolve to continue did not falter. Nothing was going to deter her now — she kept on swimming.

Sue was a good swimmer and exceptionally strong, so she met with no difficulties. The unaccustomed exercise made her glow and the cool water running over her flesh invigorated her senses. With strong strokes she allowed her body to go with the flow, but kept a careful lookout on the banks, watching out for any breaks in the greenery. It was only when fatigue reared its ugly head that she realised she had been in the water for ages and it was still too deep for her to stand. There were no breaks in the foliage where she could clamber out. The sun was very low, in-fact she could no longer see it above the trees.

Her breath started to rasp in her throat and her lungs were burning from exertion. Panic rose within her. The stream had to lead somewhere — maybe to a village, where the people would take her in. Exhaustion began to take its toll. Her strokes were becoming feeble, but her resolve to get away was stronger than ever. Doggedly she continued swimming and her body took charge. Agonizing cramp shot up her legs, making her strokes falter. In her mental anguish she thought she was going to drown but she would rather do that than go back.

Then a roaring in her head overwhelmed her senses, and through a mist she saw a rock. As a dying person would, she clung to it and for several seconds to gulp down air. After she had recouped enough strength, she was about to clamber out when her eyes stared at the rock surface. A patch of blood was visible there, blood from her knees where she had knelt earlier. She realised again she was in shallow water but barely had enough strength to stand up. Desolation swamped her and made her feel sick. All her efforts had been for nothing.

On the further bank, the bizarre man stood watching her. The elongated shadows masked his face. He drew on his pipe and said pleasantly, "I see you found the water. Have you enjoyed yourself?"

Sue's mouth opened and shut like a landed fish. She drew in a ragged breath and out of sheer desperation, snapped, "Yes I have — so much so — I'm going to do it again," and as good as her word, she flung herself back into the deep water. A wave of dizziness assailed her and

319

she put a hand to her head. Only in the distance did she hear his voice, cold and dismissive, saying "I think not," and before she realised what had happened, she found herself lying on the grass, completely alone. There was no water, no path and no old man, but in the distance was a cottage, its windows full of light and a door wide open, as though to welcome her.

* * *

Ignoring the giddiness which assailed her, Sue raised her head to take further stock of the situation, but she felt very sick. Her body protested at the action and it was then she realised her clothes were bone dry. There was nothing to show outwardly of her time spent in the river. Inwardly, she wanted to curl up and hide until her strength returned, but she brushed this thought aside; to get away from this place was her main objective. She was determined not to let any more illusions sway her mind. Narrowing her eyes, she studied the cottage and wondered if it was real or her imagination playing tricks again. Such places as this one did not exist — except in fairy tales. After meditating for a long period, she decided the place was not real and she was not going to investigate. It was another figment of her imagination.

The cottage, with a backdrop of trees, had a low thatched roof with two dormer windows and she could clearly hear the birds, which were nesting in the eaves, as they chirped. A curly plume of smoke rose to the sky where it dispersed. The yellowish stonewalls which were covered by climbing vines held two more lattice windows, one placed either side of the open wooden door. The wide aperture allowed light from within to spill out on the path leading up to it.

To Sue, the light was off-putting and unnecessary because it was not yet that dark. A strange sort of twilight hung over the area, which to her seemed unnatural. In this land it was either dark or light. Twilight was a phenomenon that did not exist in Therossa. Anyway — why was it she had not seen this cottage earlier while she was doing all her walking? It never crossed her mind that illusion may have masked it from her eyes.

While she pondered, an aromatic smell drifted through the air, teasing her taste buds and making her mouth water. Hunger made her an easy prey. It was coming from the cottage and enticed her to get to her feet. Gingerly she rose and walked towards it. Someone inside had obviously sensed her approach and stood framed in the doorway, a rotund woman whose form took up most of the space. With the light behind her she acquired a halo. Her dark hair was drawn off her round face and instead of making her look severe, it did quite the opposite because she had a friendly smile, and the moment she stepped out onto the path, Sue could see she wore a white apron over a long voluminous dark skirt. Looking at Sue, she beckoned with a plump hand and said, "Come along, my dear. You're late. I've been expecting you."

Instantly Sue halted and was on her guard. Suspicion immediately flared up. She didn't know this woman, so how could she be expecting her? Some one here was swamping her with illusions again and her initial reaction was to run. The hesitation was not lost on the rotund lady who shook her head and started to walk purposely in her direction. Sue watched her advance, mesmerised as her ample form swayed to and fro, and her huffing and puffing sounded very real. As she got close, her head only reached as high as Sue's shoulders, but her lack of height was no obstacle to her. She ignored being out of breath and smiled broadly, her eyes twinkling. She linked her arm into that of Sue and tugged her towards the cottage. Almost as though she could read Sue's thoughts, she said,

"Don't hang back. You've nothing to fear from me, my dear. I do not bite and I've cooked you some of my special dishes. You must be very hungry."

That speech was plausible but Sue still hung back. Memories of the bizarre elf-man were still smarting within her, and because of him, she didn't trust anything in front of her. The rotund lady shook her head and added in a vexed voice, "If you don't come back with me now, my food will all spoil," but Sue could not help asking. "How did you know I was coming?"

The woman's dark eyes opened wide with surprise. They looked like two buttons. Sue's question genuinely astonished her and her guileless answer came out perfectly naturally. "But I saw you arrive, dear, and because you were so tired and went to sleep I left you where the horse dropped you and decided to come back later when I had cooked a meal, to welcome you, but..." she waggled a finger playfully under Sue's nose, "You decided to go off exploring by yourself — you naughty child."

Stunned because at last she had heard a glimmer of truth, Sue retorted without thinking, "He made me go."

Her words had a surprising effect on the rotund woman because her eyebrows rose to make a perfect arch and her amiable smile vanished. "He?" she queried archly, "There are no men here,"

Sue floundered, wondering if she had dreamt everything — but her sore feet and aching limbs told a different story, so she tried again.

"It was a man," she protested. "He looked... looked... " She broke off abruptly because the woman's eyes were boring into her and a scandalised expression crept over her face.

"Are you speaking of the Keeper, child?" she demanded, and her voice was tinged with asperity, "Because if you are — you must be careful. He is not human and he hears everything."

"Well I don't care," Sue retorted, feeling nettled, she hadn't done anything wrong. "I've got no idea who this Keeper is — as you call him — but if he's got a long nose and ears, combined with straggly hair and wears disgusting clothes, then yes, that's to whom I'm referring. He made me walk miles today, and I think he found it amusing."

The little old lady showed no emotion at her outburst, but she stood on tiptoe to whisper in her ear. "What colour were his eyes, my dear?"

"Blue."

"Ah," the old lady sighed, and said no more. Her whole stance relaxed and she tugged once again on Sue's arm. "Now stop all this chatting and come with me. I don't want the meal to spoil."

Completely at a loss, Sue stumbled after her — not that she had any choice. In spite of her smallness, the woman was immensely strong and her grip dug firmly into Sue's flesh. It was not until they were nearing the cottage door that she made an effort to stop the momentum of her feet, which surprised the rotund lady. "You said you saw me arrive?" she cried out desperately.

"Yes, my dear." The woman pulled at her impatiently to make her move, but an expression of naivety filled her eyes and she said it was such a lovely sight. The flying horse had not been here for ages. "It is such a pity it did not stop, but I guess it has a lot of work to do." Her voice then changed as she asked, "Are you feeling all right, my dear? You do look flushed." The old lady stopped and lifted a hand to Sue's brow. "Goodness me," she exclaimed, "You are burning up. Come inside now quickly — and rest."

Sue did not remember lurching through the doorway after the woman, but once inside she wondered if her actions had been too hasty. Her hostess was very persuasive and she had followed like a mindless chicken, no longer coherent. Tiredness overruled her common sense. Thoughts of the day's events started to swamp over her and she ended up confused and muddled. She felt hands pushing her into an easy chair but sleep still eluded her. In the background the air was filled with the clatter of pots and pans and the sound of the rotund lady humming under her breath as she moved around. Heat from the roaring fire before her seeped into Sue's limbs and relaxed her body. Glorious warmth spread through her. Someone pressed a cooling pad to her brow and Sue allowed her eyes to close – but only for a second as something solid landed heavily in her lap.

A large black cat, purring loudly enough to deafen her, started to knead her knees with huge paws, in which the claws were only half retracted. One or two claws dug into her flesh and tore at the material of her trousers as the cat proceeded to make its bed. She winced, but had no intention of moving it off — she didn't know how the rotund woman would take such an action.

"Knock him off, dear," the rotund woman said automatically as she passed, "I'm afraid he likes to be made a fuss of."

Sue stared at the larger than normal cat, who looked back at her through the slits of his green eyes. He was definitely a cat, but the size of a puma. Before she knew it her hand was stroking his sleek firm head and he was pressing back hard against her hand. Eventually the cat reciprocated by nuzzling round her neck. His whiskers tickled her chin. She sighed. It felt so safe, so homely to have a cat on her lap, but out of the blue came the thought, *but is this real*? The cat sensed her distrust immediately and with a hiss, sprang back to the floor. Sue was surprised at how much she missed the contact, but the rotund woman surprised her even more.

"I didn't expect you to throw him off," she stated disapprovingly. "Rajah is a friend for life if he likes you."

"I didn't push him off," Sue answered, "he jumped." She felt an unreasonable surge of indignation. "He obviously doesn't like me."

The woman shook her head and moved away, a moment later returning with a basin of milk which she placed before the cat. Only the sound of his rough tongue rasping round the basin could be heard for the next few minutes. Having satisfied himself, he rubbed his solid body round Sue's legs. The plump lady beamed, suddenly happy. It seemed the cat ruled this household. She busied herself in the kitchen leaving Sue contemplating the fire. The heat from it was overpowering. When she reached down and touched the cat's fur, it seemed to burn her fingers. The cat stopped seeking her attention and looked up at her. The wide green eyes started to probe her mind. If she didn't know any better, she could believe the cat was asking her where she came from. Sue drew away from him at once, scared she was hallucinating. After a day like the one she had just spent, nothing surprised her anymore.

"Everything is ready now," the old lady's voice floated to her. "Come into the kitchen." Sue attempted to stand but her lack of equilibrium made her stagger. The rotund woman was there by her side instantly, and she helped Sue to the table. Sue never clearly remembered the meal, which was served to her in a spotless kitchen. The food was very good and tasty and she ate because she was hungry. Yet with each mouthful she swallowed, she became more muddled and confused. The rotund lady shook her head and contrary to her former actions, kept shooing the cat away from her. Sue tried to scramble to her feet, but exhaustion had taken all her strength away. Drowsiness made her head fall onto the table and her soft snores filled the kitchen.

The rotund woman contemplated Sue for several moments, biting on her fleshy lips. Then suddenly she made up her mind and took a bottle from her cupboard. Carefully measuring out a dose into a cup, she walked up to Sue and lifted her head by grabbing a handful of hair in her chubby fingers. With expertise, she forced Sue's mouth open and poured the liquid down her throat. A few dribbles trickled down her chin, but Sue never stirred.

"You shouldn't have done that," hissed the cat, "The Keeper will be livid. He wants to be able to manipulate her."

"This has nothing to do with you, Rajah — so keep quiet," the woman retorted sternly, "Help me get her to bed."

CHAPTER 24
A WAY UNDER THE WATER

After several days of trekking through the forest, the travellers had their first sight of the wide river which was rushing by below them. The sight filled them with alarm. It was more than an obstacle preventing further progress, its speed and fury of movement prohibited them from getting any closer to its banks. Raithe and Thane dismounted to stare with mixed feelings towards the far shore where the sinking sun covered the tops of trees with a splash of gold. It all looked so tranquil. Yet the third member of their party had itchy feet and she wanted to get away from them. Things had changed dramatically for her since Alfie had been spirited away. The lads were unaware of her intentions, but White Hawk still watched her through half-closed eyes. He growled when Fleura moved, which made Thane switch his gaze from the Enchanted Land, in time to see her sneaking away amongst the trees.

"Hold it there, Fleura," he called out, and strode firmly up to her, ignoring her glowering eyes. "You're not going anywhere. You're supposed to see us safely to the land on the other side of that river."

Fleura was annoyed at being caught and wished the wolf to be consigned to an unpleasant destination. Taking a deep breath, she retorted aggressively, "Only to the Enchanted Land, which you can now see. My job is done and you're on your own." So saying, with a defiant toss of her head, she marched further away.

Thane swore under his breath, sprang forward and caught her roughly by the arm. Swinging her round none too gently and disregarding the angry vibes she gave off because he had dared to touch her, he said crisply, "You were told to see us safely to the actual land, and in case your eyesight is poor — there is water separating us from it."

"Then swim," Fleura retorted churlishly.

Thane's eyes narrowed. "I think not, young lady," he retorted. "Your Goddess put us in your hands — expecting you to be grown up enough to carry out..." He broke off with a furious yell as, unprovoked, she stamped vindictively on his foot and took her chance to run swiftly away. White Hawk sprang effortlessly and, with his big paws brought her down flat on her face in the earth. Then he looked enquiringly from her to his master, wondering if Thane was going to take it any further. Thane wanted to grin, but decided now wasn't the time.

Fleura squirmed and choked, spitting out a mouthful of leaves. Her baleful eyes glared at him, and the wolf she ignored, but Fleura had her own way of dealing with this situation. So while Thane was otherwise engaged, she lifted her hands with evil intent to blast him away. At that precise moment Raithe stepped through the foliage and joined them. He took the situation in at a glance, his eyes locking with those of Fleura. "Are we having a game?" he asked with eyebrows raised. "May I join in? I rather like shooting bolts at one another."

"Let it drop, Raithe, we've just had a difference of opinion," said Thane, limping away to find a log to sit on and take the weight off his throbbing foot. She must have claws growing on her feet to hurt him so easily, he thought ruefully. With little love for her at this moment, he watched as she fastidiously brushed herself down. Then he was aware of other eyes watching him, because the hairs on his neck rose. He didn't see the Goddess at first until he looked around and saw her clad in a concealing cloak, a perfect camouflage amongst the trees. Only her shimmering halo was missing. Thane struggled to his feet, but Raithe did the honours by walking up to her and leaving Fleura behind.

"We have been very grateful for all the help you have given us." His voice sounded servile, but that was due to Raithe's upbringing. "I think I should point out Fleura did all that you asked of her. It may not have always been spontaneous — but at least she helped us in the end," he added ruefully. "I'm only sorry Fleura would never let herself be friends with us."

The Goddess smiled, "I'm afraid that was your fault, Prince Raithe. She reacts to the way you treat her. She likes to be in charge. Having you along has been a great lesson for her — but I am not here to discuss my protégée, it would take too long. There are things about the Enchanted Land I must tell you before any of you set foot on it."

"Then it can be visited?" Thane burst out excitedly. He felt a load had been lifted from his shoulders. Her eyes were on him and his face coloured up for acting like a gauche boy. "Only we were told no one can land there — men in particular."

Now she gave him her full attention. "That is perfectly true. The land is surrounded by a force-field of magic which is insuperable. Because the Princess did not arrive there voluntarily, I feel I can lend you a helping hand by disclosing the whereabouts of a secret way under the river. The way is very dangerous," she cautioned, as their faces lit up. "The wolf would get through all right but you humans only with difficulty. It really depends on how great your need is to get there. How much you want to get your Princess back home."

"I need to be with Sue," and, "I need to be with my sister." The answers came from them simultaneously and the Goddess looked thoughtful. Then she said regretfully, "Only one of you can go."

The two lads stared at each other. Raithe saw the anguish in Thane's eyes, but before he could utter a word, the Prince said gallantly, "Then it must be you of course, Thane. I know she's my sister — but on the other hand there is a strong bond between the two of you. I can wait with the horses and be ready in case she contacts me on our rings."

Thane was too choked to answer and the Goddess expressed her relief saying, "I wish all my subjects could make up their minds like you two. Still, I must stress again, it will be very dangerous for whoever goes. Too many people are under the illusion that the Crystal Horse is an object of power to steal." She saw them both stiffen in surprise before concluding, "They are so wrong. The name 'Crystal Horse' is symbolic. It is the symbol of Hope and Endeavour — not some artefact used by so called magic-wielders. Only performing feats of great difficulty and enduring hardships, which stretch one almost beyond endurance, can obtain it, and a hard task-master sets these. If anyone succeeds in these against all odds, they have the power to change anything in Therossa, but they also have to pay a price. A price usually harder than the tasks they may have performed."

Thane could not remain silent any longer. Seething with indignation, he began, "Sue did not ask to do this," but the Goddess silenced him. "Since you brought Sue to this land, she has shown a compassionate heart for the underdog, and because of this, someone has chosen her to be his or her champion — not that Sue is aware of this. We must wait and see what the outcome is."

"Deena," muttered Thane bitterly, but again the Goddess interrupted him. "I am not at liberty to tell you who has done this, but I will ease your mind a fraction. The Snake Queen is free of blame. Now, Thane, I take it you and White Hawk are going to the Enchanted Land? The wolf is a good choice for your companion. You must follow me now and I will point out the way. You, Prince Raithe, have the unenviable task of waiting with the horses. I could call Fleura back." She caught sight of his horrified face, and smiled knowingly. "Well, perhaps not," she added and the Prince sighed in relief.

* * *

Events once again changed the dynamics of the group. Thane turned and gave one last salute to Raithe before passing an outcrop of rocks that hid him from view. Raithe had misgivings about this whole affair — and it was not sour grapes on his part because he wanted to go after his sister. He felt genuinely concerned for his friend who was heading into no man's land. The Enchanted Land was an area no one knew anything about. He braced his shoulders to stop himself from moping and tried to use his time sensibly by building a makeshift shelter in case it rained. He needed a campsite. He was so absorbed in his work, he was not aware of what was going on around him until a soft footfall at his back made him spin round in alarm and he saw two ugly looking characters stealthily creeping up on him, one fondling a rope with his thick fingers, and the other brandishing a naked knife.

Raithe cursed silently. He should have thought about something like this happening — especially since he was alone and so near to gypsies. It was too late now to regret not having had the foresight to place a weapon within reaching distance. If Amos or Thane ever heard of this he would receive the rough side of their tongues; Prince or no Prince Raithe drew himself up, trying to look unconcerned.

"Can I help you?" he inquired imperiously, allowing his upbringing to take over. With soldiers, this attitude was very effective, but it had no impact on these two uncouth gypsies. The one with the rope laughed harshly, making his shoulder-length earrings swing to and fro.

"Good try, sonny, but you've got no choice," he said and leered into the Prince's face. "We've come for the horses. One person doesn't need that many." He jerked his head in the direction of where they were grazing. "It's about time you lot learnt not to trespass on our land. Now! Are you going to let us have them or have we got to make up your mind?"

Raithe held himself perfectly still and in spite of the way he was feeling, he made his voice sound scornful. "I'm not letting you touch them, you thieving band of ..." He ended with a quick intake of breath as the rope flew through the air and wound itself viciously round his body, pinning his arms to his sides and rendering them useless.

"Grab the horses, Juan," the one with the rope instructed in his guttural voice, and he smirked at the helpless Prince. Juan approached Saturn, but directly his hand touched the stallion, Saturn reared and kicked out with his hindquarters. At the same time a bolt of light hurtled across the space just missing Juan's head and making him shake. A petite figure followed it, hurling a string of abuse at the gypsies. They backed away in alarm, but Fleura continued to advance. They fled into the forest. Raithe eyed the girl warily. Her presence came as a great shock to him. He thought she had vanished with the Goddess. To his surprise, she came over to him and released the rope, which imprisoned his arms, then she said simply:

"I'll stay with you to protect the horses. The gypsies will not return all the while I'm here," and she did not give him the chance to reply, she was already lighting the fire.

* * *

Thane had been given his instructions, but before they sank into his bemused mind, his mentor vanished. The wolf waited patiently by his side while Thane surveyed the maze of rocks, brambles and vines in the area before him. He had seen places like this before and only an idiot would attempt to break through the tangle — but Thane was that idiot. He would do anything to get Sue out of the Enchanted Land, even if it meant being torn to shreds by the spiteful thorns. White Hawk pawed the ground, emitting a low whine from his throat as he tried to gain Thane's attention, but Thane just patted his head absentmindedly and continued to study the impregnable area ahead. The Goddess's last words still rang through his head: "the entrance is in there, straight ahead, but remember — caution at all times. The way is deadly. Always be wary of where you are going." White Hawk gave up trying to get his attention, and took matters into his own hands by digging under the nearest bush. He worked his way through the maze of roots on his belly, pushing with his hind legs to gain leverage. At last he reached one of the larger rocks standing proud in the middle of the thorny outcrop. Bunching his muscles, he sprang up, his supple body landing gracefully on one of its lower ledges. Shaking the bits of dead leaves and twigs from his coat, he lifted his head and howled to gain Thane's attention. Thane broke out of his reverie immediately and stared at the wolf in disbelief. Then he looked in all directions, in case his howl had attracted unwanted attention. Staring at White Hawk, he exploded, "I don't suppose you want to come back and show me the way?"

White Hawk bared his teeth almost as though he was laughing, and to Thane's exasperation, bent his head and sniffed his way along the ledge as far as he could go. After that, he looked back at Thane and pawed the ground. Thane's annoyance increased. "I'm not in the mood for your games. Just stay where you are and I'll find my own way."

As he turned away from the wolf, his eyes inadvertently swept the ground and he saw the signs of broken stems and crushed grass. He realised White Hawk had left clear evidence of the way he had taken, which wasn't the way he wanted to go. Thane looked back at the wolf, who had now settled himself down to wait for him. With a wry grimace Thane fell to his knees and studied the uninviting way a little closer. There was nothing for it but to wriggle his way through. The wolf had done the hard work. His bulk had smashed out a tunnel. Tying a bandanna over his head and part of his face, he carefully moved his body over the ground. After ten minutes of pure hell, he decided White Hawk must have a hide of leather.

Thane's body was punctured through his clothes by razor sharp thorns and they made huge rents in the material of his clothes — this was finished off as brambles ripped them even further. An agonised yelp escaped his lips as a strand of his hair knotted itself around a forked branch. He was sweating profusely by the time he had managed to cut himself free. How much further did he have to go? Clenching his teeth, he made one last painful lunge and came up against a wall of granite.

Thane caught hold of it, thankful that at last he could stretch his legs and remove the bandanna. He tore himself from the vines, which still tried to hold him back, and leant against the rocky wall until he had sufficiently recovered his breath. Then he started moving round the rock to find White Hawk, who was now several yards away on another rock surrounded by impenetrable greenery.

Thane swore, cursing that he had not followed the wolf's tracks. "I'm coming to you," he shouted and moved to retie the bandanna, when the ground beneath his feet gave way and with a startled yell he fell into an underground cave. White Hawk dived into the tangled undergrowth and headed unerringly to the last spot he saw Thane before he disappeared, stopping only in a shower of dust when he reached the brink of the newly exposed cavity. He peered down into the depths, sniffing the air. Only when his ears picked up a faint rustle and he heard Thane's voice mutter something unintelligible, did he leap down to be by his master's side.

Thane sat up rubbing his shoulder gingerly, thankful it was the only part of him giving any trouble to his limbs. As dust and stones rained down on his head, he looked upwards to where jagged edges of rock and grass were silhouetted against the sky. For one brief moment this sight was blotted out as White Hawk jumped. He landed on top of Thane who now had another shoulder hurting to match the first one. Thane fumbled for his tinderbox, trying to take stock of his surroundings. With hardly any room to move, he soon discovered they were at the beginning of a subterranean tunnel. A tunnel through which there was a through-flow of air.

Thane pressed a warning hand on the wolf's head and slowly proceeded forward. By the faint glow from his tinderbox, he could see he was walking over a slime-covered floor, shining a dull green. In spite of the air touching his face, the smell arising from the slime became sickly, and the rocky path, being full of potholes, made the going hard because it was slippery. Before long, the pace they were moving at was reduced to that of a snail. Thane paused, listening.

Nothing could be heard except the monotonous sound of dripping water. The glistening walls inclined inwards, forcing Thane to stoop. In this uncomfortable posture, he proceeded further along the tunnel. In spite of the cold atmosphere, he was now feeling hot under the collar, and when the walls unexpectedly fell away, he found he was standing in a fairly large cave. Another smell added itself to that of the slime. It was hard to detect, but it worried his senses. He felt he should know what it was.

Wolf and man took a breather while Thane studied the situation. The tunnel continued onwards, but not very far. A rock fall blocked it completely and the granite was too heavy to move by hand. But there were still two more exits. One seemed no more than a bolthole near the floor and the second one was much higher, near the roof. Thane pointed to the lower one for White Hawk because he couldn't climb and immediately started to scale the wall to reach the higher exit. The walls were unstable. More than once the rock shattered beneath his feet. This should have warned him to take more care, but thoughts of reaching Sue were uppermost in his mind. More of the wall became dislodged when he touched it and his feet often lost leverage in the scant foot holes. He never noticed White Hawk had not moved and was watching him. Near the top a jutting slab moved, throwing him off balance. With superhuman strength he flung his body forward and grabbed at the edge of the opening. Sweating profusely, he painfully hauled himself over the edge. For a moment he lay there gasping. Unexpectedly the rock beneath him gave way and he fell forward with the masses of falling rubble and chunks of stone. Dust choked him and blood smeared his face as a sharp pain pierced his head. The smell made him gag. Thane feebly felt for his tinderbox and held it aloft. The way behind him was now blocked, cutting off his retreat, but the sight before him made his blood run cold and he knew now why no one ever reached the Enchanted Land. Ahead was a moving pit of blackness. Snakes were mindlessly slithering over each other. He felt their red eyes watching him and knew he had no hopes of escape. One bite from them and he was dead. Could they reach him where he was trapped? To think Sue kept a couple of them as pets. Sue! His mind was clouding over. "White Hawk!" he yelled hoarsely, "White Hawk! Can you hear me? For God's sake you must find Sue…" and he slipped into a coma.

CHAPTER 25
WHITE HAWK

Sue woke to a new day feeling completely refreshed. After a dreamless sleep, she was lured into the spotless kitchen by smells, where the rotund lady had laid out everything she liked to eat on the table. It was as though her thoughts had been plucked from her mind during the night. Determined to give the impression she was completely fooled, Sue played along with the illusion, while all the time actively looking for a way of escape. The situation in which she found herself was deceptive. The lady was too friendly to be sincere — the cat an enigma, much too large and she did not trust that either. Then there was the Keeper — she was pleased he was not in the house. He was the one person she did not want to meet. No one stopped her wandering, so she spent her time looking for a means of escape, there had to be one. The cat was a constant companion, following her everywhere, and the rotund woman was delighted they seemed to get on with each other. By the time night fell for the second time, she had not gained any ground.

Sue went to bed frustrated, and drank the milk offered under the guise of friendship, even though she guessed it was drugged to keep her from wandering in the dark. She just hadn't the spirit to refuse it and make trouble.

The following morning she awoke once again refreshed and ready for anything — and her determination to get away was now stronger than ever. As she entered the kitchen, the rotund woman beamed at her and said, "You really are looking better, my dear. There is someone outside to see you. We must not keep him waiting."

It took all Sue's willpower to prevent apprehension showing on her face. She knew without looking through the window who was going to be there. She fixed a smile on her face and said lightly, "I'm sure he will wait a little longer while I have my breakfast," then sat at the table waiting expectantly. The rotund woman's smile slipped, showing a completely different side to her nature. She raised a plump hand to chastise Sue. The cat hissed at her action and the woman allowed her arm to drop. Having prevented the attack, Rajah sprang onto Sue's lap, but his green eyes were fixed on the woman. He purred loudly and thrust his head all over the girl's face. Sue was not exactly happy with the sudden display of affection, and he was heavy. She attempted to push the cat away, but his claws dug into her shoulders, making her wince and she had the distinct impression he said:

"If you want to get away from here you will have to meet the Keeper. Stop overplaying your hand and go while you have a chance. I will not be around all the time."

Sue pushed the cat off and at the same time risked a glance at the rotund woman, who had not had enough time to resume her normal expression. The naked animosity she saw there shocked her. She knew now she had been right — but strangely she was not happy at finding out she was correct. They were all in this deception. She forced herself to act nonchalantly, and

341

walked from the table, straight out of the cottage without a backward glance. She saw the Keeper immediately, sitting on his rock and still puffing away on his pipe. She wondered ironically if he carried the rock around with him. Still dressed in his mismatched clothes, he looked as obnoxious as ever. Making no attempt to rise and greet her, he watched her approach with steely blue eyes, and Sue, for some reason, was pleased the cat padded silently behind her. She saw the sudden narrowing of the old man's eyes. "Be careful," she heard the cat say, "do not antagonise him. You do not look subdued enough."

Sue wondered how she could avoid antagonising him. The very sight of him put her back up. Determined to be civil, she stopped within feet of him and said, "Good morning."

He rudely ignored her greeting as though it were beneath him to acknowledge her presence. "I have a task for you to do," he said without any preliminaries. "You have kept me waiting — so come with me now."

"I'd like my breakfast first," Sue demurred, and almost jumped out of her skin when he snarled, "I said *now*," emphasising the word now. She could feel her jaw dropping with shock and quickly snapped it shut. There was no way she could control her temper. "I'm not here to do things for you. You look capable enough to do them for yourself. I want to go home, as you well know."

The old man showed his yellow teeth, in what Sue suspected was supposed to be a smile, but the sight of them made her go cold. When he spoke, his voice cold and impersonal. "You can abolish that idea forthwith. You will not see your home again unless you carry out the tasks I have set you. This is the first of many. I can see you need to be taught a lesson, and this is your own fault. You should never have come here."

Sue was livid. "I didn't ask to come here. The horse brought…"

"Don't go all through that story again," he interrupted sharply. "You have a task to carry out. Bring me back what I want — and then," his eyes gleamed evilly, "then I will reconsider your position here."

The cat hissed a warning and came to Sue's side. The old man swung round on him with fury twisting his face, making it appear more bizarre than it already was. "Get out of here, Rajah, and see to your own business. This has nothing to do with you."

Rajah disagreed. His sharp feline teeth showed in a snarl as his lips curled back. His back arched threateningly and the black fur stood on end. Unexpectedly the Keeper raised his stout stick and threw it with force at the animal. Sue saw what he was doing and lurched forward to give the cat some protection, ending up by taking the full impact of the blow on her own body. There was a pregnant pause as she clenched her teeth to keep from crying out as the pain seared through her.

The Keeper cursed her as the cat ran. "What's the matter with you, woman, interfering in what does not concern you? Are you incapable of standing still?" There was no sympathy or apology in his voice as he noted her distress. "You wouldn't have been hurt had you kept your nose out of it. Now you've made your task ten times harder." He raised his hand and pointed with a gnarled finger to one of the three paths. "That is the way you go, girl, and look for a valuable jewelled casket. Do not, and I mean do not come back unless you have found it, otherwise I shall have to punish you."

Pain made Sue feel sick, but she showed no reaction beyond tightening her mouth. "Then there's nothing to worry about," she gasped, "I'm not going. I've walked that path before and it leads back here. You had better start the punishment."

His blue eyes were dangerously bright as they surveyed her. He removed his pipe and stood up — showing Sue he was a lot taller than she had imagined. She wondered what his real form looked like. However, the Keeper left her in no doubt where she stood.

"This is my domain," he asserted, his words clipped and icy. "Your life depends on my decisions. It is of no consequence to me if you live or die, but it may upset your friends — especially those who sent you here. Each task you carry out successfully brings you one step nearer to seeing them again. That is all I have to say. Now go!"

There was no chance to answer. A flash of light blinded her eyes and it was several minutes before she could see again. When sight was restored, she looked around in bewilderment. Everything had changed. There was no cottage or rotund woman — not even any Keeper. She was staring down into a vast valley, overgrown and full of ruins. Jagged inhospitable mountains surrounded the valley on all sides, and behind where she stood was a black cavity, swirling with a malevolent mist, daring her to retrace her steps.

* * *

Sue sank to her knees, hugging her bruised body tightly. She felt swamped with utter despair as she tried to comprehend what was facing her in this valley. Somewhere in this vast area of tangled undergrowth and ancient trees was a tiny jewelled casket, which was hidden from her eyes. It would take months of searching through this desolate valley to find such a small item. If she were to escape from this place, it had to be found. The Keeper was asking for the impossible. He knew exactly what her chances of success were. It made Sue wonder what she was doing here.

Why had that mare brought her to this Enchanted Land? Did it want her to find the Crystal Horse? Also, why was the Keeper so adamant about the horse not being here when even the rotund woman had seen it? Could the mare be the Crystal Horse? It was a far-fetched idea but a possibility. She shut her eyes in the hopes of blotting out everything and mulled over the dilemma she was facing. Sitting where she was, high up the side of the valley, her position was very precarious. A strong breeze tugged at her clothes and blew her hair back from her flushed face. She shivered and decided not to remain there any longer, especially if she wanted any chance of success. Grimacing at the pain as she stood up, she descended to the valley floor where she hoped to find shelter, and maybe light a fire for warmth. She doubted any other people would be there. It was not the Keeper's intention. He liked his victims to be entirely alone.

Slipping and sliding, Sue stumbled down the hill. She needed the use of her two arms if she didn't want to have a nasty fall. One hand was completely out of action and an ugly mauve bruise covered most of her forearm.

She sucked in her breath each time she accidentally brushed against an obstacle because of the uneven ground and treacherous rabbit burrows. Her stops were frequent, each time accompanied with tears of self-pity. At last she came across a patch of grass with a tiny stream bubbling over rounded stones. She fell to her knees on the bank and stretched out her neck to drink from the cool water.

She had not travelled very far to reach this destination, and already the sun was sinking behind the mountains. Some peaks were in darkness, but the tallest of them, covered in snow, were bathed with a rosy glow. It was too late to forage for kindling, and besides that, she was exhausted. She decided she would sleep here for the night. The water had taken away the edge to her hunger, and if there were any predators around, she was too miserable and confused to care.

It was not so much sleep which took over, but total exhaustion that sent her into oblivion. A few curious nocturnal creatures worked up enough courage to get near and sniff at her skin. One ran over her face, his whiskers twitching, but Sue did not stir. Yet something made her open her eyes, although she did not move from her recumbent position on the grass.

The most beautiful mare Sue had ever seen lowered her graceful neck to drink thirstily from the stream. Her whole body was translucent. Sue could see the trees through her form, which glowed with every movement of her anatomy. No colour could be attributed to the mare, she looked almost as though she were constructed of glass, and as Sue watched, it was as though the mare sensed her observation. She lifted her head and looked towards Sue with soft brown eyes, then delicately stepped towards where she lay, and lowering her nose, blew softly on her face. The next instant she was gone.

The morning sun blinded Sue's unprotected eyes and she awoke with a start, wondering why she felt so different. Without thinking, she sat up, putting all her weight onto her hands to support her body and, with a shock, realised her arm had been healed in the night. It was only then that she recalled fragmented scenes from her dream. Her thoughts of the Crystal Horse must have merged with her subconscious mind — but that did not explain how she had been healed, unless the injury had been an illusion in the first place. She smiled ironically because she didn't believe that. The pain had been very real.

Sue jumped to her feet, brushing dead leaves and bracken from her clothes. She needed to make an early start with her searching — there was a lot of ground to cover. Which way to go, was to her a problem. In the end she decided to follow the flow of the stream, and along its banks she found plenty of berries to sustain her in her search. Every time she passed a ruin, she gave a cursory glance within to make sure it was empty. Two or three times it was impossible to follow the water since gorse and bramble covered the whole area and she had to make a detour.

By mid-morning, fatigue forced her to rest. She wiped her face, which was moist with perspiration, and sat beneath a tree with her head pressed back against the bark. This was hopeless, she thought, staring moodily at the endless rows of bushes. To find anything here was like looking for a needle in a haystack and she had only the Keeper's word the casket was here. She would be better employed finding her way out of this valley, except that if this place were all an illusion, there would not be a way out.

"Ten out of ten for coming to your senses at last, girl."

The voice that uttered these words was clear in her head. Sue recognised it at once and sat up. She gazed from left to right, not seeing anything except the monotonous landscape. Something fluttered past her eyes and automatically she looked up amongst the branches and met the inscrutable unblinking stare of Rajah. With languid grace he sprang from the tree and fastidiously groomed himself in front of her, in no hurry to explain his presence. Even the cat was company, and Sue felt uplifted — but his sudden silence made her gnaw at her bottom lip. "You spoke to me," she ventured at last, and thought back to the time of her imprisonment with the Drazuzi and the Priest. There was hardly any difference in the situation. "You picked up on my thoughts," she said.

"True," answered the cat and then ignored her and washed his whiskers. After watching his ablutions in fascination for quite a while, Sue asked slowly, "What are you doing here?"

Rajah lifted his head and his green eyes bore right through her as though he wanted to assess her innermost thoughts before he spoke again. "In my book one good turn deserves another. You took a blow which was meant for me."

"So?" Sue prompted him. The cat's ears twitched. "You tell me," he countered.

"Then," Sue murmured daringly, "perhaps you could tell me where it is best for me to search for the jewelled casket?"

Rajah hissed in annoyance. "Don't you realise what I'm offering you? Why just the best place? Wouldn't you like me to tell you where it actually is?"

A prescience of danger pressed down on Sue. She could feel the hairs prickle on her arms and legs. Someone was trying to warn her to be careful of falling into a trap. She jumped to her feet — the movement startled the cat. "No!" she answered vehemently. "I want to be able to say I found it myself. The Keeper would know if I lied."

A growl came from the cat and his tail swished furiously. When he saw she was adamant, he pushed himself against her legs to ingratiate himself with her. "The Keeper will not care how you come by it, so long as you return with it. Come on now, follow me."

"No!" Sue was unyielding. "I'm not cheating. I'll search for it if you tell me in which direction to proceed."

"You're mad," the cat hissed disgustedly, "you'll be here for months and by then you'll have no strength left because there is no food here to eat. Forget your principles, girl. He will never know I told you."

"But I would — and I intend to carry out the task the Keeper gave me." Sue turned away and was halted by the cat's screech of "Danger." There was no danger as far as she could see, but turning back she saw the cat's fur standing on end as he shot back up the tree. Something crashed through the undergrowth, and she was flattened to the ground. A cold nose pressed on her ear and she heard a soft whine. Picking herself up and hardly daring to believe her eyes, she looked into the face of a big white wolf. From that day onwards Sue believed in miracles.

"White Hawk," she choked, and Rajah was sickened when she threw herself on the wolf and put her arms round his thick neck. With tears running unashamedly down her cheeks, she hugged him, and his long pink tongue washed her face. Her hold tightened and she knew the cat's thoughts were scathing as he said, "For goodness sake, girl — are you trying to choke him to death? If you know what's good for you, you'll get rid of that animal. The Keeper will go ballistic if he finds out he's here."

"Why should he be worried about a wolf?" asked Sue. "I thought he was all-powerful."

"Wolves do not live in the Enchanted Land, but somehow this one has got through the magical barrier. It's something that has never happened before. The Keeper is very particular about his force field."

Sue glared up at the cat. "So the Keeper is not infallible. He can make mistakes as well. White Hawk is my friend and bodyguard — and he's staying," she added defiantly.

Rajah made a move to come down the tree, but at his first movement White Hawk showed his teeth and added a warning snarl. Sue laid her hand on his head and whispered in his ear. No matter how hard the cat strained his ears, he didn't hear what she said. Sue was happier and safer than she had been in ages. She took pity on the cat. She didn't believe he was her enemy.

"He will not harm you if I introduce you as a friend – so come down," she invited.

The cat arched his back and spat out, "What kind of a fool do you think I am?"

White Hawk dismissed the cat as a nonentity. He remembered his master's last words and caught Sue's arm gently in his mouth. He tried to pull her away with a small whine. When Sue resisted, he pawed the ground and moved off a few paces, looking back at her. Sue knew he was asking her to follow him and that meant something was seriously wrong. She took one step towards him and Rajah leapt from the tree, blocking her way, and he suddenly seemed twice his size. There was nothing friendly about him now. Aggression oozed from his body. "Fool!" he hissed, his green eyes glinting. "The wolf might be able to leave this area — but you can't, girl. You are locked in here by the Keeper."

Sue automatically stiffened and stared at the cat steadily. "I'm not leaving. I shall come back and continue my search — but right now, someone is in trouble and I must go with the wolf."

Rajah looked like a porcupine with his fur all bristly. "You can't," he snarled — but Sue took him by surprise and sprang past him straight onto White Hawk's back. There she clung with her arms round his neck. Wolf and cat made eye contact, measuring each other up. White Hawk was twice the size of the cat so it was not surprising the cat gave way. White Hawk made good use of his chance and was away swiftly. Rajah watched until they were just a blur, then lay down and bided his time. There was plenty of time before he needed to make contact with the Keeper.

CHAPTER 26
DECISION TIME

Thane dropped in and out of consciousness, lying in a state of delirium in the dark subterranean cave. The cloying smell from the reptiles filled his lungs and had almost become an anaesthetic. In his few lucid moments, he discovered that if he did not light his tinderbox, the snakes ignored him. Thane wondered which was worse — lying in that oppressive chamber in complete darkness or listening to scratching sounds as their bodies slithered over each other. He could hardly hold the tinderbox and lit it once again, watching as they climbed up the wall in their attempts to reach him. There was something about the wall which repelled all their attempts and he could keep his nerve admirably until he wondered what it was they lived on. Thane had been in here for a long time. He was cramped and did not dare to move his body in case more of the wall gave way. Another fall would be the end of him because he would land in the pit with the snakes. Cramp became unbearable. He wanted to move his arms. He tried to move the one he was lying on and it protruded over the edge. Something leapt from the pit, missing his hand by a fraction. Then others followed suit. Darkness filled his mind as a wave of nausea took over. Thane knew there was no escape for him. He had let everyone down. His eyes blurred and he still remembered Sue's stricken face as it had been that day he had turned his back on her. "You like dragons so much – you have them. I don't need you." Why on earth had he said that?

Meanwhile, quite a distance away, White Hawk had accomplished his mission and was on his way back to his master with Sue. The wolf knew exactly where he was going — he was immune to all the magic. Unlike Sue, his eyes were not affected by illusion. He saw no mountains or high-sided valley, only trees and the far away river, which divided this place from the mainland. His one aim was to return to the spot where he last saw Thane, and this he did with all the speed he could muster. Sue clung tightly to him, arms wrapped round his neck and her face pressed firmly in his ruff. This was a journey she could never have made by herself — and it was just as well she couldn't see where she was going. White Hawk had his own unique power to shatter the illusions the Keeper had built around her.

High up on a slope, unseen by either of them, the figure of a man watched them go by. He easily picked up on the wolf's urgency and wondered from where and how it had got here. His blue eyes suddenly narrowed as he realised who it was on the wolf's back. Had it not been for that animal, she would still be locked safely in the valley, which he had conjured up to keep her confined. He chewed on his lower lip thoughtfully. From the very beginning he knew there was something different about this one. Several people had passed through his hands, but all had been useless. He knew he could stop Sue and the wolf right now, by snapping his fingers, but he was curious to see what happened, and this made him refrain from doing anything. The way the wolf was heading spelt certain death, so he just watched. He was not in the least disturbed to know she was going to die.

The Keeper had already made his assessment of Sue's character, but he wanted to see what the outcome was going to be. Other participants had died going in that direction. Yet something in him was uncertain this time. Where did that wolf come from? He sat down with his pipe and puffed away, biding his time. There was no way they could get off his domain — well, maybe the wolf might, but he was interested only in Sue.

White Hawk's sides were heaving when at last he reached the accumulation of rocks, which directed him to the subterranean tunnel. There he stopped running and collapsed on his belly. Sue hastily rolled off his back and saw with alarm the distressed condition he was in. Her eyes were anxious. She expected Thane to be here, but the wolf was alone. Sue shifted her gaze to her surroundings, giving him a chance to regain his strength. For the first time she saw the fast-moving river which no man could cross, unless he wanted to die. She sighed, so near to escape was she, but unable to take it. On the far side of the water were several colourful gipsy caravans. Their crooked chimneys were issuing smoke that curled and evaporated in the air. Plenty of children were running around, but their guttural voices jarred on her ears and not one of them looked across the water.

Sue looked back at White Hawk and at last he rose to his feet, and taking her hand gently in his mouth he guided her amongst the rocks to where there was a black cavernous hole, the sight of which made her bite her lip. She hated underground tunnels, and hung back slightly. But without a pause in his steps, the wolf led her inside and suddenly she was blind. White Hawk was not bothered because he could see in the dark, but Sue was completely lost. For a while she fumbled, trying to feel her way. Then her hand felt the wolf's back and he guided her further in. It suddenly crossed Sue's mind that she was being shown an escape route, until her head banged on a piece of rock jutting out from the wall. She stopped, muttering one of Barry's profane expressions, and wondered, since they were now under the river, whether her ring would work down here. Experimentally she rubbed it and to her ecstatic joy the green light flared out, bathing everything in light.

Her surroundings were now visible and Sue felt a lot happier. White Hawk's eyes shone like gold coins and he proceeded to walk deeper into the tunnel. It was at this point Sue picked up on the smell, which tickled her nose. She recognised it and went cold as visions of Deena filled her mind. Now she knew why the wolf had found her. Someone was trapped in here — and that someone could only be Thane. He was the one in danger. Fear almost paralysed her when she realised he must be in contact with the deadly snakes Deena had introduced to her.

The wolf suddenly stopped and for the first time Sue realised the tunnel had two exits. The very low opening at ground level was obviously the way the wolf had used. Higher, and much larger, loomed another opening. White Hawk pressed against her and whined. She knelt and hugged him. "I know," she whispered softly in his ear, "I feel the same way."

She began to climb to that high opening and White Hawk sat on his haunches, watching her. She was careful where she placed her feet and before long she reached the cavity. The smell became stronger.

At the top, she turned and looked down at the wolf, and he whined. She swallowed painfully. The tunnel she was now in was short, but the stench nauseated her. She had forgotten how strong it could be. She proceeded along until she reached the pit. At the lip of it she fought away a bout of dizziness. The green light showed everything. Feeling sick in her stomach, she stared at the heaving mass of snakes below and nearly retched. Her eyes roved carefully round the pit and then she saw Thane's body lying half on a very narrow ledge, half covered in rubble.

Her first impression was that he was dead, but by the light from her ring she saw his chest rise and fall and knew for the moment he was safe; but he could easily roll over the edge. The snakes could not reach him, although several were trying to do so. She called his name softly, but her voice quivered.

He heard her voice and thought he was dreaming — hardly daring to believe it was Sue. Thane raised his head with difficulty, seeing at first only a green haze. Then his eyes cleared, and he saw her stricken expression. Emotion choked his voice. "Sue! Sue, my darling. White Hawk found you." His throat hurt and was unbearably dry after breathing in so much dust. Everything went black.

He desperately fought his way out of it. He couldn't lose her now. He coughed and cried, "Sue! Am I hallucinating? Is it you I can see?"

Just for one terrible moment Sue couldn't speak because he thrust out an arm over the pit and two snakes leapt for it, crashing into each other and falling back into the pit. She wondered if she was still immune from the snake's venom. These were different from the ones Deena had bred and it was a long time since she last handled them — but looking at Thane decided her. She could not lose him. He must be saved because she loved him, no matter what the cost was to her. She lowered herself carefully into the pit, holding her breath. If they bit her, then they did. It would all soon be over. To her relief the snakes veered away, immediately making a path. She started to breathe again and felt Thane watching her. Their eyes met. She walked slowly and steadily towards him and when she reached his side he put his arms around her body. With a coherent cry she buried her face in his shoulder and he felt her hot tears on his cheek. Contact with him after all this time had the power to remove her stress. To feel him so close filled her with contentment. It was White Hawk's howl that made her remember where they were. Thane came to his senses.

"We can't get out from this side," he muttered, "it's all blocked behind me. The roof caved in."

"Then we must cross the pit," returned Sue quietly. "Do you remember the last time? Take my hand and keep contact with me — then the snakes will not touch you. Can you walk?" she asked anxiously.

Thane moved slowly and groaned, "If you remove the rubble from my legs, I think so. I'm a bit stiff from lying here for so long." Hanging on to Sue tightly, he gingerly slid from the narrow shelf and lowered his legs over the edge, feeling sweat stand out on his forehead. He tensed because he expected to crunch a few snakes underfoot as his feet touched the ground, but they all slithered away. With her supporting him, he struggled to the other side, but his eyes were fixed on the roof all the time, not on the heaving mass of reptiles. She helped him swing up his leg over the edge of the pit and sat by his side until he felt stronger.

Eventually Thane's arms wound round Sue and he kissed her trembling lips. "You'll never know how much I love you. Can you forgive me for my jealousy over Silver?" At that moment White Hawk howled impatiently — they smiled at each other, got to their feet and made their way back to where the waiting wolf stood.

* * *

Half an hour later, all three broke out into daylight and the ring automatically lost its glow. From his position amongst the trees, the Keeper frowned thoughtfully, his mind whirling. It was the first time he ever recalled seeing a man emerge alive from beneath the river, and he pondered on what power it was which had helped the girl. Sue breathed in deeply now that she was out in the open and White Hawk danced ecstatically around them. Thane, however, was conscious of being watched — his skin prickled and he glanced curiously at what he could see of the Enchanted Land.

"Where to now?" he asked uncertainly.

Sue sighed as realisation returned. Thane was alarmed at the way the glow faded from her face, which a few moments ago had been radiant. "I must go back," she said, but her voice was now curiously flat. "I must finish what I was asked to do. White Hawk dragged me away and only he knows the way back. I can't see the mountains from here."

"Of course you can't because there aren't any," Thane began hotly — then paused, this was the Enchanted Land. Someone had woven a spell over Sue's eyes and she believed what she was saying. He turned her round to face him. "Must you go?" he asked grimly, "we could try and escape across the water. After all — you didn't ask to come to this place. They can't keep you here."

Sue released herself gently. "It's a matter of honour. I've been given a task and I intend to carry it out. You wait here for me."

Thane's eyes blazed. "Not likely. I'm not letting you out of my sight again. I'll come and help you."

Sue hugged him, which Thane thought was a fair answer. "Thank you. Come on, White Hawk, show me the way."

The wolf was only too happy to oblige and headed towards the trees with the other two following hand in hand through the dappled sunlight. They were happy just to be together. The Keeper stiffened. He didn't understand this holding on to each other. The only sound to be heard was the crunch of dead leaves under their feet and the drone of insects flying by. Sue and Thane were blissfully happy until White Hawk shattered their illusion by growling and the Keeper stepped from the trees and blocked their way. He also grew bigger and matched the wolf in size. The unexpectedness of it made Sue gasp, but one look from his piercing blue eyes, and the wolf retreated behind Thane. Thane was wary. He measured the man up and felt the power radiating from him but the Keeper ignored him. He had eyes only for Sue and attacked at once.

"How did you break out of the valley?" he asked in an aggressive voice, and undaunted, Sue replied, "I have no idea. The wolf fetched me, but just in case you're wondering, I'm on my way back now. I told Rajah I would return and search for the jewelled casket — even if it takes me months."

"The cat had no business to be with you," was the Keeper's harsh rejoinder. "It's a wonder he didn't offer to do the searching for you."

Sue's mouth opened and shut, but she decided not to answer. It had nothing to do with him, but the Keeper insisted. "Well, did he?" he prompted imperiously.

"Yes," Sue retorted, "but I happen to like a challenge and intend do my own hunting, even if things are unfairly stacked against me." When there was no answer, she could not resist looking at the Keeper's face, which was nowhere near as grotesque as it previously had been. She now saw a smile there. It transformed him completely. To her surprise he reached out and touched her. The unexpected action took all Sue's willpower not to flinch away; but with Thane holding her hand, she drew courage from him and pleaded, "Please do not be cross with Rajah. He has been a good friend to me."

"You seem to have many friends," returned the Keeper dryly, "and you also have the power to charm my guardians of the tunnel — yet there are no marks of initiation on your arms."

"That is because the Princess must not be marked," cut in Thane coldly before she could answer. "I take it you did know who she is?"

The Keeper drew himself up. "I am not interested in who gets sent to my land. I only test them. That is my job."

Thane gestured towards Sue. "But you're still testing her, aren't you?" he asked harshly.

"No, young man, I'm not. I've finished," replied the Keeper. "You being here does not make any difference to the outcome and that can be very harsh. She will be given a choice. This is not a game."

"I would suggest you allow the Princess to leave with me now." Thane glared at the Keeper. "The king will not allow you to keep his daughter here as a prisoner."

"The king has no magic. He is powerless against us."

"Then you haven't done your homework..."

"Stop it," Sue interrupted, looking anxious. "I haven't found the jewelled casket yet."

Thane didn't answer but his grip on her tightened. They were both bewildered. The Keeper turned away from them and indicated that they should both sit down on a log, which miraculously appeared beside them, exactly as a rock appeared for him, and once they were settled, the old man said ruminatively:

"I am going to bore you both with a history lesson. The Therossa you know today is like it is because years ago someone placed an artefact of omnipotent power in the safe keeping of the Enchanted Land. I was chosen to guard it against all the thieves and marauders who wanted to steal that power for themselves. I have been the guardian for many years. Many people have come to retrieve it legitimately — and just as many have failed the tasks presented to them. I have been looking for the right person for years. A person with the best qualifications, and who can accomplish the demands made on them without showing any ill feeling. If I find that person, then I shall know I have found the one who is capable of wielding this colossal power and taking my place."

The Keeper's stare was fixed on them both and Sue looked extremely uneasy. She edged closer to Thane and he responded by putting his arm round her and giving her a reassuring squeeze. "I'm so glad I don't qualify," she said huskily. "How awful to be the person with all that power — knowing that anything they ordained would come to pass. It's not right someone should have all that power at his disposal." Unbidden, the face of the Priest came into her mind and a shiver went through her. A smile touched the Keeper's lips.

"You are misunderstanding me. My job is to pass that power to someone else. But whoever touches the Crystal Horse is not allowed to keep it. All they will have done is to make one wish that will change something they know is wrong, and for using this privilege, he or she will have to pay a stiff price."

Another silence fell over the group. Sue could feel her anxiety increasing. She could not grasp what the Keeper was getting at, but Thane was more astute and came to her aid by asking him why he was he telling all this to Sue.

The Keeper pressed his fingertips together and then touched his chin. He stared intently at Sue as he said, "Because someone sent Sue here in the hope she would win this chance to rescue them from the hell they were living in. He picked his champion well because she has passed all my tests. She has shown she will not be bribed to take the easy way and has shown compassion for her companions. Also she has the right outlook to do well. It leaves only one question — will she abide by the last test?"

Sue stared at him, apprehension uppermost within her. She licked her lips. "There is still another test?" she asked tentatively.

"Not exactly a test," he replied, "but a stipulation by which you must abide."

Sue was lost for words, so Thane demanded grimly, "May we know what this stipulation is?"

The Keeper shook his head. "That is not permitted at this moment. If Sue is dedicated to her cause, she will willingly abide by it. If not — she may leave this land now, but will never be allowed to return, except under the threat of death." Sue stared dumbly at Thane, and White Hawk nuzzled her hand. They both knew what was in her mind. She turned back to the Keeper. "How long have I got before I need make my decision?"

"Until sunset," the Keeper returned gravely. "No longer than sunset."

Sue and Thane stared up at the sky where already the sun was on its downward path. The three of them huddled together. By the time only a sliver of sun remained on the horizon, the Keeper reappeared and approached Sue, who now was on her own, hunched up on the side of the hill. This was not Thane's idea, it was the way she wanted it. Thane's face was set like a mask, veiling his emotions and he kept a restraining hand on White Hawk's head, to stop him from breaking through the fragile veneer Sue had built about herself. The

Keeper's face showed no emotion. He asked Sue to stand, which she did, very slowly. The Keeper held something small in his hand and walked up to her. "Do you wish to use the power you have earned?" he asked carefully.

Sue nodded, unable to speak for the moment because she was overcome. She looked at Thane, her eyes brimming over with tears — then back to the Keeper. A lump came up in Thane's throat and he wanted to gather her in his arms, but under the Keeper's stare, he restrained himself with an effort. He admired her for what she was about to relate. Fighting to remain composed, Sue said, "Many months ago I was held a prisoner by the Priest Oran and I saw what a degrading life the Drazuzi people were forced to live, wearing nothing but rags and forced into slavery in their own homes. He humiliated them by making them work to keep him and his followers in luxury. One Drazuzi woman helped me to escape from the caves and I vowed if ever I had the chance, I would do everything in my power to put things right for them. My chance has come now. Yes, Keeper — I — " she broke off because he pressed a stone into her hand, and then bade her continue. "I want to wish that the Drazuzi people break free of the bondage which holds them prisoners in their own homes. I want the downfall of the Priest," she declared.

There was a silence in which the air vibrated. The stone in her hand flared with light and she fleetingly caught the glimpse of a miniature Crystal Horse. The Keeper gently removed it from her almost lifeless hand and looked towards Thane. "Before anything else happens, you might like to know that the Drazuzi people sent Sue here and faced the possibility that she might not even do anything for them. Also, I must tell you that it is as perilous to leave this land as it is to enter. Now that Sue's wish has been granted — only one person is allowed to leave. The other stays here for eternity." With those words he looked back at Sue and just as he turned to leave, Sue cried out piteously, "Please let White Hawk go with him."

The Keeper vanished and Sue clung to Thane, crying, "I'll find a way — you see if I don't." His arms enfolded her, then suddenly she was on her own, trying to grasp for air. Thane and White Hawk were gone. In utter misery she flung herself down on the ground and cried, until the rotund woman found her.

CHAPTER 27
THE SACRIFICE

"I think we should go this way," Barry said because he felt someone should make a decision, but his voice sounded hollow as it echoed round the large amphitheatre where they were standing. Arctic conditions prevailed and any exposed flesh soon became covered in goose pimples. Zeno shivered and let Barry's remark sail over his head. He stared in distaste at the tiers of seats surrounding them. There was a feeling of evil in the atmosphere. Sconces flared from brackets around the circular walls casting strange shadows. Why should the Drazuzi want light when they could see perfectly well in the dark? He shied away from the thoughts entering his head and muttered fearfully, "I think this is the place where they intend to sacrifice us. What on earth possessed us to come here?"

Barry snorted. "We haven't got a map, that's why," he retorted sarcastically. "Have you got a better idea?" He eyed the sconces placed alongside each row of seats where they joined the stone steps leading down to the central arena. The vast layout of the place with its nearly invisible roof made both of them feel small. Zeno stepped back a pace. "Yes," he answered tightly, "we must beat a hasty retreat before someone comes along and catches us."

"OK." Barry took charge and gave a quick look around. "Let's go down here." He chose a tunnel at random since he had the choice of many. It was darker than all the others and much narrower. It appeared to be unused.

In trepidation they started on their journey through the gloom of the uninviting tunnel. It had jagged walls and many potholes. They were getting tired, a lot of time having passed since they had broken out of the sphere in a bid for freedom, and spent hours of wandering aimlessly through endless tunnels, jumping at shadows and avoiding bright areas. Coldness was eating into them. Zeno worried all the time that they had not encountered any Drazuzi, but Barry worried much more that they had not found a way out of their underground prison. Inadvertently he touched the icy wall and grazed his knuckles, so he stopped to suck the blood away. Zeno gave him a shove and said, "Get a move on there before I turn into an icicle."

Barry's expression was pained as he moved on. It soon became apparent their insignificant tunnel was at last widening and before they knew it, they were out in one of the main thoroughfares used by the Drazuzi. Barry realised he had made a bad mistake when choosing this way — there was nowhere to hide. The walls arching over them were smooth, and gave off an eerie glow, but the coldness exuding from the rock increased. It was an automatic reaction for both lads to pump their arms up and down to stimulate circulation. Zeno took a cautious look down the thoroughfare in both directions, and since neither way appealed to him, he shrugged and said, "We've got another choice to make. Right or left?"

Barry sighed. "Suppose you try your luck this time?" he suggested.

Zeno refrained from answering and immediately turned to the right — only because he saw a bend in the distance. Stumbling along, the boys still kept their eyes skimmed for the slightest indentation in the walls. Luck was not with them. Nearing a bend, Barry halted. There was disbelief in his eyes. He lifted a hand to his mouth and hissed, "Someone is coming towards us. He is just round the corner."

Zeno tugged at him urgently. "Let's run back. I don't want to be caught again."

"It's far too late for that," Barry retorted. "He'll be round the corner any moment now. Anyway, I expect he's already picked up on our being here."

His words sparked off panic at the thought of their freedom ending. Neither was prepared to be recaptured. Unanimously they were determined to make it hard for the Drazuzi to catch them a second time. Zeno stiffened, though he tried to look composed. Barry glowered like a cornered animal. "Don't let him see you're afraid, Zeno," he muttered unfairly, and Zeno glared at him fiercely. "I'm not!" he exploded, forgetting to keep his voice down — and would have said a lot more had not the Drazuzi turned the bend at that moment. There was a stunned silence, broken by a deep voice.

"My God, it's Barry," someone said, and Barry found himself being hugged by strong arms. Zeno's jaw dropped incredulously when he saw the king and Rainee smiling at them, but years of soldiering made him jump to attention — although his shivering rather spoilt the effect.

"Relax, son," Tam smiled, "no one is on parade here. You don't know how great it is to find you both without having to overcome any Drazuzi." He was suddenly aware of Barry's cold body as the boy fought to be free of his embrace. "Rainee!" he exclaimed in disbelief, "The lads are freezing." Quickly removing one of his outer garments, he draped it over Barry's shoulders. Rainee came forward and did likewise for Zeno. She found it hard to keep her composure on seeing their pathetic gratitude. Barry's dazed mind started to function normally. He focused his attention onto Tam hungrily, almost as though he thought he would disappear. A lump rose up in his throat making it hard for him to swallow; consequently his words were nearly incoherent. "Tam, Rainee! What on earth are you doing in here? Have you come to rescue us?" he asked.

Finding his nephew unharmed had robbed Tam of a ready answer, but Rainee, more alert, stared anxiously along the tunnel. She drew the king's attention back to her by saying, "This isn't the best place for a reunion. If we know what's good for us we must leave this place at the first opportunity. Anyone could come along and ask awkward questions. If my memory is correct somewhere down there is a narrow tunnel which turns off from this one — and from there it will lead us to Oran's private quarters."

At her words, Barry gasped. "The Priest," he echoed almost in dismay. "I had no idea we were travelling in his direction. What fools we were." At Tam's questioning look, they poured out their story, not only about their imprisonment in a sphere, but about the two bands of Drazuzi living in these underground passageways, fighting each other along with the Priest. Just as Tam and Rainee digested the information, Barry added carelessly, "This is how you happened to find us. We had escaped from the sphere and were running away because the Drazuzi were going to sacrifice us to their God Raga. We didn't feel like being cooked."

"Barry!" exploded Tam angrily, "this isn't the time to be flippant. You should have told us this from the first. We're wasting precious time standing here." He exchanged a worried look with Rainee. "What do you think?" he queried. Her face creased up in a frown, which confirmed what he already thought. No Drazuzi around meant only one thing. The threat of sacrifice was very real. The Drazuzi must all be assembled somewhere else — and if Barry was to be believed, it would not be long before they were accosted by a search party. Looking for Oran and rescuing the Professor became secondary goals, and Tam came to an unexpected decision. Instead of retracing his steps, he turned to his nephew.

"Show us where this amphitheatre is, Barry," he ordered tersely, "is it far from here?"

"Are you sure you want to go there?" asked Barry doubtfully. "It's not a very nice place and by now it must be swarming with Drazuzi. I'll draw you a map."

Tam's eyebrows raised a fraction. "What a pity I forgot to bring pen and paper," he said mockingly. "So you think they are all there waiting for you and Zeno to turn up — and if you don't turn up they will make plans for another day?"

"That makes it worse," interjected Zeno. "They must be searching for us and getting madder by the minute."

"How right you are," the king said, smiling grimly. "I want to meet them. My fight is not with them. Don't look so alarmed. You will be safe with us."

* * *

Barry wished he shared Tam's optimism. He could not get rid of that niggling fear in the pit of his stomach. The last thing he wanted was to go back and deliberately meet the Drazuzi. He exchanged glances with Zeno as they reluctantly retraced their steps. How could you argue with a king? Even with grownups in tow, they felt decidedly nervous as they neared the amphitheatre. Barry chewed on his lower lip. The prescience of danger overcame him when the end of the tunnel came into view and light flooded towards them. The amphitheatre had changed dramatically; it was now overflowing with Drazuzi, and every seat was taken. Many struggled to find a place where they could be sure of a good view. From where Barry stood, lurking behind Tam, the central space appeared very small and crowded with white shrouded disciples of Raga. It was when the disciples moved, and he caught the glimpse of two wooden stakes erected side by side, that the world spun and he and Zeno were rooted to the spot. Shivers ran up and down their spines. Rainee tried to calm them, but all the soothing words from her could not erase what, in their eyes, those stakes meant. Even Tam had second thoughts on seeing such an organised event. His sharp hiss of "Stop!" was too late — the Drazuzi surrounded them, coming up from behind on silent feet. Unless he wanted to appear a coward, the king had no option but to go forward and meet the tall Drazuzi who seemed to be in command.

Behind him, Rainee felt her hackles rise. The scene revolted her so much, her hand sneaked towards her throat where the talisman was hidden — and to her chagrin, a power stopped her hand before it reached there. A stern voice rebuked her. "Do not do anything silly, lady. Our powers are stronger than yours. You were not invited here, so please stay out of our affairs."

"We came for..." Tam started grimly, but the Drazuzi cut him short, saying, "We are indebted to you both for bringing our runaways back to us, but there was no need since we already had them under our surveillance and knew exactly where they were. It makes them happy to run free for a while and a happy sacrifice is much better than an unwilling one." The callous words came out with no feeling at all as to the effect they had on the listeners. His large dark eyes bore into Tam as he continued unemotionally, "At any other time, Your Highness, I would be pleased to converse with you, but today is a special occasion and I have not the time. You may stay and witness our ceremony if it so pleases you since you are here."

Tam was nonplussed at being recognised. "So you know who I am," he answered guardedly, and nodded towards Rainee and the boys, saying, "In which case, would you please allow us to continue on our journey. We have no wish to interrupt you."

"You, Your Highness, are welcome to proceed," the other retorted smoothly, "but you cannot take the boys. They are my guests."

"Guests be dammed," spluttered Tam, his eyes hardening. "They are your prisoners."

"In that assumption you are mistaken," the Drazuzi returned composedly. "We have looked after and fed them for several days. Now they are both repaying us by taking part in our ceremony and..."

"Ceremony," Tam blazed, rudely interrupting him. "I'm not going to stand by and watch you kill off members of my family in what you have the nerve to call a ceremony." At those words the Drazuzi closed in on him. The white-clothed disciples were so close his arms were pinned tightly to his sides, and a peculiar hissing sound came from their mouths. The one in charge remained calm, showing his large teeth in a smile and replied politely:

"His station in society is of no consequence to us. If he is related to you, then we apologise, but he is here because he has a destiny to fulfil. We need his blood."

Rainee tried to suppress her gasp of horror, but Tam was livid. "My nephew has no destiny to fulfil," he thundered, "and certainly does not have to give you his blood for a barbaric ceremony. Unless you want trouble, then I demand you release him this instant."

"It is too late for that," the Drazuzi answered unemotionally. "It has to be this way. We are a people fighting for survival. Maybe royal blood will be a good thing and bring us success. We need to overcome the Priest."

"So do I." Tam took a step forward. It was an unwise move but he didn't care. With disciplined control he stopped himself from shaking the man. "I've got powers of my own," his voice growled, "and you will be on the receiving end if you so much as lay a hand on these boys."

The Drazuzi man lifted his hand contemptuously, and before Tam realised what was happening, he was completely enmeshed in a fine golden net, which bound him tighter than any rope. It not only curtailed the movement of his body, it also stopped him from speaking. Rainee rushed forward without thinking, and tried to claw it away, then found herself suffering the same fate.

Barry was now bereft, utterly dumbfounded at seeing his elders trussed up like chickens. He didn't think anyone could ever overcome Tam, and the knowledge that they could, lowered his morale considerably. Before he knew it, the Drazuzi turned their attention on him and Zeno. They both fought with a wild frenzy to escape but, outnumbered, they were soon dragged to the central floor where they were put on view to the waiting masses.

There was nothing dignified about the way they came. Zeno kicked like a mule and tried a few life-saving moves Amos had taught him for survival — and had the pleasure of hearing rasping sounds coming from those who attacked him. Barry acted like an animal and bit an arm, which he instantly regretted, but had the satisfaction of seeing blood. However they were soon overcome, as it was a one-sided battle.

Tam tried thinking up all sorts of incantations for the downfall of their captors, but the golden mesh acted as a deterrent. His magic was useless. Barry tried a magic of his own — brought on because he suddenly visualised Sue's face and realised he was never going to see her again. Or Tamsworth Forest and Aunt Moria. Something

374

exploded in his mind. His eyes glazed over as he screamed out vehemently, "You've had your fun now — but have you considered the consequences when Golden Hair hears what you have done to her brother? Believe me you will suffer. Golden Hair is my sister."

Barry felt a tinge of remorse at the lie but forced himself to ignore it. Everyone in the amphitheatre heard his words, which caused an uneasy silence and brought moisture to Tam's eyes as he looked at the devastated boy sadly, unable to help him. "She will never help you again," Barry continued to yell out, "she might have stood up for you once — but after this," he gulped, "after this she'll never do it again." His voice cracked and ended in a sob.

While the Drazuzi looked at each other, undecided, Tam struggled afresh to free himself. Barry would never know how near he came to upsetting the ceremony — but one person was adamant it would go on. A loud bang on a drum drew everyone's attention to the disciple who walked regally down the steps to the central space. With hard eyes, and not showing a glimmer of remorse on his face, he proudly carried the sacrificial knife towards his intended victims.

A light from the sconces lit up the blade with a red glow and the boys followed him, each holding a silver dish. The tableau was self-explanatory. Barry swallowed convulsively and Zeno changed colour as nausea choked him.

"Secure them," snapped the newcomer, and in the midst of battling with his fear, Barry realised that all the white-clad disciples spoke with words — not that it was going to help him. Within seconds of the order being issued, he and Zeno were lashed to the stakes by eager hands and their heads were pulled roughly back against the wood. One of them took great pleasure in baring their throats. The king's coat and the shawl of Rainee were trampled underfoot. Rainee sucked in her breath and wished this was all a dream and she was back in her caravan. Tam could hardly think coherently while desperately trying to escape from his bonds, but the gold mesh held him cruelly. His magic was no match against the Drazuzi.

Unconsciousness overtook Zeno — Barry was not so lucky and tears ran down his face as his emotions let him down and his screams filled the air. The noise in the amphitheatre pulsated through his head and when the boy stepped forward and placed the silver dish under his chin, nausea became a reality. The sacrificial ceremony began. The disciple held his knife aloft. "Raga!" he shouted out. "Raga, we all wait for your command."

"Raga, Raga!" repeated the crowd, and they surged to their feet. "We are ready."

Still in the same position, the disciple intoned, "The sun over our world has at last set, the time is right and our sacrifice is willing to help our cause. Accept our offering, Raga. Take the blood of these boys for our salvation."

An unnatural silence spread round the amphitheatre as the knife started on its lethal downward sweep, but above the hush of expectancy, another harsh voice roared out, "Stop this barbaric stupidity at once," and the whole cavern was suddenly engulfed in flames. The phenomenon lasted seconds, and no one was hurt, but when the air cleared and normality returned the disciple with the knife had vanished and the bonds securing the prisoners fell to the floor. Freed from their bonds, Barry and Zeno toppled senseless to the ground.

Tam sprang forward as the gold mesh binding him disintegrated, and picked Barry up, cradling him in his arms. Rainee did likewise with Zeno and no one standing nearby stopped them. They looked at each other, neither one of them ashamed that they had tears in their eyes.

"Who saved them?" asked Rainee huskily, and simultaneously they both gazed around the amphitheatre searching for the cause of their rescue and their eyes fell on a gaunt, tattered figure almost falling down the stone steps. The Drazuzi shrank away from this person, allowing him room to pass unhindered. In spite of his unkempt beard and sallow complexion, Tam recognised an old adversary from his youth.

"Graham Harding," he ejaculated, his astonishment barely concealed. "Well I'll be damned. I never knew you possessed so much power."

"If only I did," muttered the Professor stumbling up to them. Although weak and emaciated, he still maintained his hauteur. "I had nothing to do with that fire. It was purely coincidental that I shouted out at the same time. If I had that sort of power, I would have broken out from this hell ages ago."

Rainee ignored the pathos in his voice. She had heard a lot about him from Barry and was prejudiced. With critical eyes she studied him, and didn't like what she saw. "I've heard a great deal about you," she said. "Because as well as Barry, you were one of the people we came here to rescue. I was under the impression there were two of you. Where is the other one?"

The Professor's sunken eyes were suddenly distorted with fury. Her tone of voice caught him on the raw. He didn't know her but he turned on Rainee so viciously she drew back in alarm. "You think this is all a game," he snarled venomously. "You've got no idea what I've been through, and the 'other one', as you call my friend Cyril," he paused to draw a rasping breath and saliva dribbled from his bloodless lips before he added, "my friend Cyril is dead." He ignored her quick intake of breath. "He was killed just as the Drazuzi were about to kill them," he said as he jerked his head towards the unconscious boys, "only I didn't save him although he was ten times better than that precocious kid who's got no respect for his elders."

It was obvious to Tam the man was existing on nervous energy and not aware of what he was saying. He laid Barry down beside Rainee, gripped the Professor by his thin shoulders and felt him totter. "Calm down, Harding," he said, "we had no idea what was happening to you or we would have been here sooner. Where is the Priest now?"

The Professor's eyes filled with a wild light, his laugh almost maniacal when he said, "He's dead as well and I call that justice. That's how I managed to get away from him. I've been locked up for ages in this underground hell, putting up with him probing my mind. Then suddenly he had a seizure before my very eyes and I was able to escape — only I didn't escape. I walked straight into this amphitheatre and saw the Drazuzi sacrificing a couple of helpless boys." His whole body shuddered. "I couldn't let that happen so soon after

Cyril's death." He was shaking, almost out of control, and Rainee found it in her heart to pity him.

Tam pushed him down onto a seat, which was miraculously empty in spite of all the people crowding around them. "Thank you for doing that," he answered, but then the professor slumped over from sheer exhaustion and was out of this world. Tam suddenly remembered all the disciples and the Drazuzi who were watching proceedings. His eyes flickered around the amphitheatre, and what he saw made his breath catch in his throat. "Rainee," he choked, and managed to get her attention by the very way he said her name, "am I having hallucinations?" Rainee rose to her feet and stood by his side.

The Drazuzi people were now completely different. They had changed from being grotesque creatures into well-dressed human beings. No longer skeletal, their skulls were covered with healthy flesh. All deformities vanished. Men could be distinguished from women. Their hair hung to their shoulders, thick and lustrous and their formerly expressionless eyes were now full of compassion. They grouped together, silently watching the king retrieve what was his. Not only had they changed, but so had their surroundings. The icy chill in the air had vanished and, to their astonished eyes, the sconces on the walls turned into elaborate lanterns. Dark wooden seats now took place of the stone ones, and each had a red velvet cushion placed on it for comfort. The stark rocky walls were covered with intricately patterned tapestries of gold and crimson. The whole place had the appearance of a holy temple.

"What has happened here?" Rainee was completely overwhelmed. Her eyes tried to comprehend what they were showing her. "What magic is this?"

"I think we are about to find out." Tam took hold of her arm to give her courage. "We have nothing to fear so stay calm and let me do the talking. Just watch, because we'll never see the likes of this again."

Rainee gazed in the direction he was looking, and her husky whisper of, "Is she a priestess?" was barely audible. Coming down the steps, dressed in a white gossamer robe with flowers entwined in her long dark tresses, an ethereal woman glided towards them. She paid homage to Tam, who stood spellbound, unable to take his eyes off such exquisite beauty. He knew who she was — but never expected to meet the Goddess in person. Before speaking to them, she stooped over Barry and Zeno, placing her delicate hands on both their heads. Her sweet melodious voice drifted to every part of the amphitheatre. "When you wake up, this will all seem like a dream." She turned to Tam and Rainee, her expression calm, and her serenity encouraged them both to relax. In a soft voice she said to them, "The Drazuzi people were once a proud and noble tribe — but other people's misuse of them ground them down to what they are today. They were near the end of their tether when unexpectedly they were shown a way to regain their own salvation by breaking the tenacious hold the Priest had over them. They were shown a champion, ironically brought to their notice by the Priest himself, and, without this person being aware of their intentions, they sent this emissary to the Enchanted Land to fight their cause. Their emissary was your daughter — the Princess Sonja."

At Tam's gasp of protest, the Goddess held up her hand to silence him and continued. "She remained ignorant of who sent her, so that she was biased. This whole venture could have worked against the Drazuzi, but they chose well, for she succeeded in all the tasks laid before her and won the right to use the Crystal Horse — in favour of the Drazuzi. The curse, which had lain over them for centuries, was broken and the people who prolonged its effect were eliminated. You should be very proud of your daughter, King Tam." Tam fought between pride and torment, his face drained of colour. "And where is she now?" he questioned harshly.

The Goddess smiled. "She is still there. The law being that once someone has a wish granted, they remain there for ever." Tam opened his mouth to protest furiously, but she said sharply, "Wait! Sonja's love for certain people will melt the hardest heart. Do not worry about her, Tam. She will break away. Your daughter is very resourceful." She gave him no time to reply. In a flash, the Goddess vanished, just as Barry stirred at their feet. "Gosh, have I missed anything?"

CHAPTER 28
FREEDOM

Sue never remembered arriving back at the rotund lady's little house, until she woke up to find herself sitting before a roaring fire with Rajah at her feet. Outside. a storm was gathering strength and the wind howled eerily around the cottage. It was too dark to see anything beyond the windows and Sue was too distraught to care. The words thrummed through her mind. A lifetime here on the Keeper's land was too devastating to think about. Her cheeks felt stiff where so many tears had run down, and it was useless to keep wiping them away because there were too many of them. She looked into the fire with her swollen eyes and seemed pathetically lost.

The woman came beside her and pressed a mug into her hands, telling her brusquely, "It will pass. By tomorrow you will have forgotten everything. Drink this up while it's hot."

Forgotten, thought Sue miserably, I'll never forget as long as I live. I've lost Thane and White Hawk.

The curtains flapped at the open window as the wind caught them, causing a draught to fill the room and smoke to issue from the chimney. Sue shakily raised the mug to her lips, inhaling the steam rising from it — but before she could drink, Rajah decided to jump onto her lap. Sue gasped and the mug jerked wildly because she could not control it and the contents splashed over her arm and over the cat. He hissed and returned to the floor. The rotund woman lost her sunny smile. She glared at Rajah. "What did you do that for, you great big lummox?" she snapped, looking aggrieved. "Now I've got to make another one."

She snatched the mug from Sue's hand, ignored her embarrassed "please don't bother" and swiftly returned to the kitchen, where a few bangs and crashes indicated her mood. Perplexed, Sue looked at the unconcerned cat, which had nearly been scalded. "What's making her so short-tempered?" she asked.

Rajah's eyes gleamed as he looked at her. "Because that drink was special," he answered. His pink tongue licked his lips with relish. "When she returns with the next one, just pretend to drink it — if you don't, you really will forget everything."

"What do you mean?" Sue was shocked. "She wouldn't harm me. She has given me great comfort. Why don't you say what's on your mind? You deliberately made me spill that drink." Her voice was accusing.

Rajah twitched his ears and swished his tail round to cover his front paws. The green eyes glittered as they surveyed her. "I'm glad you've still got enough sense to see some things — even though you can't see I'm trying to help you. Go ahead and do what you want," he ended dismissively, and turned his back on her to dry his fur by the heat thrown out by the fire. A strong gust of wind surged through the open window and this time it shut with a bang. A large cloud of smoke poured down the chimney and drifted across the ceiling. "That's where you should be," the cat warned under his breath. "Get up high. You need to be able to think straight."

"Why? Am I still being tested?"

"Of course not, my dear," retorted the rotund woman, returning with a freshly filled mug. The smile was back on her face. "If you don't go to sleep soon, it will be morning and you will feel like nothing on earth." She placed the mug once again in Sue's hand, adding, "Drink it down now – and as for you" she turned to Rajah, "stop pestering her."

"I'm trying to help," the cat sniffed disdainfully. "All you're doing is helping her to sleep but she really needs fresh air to blow away the cobwebs."

"Not on a night like this. Maybe in the morning she can go out if she feels like it. I'm only carrying out what the Keeper advised," the woman said, defending herself, but the words she uttered cleared the depression clogging Sue's mind. Even now, after all that had happened, she still didn't trust anything that the Keeper had had a hand in. The lady was still waiting for Sue to drink the contents of the mug, so she lifted the mug to her lips with one eye on the cat. Directly the liquid touched her lips, she jerked her head away, and it was a genuine reaction. "It's too hot," she said, "I'll drink it in a minute," then she turned crimson, noticing the disapproval etched on the plump lady's features. It was obvious she did not believe her. "There is nothing in it. What nonsense has Rajah been filling you up with?"

"None," retorted Sue hastily, and inadvertently slopped some. "It really is too hot. You try some."

The offer was rejected and the rotund woman turned away. "Well you know where your bed is when you've drunk it," she said. "If you go to sleep in that chair, you'll be asking for trouble. You will not be refreshed in the morning. Watch over her, Rajah. I have other things that need to be done. The shutters must be closed before the storm worsens. It's going to be a real bad one tonight." She waddled purposely to the front door and her long skirt billowed out like a tent as she opened it. Without looking back, she slammed it behind her and disappeared in a swirl of wind.

Rajah stretched his body and dug his claws into Sue's knees, making her suck in her breath. "You don't have to act like that, I haven't drunk any," she said angrily. "There is no need for you to display your persuasive powers."

"Good," he answered. "Pour the drink over the logs and go to bed. She is watching us." In spite of the heat, a shiver ran down Sue's back. "Why is she doing that? What reason…"

"Pour it out now — quickly — and then raise the mug to your lips as though you are draining it empty." There was so much force in his voice that Sue complied, even though she thought it was a bit over the top. The logs steamed and, should the woman return, she might notice this. Sue stared at the cat inquiringly. "What now?" she asked.

Rajah turned away from her to face the fire and proceeded to wet his paws and clean behind his ears, but all the time his voice came to her clearly. "The drink she gave you was drugged — to keep you asleep for the next two days. I tasted it, so I know. When you eventually woke up, you would have no idea of the time lapse and it would be a good few more days before your memory was fully restored."

Sue's eyes opened wide with astonishment. "But I don't understand," she said, staring at him incredulously. "Why should she want to do that to me?"

"Because the Keeper suspects you have power," he replied.

"That's stupid." Anger laced Sue's words. "His power is stronger than anyone else's I know. Is it because I can control the snakes?"

"It's more than that," Rajah hissed. "It's something he sees in your aura. Now listen to me carefully. To grant you your wish with the Crystal Horse, the power used was colossal. It has left the Enchanted Land unprotected, but in two days' time, the magical barrier that keeps everything out, and you in, will be restored. In the meantime, anything could happen. Suppose you, with this power that he suspects you have, called to someone for help — they would be able to come and not be harmed while the barriers are non-existent. Are you following my meaning?"

Sue was — and it stunned her. The cat's eyes pierced right through her and saw the tremendous excitement building up in her face. He wondered how she was going to get Thane back, but to see her looking like she was right now, it was well worth the risk. Sue's eyes lit up and transformed her face as she realised there was a real possibility of following Thane and White Hawk. Giving her the drug was a wise move on the part of the Keeper. If she were asleep, then the escape bid could never happen. Thanks to Rajah, she now knew she had a chance to get away and she knew exactly how she was going to do it.

"Rajah," she breathed, "I could hug you."

Rajah brushed against her legs and murmured, "Then don't spoil things now. Act as you've never acted before, because your freedom depends on it. Pretend to take one last gulp of whatever's in your mug, and yawn. Then go to bed and feign sleep. I will come to you directly the woman has come in and gone to bed. If you are going to try, it must be tonight, storm or no storm."

Sue rose to her feet and gave a realistic totter. She sensed someone watching her from the window, which was still not shuttered. Slamming the mug down carelessly on a small table nearby, she reached the door and yawned loudly, mumbling a little incoherently, "Wake me up tomorrow, Rajah," and disappeared to where she knew her bed would be.

* * *

Sue and Rajah had been on the move for over an hour, battling against the storm. From the moment of leaving the cottage, the prospect of the forthcoming trek was daunting. They were swept along by a violent wind, and a stinging rain made progress even more difficult, but they persevered. Sue hadn't realised how out of condition she had become.

Drenched to the skin, Sue caught hold of a slender trunk for support. It was swaying drunkenly in the squall, but she needed to regain her breath and ease the pain in her side. It was hard work following someone like Rajah in the dark. He could so easily slide through the undergrowth; showing himself only now and again. She felt she was running a hazardous course with her eyes shut. The ferocious wind roared in her ears and whipped strands of hair across her eyes. Her clothing was so wet it plastered around her body, almost as though it was trying to stop her limbs from moving. The cat, being black, was difficult to keep in focus — and should he suddenly decide to abandon her, the situation she was in would become treacherous. It was only when Rajah turned to look at her that she knew where he was, by his luminous green eyes. "Wait, Rajah," she gasped, doubled up with the stitch. "I've got to rest. Where are you taking me?"

The cat's stare was unblinking. "You haven't got time to rest," he replied. "Are you changing your mind?"

"Of course not, but it's hard to see you and almost impossible to follow you. Furthermore, we don't seem to be getting anywhere."

Rajah walked back to her looking a sorry sight. Water poured off his bedraggled fur, matting it down so that he looked only half his size. At times like this, telepathy came to the rescue because voice-sounds would be fragmented by the wind. "We've got to get to the best point around here where the power lapse is worse," Rajah said. "We need to get as high as possible. I just hope Thane has the ability to work this out for himself and find you."

"Thane!" choked Sue, trying to suppress her surprise. "I wouldn't bring Thane out in weather like this. I intend to leave this place and do it swiftly. Just let's get to where you are taking me."

"Then how—" the cat started hedging and Sue interrupted swiftly. "Rajah, it will be dawn soon and the Keeper might see me. Please lead on. Don't leave me here."

He sensed her desperation and moved forward. With breath quickening in her throat, she followed. Everywhere looked so different at night — bushes and trees were waving like ghostly phantoms, dark and sinister. The roaring wind gusted over them. Rain stung her face with regular monotony. She knew they were getting higher because she started to shiver uncontrollably and the wind whined in her ears. But the climb was taking its toll and seeping away her energy. Breath started to rasp in her throat. Suddenly a break in the fast moving clouds showed up a watery moon, but it did nothing to alleviate the situation. The rain ceased for a while, but the wind remained strong. When cramp attacked Sue's legs again, she stumbled with the agonizing pain, falling to the wet ground. There she crouched low, unable to move for a while. Rajah came back to find her. "Come on," he urged, "don't sit down here, the spot is just ahead."

"I can't walk any further," she groaned.

"Then crawl, woman — crawl," came the unsympathetic answer. "Directly dawn breaks, the Keeper will be about. Don't let him stop you at this point."

Sue bit her lip and started to crawl over pieces of twig and wet grass until she reached an open rise surrounded by trees. Lightness began to appear on the horizon and it didn't need the cat's urgent cajoling to make her stagger to her feet. The wind buffeted her body, trying to bowl her over, but Sue stood firm. She lifted her arms to the sky and called out, "Silver! Silver! I need you. Come swiftly."

"Who's Silver?" Rajah hissed, feeling annoyed he had missed something. "Why isn't he or she here? You haven't got time to hang around."

"She will come," Sue retorted calmly. "Wait and see."

"There isn't time to wait, I tell you," the cat growled. "Look to your right."

Sue looked. The first glimpse of red showed itself on the horizon, and in the same direction appeared a small dark speck coming at speed. That had not registered yet on the cat. Rajah pushed himself against Sue's legs, agitated on her account and worried on his own. "We've got to move from here, the Keeper has already sensed our presence. Run!"

Sue smiled at him. "You go, Rajah. You've been a good friend and I shall never forget you. But look before you go. Here comes Silver."

One look at the approaching dragon and the cat vanished from sight. As Silver slithered to a standstill, Sue attempted to run joyously up to her, limping badly. The Keeper appeared from the trees. Silver saw him immediately and roared threateningly. Smoke and flame poured from her mouth — but she knew better than to attack him, even though he was an old adversary. The Keeper remained where he stood, not lifting a hand or attempting any magic. He knew he had been right about Sue's powers. He watched Sue hugging the dragon's long scaly neck and saw its huge head turn round towards her, nearly touching her cheeks.

"Let me take you home, Princess. It's been a long time and we have all missed you," she rumbled. At her words the Keeper slowly retreated from sight.

Sue scrambled up on her back, Rajah forgotten, and lay hugging her neck tightly. "Yes," she breathed happily. "Take me home."

* * *

The first rays of sun dispersed the fingers of mist lingering over the water, separating them from the Enchanted Land. Raithe smothered a yawn and glanced towards a bleary-eyed Thane who had arrived at his camp in the middle of the night. With White Hawk beside him, Thane had slumped to the ground, saying, "That was one hell of a journey," and had gone to sleep.

So Raithe extinguished the fire and packed all their belongings on the spare horse. Then he smothered another yawn, trying not to appear too curious. "So where are we heading?" he asked at length. "Where have you left Sue?"

Thane stared at him vacantly. "Sue?"

"Yes. You went to rescue her. Remember?"

Thane gave the impression he had not heard a word. He was bemused and wondered how on earth he had got back here. Where had the Keeper gone? He showed signs of being distraught and was barely under control, moving around like a caged animal. After refusing food and refraining from conversation, he sat hunched up with the faithful wolf by his side, and stared back at the land from which he had been expelled. Fleura waited long enough to make sure he had no injuries then she departed. There was no need for her to remain, and it surprised Raithe that he was genuinely sorry she had gone.

391

At times during the next day Thane spoke incoherently of Sue, but more often than not he lapsed into long silences. It was then Raithe became annoyed. He was just as gutted about his sister as Thane was. He wanted some news. Pursing his lips, he looked back at Thane who was still preoccupied with his thoughts.

"Sue's not suddenly going to appear, you know," Raithe said at length, regarding him with a mixture of sympathy and sternness, "and there's no way you are ever going to get back there. We need to get help and our best strategy is to seek the Shaman. The only way to fight magic is with more magic — so what do you suggest, back to Therossa?"

"Sue was devastated," Thane muttered, still living in his own little world. With a bleak face and his voice full of frustration, he added, "It was so unfair. The Keeper acted like a god and penalised her for doing a good turn. I think we should go back to Rainee and then I'll have a chance to have it out with the Drazuzi."

"That's a damn fool idea." Raithe glared at him. "If that's your intention, then we're parting company right now. I'm seeking my father. He's sure to have an answer. It's just a matter of who is going to take the packhorse. You, or am I?"

"What!" The question jerked Thane back to his senses. "I've got a better idea. Why don't you contact your sister with that ring?"

"It didn't work the last time I tried."

"Then try again. Things are different now because she's used the Crystal Horse for a wish."

"Why didn't I think of that." Raithe lifted his hand to examine the ring with a wolf's head engraved on the stone. He was still a little sceptical because the last time he tried to use it nothing worked. "Well, here goes." He rubbed it carefully, calling for Sue, and was pleased the action seemed to satisfy Thane because he edged closer. With their eyes pinpointed on the ring, they waited. They were rewarded when it pulsated into life, and from the stone came Sue's voice, very breathless as though she was far away. "Raithe — is that you? Can you hear me?"

"Yes. Just tell me where you are so that we can organise an escape."

A funny noise reached their ears — maybe it was Sue laughing, but the pause was too long and Thane had to contain himself from snatching at the ring. Eventually her voice came back, rather disjointed. "There is no need. I'm — I'm flying."

"Flying," echoed her brother in disbelief. He was immediately concerned. "What do you mean? Are you ill or something?"

"I'm flying home — on Silver. I'll — I'll see you there and give my love to Thane," she cried.

"Sue!" shouted Thane excitedly before Raithe could answer. "How did you get away from the Keeper? Sue?" but long before he stopped speaking, the ring had gone dead. He glanced at Raithe's radiant face and then said with excitement filling his voice, "That's where we are going." He jumped on his horse and kicked it to a gallop, leaving Raithe to follow with the packhorse.

CHAPTER 29
HOME COMING

Some phenomenal changes came overnight to the land that touched the base of the Bluff. When the troop of soldiers camping nearby woke the following morning, they were bemused at the change. The overgrown foliage and well-worn tracks had vanished. Sheeka flew some distance away to watch proceedings, and the other two dragons went with him.

A gentle paved slope now led the way to a massive ornate opening in the Bluff. Entry was barred to anyone trying to get in by the two golden doors. Vance kept the soldiers well away from them, and until the king returned, they would stay camping where they were. Only one person ignored the ruling. Scrap seemed to know his mistress was inside. He lay outside the doors with his nose on his paws. It was a daily occurrence for the two soldiers looking after him, to go and fetch him back.

Inside the Bluff, the trauma of the ceremony had left Tam and Rainee emotionally drained. The now fully restored Drazuzi people could not do enough to help them. They were attentive and very supportive in anything they needed. Barry and Zeno were cared for and completely spoilt. In fact, with no memory of events to fall back on, they both wondered where on earth it was they had wandered after leaving the sphere.

"I can't believe I passed out and missed the transformation." Barry was disgusted with himself, and because of it, he glared at Tam and Rainee as though it were their fault. He was reclining with them on an old-fashioned, high backed sofa, although to call it old-fashioned was an inadequate description of such a beautifully made and upholstered piece of gilt-edged furniture. Professor Harding sat in an equally magnificent chair, and his eyes were calculating the value of everything around him. He was a grotesque representation of the man Barry used to know, but he had also lost a lot of his memory.

This was not the time to dwell on the likes of him, and Barry's eyes slid past him to study his surroundings. They were resting in a sumptuously tiled hall where fountains played, sending spurts of water high into the air which made a delicate tinkling sound as it fell back into the basins.

On the wide curved edge around the fountains sat one or two people, idly gossiping. Cushions were thrown about the floor for the benefit of anyone wanting to relax and nibble at the food, which was supplied on low tables. Through a high, wide archway, which Barry had never seen before, he could see the rest of Tam's soldiers enjoying a feast out in the sunshine, and further away still, Sheeka and two other dragons were sleeping with their long necks stretched out on the dry grass.

But even as he watched, the vision vanished and he was staring at a tapestry. The metamorphosis of the Drazuzi people made them almost unrecognisable. "If only Sue could see all this," Barry breathed. He turned to

Tam, his eyes bright with expectancy. "How soon can we leave here?" he asked. "I want to tell her everything."

"Our hosts will not be very happy if we run away so fast," Tam admonished. "They are doing their best to make amends for keeping you and Zeno prisoners. You must try to understand, Barry, that the debilitating curse put on them for a great span of time changed their personalities and made them as harsh as the cold caverns in which they lived. Now they are normal and the place is warm and exactly as it used to be. It must be very strange to them — as strange as it is for us to watch." He saw no reason to expand on Sue's whereabouts at this moment.

"Would it be permissible for me to go outside?" Barry asked, knowing that this was where the soldiers were. Tam was just about to nod when Rainee pointed out that two Drazuzi people were approaching them. "They look important," she added in a low voice. The man was tall and dressed in a long golden robe, with a golden band encircling his head. He held himself with hauteur, which suited him — whereas it didn't suit the watching Professor. He still remembered Cyril Grant. Beside him stood a woman, identically clothed, and from behind her she pulled forward a young boy who was desperately trying to hide. She placed one hand on his shoulder to keep him in place, and Barry's eyes goggled, recognising him.

"Our son," said the man in a deep pleasant voice. "He wishes to apologise to your nephew for running away from him." Barry stared at Honda, looking resplendent in his high-collared coat and turban covering his hair. The young boy held out his hand regally. His handshake had remarkable strength.

396

"I hope there is no bad feeling," he said. His voice was perfectly modulated and his eyes expressive, but behind them lurked a sparkle of mischief, which showed that at heart he was still a boy. "I want you to know that I refused to carry the silver dish," he said unexpectedly. "I had too much respect for you. In fact I did not even want to be there."

"What silver dish? What are you on about" echoed Barry, completely lost — yet at the back of his mind the words 'silver dish' rang a bell. Determined not to appear a fool before this self-possessed boy, he muttered, "Oh yes — the silver dish. It was — was —" He paused expectantly, and Honda fell into the trap and filled him in with, "At the ceremony to Raga. Do you not remember?"

Tam cursed under his breath and Barry shivered, feeling that his memory was returning, but he could not quite grasp the situation. He did remember hearing about Raga, when in the sphere, and it had upset Honda. He stopped thinking because Tam broke in with an edge to his voice and said, "Thank you, Honda, for your consideration. Your apology has been accepted by my nephew. Some things," and as he spoke he turned to the man, and added pointedly, "Some things are best left unsaid."

Honda's father was anxious not to offend. "I understand perfectly. Now, for my son's benefit — he would like Barry to return here at some time in the future."

"Please," broke in Honda, and by the expressions on his parents' faces, he had broken all protocol by butting in, "I should like a friend to show me the outside world. I've never been out there."

"You can come and visit him at the palace," Tam interjected smoothly, relaxing now that the conversation was back in safer channels, "and if you're lucky, you will meet the Princess Sonja."

Honda was ecstatic and his father beamed his approval. For the time being, Barry had been side-tracked. Honda's mother gave them a slight bow and said with dignity, "Before you think of leaving us, you must attend the banquet being prepared for you all. You are invited as well as all your men outside — only the dragons are barred, they are too big," she added hastily, seeing Tam's eyebrows rise. He bowed to her. "Thank you, Madam. We look forward to it — but at midday, a few of us must leave."

* * *

"Whatever you say, Annalee, I will not change my mind," Tansy said, "you're being awkward. Priscilla has changed. She's not quite so unapproachable. Come on — where's your sense of adventure gone? Be a sport and let's have a day out riding on the dragons. You know that's what you really want to do."

"I know — but why with Priscilla?" asked Annalee, reluctant to show any enthusiasm. "If you really want to know why I'm refusing, it's because I can't stand all the dramatics we have to put up with when she's around."

Tansy knew exactly what she was getting at and grinned, then said in a cajoling voice, "It's a small price to pay for the exhilarating feeling of the wind blowing through your hair, and besides that, the dragons love taking us around."

"I'd love to, Tansy, but please tell me why we have to put up with her every time."

Pursing her lips, Tansy glanced surreptitiously towards Barry's sister who still went around with a petulant look on her face. She wondered for the umpteenth time why the girl shied away from their friendly advances. The way things were between them, she might just as well have built a wall around herself. "There must be some reason for it," she mused thoughtfully. "I would love to know what motivates her each day — other than thinking she's the cat's whiskers."

"Men," retorted Annalee tartly, dismissing any other reason. "Haven't you noticed her? She's like a leech where Alfie is concerned."

"She likes him," was Tansy's answer.

"She wants to own him," Annalee glowered.

Tansy disagreed with her friend. "Alfie might not know much about girls, but he's no fool and it's easy to see he is giving her a hard time just lately. Our young lady, who likes to think she is so sophisticated, does not understand men very well. She needs someone like us to show her the way. So — Annalee, after that appraisal," she turned back to her friend, "let's take them both for a ride and clear the air between us. After all, we did promise Tam. I could take Alfie, and you can have…"

"Oh no." Annalee spun round, cutting Tansy short. "Make it the other way and maybe I'll change my mind."

"That's blackmail."

"Poor Priscilla," laughed Ruth softly, breaking up the argument as she came to join them. "You're not giving her much of a chance, are you? Suppose you let her decide with whom she will fly, and I dare say she will surprise you by saying… "

"Alfie!" the two trackers exclaimed in unison. Then they turned red because their voices carried as far as the lad in question, who was working with Priscilla in attendance. She wouldn't like that. She didn't like their having anything to do with Alfie, and it wasn't always possible for them to oblige — not that they tried to do so.

Priscilla was perched most uncomfortably on a log — it was the nearest she could get to Alfie without hindering him, but on hearing the voices of Annalee and Tansy shouting out his name, she raised her head and stared at them belligerently. It looked as though she had been following their conversation, and they had the grace to look sheepish, but Priscilla thought they were making fun of her. She was always self-conscious when in their company. They were so self-assured it gave her a feeling of inferiority. Only with Alfie was she happy. Alfie groaned and kept his head bent low as he continued to work on his task. He made no attempt to get involved in girlish squabbles. It pleased him to stay occupied; that way he was not compelled to make small talk, which he hated. He actually hoped at times that his silence would drive Priscilla away to find new friends.

Alfie loved the redwood forest. From the first moment of his seeing it, he was lost to the beauty of the magnificent trees. He got on well with the people who lived here, and they made him welcome. As for Priscilla's Aunt, he adored her — queen or no queen, she was a gentle loving woman. He could not understand why Priscilla wanted to go home when there was a place like this to live. Alfie hoped he would be asked to stay. If

Priscilla had no love for the great outdoors — that was her problem.

Alfie admired the two trackers. They were uncomplicated and easy to get on with, although he could always feel the tension when Priscilla was around. Annalee taught him how to shoot with a bow and arrow. Because Priscilla was not adept at this sport — or didn't want to be — she made a scene, which erupted into a furious row between them, and ever since then Priscilla never vouchsafed another opinion, but her actions spoke louder than words.

Ruth took it upon herself to approach her guests, and Alfie, sensing her presence, immediately gave her a smile of welcome, to which Priscilla added a poor imitation. Ruth wondered how the two of them were getting on and her heart sank on noticing the extra brightness in her niece's eyes, which indicated tears were not far off. Another demonstration was the last thing she wanted today. She laid a hand on Priscilla's head, ruffling up her hair, and winced as she felt the girl stiffen beneath her touch and jerk away.

"So how are you both enjoying my forest?" she asked casually and was touched by Alfie responding swiftly. "I think it is the most beautiful place I've ever seen," he replied. "I would give anything to call this my home." He stopped abruptly, catching sight of the expression on Priscilla's face. Ruth glanced at her niece and enquired, "What about you, my dear?"

Priscilla would have loved to evade the question, but with all eyes on her she felt her skin become clammy and her mouth dry. She hadn't got the ease of making conversation. Licking her lips she said awkwardly, "I — I need to see more of it."

"Then you're in luck," Ruth smiled, and said to her dismay, "Tansy and Annalee are just about to fly the dragons and they want you to go with them." The lie slipped out so easily. Alfie jumped to his feet with agility. Placing his work on the bench, he unexpectedly hugged the queen and she was touched by the sincere gesture. Priscilla's jaw dropped in horror on witnessing his familiarity. "That's a good idea," said Alfie approvingly, glancing from the queen to the trackers. "Thanks for asking us." He turned rather belatedly to his companion. "Are you coming along, Cilla?" he asked.

She glared at him. "My name is Priscilla," she snapped.

"Oh stop being so stuffy," Alfie retorted crossly. "It's about time you let your hair down. Cilla is not such a mouthful as Priscilla and it sounds a darn sight more friendly."

"I don't call you Alf," she blazed back at him.

"Then more fool you," retorted Alfie, stopping her in her tracks. "Are you coming or stopping here?"

She didn't move until Ruth nudged her — then reluctantly Priscilla got to her feet. The queen turned back to the two trackers and said guilelessly, "You'll be pleased to know they are coming with you."

As she moved away, Tansy said in a low voice, "You're very diplomatic, your Majesty. I suppose you wouldn't consider coming along with us — would you?"

Ruth backed away. "I'm much too busy. I had word this morning that Tam will be back later today with Barry and a mystery guest. I'm going to see about preparing a banquet beneath the trees."

Priscilla was suddenly clutching at Ruth's arms. "Please let me help you, aunt," she begged, volunteering herself without thinking — but Ruth pushed her gently away. "You're looking a lot better, but your cheeks could do with more colour in them. A spot of flying is what the doctor ordered. Now who is flying with whom?"

"I'll go with Alfie," Priscilla answered swiftly, and her face became suffused with anger when Alfie pushed her aside. "Don't be stupid," he remonstrated. "Neither of us can ride a dragon. Who do you want to be with? Annalee? Or Tansy?"

Priscilla was full of chagrin. She wanted neither. Because she dithered for too long, she was completely humiliated when Tansy said carelessly as though she were a package, "I'll take her along with me," then seeing Priscilla's face, added a little more kindly, "We have flown together before. Don't you remember?"

CHAPTER 30
DRAGON CONFLICT

Annalee and Alfie made themselves comfortable on Griffin's back and he took off gracefully. The sun on his scales shone like a golden globe. Alfie was jubilant and he looked down on Priscilla still on the ground. He waved. Annalee deliberately kept her eyes averted, relieved at not having to be a nursemaid to her. Down below, Priscilla watched them go, envious of Annalee because she was sitting beside Alfie. Griffin soared over the top of the redwoods, and from this high vantage point Alfie could see the sea in the distance. He was so excited he could hardly contain his enthusiasm. Up here on the back of a dragon was a brand new world. The redwoods looked beautiful. This was a marvellous country and Alfie was determined to stay here. If permission to do so was refused then he would go off on his own and live like Rainee in a caravan. No way was he going back to be a chauffeur for his uncle — taking it that his uncle was still alive. The thought struck him as funny and he suppressed a grin. It would take a lot to kill Uncle Graham. He suddenly caught sight of Annalee studying him and felt foolish for showing so much exuberance but she gave him a broad smile, sensing his oneness with the environment. She was secretly pleased with the thought that Priscilla was heading for a great shock. That girl had to learn that the world did not revolve around her.

Tansy seated her unwilling passenger onto the back of Firefly. She made doubly sure that the harness was firmly in place, knowing the girl's nervous disposition. She was just about to scramble up beside Priscilla when Ruth came hurrying over to speak to her. "Won't be a tick," Tansy muttered, and went over to the queen. Ruth drew her out of earshot, not wanting her words to be heard in public and certainly not by Priscilla.

"There is trouble, Tansy, and I'm rather nervous. Evonny is out for revenge. No! You mustn't look startled, it's not you he's after — he's looking for Silver. Somehow he's found out it was she who helped remove Priscilla from his clutches. No one seems to know where she is. She flew off before sunrise. The thing is — should you see her while out flying, will you warn her of the danger? Oh dear! Why is it everyone vanishes when you want them?" Ruth sounded distraught. "Sheeka went off with Tam the other day and hasn't returned. It's always the same when you want someone."

"Calm down, Ruth," Tansy laughed, "you're making mountains out of molehills. There is nothing to worry about. We shall not be gone long and I promise you if we see Evonny we shall return. Now go and take your mind off things and prepare the banquet while you can."

Tansy hurried away before Ruth could add any more and, slightly out of breath, took up her position beside Priscilla. The girl looked at her curiously and Tansy said brightly, "Are we ready to go?"

To her surprise Priscilla shivered and said, "Something is wrong. I can feel it."

Having just listened to Ruth, Tansy's stomach turned over and a few goose pimples came up on her arms. She laughed it off by saying lightly, "Are you a soothsayer? Or are you looking for an excuse not to go flying?"

Priscilla stared at her helplessly. "It's not that at all. I know you and Annalee don't like me," she said with unexpected candour, "but I tend to get these premonitions from time to time. Barry or Sue could have told you, but they're not here to back me up. Honestly, Tansy, there's this feeling in the air which I can't shake off."

Firefly moved restlessly beneath them and rumbled. "We shall lose the others if we dither here much longer," Tansy said and turned to Priscilla, concern in her eyes. "If you want to get off Firefly I won't hold it against you. I'm sure your aunt would welcome some help, but I must fly off and join the others."

She quite expected Priscilla to jump at the chance and start to fiddle with the harness, but through clenched teeth she answered, "If Alfie can do it — so can I. Let's go."

Tansy looked at her in surprise. "At times you really do amaze me, Priscilla," she said approvingly. "Maybe you're a chip off the old block after all. OK. Hold on!"

Priscilla's cheeks reddened, but inside she glowed and forgot all about her premonitions. She meant to enjoy herself. Thankful to be airborne at last, Firefly took off amidst the oohs and ahs from the few children watching, and within seconds was up with Griffin who lazily circled around while waiting for them. Under Annalee's guidance, they ignored the sea and swept inland towards the distant mountains. It was chilly at the best of times but riding against the wind they felt the temperature plummet as they skimmed over snow-capped summits.

Priscilla hugged her arms round her body but she didn't complain. The views below them of jagged rocks, soaring up hundreds of feet, opened up an entirely new vista. Waterfalls, plummeting to hidden depths, looked like small cataracts. The wild scenery was stunningly beautiful. Priscilla's eyes tried to comprehend everything. Her face was flushed with animation, and when Firefly flew side by side with Griffin, the sight of her astounded Annalee and Alfie. This outing was proving to be a great success until compunction hit Tansy. They had been flying for ages, time meaning nothing to them, until she remembered her promise to Ruth and yelled across to Annalee that they should start to think of returning home.

"Well thank goodness for that," snorted Griffin dourly. "There is another dragon following us. I cannot see who it is but I sense they are using the magic of invisibility."

Alarm immediately assailed Tansy. Twisting her head, she searched the empty sky with her eyes, remembering Priscilla's premonition. "Are you sure?" she asked; there was more dismay in her voice than she intended and Annalee sensed it. "Is there something wrong?" she queried.

Tansy shared all her misgivings about Evonny and what the queen had told her with the others, whereupon Priscilla looked terrified. The mention of Evonny made her clench her jaws. But with Alfie, his memory of the black dragon was seeing it scooping up Priscilla in his talons. Out here on Firefly's back she was vulnerable if he should suddenly attack them again. He didn't think any further. He bellowed out firmly, "Head for home, Annalee."

Firefly roared in agreement. "We can out-fly whoever is following us — but in case you haven't sensed it yet another dragon is approaching from the direction we must take, and this dragon is not using invisibility magic. If I'm not mistaken, it's Silver." He refrained from mentioning there was someone on her back.

"Then let's hasten to Silver," Tansy snapped. "If there is any trouble, three dragons are better than two, and she needs to be warned about Evonny."

With the speed at which Silver was going, they met up in a very short time and received a shock. Greetings were yelled out and Priscilla nearly unseated herself when she recognised the rider on the white dragon. "Sue! Sue! Look, it's me," she shrieked.

From Silver's back, Sue raised her weary head; she was almost asleep. Priscilla's high-pitched voice jerked her rudely awake and she saw her sister being held down by Tansy. A few tears of joy trickled down her face. "Priscilla!" she cried.

"We're not stopping, Princess," Silver roared before she could say any more. "They will have to follow us. I sense treachery in the air. A dragon is using the forbidden magic."

Griffin and Firefly came alongside either side of them, and while the dragons conversed between themselves, Priscilla was nearly committing suicide in her efforts to reach her sister.

"Sit still, Priscilla, before you fall," yelled Alfie on seeing what she was doing. "What are you trying to kill yourself for?"

Priscilla immediately got the wrong impression; her face was drained of colour, but to everyone's relief she sank back in her seat and put a hand to her confused head. "I'm scared," she said jerkily and Tansy put an arm round her shivering body. "So am I," she muttered, "but with luck we shall soon be home."

Luck was a commodity which had just run dry. The sun was blotted out as something fell from the sky above. Blacker than darkness, the huge shape thundered over the tops of their heads causing a great downdraught. The black-winged dragon turned, and almost halted in mid-air, towering above them. Evonny exhaled fire, watching for their reaction in his mean spiteful eyes. His ploy was rewarded. The three smaller dragons automatically separated and with a roar of defiance, he bore down on Silver.

"You made me look like a fool," he thundered, heading straight at her. "No one lives who betrayed me like you did — and it's worse because you did it for a human."

A blast of heat hit Sue. She felt as though she were burning up as she lay flat on Silver's back. Pain seared her flesh and she was terrified, unable to do anything to save herself. She knew a moment of nausea. Silver nimbly swerved out of his way and Evonny rushed past, unable to stop. Priscilla screamed out above the roar of the dragons and Evonny swooped round, recognising her voice. He came back straight at her, his evil venomous eyes full of recognition. She was not going to get away a second time, he would kill her as well as Silver. Before Tansy realised what was happening, his talons caught hold of the hysterical Priscilla and tore her ruthlessly out of the harness, in spite of Firefly's evasive action.

Alfie never knew he possessed so much anger. He grabbed Annalee's bow and shot a couple of arrows indiscriminately at the black dragon. The first found its mark in one of the black dragon's eyes, and the other missed Priscilla by inches. Annalee pulled the bow furiously from his hands before he could kill her. With an explosive howl of rage, Evonny released his victim and she hurtled towards the ground to what would have been certain death, but Silver dived with phenomenal speed intercepting her fall. A demented Sue who was clinging on for dear life felt the world tilt about her head.

The roar from Evonny was deafening and the great winged dragon turned. With murder in his one remaining eye, he swooped down on Silver, flame and smoke issuing from his gaping mouth, intending to destroy her. His larger bulk gave him extra speed. As he plummeted down and almost reached her, a third dragon came out from nowhere to intercept him. Too late did Evonny see the blue scales that sparkled in the sun, and they collided head on. A roar like thunder filled the air. An inseparable bulk of broken leathery wings mixed with black and blue scaly bodies plummeted down to smash on the trees below.

None too gently, Silver caught the unconscious Priscilla before she reached the ground — Firefly and Griffin were right behind her. Alfie was yelling out hoarsely, "Stop! Let me see her."

"I'm not stopping," Silver roared. "She's been harmed enough. Anyway — we're too near home."

410

Silver's voice cracked as she made her way to a gap in the forest, where the queen had her home and preparations were well under way for the banquet. But the noise of the fight had attracted attention and many people were gathering below. Silver was devastated. Things would never be the same again because her old friend Sapphire had given her life to save her, Priscilla and Sue.

The three dragons stopped short of the forest dwelling, and in the glade where they landed, the people who were preparing the forthcoming banquet were there to help them. They took little notice of the three dragons returning. It was commonplace to see them coming and going. Ruth however, busily overseeing the cooking, glanced up, saw them, and waved, relieved they had returned unharmed. She continued to converse with the two lads who had recently returned from their own journey. But at the sight of Silver, they quickly took their leave of her and raced towards the passengers on her back. White Hawk bounded ahead, sensing Sue's presence. It suddenly occurred to Thane and Raithe that there was no banter from the girls. A subdued silence hung over the riders and it immediately made them wary; then they saw the limp form Silver placed on the grass and their worst fears were realised, there had been an accident while they were out flying. They spurted forward, suddenly anxious and wondering whom the unfortunate victim was. There was something vaguely familiar about her, and Silver was keeping White Hawk at bay.

"Someone get the Shaman," ordered Raithe loudly, looking down on the unconscious girl on the grass who was bleeding profusely, and, before he could say any more, Alfie was there, cradling her in his arms and his voice was tinged with hysteria — saying brokenly, "Priscilla, speak to me."

Thane dragged his eyes from Priscilla and stared up onto Silver's back where Sue lay motionless with one arm dangling uselessly from her neck. He drew in a ragged breath, his face blanching. Her clothes were literally smouldering, giving off an obnoxious smell. Her hair was singed and matted. He yelled hoarsely, "Raithe! Quickly, help me down with Sue."

"Do not touch her."

Silver's voice stopped him in his tracks. Sue heard it all, but their voice seemed far away. She tried to struggle through the mists of semi-consciousness, but the pain was too much. Silence surrounded her. The villagers gazed upon their princess, seeing her skin red and blistering. She had lost some hair, but her ruined clothes had saved her from a lot of damage. Raithe's cry had drawn a crowd of people around them and the queen threw down what she was doing and hastened to see her daughter. Silver did not stop her. Sue gasped as hands touched her and she winced with pain. Tears stung her face and Silver's head snaked round to look upon her. "Princess, I'm sorry that I could not save you from Evonny," she growled.

"What's been going on?" Raithe demanded grimly, appalled at the sight of his sister. "Whoever did this is going to pay dearly."

"Evonny," answered Annalee in a low sombre voice, coming up to them, and in her white face fear still lurked. Tansy joined her, holding on because she was still shaking.

412

"He tried to kill Silver by burning her up," she said, her voice barely audible. "Then Priscilla screamed and it drew the dragon's attention to her. He thought he would have two for the price of one. He..." she shuddered, her voice choking as she remembered, "he ripped her away from me then went on to pursue Silver. She didn't stand much of a chance, neither did Sue, and we couldn't do much to help her. Evonny was demented after Alfie shot an arrow in his eye."

"Alfie shot an arrow!" Thane ejaculated incredulously. "He can barely use a bow and arrow, let alone have superb marksmanship." He dragged his eyes away from Sue and looked down on Alfie with new respect. Alfie was completely unaware of his approval and was still holding Priscilla tenderly. By the time Ruth reached his side, apart from Raithe, Thane and the girls, everyone else moved discreetly away. This included the three dragons but on seeing Silver retreat, Raithe motioned to a few men to follow her as best they could. She went no further than the damaged body of the blue dragon. She was still intertwined with Evonny, and many torn off branches. The men backed prudently away and allowed her to mourn in privacy.

Ruth wanted to hug and give comfort to her daughter as Alfie was doing to Priscilla, but she did not dare to touch her. Thane met her eyes and said gruffly, "She will be fine when the Shaman gets here — so will Priscilla."

"Thane," whispered Sue, struggling to sit up, but everything hurt too much and she fell back, her eyes closed.

413

CHAPTER 31
PROFESSOR HARDING

Disaster was averted when a sudden squall swept through the forest and threatened to upset the banquet. Its duration was short-lived, but while it lasted most of the paraphernalia and food laid out for the people to enjoy later on was covered. The Shaman discharged his patients saying he had done all he could for them — only time would heal their minds. It was the first time Priscilla became aware of the magical powers that could be summoned for healing in this land. She had not believed her aunt when told for the first time how dreadfully ill she had been. To her it had seemed a way of keeping her movements curtailed. Now suddenly she was seeing life through different eyes and began to wonder how many other things she had been wrong about.

By the time word came to everyone that Sheeka and another dragon had landed on the outskirts of the forest, and dropped off their passengers there because they were too big to get through the trees — Ruth and Raithe had ridden out to collect Tam and his companions, taking two spare horses with them. When asked to accompany them, Sue declined, preferring to stay with her sister and catch up on things. Outwardly, the two girls looked in the best of health and, thanks to Tansy's work, Sue's hair was now fractionally shorter. She laughed and joked about the attack from Evonny, but the stark terror of the incident would take a long time to recede.

When the sisters settled on a log, away from the hustle and bustle of all the workers, Alfie made a bee-line towards them. But Thane intervened and drew him to one side, telling him to give them some time on their own. With Tansy and Annalee backing him up, Alfie conceded to their better judgement. It was almost like old times. Sue imagined she was back in Tamsworth Forest, having a tête-à-tête with her sister, until her eyes rested on the magnificent redwoods. Priscilla had a lot to get off her chest but she skipped through the account of being hijacked by Professor Harding, and was more elaborate about her meeting with Alfie. Sue would have to have been blind not to notice how Priscilla's eyes shone when she mentioned Alfie. She remembered very little about the spider bite and her illness or who saved her, but Evonny had been etched clearly on her mind. Most of her recollections of living in the palace with her aunt were sketchy. She had not been a very sociable character. Priscilla ended her narrative by saying ruefully, "Annalee hates me."

Sue grinned, and ignoring the self-pity replied, "She hated me when I first came here and ended up by saving my life," which made Priscilla stare in surprise. Sue went on to tell her what her life was like, missing out quite a few unsavoury topics, but she did let her sister know how much she loved her newly-found parents and twin brother Raithe. She ending up by saying she would never leave this country again. Aunt Moria was now in the past. This was her home. She looked at Priscilla quizzically. "It's not for you — is it?" she queried.

Priscilla flushed at the censure and said defensively, "I will stay with Alfie." Sue touched her arm, her eyes serious when she said, "I heard Alfie say he wants to make his home here. This place has everything he's ever wanted. Be careful what decision you make. If you hate it here — he will sense it and you will lose him."

Her sister's face grew blank and she wondered if Alfie thought of her as an incredible nuisance — but Sue put her right on that score, remembering hearing Annalee say Alfie was scared to death Priscilla might die. Priscilla clutched at straws and declared, "I shall be fine, Sue, if you help me."

She shook her head. "No, Priscilla! I'll always be around but, if you stay, you must make your own life with or without Alfie and you must love this country."

"But..." Priscilla's protest was hastily interrupted by Sue. "Thane has other ideas for me," and she flushed when her sister gave her an affectionate hug. The old Priscilla would never have done that.

"You've helped me no end," Priscilla murmured, "but so long as you're around, I'll be able to face everyone without feeling a nonentity."

"Whatever else you might be, you're not a nonentity," Sue retorted. "Now come — we've sat here too long. Let's mingle with the others. If you show the people you're one of them, they will love you. Don't hanker after Alfie all the time and you'll find you have the approval of Annalee as well."

Priscilla grinned. The petulant look on her face disappeared. The whole world took on a different aspect. The forest was suddenly a beautiful place, and when a villager saw her grin and smiled back in return, she felt she was being accepted. Sue moved away, knowing she would stay here, and was happy at the thought.

* * *

The Drazuzi people asked Professor Harding to stay with them, but very churlishly he burnt his boats by refusing. His reason was, he could not stay where his friend had been brutally murdered. But he quickly accepted Tam's offer to meet Ruth. In spite of what had happened to him, he still remembered her; and in his conceit, he thought she would be thrilled to see him again after living in this savage land for so long. When he realised the mode of travelling was to be on the back of a dragon, he was aghast. They couldn't be that primitive here, he thought. This was such a barbaric land. What possessed him to come here? Then his thoughts went back to Ruth again, and he conveniently forgot he had jilted her. Watching his outraged face, Barry remarked nonchalantly:

"You could always travel with the army — you would fit in seeing you used to be a soldier."

"Soldier!" roared the professor in fury, "I was a captain, and I didn't play with bows and arrows like this supposed army take pleasure in doing."

"Humph! I'd like to see you shoot one — but you please yourself." Barry shrugged his shoulders and turned away to help Rainee climb up onto a dragon's back. The sight made the Professor shudder distastefully. In his classification, dragons came under the heading of slimy lizards. It was bad luck his thoughts were picked up by Sheeka, who carefully scrutinised the emaciated old man and deliberately blew out a puff of smoke and flame with the idea of intimidating him, and it worked admirably. The Professor backed away with alacrity, inwardly fuming, wishing he had the nerve to retaliate, but did not dare to be objectionable to the huge red creature towering above him. Then he received the news that he was to share another dragon with Barry and Zeno.

"What kind of organisation do you run?" he snarled at Tam. "I'm not risking my life on a thing like that with a couple of kids to keep me company. Anything could happen and I should be defenceless."

"I wouldn't call you defenceless," Tam objected calmly. "You look well able to take care of yourself. I thought you wanted to come and meet your old girlfriend."

"Yes, I do, but not on that." The Professor's remark was disparaging as he eyed the second dragon. "Nothing will get me on his back."

"Then I'm afraid you'll have to stay here." Tam made to move off, so Professor Harding looked around. The Drazuzi people no longer looked friendly after the way he had spoken to them earlier. Some soldiers came along, one carrying a squirming dog which he handed up to the woman sitting on the dragon behind him. The others looked towards the Professor. The fact that they did this made him grind his teeth, and he allowed Tam to help him up on the dragon's back. His clumsy movements made the dragon in question roar out, "Mind where you're putting your feet, man," and the Professor nearly fell off in horror, having no idea dragons could talk.

The ride unnerved the Professor, and the dragon sensed his agitation. He had been seated at the back by his own request, because he wanted to keep an eye on Barry. From that position, the fear of falling off was constant because the dragon decided to do more swoops and banking than was strictly necessary. The Professor dug his nails into the dragon's scales to cling on, and the huge head snaked round and thundered, "Have a care with my body, man."

At last the nightmare was over. The dragons headed towards the forest and landed smoothly on the outskirts of the trees. Nothing could be seen in any direction except trees and overgrown shrubbery. No building or any other people were in the vicinity. Once the passengers had scrambled to the ground, Sheeka and his companion made off. Thankful to stretch her legs, Rainee put Scrap down on the grass and he immediately started to race around like a lunatic, barking at anything that moved.

Each bark hit a nerve in the Professor's head, and he shouted out, exasperated, "Keep that pest of a dog quiet, woman," then he turned to Tam and demanded, "So what do we do now? Don't tell me you expect me to walk in my condition?"

It was on the tip of Tam's tongue to say 'yes' when a sound came from the forest and a flock of startled birds took to the air. With a side glance at the Professor, who looked as though he was suffering from shock, Barry said solemnly, "Is that man-eating monster coming for us, sir? Should we climb the trees while we have a chance?"

Graham Harding's face turned ashen and he looked nervously over his shoulder. Then he heard Tam say, "That's enough, Barry. He's had enough shocks for one day," and the Professor was filled with livid fury and itched to get his hands round Barry's throat. He masked his feelings with difficulty as two people and four stallions emerged from the covering of trees and he saw the beautiful elegant woman whom, years ago, he was once pledged to marry. To his disquiet, her eyes passed over him as though he were not there and she went straight to Tam and gave him a hug, placing a light kiss on his cheek. The other rider, whom at first he thought was Sue, jumped off his horse and greeted Barry warmly, then made a fuss of the excitable dog. Realising he was being completely overlooked, the Professor coughed and Tam drew Ruth's attention to him.

"An old friend has come to visit you," he said with tongue in cheek. Ruth's eyes settled on him; her impartial look made him squirm inwardly and very casually she said, "I do not recollect your name, sir."

The Professor clenched his teeth to keep his acrimonious feelings under control. She hadn't changed in all these years. "Graham Harding," he retorted in a tight voice, and she gave a slight shake of her head. "I do apologise, you've come all this way and I don't remember you. Still, you must come and join in our banquet as compensation." With that, she turned her attention back to Tam and only he saw the wicked smile on her face.

Having settled her on the same horse as himself, Tam turned to the others. "You work the seating arrangements out amongst yourselves and follow us," he directed, and vanished with Ruth amongst the trees.

* * *

420

The visitors approaching from the forest were heard long before they reached the area set up for the celebration. Arrangements were proceeding smoothly as jobs had been assigned to appropriate people and were going ahead smoothly without the queen's presence. Tables had been set up in the form of a circle, allowing everyone to see everyone else when they were seated. Eager hands decorated the colourful table-tops with garlands of flowers, which created a festive feeling.

Tam on his horse came trotting from the trees, carrying Ruth before him, and directly they were seen, eager hands were there to help them down. They were followed a little while later by Raithe, with a nervous Rainee sitting behind him clutching her dog. She was bemused at seeing so many of her own kin after all these years and it was quite an ordeal to face them. Most of the villagers gathered here knew her from the past, but they had forgotten why she had been outlawed. Now they gave her a smile of welcome. Barry cantered into view with Zeno riding pillion, and his first action was to look around for Sue and Tansy — and directly he saw them, he made a beeline in their direction. Bringing up the rear and riding a horse with no one else on it but him was Professor Harding. He looked even more supercilious now that he had removed the growth of hair from his face. His demeanour and actions did not make him very acceptable to the villagers, and because of that they shied away.

Sue, with Tansy, Annalee and Priscilla, ran to greet Barry. "How come he has a horse all to himself?" asked Sue, giving her brother a hug and nodding towards the Professor. Barry answered, "Surely you don't need me to answer that one. He objected strongly when he had to share a dragon with Zeno and me, and it was really funny because the dragon took a dislike to him, gave him a bumpy ride and told him off twice."

As hails of laughter erupted from his friends, Barry slid off the stallion and suddenly realised Priscilla was hanging back, arrayed in clothes she wouldn't have been seen dead in a year ago. She had lost that look of languor. He embraced her and then held her at arm's length. "It's great to see you, sis," he said, "especially living in Therossa. How do you like the place?"

"It's fantastic," Priscilla's answer was unexpected, "and I've made a lot of friends." As she spoke her eyes met those of Annalee, who after the briefest hesitation, rose to the occasion by saying, "Anyone like you who has Barry for a brother has to be nice. Great to have you back, Barry. We've really missed your sense of humour. You've got no idea how much Tansy's missed you."

"Well I've missed her," he returned, unabashed.

The teasing bought forth more general laughter as they moved away, happy to be in each other's company. Zeno collected the horse and took him to the picket line. He did not mind being on his own, in fact he enjoyed it. The Professor, through narrowed eyes, watched them all disperse. A sneer settled on his thin angular face when he realised there was no welcome for him. The young people here were no different from the youngsters at the hotel. Their manners were appalling and they had no respect for the elderly — not that he classed himself in that category. He had wasted his time seeking out Ruth, and there were no fabulous buildings in this uncivilized country either. Scanning what he considered to be ill-bred country yokels, his eyes fell on a strange bald-headed man watching him almost as though he were a peculiar insect. Incensed that no one was ready to help him, the Professor struggled off the horse and held out the reins to him.

"Brush him down," he ordered arrogantly. "I suppose you do have a stable in this godforsaken place."

The Shaman declined to take the reins, and said before he moved off, "Here, my son, we all see to our own mounts," and he left the Professor full of chagrin. At a complete loss, he stood there on the outskirts of all the activities, and wondered now why he had insisted on coming here, when even his nephew had ignored him.

CHAPTER 32
FAREWELL AND REUNION

By the time dusk fell, the events of the day had wound down and people started to relax and enjoy themselves. The well banked fires gave off comforting vibes and threw their flickering light onto the nearby trees, making the shadows in between them appear extra dense. Colourful lanterns, strung haphazardly from redwood to redwood, gave enough light to distract the gossamer-winged insects away from the revellers. People who had received an invitation from the queen took every seat around the circular table, but many other villagers placed their own tables within the vicinity and were not left out of the celebrations. They wore their festive clothes with abandonment, and gave the impression of a moving colourful kaleidoscope. White-clad servants waited on everyone and succulent food whetted the appetites. The crystal-clear beverage which was passed around and poured liberally into mugs, had ingredients which were a well-kept secret, because the drink had the power to relax people and break down barriers, thus making this event a very happy occasion.

Ruth had planned the seating arrangements with great care so that family and friends were within easy speaking distance. Etiquette compelled her to seat important visitors near to where she and Tam sat. Alfie and Priscilla were no worry since Sue and Raithe took them under their wing, but Rainee and Professor Harding were a different proposition. Rainee had great difficulty in deciding what to do with her dog. She was loath to let him run free, until a village woman took him from her. The Professor walked a tightrope of his own making because he considered the people were beneath him, and was the cause of many feathers around him to be ruffled.

As the animated hum of conversation filtered into the air, Ruth let out a sigh of relief. To have her ex beau back in her presence after so many years absence filled her with unease, and she was counting the time to when she could dismiss him for good. It was noticeable that the Professor did not contribute to the conversation and answered only when someone forced a question on him. Also, he only picked at his food — as Barry said afterwards, 'That was his loss.' At last, when the servants cleared everything away except for the drink, lots of differently shaped mugs were still filled to the brim. Villagers had the queen's permission to depart and start up the dancing, but a few of them remained, mainly men who were trying to look inconspicuous because they were bodyguards of the Royal Family when they resided in the forest.

As Ruth had declared at the very beginning, this was a celebration because everyone had returned unscathed from wherever they had been, and at last were all together. She was sorry only that Amos could not be with them. "But I have been compensated," she said with a broad smile, "because besides having my nephew here, I've now got my niece." Priscilla blushed at the sudden attention, and Alfie, sitting beside her stated boldly, "You've also got me."

"And you're welcome to stay," added Tam, his face crinkling into a smile. A murmur of approval arose on all sides, to be instantly shattered as the cold voice of the Professor shouted, "What do you mean!" as he lurched to his feet spilling drink everywhere. His tone immediately braced the hunters for trouble. "Alfie needs my permission to stay here, and I've not given it and am not likely to do so. It's got nothing to do with you." He glared at Tam, then turned to the startled Alfie and said, "I must remind you, boy, that you're still in my employment."

Amazement crossed the face of Alfie which he instantly controlled. "You mean was, uncle, was!" he retorted, unperturbed, and, not moving from his seat between Thane and Priscilla, added, "My employment with you, as you call it, ceased when you came to this land. Now I've found a new life here, which I love, and I've also found a girl. You cannot compel me to leave."

"Girl," spluttered his uncle, outraged, and looked almost as though he had been insulted. His flinty eyes settled on Priscilla, making her draw back in alarm. "Are you demented, boy?" he asked scathingly, "She's just a brainless idiot."

Alfie was on his feet immediately, knocking the bench back in his haste and making the others jump. His size was daunting, twice that of his uncle and he looked a force to be reckoned with. Thane also stood and pressed his shoulder warningly so that he did not do anything stupid in front of avidly watching eyes. Alfie shrugged him off, his anger barely concealed. "You may be my uncle," he said, his voice cold and clipped, "but that does not give you the right to run my friends down with your

426

insulting remarks. If it's a fight you want," he looked at him threateningly, "I'll see you later, but it will make no difference to my plans."

Captain Harding was nearly convulsed. Blood rushed to his face. "You dare to speak to me like that when I've practically brought you up and been a father to you. I'm not standing by and letting you throw your life away on the likes of her. You're coming home with me, boy."

"I'm afraid not," declared Alfie shaking his head, and the action riled his uncle all the more. "Yes you are," he snapped testily. "We leave tonight."

Tam did not give Alfie the chance to reply. He surveyed the hostile man impassively. "Do you know the way?" he asked, raising his eyebrows.

"No I don't," the other man retorted, "but you do. You've trespassed enough times in Tamsworth Forest without permission — the same as he has." He glared frostily at Thane. "What's more, you've brought savage wolves to create carnage. Do you know, sir," he continued with a snarl, "one bit me." He raised his sleeve to show the jagged scar. "It bit me in my own forest."

At that moment White Hawk decided to make an appearance and he advanced towards the raised voices. The Professor nearly suffered a spasm. His eyes dilated with fear as the wolf padded in his direction, recognising an old adversary who had attacked Sue. White Hawk curled his upper lip, showing a row of sharp pointed teeth, and he growled. Suffused with rage because no one did anything about the wolf, Professor Harding glared at Tam and demanded, "Keep that carnivore chained up. He's a savage."

"That is not our way," put in the Shaman from behind him. "I cannot understand, my son, why you ever came to this land when it fills you with such revulsion. I think I am correct in saying you have tried several times to get here." He surveyed the man quizzically through his watering eyes, and the Professor felt he was being patronised.

"I didn't come here to enjoy your land — I came because of her." As he spoke, the Professor glared insultingly at Ruth sitting composedly beside Tam, but his lack of respect for the queen brought forth angry murmurs from the villagers, and what was once a friendly atmosphere was now charged with tension. The Shaman regarded him solemnly over his bulbous nose.

"There are others sitting around this table who are of your kin. They are happy to live out their lives here."

Professor Harding clutched the table, making the wolf snarl again. His knuckles showed up white, and spittle gathered on his lips. The idea that Sue and Barry could be called his kin infuriated him. "They are not fit to be called my kin. They are disrespectful hooligans — especially that one — she tells lies," and he glared venomously at Sue. Raithe sprang to his feet like a coiled spring and took two steps towards him — dagger drawn and his intention to use it very real. The hauteur on his face put the Professor to shame.

"Do not speak to my sister that way," he growled between his teeth. "You, sir, are not welcome at this gathering."

Tam stood up swiftly, as did the guards. He stepped between them, one hand resting on the quivering Prince to calm him down and said, "While he is sitting at our

428

table and eating with us, he is a guest and will be respected as such. — but when the banquet is over, he will be sent back to his own country, alone." He ended his speech with a certain amount of satisfaction.

"Well, it's over now," Raithe acknowledged, and Tam smiled. "So it is, son," he said and turned to the Professor who was watching him like a snake. "To show there are no ill feelings between us — will you have a farewell drink with us all?" he asked. He glanced at the Shaman, who inclined his head and clapped his hands. Almost on cue, Neela and Tug came forward carrying a small tray of glasses and the Professor's eyes narrowed, smelling a rat. Each glass was almost overflowing with golden wine. Neela handed them out to Tam, Ruth, Thane, Raithe and Sue. Tam handed one to the Professor, who eyed it suspiciously. "Where's yours?" he asked the Shaman, looking distrustfully at his empty hands. The Shaman looked at him reprovingly.

"Normally I don't drink. My religion prevents me, but on this occasion I will join you. Neela!" he called out and held out his hand and the acolyte brought him another glass. Tam raised the golden liquid in a salute as he faced the querulous old man. "Here's to your health and safe return back to your country," he said.

"Not without Alfie," Captain Harding retorted and glowered at them all, while Ruth smiled sweetly at him and murmured, "We realise that. He is your kin and we will get him ready for the journey." Someone gave Alfie a kick because he was about to protest. Ruth held up her glass. "Your health, Graham," she toasted and drank. Tam and the others raised their glasses and drank the wine. After the briefest hesitation, the Professor also drank. He expected some vile concoction, but the wine was palatable. He drained his glass, feeling strange warmth in his chest. The next moment he slumped over the table. Alfie sprang towards him, a shocked expression on his homely face and his suspicion was plain.

"What have you done to him?" he demanded angrily. "Have you killed him?"

"No, my son," interjected the Shaman quietly, "only drugged him so that he does not remember the way back. The men will take him now." He noticed Alfie only half believed him, so added kindly, "Do you wish to go with him?"

Alfie shook his head. "No, I only wanted to make sure he was not harmed."

"Then do not fear," answered the Shaman. "He will wake up in two days' time, feeling very confused, and in about a week he will start to remember where he has been, only he will think it was a dream."

Sue gave a start. "That was what Rajah told me," she interrupted, "when the Keeper wanted to keep me in the Enchanted Land, Rajah stopped me from drinking the concoction. That's how I got away…" Her voice trailed off as she remembered her parting from Rajah, and Thane poked her in the ribs.

"You don't seem very happy about it. Do you miss the place?"

"I miss Rajah. He was a special friend," she said.

"Then invite him here," Tam insisted. "We've got room for one more — haven't we?" He looked at Ruth.

"It's not that easy," Sue answered before her mother could speak. "I don't think he could leave. He's part of the set-up there, and I doubt very much he would fit in here."

Ruth was indignant. "I'm sure we would make him welcome. How old is he?"

How old was Rajah? Sue tried to suppress her smile. "He's ageless," she declared, "but it's not you I'm worried about. White Hawk took a dim view of him when they met."

"We'll tell him he's a friend," Thane said cheerfully, wanting to meet this Rajah.

"I already have," retorted Sue, desperately trying to keep a straight face, "but White Hawk objects."

"You didn't tell him with the correct tone in your voice," Thane laughed, giving White Hawk's ruff a scratch. "He will do anything for you."

"Not when it's a cat," Sue muttered.

"Cat!" everyone shouted.

There was a sudden silence — then the comical side of it hit them and everyone laughed, but as the laughter faded away, Thane saw Sue still looked sad when Barry asked jokingly, "What's so special about this Rajah other than having a long tail and four legs?"

"He talks," answered Sue.

The subject was suddenly dropped because Tam suggested they should all start to enjoy themselves before it was too late, and Thane drew Sue away to join in the dancing. Priscilla watched them go wistfully. Alfie dragged his eyes away from his uncle, and tapped her on the arm. "Are you going to teach me to dance?" he inquired, and as her eyes lit up, he added, "I had better warn you. I'm not very good."

431

Tansy winked at Annalee as they left, and turned to Barry and Raithe. "Come on, you two. Let's have some fun before the festivities are over."

* * *

Rubbing sleep from her eyes, Sue yawned, wondering what had awoken her other than the dawn chorus of birds outside her window. A lacy pattern of leaves shaded her room from the morning sun and a soft breeze touched her skin. She stretched her body lazily, knowing there was nothing important to worry about, so with that thought in mind, utter contentment washed over her. A great deal of noise and activity floated up from the ground below. It sounded as though half the villagers were congregated there. It was too early for things to be happening, so she closed her eyes when suddenly, a voice in her head said, "Sue — for goodness sake where are you? Get down here. I need your help."

Sue sat up with a jolt. Memory flooded back to her. Today she was leaving with Thane to visit his ideal place in Therossa. It was to be a little trip on their own before they returned to the palace with all the others — it was also a trip neither of her parents wanted her to take. An early start, Thane had said last night. Guiltily she jumped out of bed, speeding through all the jobs that made her presentable. She then made her way down to the ground by the narrow stairs ingeniously carved out of the redwood. She was looking forward to this unexpected trip, but no matter where she went, the forest of redwoods would always remain her favourite spot.

"Come on, sleepyhead," called Tansy yanking at her arm as she stepped onto the grass, looking a little bleary-eyed after her late night. "Thane's been chaffing at the bit waiting for you."

Sue grinned. "You could have come up and given me a shake," she said then she broke off, seeing all the people milling around. "What are they all doing here? I don't want a send-off. It's only a fun trip after all."

"Well, I didn't tell you everything. There is something else," Tansy answered in a low voice, and before Sue could ask, she pushed her friend forward. The nearby group of villagers parted to let her through and see what the commotion was about. A very disgruntled Wolf sat by Thane, with other bleary-eyed trackers, all trying hard to look alert at this early hour. The Shaman, with Tam and Ruth, stood in the central clearing where a large tied-up bundle was moving at their feet. Sue blinked, thinking she was seeing things. It moved as though what was concealed inside was trying to get out, and everyone gathered around was agog with undisguised interest to know what it was.

"What is it?" Sue whispered to Tansy — but Tansy never replied and stood back to stare like everyone else. Thane made room for Sue, and White Hawk pressed himself against her legs, looking almost pleadingly at her through his expressive golden eyes. Sue knelt down and hugged him, looking up at Thane with questioning eyes. "What's the matter with him? I've never seen him like this before."

Thane never answered because the Shaman looked across at her, a strange smile on his old face. It was off-putting because the Shaman never showed any emotion, let alone a smile. Tam beckoned her forward and pointed to the bundle tied up with rope, which was swaying slightly as though it had a mind to escape. It repelled Sue as well fascinated her but whatever vibes were coming from it really upset the wolf.

"This is a gift from the Drazuzi people," Tam said unexpectedly. "They hope it will compensate for all you went through to help them."

Suddenly wary, Sue stepped back, alarmed. "But I don't want to be repaid," she protested, and the Shaman with a hint of rebuke in his voice, said, "That is very unworthy of you, daughter. You must never turn down a gift which is sent with love. It is very bad manners." Sue felt her face stinging at the reprimand, and the Shaman went on in a softer tone, "Suppose you look and see what it is. We are all interested," and a murmur of agreement rose from the watching crowd.

Sue approached the moving bundle apprehensively and stared at it for a while. White Hawk's whining distracted her, and she called over to him, but for some reason he ignored her, staying by Thane's side. She was dismayed because she always felt safe when he was near her. More and more people joined the watching group and speculations as to what the bundle contained were bandied from one to another. A great reluctance to untie the knot filled Sue. She had the distinct impression this action was going to change her life, but at an encouraging nod from Thane, she untied the restraining rope and whipped away the covering and stood back at the same time as a plaintive voice said:

"Have you been asleep, girl? Do you realise that I've been suffocating in that contraption?"

The onlookers were suddenly silent — whether with awe or shock was not known. Sue's breath caught in her throat and she stared at Rajah with a mixture of delight and unease, almost expecting to see the Keeper step out from the trees. She knew now what White Hawk had sensed. He was never keen on the cat. The larger than normal cat arched its back and stretched — then casually shook itself so that its black fur fluffed up. Ignoring the villagers, it was about to start on its ablutions when the cat fixed his green eyes on Sue and asked, "Is this coming here something to do with you?"

Sue squatted down beside him, suddenly happy to see the cat again. She owed Rajah so much. Her hand went out and stroked his back, and in return he brushed against her knees, but he was still indignant at the way someone had manhandled him. She thought she owed him an explanation. "I mentioned only last night how much I missed you and what a good friend you were to me and..."

"And now you've got me for good," the cat retorted tartly, "not that I'm complaining. I'm pleased to be away from the Keeper. He's been a bit touchy since you escaped." Something different caught his eye and he examined it from top to bottom. The redwood stood there in all its glory, branches growing in every direction. It certainly met with the cat's approval and seemed to be an ideal place to live. *I can have fun here*, he thought. He turned back to Sue and said crisply, "Well, now that I'm staying here to look after you — suppose you start by introducing me to all..." He suddenly stopped and hissed, his fur bristling as he made eye contact with White Hawk, the wolf who had defied all logic and appeared in the

Enchanted Land. *So*, he thought, *I've got competition here for Sue's affection.* "What's he doing here?" he spat out and White Hawk growled to show the cat he had the same sentiments.

Some villagers thought it prudent to move away, as a cat was not enough of an attraction to keep them there. Thane saw the happiness Sue experienced at seeing Rajah again evaporate before his eyes. There was no way the cat and the wolf would ever be united and live together. Sue felt tears of vexation blur her vision and she knew she couldn't leave things like this. In a choked voice she said huskily to Rajah, "Please understand, White Hawk is also my friend, and if — if you stay with me — you've got to be his friend as well."

"There's no 'got to' about it." Although he heard the break in her voice, the cat disdainfully turned his head away and added, "Never!"

"He's a really loving wolf," Sue pleaded.

"That's your opinion," Rajah hissed, and flinched as he felt a tear splash on his fur. "That wolf doesn't like cats."

"He doesn't know you," Sue cried desperately. "Please give him a chance and meet him halfway."

Through slit eyes the cat stared haughtily at White Hawk, who retaliated by showing his teeth in a snarl. Trying to ease her distress, Thane came forward. The cat immediately fixed his eyes on him and became wary, especially when he knelt down at his own level to out stare him. Thane did no more than hold out his hand, and the cat sniffed at his fingers. *Pooh*, he thought disgustedly, *you smell just like a wolf*, and from White Hawk's direction came, "and he's going to come back to me smelling like a cat." Rajah tossed his head and looked aristocratic. At the action, Thane took the liberty of tickling Rajah behind his ears and the cat gave a contented purr and closed his eyes. Thane stopped. The eyes opened in surprise, trying to will Thane to continue but when he didn't, Rajah's tail started to swish to and fro in anger.

"Now don't do that!" Thane's voice was stern and he stared hard at the cat. Except for his whiskers twitching, Rajah made no movement to show he had heard. "I want you to understand that we are all friends here, including White Hawk. He has protected Sue ever since she came to this land, and he also protects me — but there is only one of him and he cannot be in two places at once, although he is extremely intelligent. You, on the other hand, have the advantage of being able to talk."

"And pick up thoughts," the cat interrupted smugly. "That's how I know your clever guard wolf would like to tear me to shreds." Thane ignored the cat's complacent remark and continued as though he hadn't spoken. "I and everyone here appreciates what you did for Sue while she was in the Enchanted Land, and I can't help thinking how nice it would be if you two came to some arrangement and shared the responsibility of guarding us together. You know," he gave the cat a lopsided grin, "you might even get to like one another."

Rajah sniffed, but he never moved — his eyes still regarded Thane.

"Have you ever thought," cut in Sue with sudden inspiration, "you could do things which the wolf can't? You can climb trees and attack from above. Have you

437

looked at that tree behind you? Imagine climbing to the very top. You can leap great distances…"

"Spare me," Rajah groaned, "I can't fight two of you. You'll have me in tears in a minute. You don't have to spell it out. I know exactly what the situation is. Why are you two trying to put the blame on me? What about him?" He looked indignantly at the watchful wolf whose eyes were boring into him. Thane issued an order to White Hawk, who reluctantly moved a little closer. Rajah took a few steps in his direction and they met halfway. The wolf sniffed cautiously at the ill-humoured cat, wondering if his sharp claws were retracted, while Rajah's ears twitched. With his magical powers, he tried to assess how swiftly he could move if the wolf decided to take a bite at him. Instead, White Hawk regarded him patronisingly and walked straight past him to Thane and Sue's side, as much as to say, 'these people are my property'. They both dropped to the ground and made a fuss of him. In one bound, Rajah was there as well, demanding attention for himself, and tried to push the large wolf away.

"This isn't a game," White Hawk growled and the cat was nonplussed as it picked up the wolf's thoughts. "Your strength isn't a patch on mine," he continued, "but if you keep to your place, we'll get along fine."

"And where exactly is my place?" enquired Rajah, stiffening as his green eyes flashed fire.

"Up in the trees where you can see for miles," replied the wolf. "It is an advantage I haven't got, and you can hunt birds for food. Meanwhile, I'll stay on the ground where I can track and hunt rabbits. At night —" White Hawk stared at him intently and Rajah braced himself for the next bit. "At night we'll stay together and guard them both."

In the distance came excited yaps from Scrap. Rajah's ears twitched and the wolf cringed. "That's someone I want to get away from and someone you don't want to meet. Take my word for it." Rajah quickly assessed the situation and it was to his liking. He brushed his head against White Hawk's body and they moved off together.

Rajah's purrs were loud enough to be heard by everyone, and the villagers turned happily away. Tam, Ruth and the Shaman exchanged knowing looks. They had no need to fear for Thane and Sue taking this trip because they now had adequate protection.

THE END

Printed in Poland
by Amazon Fulfillment
Poland Sp. z o.o., Wrocław